Sacred Blood: The Vatican Assassin

Sacred Blood: The Vatican Assassin

Andres Amezquita

ISBN: 0692581243
ISBN 13: 9780692581247

TABLE OF CONTENTS

PART 1
DEATH AND REBIRTH

CHAPTER 1

INSIDE BOOK COVERS

Anthony puts his pen down and crosses his arms around his body to contain the pain. He has been writing a to-do list before the trip to Rome while having Laura's laptop open in front of him with her last essays. What happens now?

What happens when the alphabet is made of digital bits, resides in an electronic cloud, and the words, sentences, prayers, and paragraphs that make our stories are spellchecked and autocorrected by robotic crawlers? Can forests of data modify history and stop it from repeating?

Anthony met Laura in the line to pick their class schedules at UCLA, just before the first day of college. By graduation day, their lives were as if they had written their private hardcover story with more meaningful and personal quotations than anything they had read as literature majors. At twenty-two—wise and seasoned with the knowledge harvested from books that animated each one of their days—they got married and soon produced their first daughter, Claudia. She was named after Claudius, the Roman emperor and the main character of two of Robert Graves's historical novels. During the next years, while they studied for their master's degrees and PhDs, books became their furniture, their three daughters' toys, their toiletries, and the wallpaper that thickened the thin walls of their apartment. Books covered all available wall space, going around doorframes and windows, lined in orderly fashion on the shelves that Anthony continued to build every weekend.

But the narrative of their existence together ended abruptly when Laura unexpectedly died of pancreatic cancer at the end of spring last year. Anthony and her three daughters survived her, and no sentence in all the books at home or in the public library could help them make any sense of it.

Anthony has become a mute, wandering minstrel, living death bursting with inexpressible grief. He has systematically embraced his daily routine: teaching at UCLA, working on his research about lost Classical Roman texts, driving the girls to activities they are now indifferent about participating in. Anthony has been taking care of Claudia, now fourteen, Virginia (named after Virginia Woolf), eleven, and Thalia (named after the poetry muse), eight. They all move with a synchronistic, orchestrated heartache that has teachers, principals, bosses, deans, and psychiatrists sending notes and emails, leaving voice messages, and finally intercepting the family for face-to-face conversation in which they share their concerns and their Zoloft.

The girls perform well in school, top grades. Anthony performs well, too. His papers are published, his students graduate. But the family has stopped reading for pleasure. They avoid even text messages. Cable TV and physical exertion sports consume their spare time.

Laura's parents are a great back-up. They take care of the girls when Anthony has to participate in the lecture circuit. They become the first to encourage him to go to Rome in response to an invitation from his research associate at the University of Milan. Doctor Francesca Malatesta has asked him to join her for a sabbatical to study ancient manuscripts from the Vatican Library Secret Archives. She has been able to gain access to the exclusive club. Every year, about fifteen hundred scholars from over sixty countries are admitted after passing strict assessment from the Vatican. The dean at UCLA's Humanities Division cheers the option. Laura's parents are very wealthy, so they quickly register themselves and the girls to study Italian at a prestigious language institute in Rome during the summer. They also volunteer to pay for the American School if the girls are to stay with their father for the full year.

Francesca is a PhD from the University of Milan. She has been Anthony's research partner for the last five years probably because the troublesomeness of her hyperactivity and promiscuity have been conveniently diminished by having the Atlantic Ocean and several time zones separating them. He is also the temperate Californian child of yoga and transcendental meditation. Together they have written several papers on Roman literature and received a few awards for their research. New technology in digital imaging allowed them to help rebuild fragments from papyrus discovered in Pompeii. Anthony never succumbed to her sexual advances. He was too much in love with Laura. Francesca had found a good friend in him who could listen to her stories of escapades with married men, priests, and assorted college students and personnel. She particularly liked clergymen.

Anthony lets himself go with the flow of going to Rome for research, not indulging in reflection. He throws clothes and toiletries in his suitcase without thinking about it, grabbing the first items in his closet. He, the girls, and his in-laws take the plane to Italy.

Now, sitting in one of the two reading rooms, Anthony looks back at the year since Laura's death—for the first time. He realizes that the long sequence of gloomy days has felt longer than the eighty-five linear kilometers of bookshelves gathered in 630 archival units that constitute the Vatican Library Secret Archives. Laura's absence made him more irretrievable than a misplaced sheet of paper within the almost two million books, seventy-five thousand manuscripts, and uninterrupted church files collected since the twelfth century in the ancient library. Still, their first week in Rome has been healing.

Anthony studies a thirteenth-century religious hymns manuscript that Francesca located and wants him to analyze. The book is small, its hymns and artwork average for the time, maybe even mediocre compared to the many other treasures produced in the Middle Ages by hardworking monks. Its leather covers seem thicker than needed for travel protection. During the Middle Ages, monks would copy religious books by hand, carefully writing with paintbrushes in calfskin pages called vellum. Vellum had the advantage of lasting longer than paper or papyrus but was more expensive. The monks also copied Classical books that their abbot identified as important. Sometimes they would copy the text from a crumbling papyrus to practice lettering. What makes the little book that Francesca found so exceptional is that the monk who worked on it inserted lines from erotic Roman poetry within the Catholic psalms. Anthony's heart beats with excitement. He glimpses the energy he thought had been completely erased from his soul after Laura's death.

Francesca believes the poetry could be from Catullus, a famous poet who was in love with one of Julius Caesar's mistresses. Anthony handles the book with gloved hands while transcribing the words into his old laptop to later compare the structure and style to other of Catullus's surviving works.

Anthony feels happy, and the feeling makes him stop in surprise. The words of the poems linger in his conscience while he hugs the little book. He caresses its covers, tracing the engraved leather details. He puts it close to his face and smells the fabric of the inner covers, catching the scent of sunlit fields from many centuries ago and tasting oranges and grapes on dinner tables that have turned to dust. He wants to rub his cheeks against the fabric. With the book so close to his eyes, he notices a hidden pocket in the inside of the back cover. Someone hid some folios in it. He runs his fingertips around the corners of the cover and, with the aid of a magnifying glass, discovers the fabric flap that opens the pocket. The stitches joining leather and cloth are different in that area: wide and loose versus tight with no space between them. They were sealed up with obsessive mastery, as the spaces between the stitches appear perfectly equidistant. The thread at the end has not been secured so he pulls it, gaining access to the inner pouch. He knows he is not following protocol for this type of finding, but a hungry curiosity thwarts his scholarly logic. He inserts his fingers in the pouch and pulls several sheets of carefully folded vellum. The handwriting is in Latin, the font Carolingian—a very popular handwriting in the Middle Ages and Early Renaissance. Although the ink is faded, he is well trained to read the words. The vellum is newer than the one used in the book. Anthony reads with the eagerness of a treasure hunter, as if the letter had been addressed to him five hundred years before.

Day 1 - December 6, Anno Domini of 1521

I pray for forgiveness to our Lord, Jesus Christ. I cannot go to my confessor as I am the keeper of secrets that he cannot hear. I cannot even go to the Pope as he is now dead. I killed him. The conclave has gathered to choose his successor. I could wait but I have twelve days to live. The poison I took will soon start affecting me. I must hurry. If you find this confession, take it to a high ecclesiastical authority. Ask them to judge my case and intercede with all the Saints for absolution of my sins.

My name is Federigo Dottore. I have been a spy and an assassin to both Pope Julius II and Leo X. I was born in Florence in the year of Our Lord of 1482. My grandfather was a very successful trader and the first in our family to be in love with Classical Roman culture. Maybe he had been inspired by the Medici, or maybe had been influenced during his travels. He acquired merchandise from other countries and cities to sell in Florence. He also traded manuscripts. He became fascinated by them, and would read them and discuss with other thinkers of the time. My grandfather wanted his only son to be more than just a trader so he sent him to the University at Bologna to study medicine with Niccolo Leoniceno, a renowned doctor and teacher.

While my father's practice had been good in Florence, he was hearing how Pope Sixtus IV and later Innocent VIII were bringing new energy to the City of Rome. He sensed the center of power was shifting away from Florence and in his foresight understood that in a few years business there would be better. When I was five and my brother, Giacomo, two, we moved. Father bought a house in Pigna, between the Pantheon and the ruins of the Roman Forum.

Some of my first memories are of going to the bakery with my mother after mass. We passed ancient edifices that had become stables for cows that roamed through the shrubbery during the day. The bakery was a recent construction. Two walls were new and two were part of a pagan temple that was only halfway above the ground. Red and brown bricks revealed competing eras.

Father soon got a good clientele of wealthy merchants, bankers, and clergy. He became very busy and would spend most of the day going from one palace to another. Still, he would dedicate a couple of hours daily to teaching me and my brother to read and write in Latin and Greek, and to gain understanding of mathematics and the basics of medicine. Inspired by my grandfather, he used a large portion of his profits to buy copies of manuscripts, allowing me to read Homer, Virgil, and Julius Caesar from an early age. Many times, he came home with a text one of his wealthy patrons had lent him and went through it voraciously by candlelight at night. If we were lucky, he read to us. I can still feel the longing for adventure that I got from his voice reading Herodotus's travels. My breath short with wonder, his voice echoing in the old walls of our living room bringing light to the shadows that the candle or oil lamp could not dispel. My mother always had a disapproving look when he read to us. She was a devout Catholic and believed people should only read the Bible and the lives of saints. Instead of pagan poetry and "The Twelve Caesars," we should be reciting the New Testament and reading Saint Paul's letters. We ignored her reproachful glances and knew that she loved my father so much that peace and Classical Culture would prevail at home as long as we went to catechism class and to church every day.

For my brother and me, the city of Rome was a paradise. I can close my eyes and recall the vividness of our days and a never-ending expanse of possibilities. We explored ruins, caves, and the thick forests inside the city walls. We hunted rabbits and played fort in a crumbling imperial palace. From the treetops, we spied foxes and deer and even a pickpocket counting his loot. We were amazed by a porcupine, by a piece of sculpture, or by a beggar chasing us because we had disrupted his afternoon nap.

Most of the city was covered with empty remnants of past splendors, so when grandfather came from Florence to live in our household, we were happy that there was one more inhabitant in the city. Grandfather had aged a lot and had begun to lose his mind to some ailment, but he still proved to be a worthy companion to Giacomo and me when roaming around. Through him, the visions of the past would transubstantiate and appear more splendid and majestic. He made us believe we were in a bustling marketplace with merchants selling products from Egypt and Spain. Instead of seeing goats walking on a cobblestone alley, we would catch sight of Caesar's legionnaires celebrating a glorious triumph where generals and centurions guided troops trailed by carts brimming with loot: jewels, armors, swords, and captives. The bushes and wildflowers would transform into garlands that rapturous crowds tossed in their way and hung around the necks of never-seen beasts. We owned Rome.

One Sunday, after mass in Saint Pietro in Vincoli, grandfather, Giacomo, and I separated from the family to go for one of our adventures. Grandfather was sleepy, so he sat under a pine tree to take a nap. I was eleven, and Giacomo was eight. We were playing hide-and-seek in a field of lavender flowers so high that we would disappear just by crouching into the bright purple bushes. With their smell and color, the flowers attracted swarms of rapturous bees that floated on top of them, forever in love. I discovered a low crevice in a natural rock wall at the end of the field. I slid into it and held my breath, hoping not to be found. I heard the footsteps of my brother, so I slid deeper into the rock and discovered I was entering a tunnel. I crawled in it, following a distant light. There was a small descent. I jumped into it and found myself in what seemed to be a room. There was light coming from above. I looked around, opening my eyes as much as I could until I felt pain in my temples from the effort. I wanted to capture every detail of what surrounded me. The midday sun was coming through the cracks and holes in the ceiling, revealing crimson walls decorated with one thousand-year-old images of gardens and skies. Flat, flowering fruit trees and vertical lakes running under tree roots and bridges encircled me while naked women and men maintained their frozen conversations, reclining on long benches. I was so excited that I squeezed my way back to Giacomo to share my find.

We were back in a moment but instead of acknowledging the beauty, he started laughing at the exuberant breasts and mocking the nymphs in heat being offered enormous, erect male organs jutting out of the hairy animal thighs of satyrs. I punched him, and he tumbled. Confused, I commanded him to pray for forgiveness from Christ for seeing the sin in the images instead of the beauty. We did not know about sin or lust, but mother would whack us and order us to pray whenever we made a reference to a woman's breast or to male parts. Giacomo sobbed, leaning against a pile of clay tablets. I now felt bad and knelt in what seemed the last rotten remain of a wooden chest turned to dust. I hugged Giacomo and asked for his pardon. He wiped his eyes and smacked me back. Then he laughed. After our brief reconciliation, we continued exploring. We wanted a treasure to take home, but the only thing left in the room seemed to be the pile of clay tablets. They were big square tiles the width of my forearm on each side. In the past, we had found fragments of ceramic with pictures in them, which had made father happy. These tablets were different. They were flat and covered with writing on a white background. There were no pictures. I struggled to read, and soon figured out they were like the recipes my father used to make potions and unguents to cure his patients. This could be a good discovery. For the rest of the morning, Giacomo and I carried them out and hid them under a lavender bush close to where grandfather slept.

That night, we showed father a sample of our findings. He read it carefully under the oil lamp. The delight and concentration in his face soon became deep with interest, amazement, and finally horror as he understood the content in it.

The following day, instead of going to see his patients, he has us guide him to the bush where we had hidden the tablets. We had a small wooden cart into which we loaded all of the tablets, wrapped in a cloth. Father then took the trove home and buried it under a pine tree in the farthest part of our property.

In the following months, I tried many times to persuade father to tell me what was written in them. He would just shrug and say they were covered in writing that could only lead to mortal sin. Giacomo and I also went back to the entrance of our tunnel but in the area of the subterranean room, the ground had sunk, blocking the entrance.

By the time I was fourteen, I had almost forgotten the incident. I was too busy as a physician apprentice to my father. I carried his bag and potions wherever he went. I was very good at measuring and mixing ingredients for the cures. I would take notes for him, as my handwriting impressed anybody who saw it. I did not relish handling or carrying leeches to bleed the patients, but still father thought I could go to Bologna or Padua the following year to study. Mother nagged him to give more money to charity but he put away money for me and my brother to become scholars. By this time, mother had a new confessor who kept filling her head with ideas about how she should vow total obedience to the Catholic Church. She and father started arguing a lot. It got particularly nasty when she tried to coax him to get rid of all his books and manuscripts. She believed they were sinful objects originating from the devil.

In 1496, Rome had a French Pox outbreak. Father and I worked from sunrise to sunset for several months. Although we had treated French Pox in the past, this outbreak was very bad, and father lost many of his patrons to it. People thought Rome was being punished for the sins of Pope Alexander VI and his family, the Borgias.

Father was not a whoring man, but he also fell sick. I tended to him during his fevers. His mouth and body became covered with sores, which I cleaned with cold water. I slept on the floor next to him, only leaving his side to prepare food for Giacomo and grandfather, as my mother spent all her time at church praying. She would come home late at night to entreat the saints for forgiveness in a very loud voice while she sprinkled all the chambers with holy water. As if father's malady was not enough, her behavior enhanced Giacomo's terrors. Grandfather had lost cognition by that time. He was truly a captive, as we kept him locked in his room so he would not wander and get lost in the city. Mother's proclamations in the dark were answered by his broken voice calling for people I never knew. He called the name of friends he had met in his travels. He banged on his door, claiming he had to go to the northern states of the Holy Roman Empire, as he had to return a ring to his friend the Archbishop. His words did not make sense.

After some weeks, father's palms and feet were covered in a painful and pestilent rash. Pus ran down his forearms and stained the sheets where he lay. To reduce his suffering, I prepared a mixture of herbs and opium. During the brief intervals when he was awake, he would talk to me, and my utter loneliness would be broken by the love in his voice. He realized that soon I would become the new master of the house. He gave me advice on how to placate my mother when she got upset. He told me secrets of his trade so I would also become a great physician. He ran an inventory of all the manuscripts we had in the living room and the importance of protecting them. Sometimes he just wept, and his tears merged with the fluids that oozed from his broken skin. Other times, I would read to him from the only book he kept next to his bed: a poem by Lucretius called "The Nature of Things," which talked about the meaning of life and death from an ancient philosophical perspective. During those times, Giacomo joined us, bringing grandfather who would be very docile with the sound of my voice reciting beautiful

Latin rhymes. One night, mother came home late accompanied by her confessor and found us huddled together. They stood in the doorway listening to the poem's claims that there is nothing beyond this life, encouraging the reader to make the most of the moment. In the darkness, I could sense their bodies tense with reproach. I did not stop. How could I? I felt I was protecting the family with the ancient verses.

During his agony, father told me the meaning of the ceramic tablets we had found in the cave under the lavender hill. The area had recently been identified as Titus Baths. He explained that the writing described procedures to create poisons. He believed they had been used by a professional assassin in the service of Emperor Titus. They were written in ceramic so the assassin could have them on top of the table where he prepared the concoctions—this way, he did not have to worry if he spilled water or other ingredients on them. The tablets had probably been a priceless and secret possession. The owner recorded that he had murdered the clay artisans as soon as the tablets were baked so nobody would know of their existence. Most of the barbarians who sacked Rome through the centuries could not read. They probably had found the chest that contained the tablets but had not been interested in them. Their protection had been their utilitarian nature instead of being beautiful: Vandals destroyed beautiful objects out of jealousy.

The poisons described in the tablets were many and varied. They could kill following any whim of the executioner. He could choose to deliver a long and painful death that left irrefutable signs of murder or a death that would appear natural, as if coming from a fever or a stomach ailment. The killer could choose instant death or a slow death that would corrode the body in a couple of weeks or create madness so the victim would kill himself.

To my father, the tablets were impure. He had been tempted to leave them where we found them but realized it would be dangerous if they were discovered by someone evil. He also thought of breaking them into fragments that could merge with the pebbles covering the city ruins. But his love and respect for Roman culture stopped him. What if the tiles were part of a bigger secret, a bigger story? Indecisive, he chose to bury them under the pine tree at the edge of our property, and to leave it to Divine Providence to define if the tree roots would feed on the ceramic and destroy it, or if someone would unearth them in the future guided by God's hand.

As father approached death, mother and her confessor became bolder in criticizing our love of pagan books. Several priests joined them in her prayers at home. There were many loud voices at night clamoring for forgiveness of our sins. One night, mother pledged her life and all our belongings to the Catholic Church in repentance for having allowed us to be corrupted by my father's books. When she got home, she was already insane with fear and grief at the possibility of life without my father. Her confessor and two priests were with her. They arrived with such loud voices that the neighbors woke up and the dogs in our street barked and howled. The clergymen ushered me out of my father's room and closed the door to give him the last rites. Bewildered, I did not know what to do and did not see my mother unlocking the door to my grandfather's room. I then heard her high-pitched voice exhorting him to repent for being the source of all our family's evils. My grandfather had been lying naked on his cot. He only wore a ring with a red stone that even in his madness he would not separate from. Scared and bullied, the naked old man howled and ran out of the house waving his arms around his head as if chased by a swarm of wasps. I tried to stop him but heard Giacomo wrestling with mother. She was throwing father's books into the fireplace. She viciously slapped Giacomo's face many times and turned the shelf full with manuscripts on him. I hurried to help while my mother recited an "Ave Maria," hurling the old vellum and paper to the flames. Her black silhouette contorted in front of the fire like a cursed witch during a midnight Sabbath. I jumped on her back and snatched some sheets of vellum from her hands. I was now stronger and taller than she, but she fought me back with supernatural strength and fury. Medical, botanical, historical knowledge—all burned. The philosophers could not be saved from the pyre by their understanding of the universe, the poets could not charm their way out, and the historians became dust with their epics as the fire spread to other areas of the house. The curtains became furnaces, the table and chairs transformed into bonfires. In panic, I broke into father's room and pushed the priests aside. When they saw the flames and smoke, they quickly ran away, *leaving me to carry my father in my arms. His body had lost most of the muscles to his sickness. He was so light that I was able to move very quickly. We left a trail of boiling pus behind us. I returned for my mother but she jumped into the fire calling to Christ with her robes and hair ablaze.*

Outside, Giacomo was wailing while the neighbors ran to us with water buckets. Holding Giacomo's hand, and with father's body slung over my shoulder, I crossed through the smoke like a fugitive and escaped. Nobody chased us. My mother's confessor had previously arranged for the Church to seize all of our possessions. We lost our fortune. He would claim that my father had agreed with my mother's donations and granted them our wealth during his confession and last rites.

At daybreak, my mother's confessor found us sitting next to the ruins of the Roman Senate building. I had cried all night while keeping the hungry wild dogs away from us with rocks. My father was dead. I had pleaded to him to remain alive. He was already stinking. All searches failed in finding my grandfather. The city had swallowed him—along with my dreams of becoming a physician.

Anthony's phone vibrates on his pocket. His father-in-law reminds him via text that they cannot stay with the girls that evening as they have a business dinner with his Italian partners. Technology could be so invasive. Anthony had always resisted digital gadgets and computers but through the years Laura had convinced him that a smartphone was a good tool. He pushes the vellum back in the pouch in the inner cover of the Psalms book. He longs to finish reading the letter but his girls are calling. He returns the book to the librarian and hurries down the streets to the closest subway station.

Hotel Modigliani has a sitting room next to the lobby. It is large enough to accommodate several groups of couches and tables. It has white floors of marble tiles that match its white walls with long mirrors. Anthony and the girls are dispersed in the area. Nobody could guess they are together. Thalia sits on a chair facing a corner while playing a videogame. Virginia lies on a couch on a separate furniture cluster immersed by her smartphone. Claudia has decided to read and is sitting on a high stool on an empty bar as far away from her sisters as possible. Anthony paces around; digesting in his mind the discovery of the erotic poems intermingled with Psalms and the hidden vellum with a firsthand account of Rome at the end of the fifteenth century. He has not seen Francesca, his Italian research partner, in a couple of days. She has been very busy with some internal business with the Curia. She will be exultant about the discoveries but somehow Anthony wants to keep them for himself a little longer.

Later in their hotel room, while the girls get their showers, Anthony finishes emptying the luggage into drawers and closets. He sits on the floor with his legs crossed and looks around at their new life. Laura feels as distant as Redondo Beach.

CHAPTER 2

LAVENDER AND POISON

A nthony tosses and turns in bed all night thinking about his discoveries in the Vatican Library Secret Archives. He longs to go back to the reading room and proceed with deciphering the text on the vellum folios hidden inside the inner cover of the thirteenth-century book. In the morning, he kisses the girls as they leave with their grandparents to their Italian class.

"Remember to come home early tonight," reminds Elmer, his father in-law. "You promised the girls gelato and dinner." Anthony assents and rushes to the subway station.

The age of the document makes the reading laborious. Fortunately, the vellum is in superb condition. Most manuscripts Anthony has explored take days to read because the ink is faded and bookworms have damaged segments of it. But, in this case, the book's inner cover served as a protective cover.

Day 1(Continued) - December 6, Anno Domini of 1521

We were now orphans and had no relatives in the city. To prevent any inheritance dispute, my mother's confessor took us to a monastery, claiming he was following my father's orders. Giacomo and I were too old to be postulants but the monastery welcomed us as novices. I was fourteen. Giacomo was eleven.

Did I heal while at Saint Andrea in the Caelian Hill? The monastery was run by a very old and pious abbot. Father Anastasius took us into his fold. He told us that through penance and prayer Jesus Christ would forgive the sins of our family and soothe our sorrow. We were very busy all day. Life was simple. We began with mass and singing at daybreak. We labored at the many chores at the monastery—tending farm animals or the orchards—and then prayed and sang again in the evening. We also invested time studying music and reading Saint Benedict. Father Anastasius was delighted with my mastery of Latin and Greek. My skills from having been a physician's apprentice were of good use in the infirmary. On many occasions, I was given the task of scribe, and the Abbot wished for me to expand to writing musical notation quickly so I could copy chants in vellum for the other monks and novices to use at choir.

The prayers helped to heal me, but I cried easily. I would hide my face, so no one would see my tears, as the chorus of male voices enunciating musical phrases drifted into the air before the first rays of sun. I asked God to help me find meaning in our change of fortune. Had He always intended my life to be devoted to prayer? Why had He given me a painful path? Why had He showed me the minds of Plato and Aristotle instead of making me a devout Catholic? The incipits and cadences would flow and ebb in my soul like a river flood, taking feeling away and leaving sediments of tranquility. I was not a good singer but I strived to follow the choir. My mind and spirit would become so entranced that, with time, I came to disremember the past.

Giacomo became very physical. He favored working in the stables or the mill until he would faint from exhaustion. He avoided me, resentful that I had neither cured our father nor stopped my mother in her madness. He would not talk to me when we were together. He chose not to sing. He would sit in the chapel with eyes closed and lips tight.

After three years and swearing our permanent monastic vows, we believed that only the now existed. We assumed we would reach old age inside the monastery, like some monks whose days had been as constant as our chants.

This way of life ended as abruptly as it had started. One day, our Abbot, Father Anastasius, died when the choir finished the vesper chants. The Abbot that replaced him decided to make Saint Andrea a monastery for the sons of the wealthy of Rome. Those of us who lacked a noble or powerful family were sent to a humbler abbey: Saint Benedictus Minor outside the walls of the city. Soon after we arrived, we discovered Saint Benedictus was a place that felt dedicated to praising Satan rather than Jesus Christ. Saint Benedictus was a slave farm. The only prayers were the silent ones the monks recited pleading to God for a way out or a speedy death. The monks worked in the fields, tended animals, or made furniture. The main activities of the abbey seemed to be producing furniture from forests around the monastery and leather from its cattle. Their woodshop was larger than the chapel. The tannery inundated the air with foul odors. The Abbot and his deans sold the furniture to raise money for vices and pleasures.

Abbot Laurentius ran the place with nine young deacons who had been assigned by the Holy See to study with him to become priests. I did not know how they studied the Word of God. I never saw them with a Bible or engaged in any theological argument. Each one of the deacons appeared to be training hard to become a scholar in sin.

Deacon Leonello was in charge of making us work as hard as our starved bodies could. He enjoyed using a whip and turned furious at the slightest mistake on our labor or any disobedience to the monastery's rule of law. Sometimes they stripped a monk naked and publicly whipped him in the central courtyard for making a minor mistake. Leonello enjoyed inflicting pain. He was feared by all—including his friends.

Deacon Lorenzo helped Leonello supervise the workforce. Instead of the whip, he used derogatory words to keep us at bay. He walked next to us with his head high while looking down as if he were in a church pulpit. He relished telling us that working monks were an inferior caste. He and the other deacons were horses; we were mules. The deacons and the Abbot were of holy human strains created by God to rule over lesser beings. They were entitled to luxury, lavish food, and fine clothes. Deacon Lorenzo repeated that we lacked the human attributes to appreciate good things, so he fed us a diet of stale bread and hard cheese. Our cells were better suited for pigs than humans. We slept in small cubicles with hay strewn on the floor. We had no space for a chair or a small table. We wore threadbare robes that made us look like the lowest mendicants instead of Benedicts.

The third one, Deacon Francesco, would boast about the great labor they were doing. He claimed as his own the designs of the most beautiful pieces of furniture we crafted. He never set foot in the workshop. He shone in the marketplace where his lies granted a higher price for the furniture than their worth.

Deacon Ottavio was the money keeper. He ensured that the tools and materials the abbey bought were of the lowest quality—good for Leonello, his best friend, because whenever the cheap tools broke, this would create an occasion for him to whip someone. I am sure Ottavio skimmed the profits. He would tell the Abbot he was buying materials to replenish the infirmary, but I knew this was a lie. The infirmary was an abandoned room with numerous empty jars and containers. Nobody was in charge of it, as having someone dedicated to this job would subtract from the work force. I took it on myself to replenish medicinal ingredients with herbs and substances I could find around the monastery. By doing this, I developed a strong bond with the cook, Callisto, as many times he furtively provided ingredients or spices from the kitchen so I could cure others.

Deacon Tommaso was a fat sloth. He would sit all day under a fig tree watching with indifference how we were abused. During fig season, Deacon Martinus would spend the day with him, although Deacon Martinus's main chore consisted of supervising Callisto in the kitchen to ensure that the feasts served for the Abbot and the deacons were on par with the wealthiest banquets in Rome. Both Tommaso and Martinus were obese and smelly, their skin unctuous with fat and sweat. They provided a sharp contrast to the other six handsome deacons but mostly to a third deacon who would join them under the fig tree: Deacon Ferdinando. While Tommaso and Martinus were obese, Ferdinando was an emaciated figure, dirty and unkempt. He sometimes stayed in bed and spent the day looking with his dull eyes to the ceiling until dinnertime. Around the other deacons, his gaunt person appeared like a giant vulture. He appeared to have taken the vow of silence the rest of us working monks were forced to take when entering the monastery— but in his case he was too dejected to speak with others and preferred mute resentment.

Deacon Ferdinando provided the perfect company for Deacon Constanzo, whose daily occupation consisted of gossiping at all times about the others with petty envy. Deacon Constanzo enjoyed chatting with no interruptions. He would go into the other deacons' rooms when they were away and inspect their possessions. He stole whenever he considered he was more deserving of an object. The disappearance of these belongings was always blamed on some unfortunate, random working monk. Some died from punishment for these acts.

The last deacon, and the favorite among his peers, was Deacon Guidobaldo. He would hang around the others telling lewd stories of sex and depravity that garnered loud laughs and good moods. While we were invisible to most of the other deacons, Guidobaldo would look at us with unsettling intensity. Sometimes we were made to work in loincloths so he could stare at our emaciated, sinewy bodies. Many times he would develop a fondness for someone who would mysteriously vanish from the monastery after a short period of time.

The Abbot was the emperor. He would go back and forth to the city to socialize with bishops and cardinals. They praised him for the money he gave to their causes and the excellent work he had accomplished at Saint Benedictus Minor.

My life at Saint Benedictus was miserable not because of the hard work or the treatment we were subjected to at the hands of the deacons and the Abbot. The vow of silence was oppressive but I did not miss talking. I missed singing. The vacuum left by the choir and prayers allowed past grief to resurface. I tried to reach out to Giacomo, my brother, but he was angrier than before. One time I touched his shoulder while working in the orchard, and he smashed my face with his fist. I was taller but he continuously bullied me. His reproachful gaze followed me everywhere I went. I started to believe that I should have been able to save my father. I reproved myself for not stopping my mother from burning the books. I would awaken in the middle of the night, all my muscles in pain from the terror of ignoring the fate of my grandfather. Guilty acid burned in the back of my mouth and flowed from my stomach, scorching my throat. How and where had my grandfather died?

Had the knowledge of antiquity contained in his flesh been devoured by the same wild creatures who had devoured Rome's proud imperial constructions? In nightmares, I saw these monsters holding a spasmodic human leg dripping blood and gore in one claw and the marble head of the Emperor Augustus with empty eye sockets and a laurel garland disintegrating into dust in the other. But the creatures were not satiated. They were always hungry for the spirits of those who appreciated beauty.

Sometimes screams of pain slashed through the silence at night like sordid talons tearing a sacred mantle. Callisto then fetched me to go to the infirmary before sunrise where I would find a young monk with injuries from torture and sodomy. I did not ask questions. I did my best to cure. I was so deeply in my grief and self-recriminations I did not try to understand what was happening in the monastery. I should have tried to escape with Giacomo. The realization of the mortal danger God had placed us in became horribly clear one night when three of the deacons, Leonello the punisher, Lorenzo the proud, and Guidobaldo the lustful, came and fetched Giacomo and me from our cells. They took us to an abandoned brewing cellar, a large room where chains hung from the beams to help move wine caskets in the past. Guidobaldo glided the tips of his fingers back and forth with his hands together as if praying. At the same time, he smacked his leering lips with relish and anticipation. Leonello and Lorenzo bound and hung us from the beams using the chains. The rest of the deacons and Abbot Laurentius joined the group. The Abbot recited the Divine Office while his deacons stripped us naked. Giacomo's eyes pleaded for help . . . as if I could do anything! I begged them to stop, begged for them to release Giacomo and kill me instead if it pleased them. They just laughed in response. I was in no position to negotiate. They had us both, and they would use us both. My pleas only confirmed to them that I would suffer more if they were to torture and sodomize my brother first while I watched. I threatened to go to the authorities. I would go to the Pope himself, if needed.

"Who do you think provides boys to His Holiness Pope Alexander VI so he can offer gifts to men who take their pleasure from boys?" The Abbot spoke to me for the first time since we had arrived at the monastery. "We break and train them so he can use them as tokens in his negotiations with nobles, bankers, and merchants. Our pupils have traveled all over the world. Some have even survived. They have amassed a great reputation as dogs dedicated to pleasing their masters." He caressed my face with a tenderness that froze my blood. "Maybe one day you and your little brother will serve in the courts of the Borgia family." He then kissed me on the lips, pushing his tongue inside my mouth while my brother howled with pain at the hands of Deacon Leonello.

I lost track of time while in the brewing cellar. At night, they subjected us to cruelties that only demons could scheme. I can't describe them or enumerate them. Each of the nine deacons sodomized us; each devised a unique torment for us. The Abbot always recited a complete mass before joining the orgy. When alone, if not bound, I would cradle Giacomo and ask for him to forgive me while washing his injuries with my tears and removing fleas and lice from his body. The pests went insane with the blood that covered us.

Abbot Laurentius did not send us to the Pope. My body ended crisscrossed with scars as if someone had embroidered patterns on my skin. Giacomo died during one of the torture sessions, his body thrown into the Tiber. Before releasing me, they nailed my tongue to a wooden column for a night so I would never talk again. I survived—thanks to Callisto the cook, who nursed me in a pantry using the unguents I had prepared to cure others. He secretly spoon fed me chicken broth and bread soaked in goat milk. I had no thoughts during that period. My memories resemble walking through a moonless night through a never-ending, flat cemetery. Nothing.

My memories resumed one day when I found myself as a kitchen helper dutifully following Callisto's orders in a mechanical manner. My skills at weighing and mixing ingredients for my father had made me a great kitchen assistant. I believe one year had gone by after Giacomo's death when I discovered myself chopping carrots and basil. I did not want to live, but God did not want me to die.

I resumed curing others inside the derelict infirmary. The deacons mocked me whenever they saw me, but they had lost all interest in making me suffer. They preferred fresh meat and unmarked skin. At night, the dream creatures from the city returned to haunt me. Instead of holding the torn pieces of Roman statues, they held Giacomo's broken body. On more than one night, I woke up hollering in terror only to find my screams mixed with the far away laments of another unfortunate in the hands of the deacons. One time, I could not take it anymore and ran like a madman seeking shelter from one building to another. My steps lead to the monastery's abandoned library, which had been turned into a warehouse for wood. In one corner lay the few remaining books that Deacon Ottavio had not been able to sell. I found a small hymn book without its covers. Under the moonlight I read its psalms and heard chants praising God in my mind. From then on, I would read whenever waking up in terror. The hymns book was my main companion but I also explored the other remaining manuscripts. One of the reasons the hymns book became so important to me was that it contained a flaw. Whoever had copied it had mixed lines from erotic Roman poetry in the bottom third of the pages. The poetry reminded me of Lucretius and Catullus, its elegant Latin evoking safer times, and the safer times brought memories of the tablets we found under Titus Baths with the recipes for murder. After that, my plan progressed in a natural way. While Callisto had me serving food from the kitchen to the Abbot's table, I realized I could easily mix poison with the meals of those I served. This realization instilled in me new power. While I cleaned my body with a wet cloth in the morning and at night counted my scars, I mused on the sort of death I would visit upon each one of them. During the numerous times that I washed my hands in the kitchen, I planned my escape route to fetch the tablets from the tree where father had buried them. I scrubbed between my fingers until my skin was red, reviewing in my mind the perimeter of the monastery wall.

I found a place where the wall had collapsed under a fallen tree. I commenced my efforts whenever there was enough moonlight. A small palazzo stood where my house in Pigna had been. The pine tree was untouched; around it, lavender bushes grew with purple liveliness and the fragrance of my childhood. I dug around it and found the tablets. They were intact. I used a tattered Bible I had found in the library to copy the recipes around its margins. Every night, I copied a segment until I had transcribed all of the information they held. I then studied them vehemently. I memorized ingredients and procedures.

My work in the kitchen facilitated gathering the ingredients. Sometimes I added what I needed to the grocery list before Callisto went to the market. With sign language, I explained to him that I was replenishing the infirmary. Callisto was a good man. He was a true believer and did not hesitate to take the risk of buying these things if he could help his fellow monks.

I continued my midnight excursions. Sometimes I scoured the forests and wilderness in search of herbs and minerals. I also returned to the tree to fetch and pulverize the tablets.

During the Christmas of 1502, I prayed to Christ and all the apostles to give me strength and to guide my actions. The Abbot had a feast on the 25th. Callisto and I toiled for many days to prepare the banquet for his guests. I had found a faraway tree that sprouted figs late in the fall when the other trees were finished for the season. On the 24th, I escaped to the distant part of the forest, where I collected the sweetest and largest figs to give as a special treat to Deacons Tommaso and Martinus. When serving all the guests, I brought the sliced fruit treats only to them. They did not thank me, but it was fine, I did not wish to be thanked for the fruit that would kill them. I had dipped the figs in a poison that, on December 31st, made it appear as though they died of yellow fever.

1503 brought a typhus plague to the city of Rome, but I had other plans for the death of the remaining deacons. Deacon Costanzo died amid horrible convulsions on Ash Wednesday after "accidentally" falling from a staircase. I had poured substances in his drink to impair his judgment. Deacon Ottavio died slowly during Lent. The mysterious affliction gradually corroded his body, signaling the loss of his physical capabilities with ever-increasing pestilence. First he stopped walking, and then lost his sight; finally, he could not talk anymore, and his lungs stopped working amid groans of suffering and a turbulent, bloody fluid drooling from his cracked lips. By this time, the silent monks were gossiping. They wondered if God was sending these mortal maladies. The Abbot locked himself in his luxurious quarters. Deacon Leonello became even more vicious and whipped as if the pain inflicted on others would remove his own grief for the death of his companions.

Nobody was surprised that Deacon Ferdinando stayed in bed the last days of Lent. They were all used to his apathy, but by Palm Sunday the stench emanating from his room revealed he had been dead for a week. On Good Friday, the proud Deacon Francesco hanged himself upon discovering that his beautiful face had caught an affliction that putrefied his skin with pustules, making him look like a leper in advanced stage. On Pentecost Sunday, Deacon Lorenzo stopped boasting as he died of what appeared to be a stomach ailment that made his intestines bloat and explode.

I saved the final executions for Corpus Christi. That morning, the monks woke up to the terrorized howls of Deacons Leonello and Guidobaldo. The deacons had gone insane and believed they were chased by demons. In their terror, they had shredded their faces with their fingernails. Deacon Guidobaldo gouged his eyes out. When the monks went looking for the Abbot, they found me in his room. The Abbot was dead—and it was clear to all that I had murdered him by pushing ceramic fragments up his anus and down his throat. He had agonized through a slow and painful death. I had used ceramic shreds from the last tablet. The pieces had sharp edges that punctured his intestines and throat. I had used a potion to keep him awake but unable to move while I punished him. The monks saw me: the mute kitchen helper standing next to the death naked body of their despised Abbot. They could not figure out how I had killed him without him putting up resistance. He was much stronger than me.

The monks locked me in my cell. By noon they had called a bishop to exorcise the monastery. Other ecclesiastic authorities were asking questions. With disbelief and horror, they uncovered the sinister events that transpired under Abbot Laurentius. The nearby neighborhoods were like a tubular organ of gossip with the many stories of suffering dispersed to the winds. Everybody agreed that the death or madness of the nine deacons was a punishment coming from the Divine Providence. The Abbot's murder was a mystery. The priests heard stories of how I cured and helped many. Callisto told them about my brother's death, and how he had nurtured my tortured body back to life. Still, I was weaker than the Abbot. To my fellow monks, it seemed impossible that I could have slowly killed him without his lashing back. Authorities came to ask me questions but I showed them the hole in my tongue. Callisto explained to them that while his brethren had the vow of silence they sometimes murmured among themselves. They were certain I was mute. The bishop still tried to make me speak. He questioned me if an angel or a demon had guided me in my atrocious crime. He asked God for a miracle, to get clarity, and to understand if I was an instrument of justice or a fiend to be punished. He spent hours coaxing me, ordering me to write about the events, but I ignored the blank pages set before me. All the time while he waited, his secretaries kept entering the room to share with him more disturbing stories from other monks as the interviews progressed during the day. I felt locked in an invisible box watching everything from a distance. I had done what I needed; I refused to justify my actions to anybody but Our Creator. The bishop gave up and left at sunset. He decided to keep me locked in my cell while he fetched a cardinal to evaluate my case.

Time became a blur. I barely ate or drank. I knelt day and night praying to God for mercy. I kept a little glass vial under my straw mat. I had saved this poison to drink after the last death. It was a shimmering purple liquid. I fancied the venom to be sweet. I had made it from the poison and honey from bees on lavender fields. The tablets stated that it would provide a speedy death. Through those days I could not gather enough courage to drink it. I asked Christ for a signal. I asked Him to show me the way.

One morning, two monks came to get me. They helped me wash and shave. They dressed me in fresh new robes. A new Abbot had been assigned to replace Laurentius while I was locked away. I noticed many good changes in the monastery. The vow of silence had been lifted. I could hear prayer and singing from the main chapel.

At the Abbot's office a cardinal waited for me. He was middle aged, slim, and strongly built. He was not sitting down but rather chose to move around the room examining everything with intense curiosity. His posture expressed power, command, and intelligence. With one look at me, I felt he understood my past and my recent actions. His presence was so authoritative that I knelt in front of him and covered my face to hide tears of shame. We were alone in the room but still he locked the door and windows for complete privacy.

I babbled, failing to form words with my deformed tongue. He intro-duced himself. He was Cardinal Giuliano della Rovere, and he had special interest in my case because Abbot Laurentius had been a min-ion for the Borgia Pope, his enemy. I did not know it then but the Cardinal despised Pope Alexander VI. Their enmity had led to his exile from Rome, forcing him to live in fear for his life at all times.

I was trying to form words again when his secretary knocked on the door. In a loud voice, the Cardinal dismissed him, asked for privacy, and ordered him to keep any eavesdropper away under threat of eternal damnation. I know now that his secretary was not surprised; he was used to his impulsivity and unusual approach to everyday matters.

I stopped sobbing when I felt the Cardinal's hand on my shoulder. His grip was soothing and transmitted self-control. I raised my face and gazed into his eyes as he commanded me to sit.

With great effort, I was able to form words. I had a lisp, but if I spoke deliberately I could communicate. I told Cardinal della Rovere every-thing: my childhood, how Giacomo and I had found the tablets under Titus Baths, the deaths of my father and grandfather, our lives in the two monasteries, and finally how Abbot Laurentius and his deacons had tortured us. He listened with great compassion. His interest enhanced when I described how I had escaped and copied the information in the tablets so I could poison the nine deacons and the Abbot. He studied me in silence for several minutes after my narrative came to a close. He gave himself time to judge and assess what to do with me and my in-formation. He asked me if I had any vials of poison left. I told him about the one I had prepared for myself but had not yet used. He asked me about the nature of the poison and the kind of death it would deliver. One had to get a beehive on a lavender field, I explained, and extract the toxin sacks from the stings of hundreds of bees and mix the fluid with the honey. Finally, everything had to be laced with a concentrated lavender infusion. Other ingredients served to hide all traces of poison in the victim; that way, it would seem that the victim had died quickly from a fulminating ailment.

"Murder is a mortal sin and you killed ten. Only the Pope has the kind of holy grace you require to intercede with Christ in your favor. I cannot absolve you . . . now." He placed a strong emphasis on the

last word of his verdict. "But I might obtain your future absolution if you give me the vial of poison you prepared for yourself. I will use it for my purposes, and depending on the outcome we will know if you have been an instrument of God, or Lucifer's assistant." He unlocked the door and followed me to my cell. Once inside, he closed the door again to ensure our privacy while I handed him the glass vial. "From now on our destinies are joined. I will use this for a good cause. The Holy Spirit should illuminate the way. Be certain, if everything goes well I will demand your absolute discretion and eternal devotion to me. You will enter my service. If the poison fails the test, I can guarantee you will live an unendingly miserable existence that will make your time under the deacons' captivity seem like happy memories. Nobody should know you can speak. You will wait for me here in in the monastery. If you try to escape, I will find you." He then commanded me to kneel, and to my surprise, he blessed me. "You will hear from me soon. Pray to all the saints and your pagan gods that the news you receive is good." He hid the vial in his robes and left with a pleased smile on his handsome face.

CHAPTER 3

RED WINE

Anthony stops reading with a brisk jolt. The voice of one of the librarians brings him back to the twenty-first century. The Vatican archives will close in fifteen minutes. His hands shake, folding the vellum letter and inserting it back into the hymns book cover. In his excitement, he pushes it and tears off all of the cloth in the inner cover. He feels terrible for damaging the thirteen-century psalms book, but knowing the monk who had written the letter had read the same book 500 years ago electrifies him. Anthony cannot help it, and hugs the book again. He feels a pang of guilt for procrastinating to transcribe the Roman verses found interlaced with the hymns into his laptop. He checks the people in other tables. Had anybody seen him damaging the book? He cannot return it to the library's front desk. They might discover the damage and not loan it to him anymore. He must finish reading the hidden letter. He is surrounded by cameras. The Secret Archives library has heavy security, as it holds documents that include the trial of the Templars, the Edict of Worms, and the bulls condemning and excommunicating Martin Luther. Its most ancient document dates back to the eighth century. He moves to the closest bookshelf and hides his treasure behind other books.

Anthony is not used to contradictory feelings. Blood flushes around his temples as he walks to the exit. Protocol dictates he should have informed a librarian before pulling the letter out of its pouch but his failure to do so does not stop him from being exultant about the events of the day. First a lost poem by Catullus, and then the confession letters from this monk! His heart beats full of adrenaline at the possibilities of everything he might discover on the Vatican bookshelves. Does he need to return to California ever at all? His one-year sabbatical will not be enough. "If only Laura had lived to share this with me." Reading about the monk's misfortune has reminded him to value his three daughters. Anthony is very fortunate. He must rush back to the hotel and talk with them, regain some of the time lost to a year of sorrow.

Outside the library is a small cafeteria adjacent to the ruins of a large Renaissance fountain. Here, the three thousand scholars who visit the library every year spend their breaks drinking their espressos while their minds wander on the world's largest dossier of Western culture. The coffee shop closed earlier, and the tables are deserted. Anthony walks quickly, avoiding human interaction. His spirit is immersed in the deep well of possibilities and wants to linger there. And, yes, there is also the little concern nagging him: what if somebody stopped him because he damaged a seven hundred year-old manuscript?

He would walk to the subway station with his eyes closed if he could.

The Swiss guards check his briefcase at the Porta Santa, one of the few entrances at the wall that separates the Vatican City from Rome. Anthony enters the river of tourists outside the Vatican wall with heightened apprehension as if the pickpockets could steal ideas from his brain. A herd of Spanish grandmothers can't stop laughing loudly as they point to an apron hanging from a street shop with the torso and genitals of Michelangelo's David printed on them. Groups of monks and nuns cut their way through a Japanese tour with determination. A group of people holds banners protesting against something: "Transparency in the Curia." A fat lady eats two gelato cones simultaneously. A father explains the history of the Vatican wall to his bored and exhausted family. A street vendor persistently sells a fake Rolex. The smell of grilled gyro meat wafts through the many conversations around Anthony while the sky turns orange against a deep blue background.

Anthony hears his name from somewhere in the crowd. There must be thousands of Tonys in Rome so he keeps marching on. Then the call comes closer and turns explicit: "Tony! Anthony Hibbert!" He recognizes the voice. The multicolored hair of Francesca Malatesta zooms in on him. Anthony wishes he could escape from her conversation. "I want to hug my girls tonight." (Since Laura's death, he prefers having conversations with himself than with other people.)

"Tony, stop, stop! I desperately need your help and my dinner is getting cold! Why are you running away from me?" She grabs his arm and pulls. Her English is heavy with a mixed British and Italian accent.

Francesca does not have children and will not understand his sense of urgency. Anthony babbles some lame excuse, and then murmurs to himself: "Aren't we supposed to have coffee at noon tomorrow to compare notes on our findings? Isn't it time for her to do whatever she does at night when in Rome? Doesn't she remember I like to have supper with my girls and need to arrive on time? I promised gelato after dinner."

"*Atorrante*! Do not ignore me! I desperately need your help right now!" She enunciates her words to leave no doubt. "If we don't act now, they will forbid access to the Vatican libraries to all secular investigators! We won't be able to complete our research. Our sabbatical will go to *la merda*!" Anthony finally stops in his tracks. Turning, he tries to examine Francesca's eyes through her wide, dark designer glasses. Her body is hopping more than usual in her two-piece fuchsia and sapphire suit. "The Pope will announce this soon! Come with me. I am having dinner with someone who is in the know." Resigned, he follows her obediently. He doesn't want to return to a depression. He doesn't want to return to California empty handed.

Walking down *Viale Germanico*, Francesca pulls him into a wood-paneled restaurant called *Dal Toscano*. It seems very crowded—more than usual, as patrons want to dine before it closes for a month for its summer break. Why does Francesca think she will get a place for them? She yanks Anthony by the lapels and sits him at a table where food is served and a man is munching on a plate of some kind of meat with arugula. Usually Francesca is fun, so sitting with her makes people feel part of the in-crowd as if the most popular girl in high school had handpicked them to be part of her entourage. Tonight is different. Francesca and the man have food in front of them, but Anthony's area is empty. The man looks vaguely familiar to him.

"*Pronto*, this is Tony Hibbert; he is the head of Classical Studies at UCLA. Tony, this is Gabriel Herrera, as you know he is the Bishop of Los Angeles." Anthony feels a firm and almost businesslike handshake.

Before he can open his mouth, a waiter puts a glass in front of him and pours red wine. Anthony asks for a menu but the waiter is gone. "Why am I sitting here?" he thinks, "Does she think that just because this man and I live in Los Angeles we should be socializing?" The waiter comes back for an instant. Anthony orders pasta with eggplant, refusing to wait for a menu. Anthony is vegetarian and ordering eggplant in Italy has proven a safe bet. The waiter leaves in a hurry before Anthony can order a beer. He doesn't like red wine but he sips from his glass, composed. Francesca and the Los Angeles Bishop are in a heated argument. Why would the Pope want to close access to secular people now? The Secret Archives library opened to researchers at the end of the nineteenth century. Why now when Anthony is one of the lucky researchers? He drinks more wine.

They turn to Anthony. Gabriel apologizes for him and Francesca having ordered food before his arrival, and for the last-minute invitation. He explains that they had met to discuss the latest news and map out an action plan. Francesca had suggested that Anthony be part of the plan, as the Holy See authorities would respect his American scholarly clout. Francesca calculated the time for her fellow researcher to leave the Vatican libraries to fetch him. Anthony smiles graciously and clinks his wine glass with theirs. Francesca and Gabriel give him the background. The Holy See has been under attack through a social media campaign demanding transparency. The media calls it "The Transparency Crusade." The Catholic Church is the protagonist of many murky scandals, and people are using new technologies to demand information. They want to know about the past and the present. In the recent decade, there has been significant public outrage after information of multiple priests abusing minors leaked to the press. Public indignation has grown after it was proven that the higher ecclesiastic authorities knew about the scandals and covered them up instead of punishing the perpetrators. Protocol to suppress the truth has been more important than the well-being of their parishioners. The origins of this "secret system" goes back to the seventeenth century, but in 1962 under Pope John XXIII, the Vatican published a document called "Instructions on the Manner of Proceeding in Cases of Solicitation" that deals with the secret arrangements for any cleric charged with sexual offense. The social media campaign recruits members who call for the Catholic Church to unveil its secret dealings. Letters and petitions from people all over the world are forwarded daily to the Vatican's Communication Office demanding to make information inside the Holy See transparent to the public. This includes protocols and, most importantly, access to all of the information in the Secret Archives, where the transcripts from Papal meetings have been held for many centuries. What started as a small group went viral and now includes millions of people on Facebook and Twitter.

Anthony tries to interrupt a couple of times to explain that actually many of the Vatican files are available to whoever wants to look at them online, even many of the items from the Secret Archives. IBM had been leading the digitization and online publishing project in conjunction with some colleges around the world since 1995. Also researchers who are cleared to spend time inside the Vatican buildings can look into the Pope's Secret Archives, which holds actual correspondence and meeting registers from the oldest files to 1935, just before World War II. The trick is to find something in the miles and piles of paper, books, and notes! Nobody really knows what is kept there.

Anthony is about to make a case against the social media campaign for lack of grounds when a plate of food is thrown in front of him. Mankind was better off when digital annoyances did not exist. He tries to say something while the waiter refills his wine glass, but the waiter is too quick and sprints away. The eggplant is stuffed with ground beef, the pasta is interlaced with miniscule sausage bits. There is no way Anthony can eat this fare, but the pungent aroma of the tomato Bolognese that covers the eggplant dish makes him realize he is extremely hungry. Francesca is questioning: How come Anthony has not seen any posts about this on Facebook? He mutters that he doesn't have a Facebook account; that was Laura's realm, she was the technology one. Gabriel, the Bishop, is saying something about how he is part of the faction that proposed forbidding access to the library to non-religious research but Anthony ignores the gap of logic in why Gabriel would then be working with Francesca, who is pro-transparency, in favor of scavenging for something acceptable on his plate or around the table. Dismayed, Anthony plunges into the breadbasket and sucks up more wine, straining to pay attention to the conversation. Gabriel is saying something about the anti-transparency faction considering terrible things that go against his principles and against the law. This is why he has asked for Francesca's help. The intended crime must be thwarted. Anthony's head swims from the wine. He asks what this crime he refers to is. Gabriel whispers in his ear: "Do you remember the events around our Holy Father John Paul I's death? There were many unresolved murders at the time. I am afraid we might be unleashing events of a similar nature." Murders? Anthony dunks his bread in the wine, spilling red stains on the pristine white tablecloth. He cannot remember the murders Gabriel is talking about. Francesca comes to his rescue, recounting the story of the murders and suicides of seven people related to the Vatican Bank after John Paul died. The then-new Pope, Albino Luciani, initiated an investigation into some turbid affairs in the bank and its branches. Many believe this same investigation led to his death under strange circumstances. The media had stirred with talk of a complex web of church corruption behind a conspiracy to poison the Pope thirty-three days after his election.

The Curia had originally ignored the social campaign—a mistake in digital crisis management—until many devout Italians joined the posts streaming from around the globe. Later, the Italian press and authorities started pressuring the Pontific for a response. The tabloids were publishing bizarre stories. The bureaucrats wanted to apply codes and laws that nobody understood. The Pope is very irritated. He is convinced the Holy See has already done even more than necessary in becoming transparent. Had they not started to publish their financial information every year? Anthony grasps his glass while his head swoons. The media is demanding a commission to investigate the matter. The Pope has decided to grant a private audience to the leader of the social campaign, a Silicon Valley billionaire named Avinash Sullivan. Anthony finishes the breadbasket. Gabriel talks incessantly but Anthony is caught up in his own anguished thoughts, as he cannot bear being ousted from the Secret Archives library. "I need to find out what happened with the monk in the letter . . . where the hell do I fit in this mess?" The acid and tannins in the wine are hitting his stomach like a punching bag. Anthony examines Gabriel's face; his Hispanic features must have made him a good looking young man many years ago. He now seems tired and wrinkled. Gabriel is explaining how Anthony must reach out to Avinash Sullivan and warn him of the danger, and then connect him to people who can help him.

"This is not Palo Alto," pronounces Gabriel. "Avinash cannot stroll around Rome carelessly. Several people want him dead. He instigated the mess. He is the figure head for the Transparency Crusade. Many view murder as the only option to stop him from talking with the Pope." Gabriel has a slight accent but his voice is tuned for a good Sunday homily. He explains that he cannot contact Avinash directly as he is part of the faction against his campaign and he got his information by listening to a confession. It would be against his vows as a priest. Anthony swipes the sweat from his forehead and gulps more wine. Francesca jabbers, her voice is perfect for an Italian soap opera actress. She tells Anthony that she cannot contact Avinash either as such an act could compromise the University of Milan. The press knows she is a consultant to the Vatican on these matters. Someone laughs loudly behind Anthony. He wonders if Laura's parents are angry for not being on time for the girls. They can be difficult. For starters, they did not stay at Hotel Modigliani but in a suite at the luxurious Excelsior Hotel just a block away. His father-in-law is a Hollywood producer.

It's hot. Francesca and Gabriel are saying something but Anthony is unable to hear them through the noise in the restaurant, so he whispers to himself. "I love the Hotel Modigliani. Our room is great, the girls love it. Breakfast is included."

"*Atorrante*! You are not listening! Tony! You are the prime contact with Avinash. You must reach to him and replay everything we have been talking about. You must warn him!"

"Why me?" he keeps talking to himself but now loud enough for them to hear. "Does she think that we, all American citizens, are part of a big fraternity? Why would he talk with me?"

"You are blessed with a perfect cover up. Nobody will suspect if you reach to him." Gabriel focuses on Anthony as if exhorting him to repent of his sins. "You have the credentials by being an esteemed scholar from UCLA."

"There are many American scholars in Rome," he blurts too abruptly for his own standards of serene communication. The alcohol and thinking about the girls with his in-laws are making him testy. "Why am I different than others?"

As if giving the closing prayer at Sunday mass, Gabriel summarizes the situation: "Avinash Sullivan started and has led the social media crusade to make all information in the Vatican—regardless of how private—available to the public. The Pope is angry because he believes the Holy See has already become very transparent in the last decades in response to previous scandals. The Pope is seriously considering shutting all access to Vatican libraries to laymen and making a point that the Vatican is an independent nation with its own laws and sovereignty. Avinash is here in Rome to meet with the Vicar of Christ. He has scheduled an audience where he will present his case. Some powerful people in Rome don't want this meeting to happen. They want the Secret Archives closed to the public and Avinash dead. I want to warn Avinash. I don't need that death on my conscience."

"But you have not answered my question. Why me? How can I get close to him? Do you want me to go and knock on his hotel room door?"

"Exactly. Because your credentials as an American scholar give you credibility and because he is staying at the Excelsior Hotel, the same hotel where your in-laws are staying." Francesca speaks so close to Anthony's face that her spit is more annoying than her loud volume. "Nobody will notice if you approach him, or even if you go knock on his door."

Anthony swallows the rest of his drink in a rush. "This is too much." He apologizes and pushes back his chair with more energy than required. He needs time to think about everything. Unfortunately his chair knocks down the waiter who then tumbles on top of him spilling a tray full of red wine bottles. Streams of the ruby liquid soak him: his shirt, his pants, his undershirt, even his socks. Anthony freezes, confused and dazed. The red stains make him appear like an executioner covered in blood, but he is too drunk to make sense of the night. He folds his napkin and rushes away. "I just need to go home and see my girls."

CHAPTER 4

THE FIRST MURDER

Some people need coffee in the morning. Anthony has jogged every day, first thing, since he was in 8th grade. Instead of waiting in line for a latte or measuring spoonfuls of coffee beans, he stretches his muscles in sequential order from his neck to his toes. Instead of the sugar rush and the fat of a pastry, he feels blood flowing in his limbs and air filling his lungs with a clarity that engulfs his brain. Even at the saddest moment after Laura's death, jogging was a consoling addiction. During the last year, he ran marathons as frequently as he could so exhaustion would block any other feelings. Claudia sometimes joined him at a slower pace, creating a father-daughter bonding rhythm thicker for them than a father-daughter school dance.

Being caffeinated, others drive their cars frantically. Anthony meditates after running. He empties his mind of words, of images and perceptions. He becomes the Now, his breathing merging with the elements, creating links with the spiritual world.

Today Anthony is at the Borghese Gardens. This was another reason why Hotel Modigliani was chosen as a base for him and the girls. The Borghese Gardens is very close to being the "Central Park" of Rome. As Anthony dashes around trees and monuments, he can't help but attract people's attention. He is a very good-looking man in a very American boy-next-door manner: blond, well-built, with baby blue eyes, and well-balanced features over a strong masculine jaw. Anthony never notices or cares. All his life he has been immersed in his own world of ancient books and love with Laura, oblivious of women and men making passes at him.

His head aches after the red wine from the previous night. He has heartburn and a hangover. The reproachful look of his mother-in-law when he arrived to pick the girls still lingers in his memory. He cannot blame her. His shirt and pants splotched with red wine made him look like a butcher.

Anthony uses the exercise time to dissect the conversation with Francesca and the Los Angeles Bishop, Gabriel Herrera, separating facts from what could have been wine-induced misunderstanding. "I don't like red wine. It gives me migraines. I drink beer. I know how to control my drinking with beer." Anthony talks to himself, his acquired habit after Laura left.

He stops to meditate at a terrace looking down at *Piazza del Popolo*. The square is almost deserted. The occasional person hurries across it on the way to work. The obelisk at its center is lonely. Too small to fill all the space around, it looks more like a lonely teenager attempting a conversation with the regal twin churches in front of it. The trees behind Anthony sway in the wind, and he tries to match its breathing to the sound. He intends to empty his mind but continues replaying the conversation at the restaurant. He lacks full understanding of the message for Avinash Sullivan. Can he approach this man at the Excelsior Hotel to deliver the warning that his life is in mortal danger? What proof does he have to say that? "Oh, my friends told me to give you this message..." It was a terrible idea. "I want to go back to my hymns book and keep extracting Catullus poems and reading the monk's letter. I better pretend nothing happened last night. I'll tell Francesca the restaurant was so loud I could not hear them . . . which is partly true. I don't have to lie. If possible, I won't see her today. I'll hide in a reading room. I'll skip my appointment to catch up with her." Anthony has to transcribe the monk's letter into his computer. It is a valuable first-hand source describing life at the turn of the sixteenth century. He also wants to analyze the structure of the poems in the hymns book. He needs to prove they were written by Catullus. "I'll become another yellowing file in the Secret Archives."

Oxygen fills Anthony's lungs. His thoughts exit his conscience. His back muscles relax. "Ommmm. Ommmm . . . " He concentrates on his breathing.

He smiles on his journey back to the hotel, satisfied with his plan to ignore the previous night. His step has a little swagger. The following day is Saturday. He will go with his family to the ruins of *Ostia Antica*. By Monday, Francesca will have forgotten and forgiven everything. The Silicon Valley millionaire will have met with the Pope and be back in America. Anthony will submerge himself in the books and manuscripts around him for the entire summer, unmolested by the outside world.

When he gets to his hotel room, Anthony is welcomed by his in-laws. Thalia, the youngest, is jumping on one of the four beds. Claudia, the oldest, is reading Plato on the balcony, and Virginia is applying glitter gel to her hair. His father-in-law, Elmer (what kind of name is that?), is very agitated, talking with his wife, Melissa. The room is full of "Oh my Gods" and "Can you believe these people?" expressed at full volume. Anthony wonders how he will manage to go around them and into a hot shower.

"Oh my God, Tony, I am glad you are here! The Excelsior Hotel is a circus! Melissa and I went to have breakfast this morning but the entire lobby is swarming with policemen and reporters. Can you believe these people? All the restaurants were closed! Even the restaurants around the hotel, including *Café du Monde*, were closed! No service. Complete disrespect for their guests' hunger. Some luxury hotel! We were stopped three times, asked to identify ourselves and show our room keys. A circus, I tell you! It felt more like the *Cinecittà* movie studios than a hotel!"

Melissa stands up holding her youngest granddaughter's hand and marches to the door. "We came to have breakfast with you. Every day, the girls have told us it is very good. Don't worry—it won't go to your account. We'll pay for it."

"If the *Café du Monde* had been open, we would be there. The *Via Veneto* is blocked by security and TV vans. I can't believe you did not see any of this coming from the park," explains Elmer as he holds the other two girls' hands, ready to join his wife.

"I came through the back streets…"

"There were people running back and forth from the American Embassy to the hotel. After all, the embassy is next door. I even think the US Ambassador came to the hotel. It should make us feel safer, but are you certain you want to stay in Rome for a year? These people are so emotional." Elmer jumps into the elevator.

"I'm not sure a year in Rome is the best for the girls. Oh my God! There were soldiers everywhere. The girls could return to America with us," Melissa concludes as the elevator door closes.

Air in, air out. Laura and Anthony never raised their voices, even when quarreling. Everything was soft. "I wonder how Laura's parents can be so loud. They criticize Italians?" Despite the invasion of his space, Anthony refuses to lose his serenity. He closes his eyes while the shower runs. He visualizes being in the Secret Archives: "Two reading rooms, one index room, an internal library, a shop for preservation, restoration and book-binding, a laboratory for photography and digital reproduction, and a computer lab, all waiting for me. I can be there in an hour. Let's not forget the Tower of the Winds, the room used for astronomical studies by Gregory XIII while surrounded by rich frescoes. So wonderful and isolated!"

He dresses quickly in a beige linen suit and a light blue shirt. Italy is more formal than America, and he wants to look good. He even con-siders wearing a tie he bought at the Metropolitan Museum of Art gift shop.

The breakfast room is a long rectangle with a coffee counter and a table with pastries, bread, cheese, and cold cuts for the hotel guests to take to their tables. Modigliani reproductions hang on the white walls and columns. After a week, Luca, the waiter, and Maria, the cook, have become friends with the Hibbert family. They wave at Anthony when he enters and signal to the area where his girls are sitting. Normally, the room is full with tourists talking about their plans for the day, but today the buzz feels different. Everybody is gossiping about the events at the Hotel Excelsior. Elmer and Melissa are under the spotlight, telling and retelling their morning adventure to a group of people who have moved their chairs around them.

"The news said the body was taken to the morgue early in the morning. He did not answer his four o'clock wakeup call and a hotel employee went to his room…." Someone is relating the information he has gathered.

Thalia is dancing around the room; she seems happy, so Anthony takes her hand gently and directs her back to her breakfast after giving her a kiss. Claudia reads while munching pound cake with fresh cheese and ignoring the racket around her. Virginia brightens up at the sight of her father. She hugs Anthony with glee; her eyes are a little scared after listening to the conversations but have left their sadness back home in Redondo Beach. Anthony enjoys his fruit and white cheese while drinking a blood orange juice. He cocks his head trying to understand the topic that has everybody riled up.

"He was very rich. A billionaire. I've been to his offices in San Jose, California, and it is one of the most modern buildings I've been to. They used building materials that would have no carbon footprint."

"The Roman police is very rude. It appears they dislike tourists…"

"You say the American ambassador was at the Excelsior this morning? Ambassador Bradbury is a good man. My father met him when he was…"

"So today is definitely not a good day to go to the Capuchin Church in *Via Veneto*. The detectives will be in the area all day."

"Five bullets to the chest?"

Suddenly, the horror becomes clear for Anthony. He interrupts his father-in-law's whining with a direct question, while the blood drains from his face: "They killed someone at the Excelsior…was this Avinash Sullivan?"

"He was on our same floor. It's where the best suites are. They murdered him a couple of doors from us. We did not hear the shots. Did you notice anything when you picked up the girls? It was late. The murder might have already happened. Did you see anything suspicious? You should talk with the police!"

"Look, I was exhausted. I had to carry Virginia asleep and her backpack in my arms. Claudia and Thalia trailed behind me. I was not touristing. I did not inspect my surroundings to check if an assassin was lurking around."

"Think! You might have seen more than you remember…"

Anthony drops his fork, not hungry any more. He blocks his feelings as if he were folding his legs in a demanding yoga position. "I want to go to work. You and the girls should also hurry to your Italian classes. We are running late." Anthony hugs the girls, reassuring them that everything is all right. "Whatever happened at the Excelsior has nothing to do with us," he says more to himself than to the girls, "We will go to *San Crispino* for gelato this afternoon."

"You also promised yesterday…"

During the subway ride Anthony schemes to stay away of the Avinash Sullivan story. It is Francesca's business, not his. He will get the thirteenth-century hymns book and find the most hidden corner in the study rooms. "I have better things to do than to get involved in a Roman murder. Francesca was trying to pull me into this with the story of the Pope closing access to the Vatican libraries. The international community will not allow this to happen. I need to focus on my research." As he approaches Saint Peter, Anthony buys a Panama hat from a street vendor. He turns the collar of his jacket to cover his neck. Saint Peter's square is full of protesters demanding transparency in the Church. The crowd is angry in response to Avinash's murder. Anthony scuttles from Doric column to Doric column of Bernini's Colonnade around the square until he gets to the *Porta Santa* guard post. Once inside the Secret Archives, with the thirteenth- century book securely in his grasp, he sits on the floor in a discreet corner under the spiral staircase leading to the Tower of the Winds. Like a child satisfied with his hiding place, sitting with his folded legs next to his chest, he opens the torn fabric of the book's secret pouch, extracting the monk's handwritten confession. He squints at the ancient fonts. He dislikes technology, but in this moment, he would love if someone invented a machine that allowed him to read ancient manuscripts more easily. He feels the weight of the vellum in his hands and inhales the smell of old leather and centuries gone by. With a contented smile, he dives back into the narrative:

"After Cardinal della Rovere's visit, I was still a prisoner but was allowed to move freely inside the monastery grounds. The monks chatted happily, prayed, and used their voices to chant for the glory of Christ. Everybody believed I was mute, so I would kneel in my pew during mass listening to the beautiful modulations. I helped Callisto in the

kitchen again, and at times missed his silence as he talked incessantly about minor occurrences. The monks at the woodshop now worked at a different pace. They were happy to make bunks for everyone's cells not to sleep on the floor anymore. I cleaned my cell as thoroughly as I could. I threw all the hay where insects could live, and slept on top of the wood planks of the new bed. I wanted everything perfectly clean so I scrubbed the walls and the floor. I washed my body twice a day. My desire to be spotless drove me to shave my head and all my body hair daily. I did not want fleas or lice. I even plucked my brows and eyelashes. My genitals were as smooth as a newborn.

I also used my time to rebuild the old library. The new Abbot allocated furniture profits to buy printed books. The carpenters made desks to hold them. I dusted the books faithfully, and organized everything by size. I also returned to the infirmary.

Early December, the Pope's soldiers came to take me to the Vatican Palace. I discovered them talking to the Abbot and pointing in my direction. My luck was sealed. I had forgotten about Cardinal della Rovere's promises and thought the Borgia Pope had called for me to avenge his minions. Callisto and all the monks gathered in the cloister to bid me farewell. Some kissed my hands, thanking me for having cured them when sick. Others threw themselves at my feet and held my legs, praying for Our Lord to protect me as they believed an avenging angel had possessed my body so I could kill and liberate them from Abbot Laurentius. The Abbot blessed me. Many in the crowd were crying; the faces of grown men were covered in giant tears. The Vatican soldiers were amazed at the signs of affection. They had been ordered to transport a criminal to his punishment and did not expect this display.

To me, everything felt very distant. I had been immersed in my isolation and loneliness, never realizing what the others felt or trying to be friends with them. I was driven to do what was right, distracted by my misery. From the monastery's open door, I could see Rome's city wall. The monks chanted to Jesus, imploring for mercy with deep voices as I was taken away. With every step farther, I sensed their voices and support closer to my spirit.

With no brows and eyelashes, the sun blinded me. As soon as we crossed the Aurelian Wall, my vision was inundated with the filth on the streets. Human refuse mixed with mud created a paste into which my sandals stuck, while warm viscous liquids swished around my toes. Used to the clean air from the monastery, I now tasted the stench of urine and excrement cling to my nose and tongue. Deeper into the city, I forced myself to look around. We were in a narrow alley. The crammed dwellings on both sides had built balconies obstructing the sun. A toothless woman with filthy babies stared at me with a hint of interest. The disgusted soldiers pressed me to walk faster but the advance became harder and harder as we entered an area overflowing with street vendors. A flower girl stood bestrode a pool of vomit. Her flowers were wilted. An orange vendor had a rickety stand next to a dead dog, the meat in the carcass almost gone. Flies swarmed on a purple paste with protruding bones. Everyone was shouting. Even the pigs submerged in their slime seemed to howl their grunts at the naked children playing next to them.

There was no improvement when crossing the river. At both sides of the embankment, wretched houses formed a dense cluster of lodgings parted by the Tiber River. The water smelled fetid. My head ached, my throat thumped with the effort to suppress vomit. My eyes were red and running. Was this the Rome where I had lived during my childhood? Who had replaced the magical ruins and lavender fields with human misery?

Finally, the houses receded as we reached the open square in front of the ancient Saint Peter Basilica built by Constantine. The Pope's palace stood next to it. Constantine had built on top of a Roman cemetery, filling the tombs and mausoleums with earth to form a vast foundation that extended to parts of the Circus of Caligula and Nero. The magnificent fourth-century basilica had decayed through the years. The open cloister was surrounded by magnificent columns; many had come from earlier Roman temples, some had even been brought from Greece. The blocks of marble used to honor Jupiter were piled on top of ones used for the Mithras cult. Inside, the majesty of the construction made me ignore its disrepair through the intricate mosaics, numerous altars, and holy relics. This was sacred ground visited by pilgrims from all lands. The air was heavy with the smoke from incense, myrrh, and exotic foreign oils used to anoint the sculptures of saints and martyrs.

Vigor emanated from the many chapels around me despite heavy walls leaning on the main construction. One wall had collapsed, and on the overturned marble blocks I saw pagan writing and images. The masons in the fourth century had wanted to keep their pagan deities hidden in the stones used to establish the new Christian religion. The focal point of the building was a bronze balustrade over Saint Peter's grave. Linking it to the main building was an arch with the following inscription: "Because of your leadership the glorious universe has reached to the furthest stars: victorious Constantine dedicates this church to you."

I was taken through a passage into the palace and to the third room of the library on the first floor of the Papal residence. I later found out that Pope Sixtus IV had assigned that room for the Secret Archives when he had the Vatican library built. Two other rooms held Greek and Latin manuscripts, and a fourth room had all ecclesiastical writing. One of the soldiers prodded me to kneel. I heard them say that the Pope was approaching. Remembering that the Abbot had been a minion of the Borgia Pope, I imagined he was coming to pronounce a horrible fate for me. The soldier now pushed my face against the floor so I would be completely prostrated. I heard the soldiers move away and the Pope enter the room with an entourage. His voice was commanding. He sounded familiar. I could glimpse his ornate red slippers covered in gold and silk embroidery. He ordered everybody out of the room and commanded the soldiers to guard the rooms adjacent to us—and to kill without questions anybody who tried to eavesdrop. Everybody left in a hurry, their feet as nervous as the legs of leashed greyhounds before a race. They were afraid.

I prayed to the Holy Trinity for a swift death. I quaked remembering the humiliation at the hands of the deacons. I tightened my muscles to regain control and retain a shred of dignity but the memories were rocking through my form. I erupted in loud laments with my arms flat on my sides. The Pope placed his hand in front of my face so I could see his ring. It was not the Borgia coat of arms. This was not Alexander VI in front of me. The ring had two keys and an oak tree. I kissed it, calming down. I then kissed the slippers. The Pope raised my head and made me look at him. In front of me was Cardinal della Rovere—now Pope Julius II. Later, I put the pieces of the puzzle in place. When I started my captivity after killing Abbot Laurentius, Alexander VI was still the Pope. In my isolation I did not hear about his death, and how Pius III had been elected pope after him. Pius III had died after only a month of his pontificate. To become the head of the Roman Catholic Church, it had taken Cardinal della Rovere three conclaves, chests of gold, exceptional political maneuvering, and poisoning Pius III himself with the elixir in the vial I had given to him. Pius III's death had been clean and, despite suspicions, nobody could trace the venom.

Pope Julius II's eyes and mine met. My grief was removed. He could see through me but I could see in him vulnerability and a secret that others would never know. He knelt on the tiled floor and embraced me, his white ornate robes a sharp contrast with my humble habit. We were acting the scene of the Church welcoming a sinner to its bosom.

"God has spoken. He has shown your poisons to be an instrument of His Will," he confided as he would with an old friend. He told me of his years of exile in France to escape Alexander Borgia's corrupt power. He shared the doubts that had plagued him while away. He was uncertain if he would ever return to Italy, unclear if he would be given the privilege of leading the Catholic Church to the great status it deserved. He had left Rome a young man. His hair was now almost white, but his deep-set, eager eyes glowed with the promise of someone emerging into life. He pressed his lips together for a moment as he narrated his rushed return to the city after learning of Alexander Borgia's sickness and death. His strong body was frail for an instant as he described the political forces that had chosen the elder Pius III instead of him as pope. France, Spain, and the Italian states had groped for the power to control the Catholic Church and won a puppet. It was at that time that he had been taken to see me, and I had provided the lavender and honey poison that killed Pius III twenty-eight days after he had ascended to primacy.

With dignity, he now changed the topic to describe his vision of a new Catholic Church, one that no doubt would become the center for all countries, the authority for every ruler to follow and consult. He would make Rome magnificent again, a place where artists from all over the known world would converge to reinvent the city as a place of wonder, where olden and novel would merge, forming the foundation for all ages to come.

With eyes aflame, he solicited my servitude in three areas. Pope Julius II was not as obsessed with ancient texts as his uncle Pope Sixtus IV had been. Still, he willed me to scout monasteries and ancient librar-ies in search of manuscripts and books from antiquity. He was not going to pay traders for books. Alexander VI had left empty coffers. Pope Julius II was the monarch of all religious orders; he empowered me to confiscate anything I found to bring back to the Vatican. He then asked me to be his spy within the papal court. My fake muteness— seemingly evidenced by the hole in my tongue—was a perfect cover up. I would eavesdrop on others and report back. Finally, he bid me to become an assassin in his service. My skills and knowledge as a poisoner were pow-erful secret weapons to eliminate opponents when necessary.

"I cannot recover the Northern Papal Estates and spread our true faith armed exclusively with sacred relics and Hail Marys."

He was the Pope, the representative of Jesus Christ on Earth. To murder under him was an act of God with no sin associated with it. He walked around the room as I sluggishly swore alliance and obedience to him. He blessed me.

I was ordered to move into a room in the nearby Belvedere build-ing, where I could be close to him and part of the court. Pope Julius II owned me, and I was thankful and relieved. I felt safe and with a purpose.

Reader, I have to pause now. The poison in my blood is making me weak. My body is covered in sweat and I can hardly breathe. Is it anxiety that comes with the awareness of an imminent death or is it the poison working faster than it should? I have eleven more days. I should be strong to finish this confession letter. I need to be careful. I will hide this part of the confession in the hymn book from Saint Benedict Minor.

The rest you can find if you follow the numbers below:

3:1: 21
4:2: 45
8:4:6

15:11:22
55:4:9
75:10:3
90:2:14

Anthony stares at the numbers confused and frustrated. Is this all? Where and how will he find the rest of the monk's story? What secrets had been so terrible to hide them in places for no one to uncover? Anthony pushes the vellum folio with force inside the inner cover pouch. The cloth rips further and entirely detaches from the cover. Anthony reddens as he realizes the damage he has inflicted on the book. He surfaces from under the staircase below the Tower of the Winds and looks around to find a surveillance camera mounted on a wall staring straight at him and the broken book in his hand.

CHAPTER 5

YOGA IN JAIL

Lieutenant Alessandro Catzola is enjoying an unexpected treat. He just picked up his eight year-old boy from school. He has promised to take him for gelato, but as he drives, listening to the news on the radio, his instinct tells him that he will be dragged into the case of Avinash Sullivan's murder. His mobile phone rings at that moment.

"Catzola, *pronto*. The boss wants you back in the office. He just got lab results from the murdered American. Mr. Sullivan was shot five times at close range in the chest. There is no evidence of a fight so we have to assume this was either unexpected or he opened the door to someone he knew. Forensics is revealing unusual aspects from the bullets in the body. They were bullets made during World War II, probably early 1940s in Nazi Germany. The gun seems to be a Pistole Parabellum mostly known as a Luger pistol."

"*Benne, benne*. I'll drop the boy at home with my mother as fast as I can. Do I have time to stop for gelato?"

"No time for gelato. There is more you should know. A video has surfaced on YouTube showing the assassin at the Excelsior Hotel. A tourist who was filming the lobby captured the image. We have identified the assassin, and we believe we can make a quick capture this afternoon."

The boy complains when his father confirms the no gelato news. He has been listening to the exchange through the car speakers.

"I'll make it up to you, *caro*. I promise."

"Will you continue the story you were telling me last night?"

"I won't be home at bed time much in the upcoming week. You heard I'm starting a new case. I'll write it for you whenever I can." The boy's smile stretches his thin lips in a crooked line. He holds his protests by staring out the window, forcing himself into boredom by gazing at the streets he has known all his life.

• • •

Francesca has sent Anthony an email at noon canceling their meeting to discuss the poetry findings. She claims she has some unexpected business to tend to, and Anthony is happy to comply and keep the questions to himself. He is busy with his own affairs. He had to find a hiding place for the damaged book until he can figure how to repair it or reveal his "crime" to the librarian. He is also busy transcribing the erotic poems from the hymns book into his laptop.

Smiling to himself, Anthony leaves the library a couple of hours before closing time. It is Friday, and he wants to dodge the subway crowd. His mind is preoccupied with solving the puzzle of the numbers at the end of the monk's confession. The Swiss Guards take longer than usual inspecting his briefcase at the *Porta Santa*. They even make some calls.

"Is anything wrong?" Anthony inquires.

Via Ottaviano next to the Vatican wall is curiously empty. The street vendors stand silently behind their merchandise with no tourists around them. They eye Anthony with suspicion, and he wonders what has made them change their bustling demeanor to eyes looking sideways and twisted whispering mouths. He finds the answer when reaching *Piazza del Risorgimento* on his way to the metro. As Anthony crosses the street from the square, he is assaulted by a troop of policemen and reporters. A man with a microphone shouts at him, and a cameraman captures the instant when a policeman binds his arms behind his back. Anthony strains against confinement but soon realizes he is overpowered. He hears shouts: "*Il assassino, il assassino!*" Now he sees the tourists standing behind a rope pointing at him and taking pictures and video with their smartphones. Someone has taken Anthony's briefcase from his hand. "*Il omicida!*" He is shoved inside a police car. "What the hell is going on? I don't think that damaging a thirteenth-century hymns book is enough crime to have me arrested this way." The driver is very busy arguing through the crime squad radio. Anthony tries to reason but the driver barks at him to shut up.

Anthony focuses his breathing, controlling the flow of air in and out of his lungs. "This has to be a big misunderstanding. Ommmm..." He forces his muscles to relax despite the discomfort of sitting with his hands cuffed behind his back. Ommmm... The police car is stuck in traffic. The siren blares but no one makes way for the vehicle. Air in, air out. The driver increases the volume of his shouts to the cars around them surrounded by heat vapor. He is scarlet with fury, squabbling with a taxi driver who cuts in front of them. Obscenities fly between the cars as the men menace each other with clenched fists. Anthony visualizes the letters for *Om* instead of getting distracted by two police motorcycles arriving with more blaring sirens and loudspeakers commanding the taxi to move.

After an hour and a half, the police car arrives at a red brick building. More TV cameras and reporters are waiting for them. Two policemen shove Anthony into the station. He ventures some questions but is shuffled from one officer to another before getting any answer. They empty his pockets. They also take his belt, his shoelaces, and his Metropolitan Museum tie. They release his hands from the cuffs as they put him in a small cell with bad neon lighting whose blinking casts sordid light onto the grey concrete floor. Anthony is still concentrating on his respiration. He has managed to stay detached from his imprisonment. He has forced himself to watch everything as if he were in front of a movie screen. He is not a loud person so he does not scream or argue in a loud voice. He is certain Italian policemen will be louder. "I am a law-abiding American citizen and civility is paramount when dealing with foreign law enforcement officials. Sooner than later they will realize I am a valued member of society and will drop the charges . . . whatever they are."

Anthony is left alone. He sits on a hard, cold metallic bench and wishes his pants were not made of linen but of thick wool. The concrete walls are covered with graffiti, and as he reads the vulgar messages, he loses control and feels a muscular spasm rising from his intestines to his lungs up to his throat and finally to his forehead like a fountain of anxiety. His body heat escapes following the muscle contractions. What if Kafka were Italian? The Italian Justice system is never portrayed in a positive light by the American media. What if he never sees his family again, and this terrible, terrible misunderstanding becomes a life-long imprisonment? Anthony's knuckles turn white as he clutches the edge of his metallic seat.

Ommmm… Anthony tries orderly breathing but ends up hyperventilating. He wants to pee but the fetid hole on one corner of the cell does not look hygienic. Is it supposed to be a latrine where prisoners crouch to do their business? The stink of urine and excrement assault his nostrils. He recalls the assassin monk walking across Roman alleys in the sixteenth century. That was probably worse.

Pacing furiously around the small enclosed space does not help. He needs to get his body under control again. He looks at his left wrist. They took his watch. The girls must be worried. In a civilized manner he calls out: "*Pronto*! Can anyone hear me? Is there anyone there?" No answer. He calls again, this time louder. Still no answer. His vocal cords rebel against being so loud. His voice increases volume. Only an echo responds. His lungs join the rebellion as he shouts: "*Fillios de putana*, bastards, open the door! This is a misunderstanding!" His arms join his mind's rebellion, banging like a mob trying to shake the prison cell bars, but the bars remain unmovable, indifferent to Anthony's feelings. "Listen to me! I want a lawyer! I am an American citizen!" Anthony's baby-blue shirt is translucent with sweat, making it stick to his chest and back.

Everything seems futile. Anthony wants to regain his composure. Panic and anger will not make captivity easier. He sits on the hard floor in a lotus position, closing his eyes. He wishes he could smoke a joint to relax. On some weekends, Anthony and Laura would send the girls for a sleepover with their grandparents. For two straight days they would smoke pot, make love several times a day, and read to each other naked. Their nudity and the sweet smoke combined with obscure poetry would detox them from the daily routine, from Thalia having been particularly difficult, from a corporate reorganization at UCLA and a new dean questioning budgets. Anthony eases his muscles through the memory of Laura's body, hard and lean even after giving birth to three girls. She had been a runner and a swimmer. Air in, air out. Inhale, exhale. The recollection of her warm, soft skin, a canvas to curl against, allows his heart to beat with a steady rhythm. His diaphragm moves up and down with calm command.

Anthony loses track of time sitting in the lotus position when he hears a door opening in the distance. Someone is speaking in English! Is the American cavalry finally coming to the rescue?

Two persons are waiting for him in a small, sterile meeting room. One is a short, stout American woman. Her name is Ellia Jones. She is a lawyer from the American Embassy. The other is an Italian detective, Lieutenant Alessandro Catzola. Both shake Anthony's hand and invite him to sit while vigilantly assessing his character. Anthony returns the scrutiny. Ellia Jones is a middle-aged woman with a square muscular body uncharacteristic for someone with an expatriate life. Her very short hair is grey, and while her features are gentle, her eyes express the fierceness of a warrior. Alessandro Catzola is sinewy and nervous. His face is young and has proud Roman traits: a wide forehead, a strong jaw and cheekbones, a powerful nose. He could have been a consul in the Roman army. However his teeth and fingertips are stained from nicotine, and his suit is rumpled as if he had slept in it for several nights.

Alessandro apologizes for not having been present during the arrest. He was supposed to be the interpreter between the police and Anthony but unfortunately had been delayed first at the office, and then Rome's traffic had trapped him for more than an hour. Before Anthony can answer, Ellia asks curtly: "Are you going to provide a written confession?"

Anthony reflects for a moment and then answers: "I can, but I believe UCLA can cover the cost to repair the damage." Restoring the hymns book to its original state should be easy.

"How is UCLA involved in this?"

"What is UCLA?" interrupts Alessandro.

"UCLA is the University of California in Los Angeles. They are covering the expenses for my research during my sabbatical year here in Rome. If anything, what happened is just an accident resulting from my investigation."

"I don't understand how the event could be considered an accident?" Alessandro exclaims staring directly at Anthony's pale blue eyes.

"Well, what I don't understand is why you needed to display so much force for my arrest. A reprimand from the Vatican library would have sufficed."

"Stop playing games, Mr. Hibbert! There is no way shooting a person five times point blank in the chest can be considered a research accident." Alessandro's hands gesture broadly, expressing umbrage at Anthony's obtuse responses. Anthony straightens up on his chair, insulted by the accusation.

"What are you talking about? I tore the inner cover of a thirteenth-century manuscript. Isn't this why I am here? I don't know how to use a gun and have not killed anyone."

Ellia smiles for the first time. Her severe predator lips have only a hint of color. "You claim ignorance of why you were detained, Mr. Hibbert?"

"I damaged a thirteenth-century hymns book at the Vatican library."

"*Merda!*" Alessandro stands up as if to backslap Anthony. His body shaking with fury sends ripples that generate waves on his wrinkled suit. For a moment, he thought the case would be over swiftly and he would be able to return home to his son. Clearly it's going to be more complicated.

"Mr. Hibbert," explains Ellia Jones, assertive and direct with the intensity of a seasoned bureaucrat refusing to make an exception to a government form, "you have been charged with the murder of Avinash Sullivan. A tourist captured you on video at the lobby of the Excelsior Hotel last night around the time of the murder. You are covered in blood from head to toes. Already, the video received two million hits after it was posted on YouTube this morning."

Anthony frowns. He has never visited YouTube. He knows his daughters use it frequently, but he believes people waste their lives watching videos of kittens on the web. "YouTube is only about cute animal videos. Why would a video of me be on YouTube?"

"The Italian police was alerted immediately after it was posted. Your face has been on news around the planet. Your arrest was televised in real time," explains Alessandro, proud of his unit's response. "Where did you hide the gun, Mr. Hibbert? Where did you get a Nazi pistol and bullets from 1940?" Alessandro and Ellia stare at Anthony for several minutes as he hesitates to respond, repressing a derisive chuckle.

"Mr. Hibbert, the video posted on YouTube leaves small doubt about your culpability in the murder. Why don't you and I speak in private to expedite the matter?"

"Do you have accomplices?" Alessandro pushes his smartphone at Anthony, who can see himself walking through the lobby of the Excelsior

Hotel on his way to pick the girls from his in-laws' suite. Anthony's clothes are covered in red.

Ellia explains that the evidence reveals that Avinash was shot the moment he answered the knock on his door. The luger gun had a silencer. He was then dragged inside the suite to his bed. The assassin had spent the next minutes searching for something in the room and in the body's pockets. The police believed the assassin could have gotten bloodstains over his clothes while conducting these activities.

"My red stains are red wine. A waiter accidentally spilled it from a tray on me. Have your Italian detectives inspected my hotel room? My stained clothes are in the dirty laundry hamper. I am certain they are trained well enough to differentiate blood from wine. If you have not taken this measure, you better hurry to the Hotel Modigliani. You have to release me from this hell hole. I can see how watching videos on YouTube has increased the IQs of police forces around the world. My stains are from red wine, and I have witnesses, a full restaurant of them."

Alessandro and Ellia are startled for the first time. They look at each other, eager to pin the blame on someone. Detective Catzola punches his phone screen as if crushing cockroaches with his fingers, "Even if your improbable story about the wine were true, that won't release you from jail. You are still the main suspect." He leans in, wrinkling his forehead and slanting his eyes, breathing closely to Anthony's face for a few seconds before he leaves the room. The embassy lawyer hails a guard and commands him to take Anthony back to confinement. She moves briskly, with short powerful movements outlining muscles that are ready to subdue anybody on her path. She too leaves in a hurry. She has to debrief the American Ambassador on the interrogation.

• • •

Back in his cell, Anthony walks in circles like a stray dog captured in the pound, worried about his family. Mechanically, he starts a yoga routine: the tabletop, the cow, the cat…He stretches to empty his mind of negativity. He feels he can touch the roof with his fingertips. Sweat returns to cover his body. The low lunge, the twist, utkatasana. Anthony flexes his legs, stretching his arms in front of him and raising them slowly.

Stretching, stretching as if he were reaching to the arms of Claudia, his oldest girl. He thinks of her. She has always been more mature than her age, asking about God and the meaning of the existence of black holes since she was five. She is an avid non-fiction reader. Utkatasana, or the awkward pose. Not as uncomfortable as the stench from the open-air toilet in the corner of his cell. Anthony releases the head of his thigh bones for comfort. Claudia is precocious but likable. She helps her friends at all times and never judges anybody. Anthony stands on his toes. His body is like a giant letter Z every muscle stretched and taut. Claudia is fourteen and already had her first period. He sent her to talk with his mother-in-law. Those are the times when Laura's absence is all too evident. Although Melissa talked to Claudia about "Mother Nature's monthly gift," Claudia returned to Anthony with a list of books on women's sexuality from Amazon so she could get the facts straight.

The bare walls are closing on him. He wonders how the sky looks. He has lost track of time. He breathes slowly, making an effort to exhale his anxiety. Tuladandasana is a strong, grounding pose—the balancing stick pose that Anthony enacts by standing on one leg and leaning his torso until it is completely parallel to the concrete floor. Then he lifts his other leg to make it also perfectly parallel to the floor. Anthony almost feels blood flooding portions of his heart that had been neglected. Virginia, the middle girl, is like that. A girl that expanded his and Laura's lives to areas they had not imagined. She is the girliest of girls. She cares about her glittery clothes and sparkling hair more than anyone else in the family. Her grandparents indulge her in anything she wants to buy so her closet is the largest in their household. She has gone through the pink phase, the lilac phase, and the multicolored pastels. She is the sweetest girl and very popular with her friends for being in the forefront of fashion and electronic gadgets. She loves video games, iPhone apps, and anything technology related. Still, she reads a lot on her Kindle and cherishes books like *Little Women*.

The walls are not there anymore. He could be inside an armored vault in a bank and not notice the lack of oxygen. The night is advancing as Anthony moves to tree pose, standing straight in one leg and folding the other until it touches his groin. His hands are on his chest as if praying. This pose brings serenity and balance, very necessary when dealing with Thalia, the youngest girl, the hyperactive hurricane who needs to exercise for a long time before she can sit to read *Junie B. Jones* or Magic Tree House books. She is a little tomboy maybe as a way of differentiating herself from Virginia or maybe because she spends so much time playing soccer, volleyball, tennis, and baseball. She is very funny and makes everyone laugh.

Every time he feels trapped again or the thick smell of urine on the air makes him gag, Anthony repeats the yoga routine, almost obsessively, until a guard brings coffee and bread for breakfast. Finally, he remembers the feeling of being inside the Secret Archives study room, the smell of old paper and wood, the long tables with lamps and screens creating the safe environment of an elementary school. He remembers the feeling of touching the old psalms book and the letter inside it. He visualizes the faded numbers at the end of the confession and repeats them: "3:1:21, 4:2:45, 8:4:6, 15:11:22, 55:4:9, 75:10:3, 90:2:14"—and repeats them again and again like a mantra. His lips move in silence as if he were praying, until he stops shifting his body into yoga positions and lies on the hard bunk on his cell. He falls asleep without touching the food. Later, he is taken back to the small meeting room. Lieutenant Catzola and Ellia Jones are waiting for him. They seem to have gone through a rough night. Their angry faces are haggard and black puffy circles crawl under their bloodshot eyes. They don't waste time in small talk and jump directly to business. Alessandro Catzola explains that he fetched the stained clothes himself from Hotel Modigliani. He has seen and smelled enough blood in his career to distinguish blood from Chianti. Unfortunately, Italian forensic protocol dictates that a laboratory has to confirm his observation, and the judge needs to be convinced of Anthony's innocence before he can be released. Ellia Jones then explains that regrettably the Italian police laboratories don't work during the summer weekends and the judges like to spend their summers at the beach. It is evident that Alessandro and Ellia have been quarreling for a while. Alessandro talks to Ellia sideways while Ellia looks at him deprecatingly. Both add that a press release is in the works in case Anthony is liberated since Avinash's murder is such a high profile case.

"Ambassador Bradbury is very sorry that you are in this situation."

"Usually suspects of your caliber are kept in isolation, but the commissioner has agreed to allow visitors." Anthony clutches his fists in response while his "thank you" smile falters on his lips and turns into a smirk.

"I have been in contact with your family. Everybody is well but understandably shaken with the events. Your daughters are at the Excelsior Hotel with their grandparents. The Ambassador has visited them in person to express his support. Your father-in-law will come soon with fresh clothes and books for you."

"Can I get my laptop?" asks Anthony in an unemotional tone disguising his fury.

"It is with the Vatican security agents. They employ an excellent cybercrime containment group that is performing forensics on it. The hard drive is being duplicated as you are still a suspect. While your laptop model is very old, and your hard drive has less memory space than a smartphone, we still need to keep it. You will get it back if you are allowed to return to the Archives library." Anthony digs both his hands into his disheveled and unwashed hair. He pulls it.

"Ambassador Bradbury wishes for me to be at your service at all times during your stay in Rome," declares Ellia Jones with servitude. "I will personally escort your callers this weekend."

Anthony nods curtly at her, and after a long silence asks for a guard to return him to his grey containment cell and as far as possible from these two visitors. Before he leaves he has one last resigned petition: "Please tell my father-in-law to bring some air freshener, preferably something with patchouli."

"I will. We want to make you comfortable. Ambassador Bradbury wishes to protect you and your family from any unexpected danger your involvement in this affair might bring."

Anthony wants an explanation for Ellia's words, but she is too far down the corridor to give an answer.

He sees her later as she sits for the rest of the day in a chair in the conference room while Anthony receives visitors but still no answers from her. She looks out of place in a cheap pastel business suit. The room is very hot but she keeps her jacket on. While Anthony thanks Elmer for the clean clothes, Ellia leafs through a magazine pretending not to listen to the conversation.

Francesca, updated of the whole situation by Anthony's mother-in-law, also stops by during the day. She talks the instant she crosses the threshold. "*Caro*, when I saw you on the news I could not believe it. I am glad the whole misunderstanding is being handled now. Who would believe our small soiree would create this chaos?" Her expensive perfume battles with the foul air.

"Let's not talk about that. I am certain my escort here, Ms. Ellia Jones from the American Embassy, does not want to be bored with the details of our conversation," his eyes flame at her, signaling there is a lot to talk about that dinner but it will have to wait until they are in private. Francesca smiles gracefully, waving multicolored H. Stern jewelry that matches her hair and Versace outfit. Ellia nods her head at her and stands up. Francesca greets her with one kiss on each cheek given in a wholehearted way.

"I think we met before Ms. Jones. You might not remember me," she blinks, "but we had a very good experimental time during a conference. It was in Milan around a year ago," Ellia nods with the failed grace of a well-mannered bulldog. Francesca winks at her again before she quickly jumps into a monologue with dramatic intonations while her hands become feverish with excitement. "The Pope is creating a Transparency Commission to look at the requests from social networks and craft an action plan. Avinash's death has made the Transparency Crusade against the Vatican the hottest topic on the web. I've been glued to the news." Was Francesca a frustrated soap opera actress? "Terms related to this have taken the top ratings on Google, Yahoo, and Bing. The Pope had to temporarily turn off his Twitter account as the agency that manages it could not keep track with the onslaught of postings. I saw in the news that the social media trackers show very diverse sentiments in the websphere. I know you are an ignorant brute regarding technology. These are programs that track what people are posting and amalgamate them into feelings, trends and topics." She pulls the bottom of her jacket to straighten it. "The Pope is currently meeting with his advisors to select the members of the commission. They want secular and religious participants. Access to the Vatican Secret Files is currently on the table. I don't think they will close it, but rumors abound." She smiles to herself, self-acknowledging her importance, and then walks around the conference room like a trapped tigress. Ellia does not even pretend to be reading. "I don't know who the US Ambassador Representative will be. I am certain the US will have someone from their office. You probably don't know this Anthony, but from what I remember when I met her a year ago, Ellia is one of the most important liaisons between the Embassy and the Vatican. Who knows? Maybe she knows now but cannot tell us. She might be the one." Ellia crosses her hands on her lap more like a goon during a police interrogation than a lady. "I was just on the phone with one person close to the whole affair. He told me in an *unofficial manner*," she whispers the last two words, "that the Pope himself has been briefed about what happened with you Anthony. He knows about your innocence! As an apology from the Holy See and recognizing your scholarly credentials, they are considering you as one of the Transparency Commission members!" Francesca claps her hands and waves her extended palms around the room signaling the two persons and herself. "How much fun! The three of us might be working together in this!" Anthony and Ellia exchange hostile glances.

That night Anthony does a yoga routine again. Once relaxed, he lays on the hard metallic bunk surrounded by the aroma of patchouli. Despite all the information from the day, his mind is not on the Pope's Transparency Commission or the mystery of Avinash's murder or even on Francesca's and Gabriel Herrera's involvement in the whole mess. A few weeks ago he was a scholar living in Redondo Beach in Los Angeles, and now he is in a Roman jail leading a very different existence and obsessed with the numbers at the end an obscure monk's confession. What do the numbers mean, and how can he break the code to can find the rest of the story about the sixteenth-century Vatican assassin?

Alone, he phrases the good nights to his absent girls and pretends to sleep.

CHAPTER 6

THE DOGS OF OSTIA

No amount of yoga can keep dark thoughts from creeping into Anthony's brain while isolated in a cell with flickering sterile light above him. No amount of controlled breathing can keep Anthony from facing the vortex of despair at the possibility of being separated from his family long term, of failing them when he is the only anchor in his household. Sweat covers his body once and again from the realization that, in his grief, he has wasted a year of his life feeling a victim instead of re-writing his story. He wakes in the middle of the night, his heart beating with wild force, short of breath and feeling guilty for having moved through the previous year in mechanical motions when he should have been the one lifting his daughters out of depression every day. He should have been the strong one.

"I'm sorry, Laura. Forgive me, girls."

He lays in fetal position on the hard bunk failing to fall asleep again. His only escape is to think again of the monk's letter and the numbers at the end of it, but he fails to decipher them. Frustration is a bad companion when one is trapped in a confined space.

Anthony is released from jail on Tuesday night. The laboratory results from his clothes showed the stains were red wine and not blood, and the paraffin test results revealed the pores on his fingertips and hands free of gunpowder vestiges.

He leaves the police station through the back door as dozens of reporters are stationed at the front entrance. As sunlight shines on his face, Anthony's muscles vibrate with relief. The air is sweet. The open space becomes a tangible surface that removes layers of anxiety and claustrophobia from days inside a prison cell. Ellia Jones has a limo from the American Embassy waiting in an alley with a discreet police motorcycle escort. She welcomes him with a short phrase: "Let's stay close by. We have reasons to believe you and your family might be in danger."

He enters the limo and settles himself into the plush leather seat, but despite the newly found comfort he bites his lower lip. "Why would you say so?"

"I cannot reveal my sources."

"It is my family you are talking about." He jerks his hand through his unwashed hair.

"And we are here to protect you."

"I need to know more."

"There is nothing more I can share at this moment. I'll stay close to you, claiming to be there in case you are bothered by reporters."

Anthony frowns and decides to continue to bite his lower lip instead of participating any longer in the fruitless conversation. He hurries the driver to get him back to his family. He wants to get away from the mastiff/woman hybrid seated in front of him. The absence of his girls has convinced him that returning to depression and sadness is not an option.

Lieutenant Alessandro Catzola supervises the operation on a rooftop from a distance while on the phone with his security contact at the Vatican. The operation needs to be flawless after the embarrassment of Anthony's arrest. During the last twenty-four hours, the world media have made the inefficiency of Italian's police and justice system the center of attacks. Talk shows around the planet stream roundtables that question if Italy is fit for the European Union. Amanda Knox's story, the controversial case of an American student charged with murder, gets replayed to substantiate that messy might be the norm in Italy's police investigations. Anthony's YouTube video doubles its views to four million. Spoofs of it are posted in the hundreds. Bloggers have a field day questioning if amateur videos interfere with justice rather than aid it.

· · ·

Sponge Bob in Italian suddenly becomes irrelevant. Back at the Excelsior Hotel suite, the girls race to Anthony. He embraces his daughters, absorbing the energy of their presence, glad the unfortunate incident is over. It's the simple things of those moments that make them permanent. Thalia jumping and climbing on him like a monkey screaming "Papa" at the top of her lungs. Virginia immersing her face in his chest and covering his neck and chin with glitter gel with a comforting strawberry scent. Claudia has an awkward embrace because she wants him to embrace her, but at fourteen she is uncomfortable with physical contact. Two men watch this reunion as they wait in the corridor. Ellia Jones has arranged for body guards to walk with them back to Hotel Modigliani.

Their room at Hotel Modigliani feels like going back home despite everything being misplaced. Their belongings are crammed in half-open drawers, and their clothes are mixed after the police conducted hasty inspections in search of evidence. The beds are misaligned, some personal toiletries missing, but the family finds order by being together. After all, they have almost a year in Rome to put things back in place, and the girls kept their most personal belongings—their stuffed plush animals, books, and electronics—with them in their backpacks at all times—out of reach of the prying hands of homicide investigators.

On Wednesday, the girls skip Italian class. Anthony resolves not to go to the Vatican library and ignores the calls from Francesca on his mobile phone. Since they missed their planned trip to *Ostia Antica* during the weekend, they decide to have a Wednesday holiday. Ostia was one of the main Roman ports during the Empire, a center of commerce and financial activity. Even after hundreds of years, the ruined buildings remain. A complete city an hour away from Rome via a train ride becomes their destination—with Ellia Jones in her business suit with a new pastel color tagging along. The American ambassador has asked her to stay close to the Hibbert family. She does not look very happy during the train ride inside a hot car with graffiti-covered walls. The girls and Anthony relish the expression on her face when a woman sitting next to her falls asleep and rests her exhausted head on the American lawyer's shoulder.

Once there, everybody steps lightly, skipping into the marvels, the beauty, and serenity that welcomes them. The city is large, with several areas dedicated to different occupations: the market place, the forum, the public baths, the warehouses, and the living quarters. Founded during Rome's early years by one of its kings, *Ostia Antica* became the main port during the Republic and part of the Empire. The sun is so dazzling, it feels as though they had suddenly come out of a dark room. The sky is an intense blue, and the girls are humming to themselves the Italian song of the summer. The Hibberts are surrounded by fascinating remains from the past that fill the girls with weightless energy and make them giggle and run up and down the stairs of an amphitheater and play tag around a square that once was the center for all trading companies of the known world. What remains of these are sidewalks where mosaic patterns reveal their names and merchandise they specialized in. These labels convey a magic from the past but mean nothing today: *CURBITANI* from Korba, *NARBONENSES* from Gaul, *SOCOF* for the corn traders.

Avinash's murder seems like the plot of a mystery novel read a long time ago. Ellia, a confused vulture.

Later in the day, the group rests under the shade of Mediterranean pine trees that create an umbrella of foliage instead of growing in a triangular shape. "I could spend just one sabbatical roaming this city," comments Anthony as the girls cling to him on the grass, "You know, Claudia, your name comes from the Emperor that invested the most to make this port state of the art for its time—Emperor Claudius."

She smiles, distracted. Her mind is somewhere else as they cluster together lying on their bellies under a cool shade. She clears her throat and purses her lips. "Papa, I thought we were going to lose you, too."

"We have been so sad about Mom that I had not realized I would not survive being separated from any of you." The girls have stopped moving. They lean on the grass and focus all of their attention on their father. The aroma of pine and leaves create a cocoon of intimacy. They have always been very articulate but feelings were meant to be experienced not congealed into words, so they do their best.

"I was very scared, too," remarks Virginia, "it felt as if we had been asleep since Mama was gone and suddenly I woke up."

"I felt the same," adds Claudia, "we cannot sleep walk anymore. I downloaded a book about the loss process and taught myself techniques to move on." Can they really move on without feeling guilty for having survived?

"I think we are lucky to be in Italy and to be together. I miss my friends but I am texting with them." Virginia pauses to gather her thoughts. She is cautious for an instant but then her expression opens up. "I am happy because I am with you Papa," she says hugging him while bouncing her toes in the air and stretching like a cat.

"We all wish Mom would be with us but in many ways she is," says Anthony, caressing Virginia's hair while Thalia lays face down so he can scratch her back. "Life happens…and it happened to all of us. It happened to you too early." The girls' expressions rearrange in a maturity pattern unusual for their tender ages.

"Don't do something like this jail thing again, Papa," concludes the youngest girl, then she explodes with delight as she signals a shape moving through the trees. "Look, Papa, a red dog!" The three girls and Anthony are dog lovers; however it had been a family rule under Laura that with three girls she had enough work so no pets were allowed. They still had a lot of contact with animals, as Laura's mother was active in many charity organizations and one of them centered on saving stray dogs. As a consequence, Elmer and Melissa had seven rescues.

"Let's follow her!" Virginia, Thalia, and Claudia jump up from the grass followed by their father to chase the dog. Ellia has kept a distance from them and remains on the grass watching them sprint away. The family moves through the ruins as if the red dog were their tour guide revealing stone recollections of what used to be a mill, a bakery, an apartment building, and a temple. The alleys and old walls dissipate what's left of their grief paralysis. Same as this city, Laura becomes a memory, a vital foundation for all of them but one that has to remain in the serenity of remembrance. The play of sunlight with ancient shapes and shadows caresses their skin, bringing a sense of renewal as the pack follows the wise red wolf.

The dog guides them to a modern building: the "*Caffetteria degli Scavi*," the cafeteria next to the souvenir shop. They are on an esplanade raised above ground level; on the steps to them, seven other dogs lay soaking the sun. The girls squeal with delight and run to the animals. They pat and scratch the dogs behind the ears. The dogs respond affectionately with their tongues out. Some are very furry, others have short hair. Big and small, this pack is together in perfect harmony bringing an unexpected flash of life to the relics around them. Going from one dog to another, Anthony notices a commonality: All have tumors on different places of their bodies. Some have difficulty moving. They bear their pain calmly. An archeologist walks past them on his way to the cafeteria and stops to admire the scene.

"I see everybody is making new friends today!"

"They all are wonderful," answers Anthony scratching a brown lopsided ear, "Where do these dogs come from?"

"It is something the other archeologists and I have done through the years. We found that many dogs with cancer are abandoned when their owners find about the ailment. We have a volunteer network through Rome that rescues and brings them here. We give the animals painkillers and a space where they can die in peace. Some die within a month, others," he signals the dog that led the Hibberts to the pack, "surprise us. That one has lived here for seven years. The vet that comes once a week thought he would not last long but he has surprised everyone. The cancer is there, but he keeps on going, like a welcoming angel for the other dogs. I'll leave you now, as I have to go back to work after I grab a bite. *Ciao*."

Anthony and the girls look at each other and then at the pack.

"Papa, I wish Mama had been here in her final days. I did not like the hospital." Virginia's eyes wander around, capturing the green foliage and the marble columns expanding in the distance next to a road.

Claudia's tone is bitter. "These dogs would have been better company for her than all of those patronizing doctors and nurses."

"We are like this pack, Papa," adds Thalia, "we stay together in grief and look out for each other."

But grief has to stay in Ostia with the dogs. "I'm the leader of our pack, same as that red dog is the leader of this one." He is determined to make them heal. He will try not thinking of Laura anymore to minimize the pain.

Going into the cafeteria, Anthony starts talking about his research with the girls because he realizes that deciphering the past gives him energy to move forward and the girls listen to him as if he were telling them a fairy tale and they were toddlers. He describes finding the poem in the hymns book and then discovering the vellum folio hidden in the secret pouch inside the cover. He describes in broad strokes the story of Federigo Dottore and how he became a monk and an assassin to Pope

Julius II. Finally, he tells them of the numbers at the end of the manuscript and his obsession to unravel their meaning, to find where the rest of the confession is hidden.

"Dad, you say there was a sequence of seven three-number combinations." Claudia proclaims with slight superiority. "That is the most basic of codes. The first number in each group is the page of the book you are reading, the second is the paragraph, and the third is the letter on that paragraph. Join the letters and you will get a clue or a message. I cannot believe you have not thought about that!" The red dog licks Anthony's face with mockery.

• • •

The girls return to Hotel Modigliani in high spirits. They each hug their favorite plush friend as if they had not seen them in years. Thalia rolls on the carpet with Mr. Panda. Virginia combs the hair of Ms. Mouse, and Claudia reads while cuddling Gatito. It would have been the perfect day, but when the girls are settling to go to bed, Anthony gets a phone call from his father-in-law. His voice is loud and even aggressive to hide fear. Someone broke into their suite at the Excelsior Hotel and went through their belongings. They found clothes on the floor and the drawers on the bathroom vanity turned over. Even the room safe box was forced open. Melissa is now with the hotel detective. The police with other people from the American Embassy have been there.

"What are you missing?"

"Our documents are here. Melissa has gone through her jewelry twice and nothing seems to be amiss. There were some emerald earrings she could not find but they were under the bed. Whoever was here, tossed our stuff around as if looking for something…I called you not to worry you but because we are going to sleep in another suite. You would not have found us if calling on the phone. The police will take fingerprints, and the hotel will dry clean all our clothes. We will be in perfect shape by tomorrow. Ellia Jones requested the surveillance tapes from the hotel to review them with security personnel at the American Embassy. It seems they did the same thing with the hotel tapes from the day Avinash Sullivan was murdered. Standard procedure when American citizens are involved. Everything will be fine."

"Call me if you need anything," Anthony trails off, but in his mind he replays Ellia's warning—"We have reasons to believe you and your family might be in danger."

"I don't know why you want to spend a year in this country. These things would never happen in America."

"I don't think it has anything to do with the country...you and Melissa can come sleep with us."

"Well, your hotel has less security than this one...maybe you and the girls should move here with us."

"Yes, it has great security but also a murder and a room break during the last week. Nothing like that happening in my budget accommodation... Sorry, I did not mean to say that. You and Melissa are perfectly safe over there. I am certain these events are very unusual. Don't worry. I am sure there will be a perfectly logical explanation for what happened today. Has Jones checked with the Italian police about a search related to Avinash's murder? Hopefully you will get a huge discount from the Hotel Excelsior."

"I know. The hotel detective says this was the work of a professional, no random thief. Whoever broke in knew what he was doing. I don't understand what they want with us."

CHAPTER 7

BLACK HAIR LIKE AN OBSIDIAN WATERFALL

Alessandro Catzola's hair is in complete disarray, matching his clothes wrinkled beyond possibility and his coarse, unshaven face. His sits at his desk chain smoking while holding his forehead in one hand. During these moments, he misses being with his son more than ever. Being a single father is tough. He has not been home for three nights but his despair is augmented by lacking a clear lead on the Avinash murder case. Based on what the Italian police knows, half of the world could have a motive to assassinate Avinash Sullivan. While millions of people are followers of the Transparency Crusade, many others oppose it. The disrespect to one of the oldest institutions in human history makes people indignant and fuels anger. After all, the Catholic Church operates innumerable humanitarian causes around the world, especially with the ones who need it the most, the ones disregarded by digital and electronic technologies. Shouldn't the Transparency Knights employ their energy and resources to solve more pressing problems (hunger, maladies, violence, ignorance) than challenging the ways of the Roman Curia?

Alessandro looks at his watch and then at the phone. Because the Vatican is directly involved in the investigation, Alessandro has to coordinate his efforts with three other parties: the Swiss Guard—a company of 110 mercenary guards that patrol the Vatican and sentinel its entrances;

the Central Security Corps of the Vatican City State—130 guards who provide surveillance across the small city state and are in charge of all matters relating to internal security such as crime investigations or protection of the Vatican's huge cultural assets; and Ghostwire—a company based in Silicon Valley in charge of protecting digital information for the Vatican and thus in charge of site firewalls, information storage shields, and cyber-terrorism defense. The call Alessandro waits for is from Ghostwire. They are not only excellent in data protection but also are very well connected in many spheres of the digital world and count with outstanding information hackers. Due to the media exposure of Avinash's case, Ghostwire's owner and CEO has taken it upon herself to handle the matter directly. Alessandro has worked with her in the past, a surprisingly young, cryptic, and brilliant woman.

The phone rings.

"Catzola here. You better have some good information or I'm in trouble."

"I've been using my contacts in Silicon Valley. We have a lead."

"Good. I apologize we could not meet in person. I know you have set a base in your Rome offices but the boss needs a status update in a few minutes so he kept me here at the police station. I'll see you later in the week." Alessandro lights a new cigarette with the stub of the one he just finished.

"You will see a lot of me. As of now, I am waiting for the list of names for the Catholic Transparency Commission. The Pope is assigning the members consulting with his closest advisors. The Commission's charter is to develop a response and action plan to the Transparency Crusade. He should have listened to me when this started. We should have nipped the movement in its bud."

"This commission idea to set new protocols and parameters for information sharing is not new. It has been around the halls and offices of the Holy See since the Legionnaires of Christ scandal. You remember that case. The founder of this movement sexually abused many young men and children."

The woman from Ghostwire chuckles, "He even had a wife and kids in Mexico."

"I knew the idea of such commission has been on and off the table."

"It's alive and kicking as a response to Avinash's social media efforts. We know some very powerful people in Rome have been driving it during the last months. My sources tell me that Avinash found about this group and, not surprisingly, that the people behind it had ulterior motives to make it materialize. They have a double agenda where their skeletons in the closet are more relevant than reaching the morally correct approach regarding transparency. They wanted information in the Secret Archives to remain secret and away from the public and media. Avinash set a trap for them. His meeting with the Pope was not to talk transparency but to expose these people. He believed that if the Pope could see how secrecy generated corruption he would be open to lower the firewalls."

"Your hackers have been very busy."

"We have talked with many people, too. This is the Vatican. More is accomplished with stealth conversations in back alleys and secret passageways than through official communications and policy. It is amazing how everyone is eager to talk as long as you don't mention their names. Avinash was very private so this is as much information as we can get. I think not even his Transparency Crusade's closest generals know the full details of his plan. We still don't know who these powerful people are or what they are hiding. Still, I am certain that the murderer is among them and will be part of the Catholic Transparency Commission when it is announced. We just need the list of names, and I will get you all the information needed. You will know what time they go to the bathroom."

"Just be careful. If they killed Avinash, I am sure they will expect you to spy. After all, you have personal motives to find the killer. Everyone knows this."

"I can take care of myself. You focus on controlling Italian bureaucracy and the red tape."

"Akemi, you are—" but Akemi Morishima, the owner of Ghostwire, had already hung up. Alessandro knows that good manners are not her forte.

• • •

Ellia Jones has promised to escort Anthony anywhere he wishes to go. Instead of traveling on the subway as usual, Ellia drives Anthony to the Vatican in a limo from the American Embassy. Both of them are on the backseat looking out of their windows in silence. As they approach Saint Peter's square, traffic stops completely. Anthony drums his fingers on his thigh. The car is taking longer than a train ride. He considers engaging in small talk with Ellia but just a look at her stout legs in stockings despite the summer heat reminds him he is dealing with a bureaucrat. Instead he repeats the numbers he has memorized at the end of the monk's confession. After half an hour of immobility, a policeman redirects them through a side street that steers them farther from their destination. Ellia is long faced, and as the car stops for what will be another half hour of paralysis, Anthony apologizes and jumps off the car. He dislikes the woman and hurries away from the limo. Walking quickly with a hunter's anticipation, he refocuses on finding the rest of the monk's confession. He wants to prove Claudia's theory on the numbers at the end of Federigo's letter. Ellia sees him walking away and quickly dials on her phone, barking an order to her undercover surveillance agent.

Saint Peter's square is crowded beyond normal. Sometimes it can be packed with devout worshippers when the Pope appears in the balcony. However, the Pope spends the summer at his retreat at Castel Gandolfo. This time the crowd is made of protesters demanding complete access to the Vatican's archives. Avinash's murder has incited marches and protests around the world. The biggest is in Rome and has been going on for days. People are carrying signs demanding disclosure of the secret archives and procedures. "The Pope has to lead its flock in the twenty-first century not the Middle Ages," reads a sign. Anthony moves close to the columns around the square so as not to attract attention. He is worried that someone might recognize him from the newspapers and television images. He pulls his coat collar up and buys a Panama hat from a street vendor. This is becoming his usual way of approaching his work place. The crowd around him is very diverse: a woman with brown skin and the features of an Inca queen, a short Irish man with black hair and hairy arms, a short Korean girl with hair down to her waist. All carry signs and a committed expression to change. Feels like the Tower of Babel had poured its contents onto Saint Peter's Square.

Finally in the Secret Archives library, Anthony holds the thirteenth-century hymns book in his hand, caressing it like it were a precious Christmas present. He knows he will have to confess his misdemeanor to the librarian. This time, with gloves on and extreme care, he pulls the vellum from the pouch of the damaged inner cover. He types the nine number triads into his laptop to decode. Claudia was right. By writing the letter that each number combination provides he gets the word: LUCRETIUS. The monk had mentioned that his father loved to read "The Nature of Things" written by Lucretius. It was also a very popular book among humanists during the Renaissance. Stylistically, it is brilliantly written, evidencing a prodigious mastery of Latin. Its content was a revelation at the dawn of the Renaissance, providing a very different vision of the universe from what the Catholic Church had dictated for centuries. Lucretius was a pragmatic and an epicurean. For him the world was made of infinitely small particles, and there was nothing after death. Life was our only chance to explore the universe through knowledge and experimentation.

There are three copies of "The Nature of Things" in the Secret Archives library. While it had been discovered by an apostolic secretary to several popes in the fifteenth century, "The Nature of Things" was forbidden by the Catholic Church a century later. Anthony waits impatiently as a clerk fetches them, but the clerk comes back with only two. He apologizes—the third one is in the restoration shop.

Back in his work table, Anthony scrutinizes the two copies. They have thin leather covers and the cloth lining is tightly glued. The text inside is even and artfully depicted. No secret messages.

By lunchtime, Anthony is sitting disappointed in the study room staring at a blank screen when Francesca shakes his shoulders as a greeting. She sits next to him with a smile so bright that it dims the new psychedelic colors in her hair. "I called you once every hour yesterday. Where were you, *Caro*?" She doesn't give time for an answer. "I've been analyzing the poems in the hymns book. The cadence and structure matches Catullus erotic poetry. I even found a fragment that matches an unpublished poem. It is identical. This Catullus poem is not known. It is a fragment the British Museum treasures from a ruined manuscript found on an Irish monastery in the nineteenth century. Words from our source match every word on it. I sent an email to the British Museum manuscript curator. He is going to send me more information. He is very excited and agrees we must have found a lost collection of poems!"

Francesca had started whispering but now her volume is loud and celebratory. The scholars around them make uncomfortable noises requesting silence. This incites Francesca to jump up and down with the many necklaces she is wearing chinking and tingling like weather bells in a hurricane. "*Caro*, this is really good. We have made a major discovery in Classical literature, and we are just at the beginning of our sabbatical!"

"Well, yes, but we spent many years tracking these things…don't get me wrong, we have to celebrate…and confirm its authenticity," suddenly Anthony is tingling all over.

"Yes, we do! Celebrate."

Arm in arm, they stroll out of the library. Because it is a special occasion, they go to the restaurant at the Courtyard of the Pine Cone inside the Vatican museum. It was built by Bramante in the sixteenth century to join the Belvedere Palace with the Vatican Palace, and Anthony cannot help but delight in the architecture of the curved three-story high wall forming a niche around a gigantic bronze pine cone that was once part of a Roman fountain next to a temple for Isis, the Egyptian goddess, in the first century. As a scholar, he knows the secret meaning of the pinecone: a third eye humans were not using to see the metaphysical universe around them. He could use it right now to find the Lucretius book.

Francesca and Anthony like the outside tables where they can watch tourists come and go while delighting on Bramante's architecture. The tourist crowd seems smaller than usual— probably scared by the protests in front of Saint Peter's but Anthony and Francesca let their bodies slump on the garden chairs at the restaurant. Francesca allows for a two-way conversation, making it light.

"So you have been seeing that Jones woman? She certainly is not pretty, but who knows? She might be more skilled in bed than most men I've been with!" Francesca laughs at her own remark.

"Hey, you are the bold one!"

"*Vivire*. Live while you can. I am certain many priests have me on their minds while listening to others' confessions. Have I told you how many times I have given priests blowjobs while they are on duty in their confession booths?"

They purposely stay away from the topic of conversation with Gabriel Herrera the night before Avinash's murder. They devour luscious panini oozing melted cheese on arugula and delicate *sorpresata* salami. The perfume of basil surrounds them while Anthony describes his trip to *Ostia Antica*. She updates him on the Catholic Transparency Commission. The idea is gaining momentum by the hour. Pope representatives have met with world leaders to outline the objectives of the soon-to-be-formed group as its outcome could have implications for other world governments. The selected members will be announced in the upcoming days.

"So I might get pulled from our work to participate in these meetings. But don't worry, it will be only a couple of hours at a time. Sooner than expected, we will be back to our study tables making more amazing discoveries."

The waiter brings a dessert menu.

"Let's keep the party going! Tiramisu for me!" orders Anthony.

"Pannacotta for me and a bottle of champagne for both!" Francesca yells melodramatically but could have ordered without words based on the frenzied movement of her arms. Anthony crouches in his seat and peers at the people around them who have suddenly interrupted their conversations to look at them. In a table slightly away from the rest of the tourists, a young woman sits by herself. Her shiny straight hair falls like an obsidian waterfall on her shoulders, splashing Anthony with warmth. Her facial features are a mix of nationalities. Her eyes could be Asian, her cheekbones Nordic, her lips and hips Latin. She is dressed in tight clothes—too tight and revealing to be inside the Vatican City State. Anthony swallows and stares at her chest but her incredibly long legs in tight skinny jeans pull his gaze down to the tips of her black pointy boots that stretch in a curve similar to the slow smile that forms in his lips. She holds a tablet in her right hand and is typing but her eyes are focused on the inside of her glasses and in his direction. Anthony is not a technology expert and cannot recognize that the screen is a designer eyeglass advanced prototype version of Google Glass 3.0 with augmented reality head-mounted display capabilities that works like a hands-free computer and smart phone responding to voice and gestures: the twenty-first century's third eye. The prototype is something you would only see at the Vegas Consumer Electronics Show. His failure to understand the technology she is using almost irritates Anthony but then her eyes meet his for an unsettling moment. Her stare is unemotional, almost aggressive in its dismissal of others, yet Anthony is pulled into her eyes by a depth he has never seen, and what he discovers awakens sexual feelings in him that have been dormant for a year. Francesca's hoarse laughter breaks the moment pulling him back to the table. Uncontrollably, he blushes while crossing his legs and covering his growing hardness with a casual hand pushing against the straining pants and underwear.

"Tony, you have to be more discreet. You are with another lady. I could get very offended if I wished to. It's not that I currently want something with you. You are too late. You lost your chance by being faithful to your wife when I was willing and available for a fling. My current boyfriend keeps me very satisfied in all aspects. It's just good manners not to stare like that when you are with another woman."

Giving Anthony a break, the waiter pours the champagne into two flute glasses. Anthony asks the first question that pops into his head. "How come you never talked to me about this boyfriend before? You were never shy to keep me up to date of all your adventures and multiple partners."

"Ahmed and I have been sleeping together almost for a year. I never talk about him because you never ask about my personal life…"

"I never needed to ask before. You volunteered every sordid detail of your encounters."

"I might be becoming a grown up. I don't like to talk about him as he comes from a very wealthy Saudi dynasty; so for the first time, I keep it to myself."

"Let's celebrate then that you are into an adult relationship! That could be considered more rare than a lost Catullus text." They clink their glasses of vibrant liquid under the luminous summer sky. The beautiful stranger keeps staring at Anthony, and he cannot stop from checking her out every few minutes. This makes him uncomfortable, so to distract himself he tells Francesca that he needs to get a connection with the Secret Archives restoration lab to find a book. However he does not share his discovery of the monk's letter. Maybe the find has become too intimate for him, and he desires to keep it to himself just a little longer.

Francesca listens attentively without asking questions. She does not normally listen without interrupting. Her mood is too festive. She jumps in her place and toasts to the sun.

"Today is your lucky day. I have a very close friend, Angelo Simone, who works at the restoration shop. I'll contact him so you can get access to the Restoration Laboratory. I am certain he will find you the copy of "The Nature of Things" you are seeking. They toast again, and as he sips and swirls the champagne in his glass, Anthony feels the eyes of the woman in the corner undressing him, assessing the contours of his limbs, back, and chest as if planning to buy a stud. However, there is more than lust in her eyes. There is the interest of a forensic doctor about to dissect a corpse. She is dismembering and cataloguing every detail of him from the color and style of his shirt to the way he ties his shoelaces.

"*Andiamo*!" Francesca invites him out of the chair. "I have a meeting later on and I want you to meet Angelo before."

As they walk back to the Archives, Anthony forces himself to focus and murmurs the question he has been postponing: "How did your friend, Gabriel Herrera, know that Avinash's life was in danger?"

Francesca looks around, gets close to him and murmurs: "He explained it that night at *Da Toscano* restaurant. He says he heard it in confession. He has been part of a faction within the Roman Curia that favors restricting access to the Vatican files and information. There are others from Italian power circles that share this view."

"Has he told this to the Italian police?"

"I cannot push. If it is information he got through confession, his vows forbid him to share these secrets. I think he was so stressed about it that he stretched his vows to share what he could with us." Francesca's eyes stop smiling, and her expression becomes serious and worried. "Anthony, while you were in jail did you tell anyone what Gabriel shared with us?"

He turns and notices that the dark hair woman is still staring at him from a distance. She has not made any attempt to hide her interest in him. He wishes he could escape the uncomfortable conversation with Francesca by sinking his face into the stranger's black hair to discover its smell, and then go down her neck to nudge his nose between her large breasts. She has some kind of electronic device at her feet. It looks like a radio-controlled futuristic toy car. He has never liked electronic gadgets. Her face is in his direction from across the courtyard as if she could listen to their conversation.

"I told them I had dinner with some friends. It was there that I had gotten soaked in red wine when a waiter tripped over me. I was resentful of them for the way they treated me so I did not share who I was with and what we talked about. The police were so surprised to discover that the stains were wine and not blood that they did not interrogate me any further."

Francesca smiles to herself, satisfied with the answer. Before Anthony exits the courtyard, he checks behind his back for the last time. The woman is still staring; it makes him feel like a schoolgirl being scrutinized by a lecherous old man.

On the rooftop of the Vatican Museum around from the Pine Courtyard, Ellia Jones observes the players below her. She knows the identity of the woman with black hair. She doesn't mind her presence. After all, Jones knows she has a larger cybernetic arsenal she can use if needed. She takes a deep breath and tilts her head under the hot summer sun smiling at the upcoming challenge. The woman with black hair will prove a worthy adversary to outmaneuver.

CHAPTER 8

HYPERACTIVITY

Rome is a city where the Italian spirit distills into a contagious mix of fun, mayhem, cultural overload, and urban pandemonium. With the passing of days, Anthony notices he gesticulates more, his voice is somewhat louder, and his concentration is diminished. He can empathize better with his girls' agility, cramming more undertakings into a day and leaving his exhausted in-laws in espresso bars along the way. Why have one small cup with two gelato flavors at *San Crispino* when he could enjoy nine flavors per trip by ordering three three-flavor large cups? Why not jog an extra mile in the morning? Why not argue with a street vendor about the price of a souvenir? An extra beer? Of course! He stops at newsstands on the streets and reads headlines revealing recycled stories of his misfortunes in an Italian jail. How can he allow a bunch of misinformed reporters have the last word about his person? With the help of the American Embassy, Anthony organizes a small press conference.

Hotel Modigliani's sitting room next to the lobby can accommodate a selected good number of reporters. Maria, the cook, and Luca volunteer to work extra hours to prepare and serve antipasti and drinks. Why not tell the world how yoga in jail helped him cope with his imprisonment and joke about how he shocked the police by revealing that the red splotches in his clothes were Chianti stains? Breathing Rome's air, walking its streets, and conversing with its past makes him and the girls laugh together before bedtime when they share the day's adventures— and everybody knows that laughter generates more kinetic energy.

• • •

When, in the late sixteenth century, the Pope ordered the Spanish Steps to be created to join two important arteries, the *Via del Babuino* and the *Via Felice*, he would have never imagined that two centuries later they would be remodeled into an iconic early Baroque space joining the square in front of the Church of *Trinità dei Monti* with the *Piazza di Spagna* below it. The Baroque project produced a cosmic point of convergence for travelers, businessmen, and city dwellers. The 135 steps are paved by a human mantle that ebbs and flows with the seasons, the hour of the day, and the day of the week. During the summer it gets bad—during a summer weekend, impossible to navigate as tourists battle for breathing space with the numerous Romans who plunge into a shopping trip to *Via Condotti*.

As Alessandro Catzola maneuvers on a Sunday afternoon with resolution not to step and tumble on a tourist sitting on a step (playing guitar, resting, snacking, or flirting), he wishes he would have received the information with better timing so he could deliver it to Ghostwire's CEO early in the morning. At least parking would have been easier. Ghostwire's owner is a history and art buff and has enough money to own a mansion in Rome overlooking the Piazza, its windows pointing in the direction of Saint Peter's dome over a blanket of red-tiled roofs. On the outside, her house is an elegant Baroque construction covered in brown stone and carved motifs, rich and alive. Inside, Alessandro finds Akemi Morishima. She is an American woman with Japanese ancestry raised in Mexico and the US. She is in her sterile command center, an enclosed minimalistic area devoid of traditional furniture with a forest of vertical self-standing glass slabs where multiple simultaneous screens surface and shift directed by her movements and her voice. At her feet, as if being there to protect her from loneliness, robots of all sizes circulate like guard dogs. In air heavy with cool ozone, nanobots drones hover, buzzing like bees around their queen. They have all kinds of shapes depending on their function: from simple geometric figures to animated RC toy animals. In that aerodynamic environment, it feels Neolithic to hand her a crumbled piece of paper with names jotted in pencil, but Alessandro does not want to leave any electronic trace of the information before it becomes official.

"Here is the list as it will be announced on Wednesday. There are still a couple of names to be confirmed. The Commission will have twenty-five members." She reads in silence while standing up, as he adds, "The American, the person we thought was the killer is to be confirmed. The US Ambassador will request his cooperation in the next couple of days. I don't like him."

"He is too pretty to be a killer." She lifts her brow and smirks.

"Precisely. The pretty face is the perfect cover up for a murderer."

"Still, same as with the others, I will learn anything to be known from him. The selected commissioners are my main suspects. Whoever went all the way to kill Avinash will be part or very close to the faction deciding about access to the files. My hackers in cities around the world have been waiting for this list and are sitting ready at their stations."

"Remember, the Italian police is not linked with any of your activities. I was never here today. What you do is not legal in many countries. I'll contact you Wednesday after the press conference. We should get together with the other investigation parties before the first session. Our mutual acquaintances with the Swiss Guard and the Vatican Central Security Corps are eagerly waiting to partner with you."

"Should I care about them? This is not a popularity contest." As if playing an empty imaginary keyboard, she manipulates a worksheet on a screen while talking. Alessandro waits for her to finish so they can continue the conversation, but in a few seconds she is multitasking from one glass screen to another. Digital talking heads appear on the surfaces as she joins conferences calls. No one acknowledges Alessandro's presence, and he realizes that all the "life" in the room would go blank during a power outage. Irritated, she signals the exit with a wave of her wrist.

Alessandro tilts his head and swears under his breath. With a promise of a cigarette in his mind as soon as exiting the mansion, he leaves with his chin high.

• • •

While Anthony waits for Francesca in the cafeteria table outside the Secret Archives, he reflects on how the weekend was smooth and sunny. Everybody in his family is exploring creative ways to exhaust Ellia Jones, who shadows them wherever go. In reality, she is helpful with the repetitive bureaucratic declarations they had to give the Italian police and security personnel from Hotel Excelsior as they investigate the break-in at Anthony's parents-in-law's suite. But he wishes she would be transparent about the dangers threatening them.

The Vatican Secret Archives shop—or laboratory for the restoration of its huge documentary patrimony—has evolved through the years. Today, the main laboratory is for preservation, restoration, and bookbinding but next to it is another area for photography and digital reproduction. The latest addition in 1979 was the laboratory for the restoration of seals—a very relevant activity when considering that many of the important documents of the Middle Ages and Renaissance such as the Edict of Worms or The Council of Constance had wax seals on them to prove the authenticity of the signers.

It is close to five o'clock in the afternoon when Francesca guides Anthony to the Restoration Shop. She knocks on a heavy metallic door to be welcomed by a man with dark curly hair in his late twenties with a white robe covering his wide shoulders forming a V shape on his fit torso. He seems out of place, more an extreme athlete than a researcher. He guides them to a lighted worktable where he has been cautiously handling small paper fragments with pincers. The illuminated piece of paper on top of the table is a sketch of a naked male body. The pen lines are very thin and graceful. The figure was drawn with its legs facing forward but the torso is winding as much as possible to the back, creating the illusion of extraordinary motion as the muscles bulk and stretch with the exertion. Even more notable is the skin of the model, covered crisscrossed with lines, probably scars, which create a web of patterns on him enhancing his anatomy and generating a counter motion to the body. The sketch seems to be centuries old.

"*Ciao*, Angelo, this is my research partner, Tony Hibbert." The two men shake hands while Anthony's head wanders back and forth grasping the busy activity from the other restorers working in the laboratory. They are leaning on their workstations gluing ancient pages of books to a new cover or looking at wax seals under a microscope or typing on a keyboard under a scanned image. "Angelo has been my most brilliant student at the University of Milan. I was able through my Vatican contacts to sign him up for a summer internship here, and he proved so talented in merging restoration science with his history of art research capabilities that they immediately offered him a full-time job as soon as he graduated from college." Francesca eyes the drawing on the lighted table. "Angelo, what are you working on? It is exquisite."

"There is a place in the underground vault of the Secret Archives where different areas centralize materials across Vatican City so they can later be catalogued and sent to the right department. This drawing is a good example. The woodshop found a bunch of old papers and documents within secret compartments and double paneling when restoring a sixteenth-century desk. They sent a box of items to the centralization area, and some of our researchers went to catalogue the items and assess their value. We were very fortunate," his face lights up as he describes the findings, "they identified drawings made by Raphael! Francesca, the hymns book I directed you to in the archives also came from that stash. The Raphael drawings are very different from other pieces we have seen. We only have one other example in which he explores sexuality in such an overt manner in his work." Angelo winks at them. Francesca's smile broadens like a wolf in mating season.

"We know that in 1516, Raphael Sanzio painted erotic frescoes on the walls of a heated bathroom for a 'Family' Cardinal, Bernardo Dovizi Bibbiena. This Cardinal got the 'Family' classification because he lived very close to the Pope, almost like real family. Bibbiena inhabited the third floor of the Vatican Palace, the Pope inhabited the second."

"Angelo, a room full of erotic frescos here inside the Vatican? That is unbelievable...and completely entertaining!" Francesca's hoarse laughter fills the laboratory, making the other researchers turn to her with consternation.

"I always thought about Raphael as the most traditional of painters..." Anthony's face is very close to the lighted drawing as he examines the details in it.

"As you know, the three great masters of the Italian Renaissance were Leonardo da Vinci, Michelangelo, and Raphael. However, after being considered a superstar for a long time, Raphael has been seen as a minor figure for the last century probably because the pre-Raphaelite art movement in Britain scorned his influence in art."

Francesca points to the lines on the sketch: "These findings could be huge. They could evidence what Raphael would have accomplished if he had lived beyond his thirty-seven years. Angelo, this is huge!"

"We found several sketches. I am restoring one at a time. This is the first. Unfortunately, this one is incomplete. If you notice the right border, a part was torn and is missing. Look here, Raphael was clearly studying the male anatomy; he drew a penis in different stages of arousal." Angelo points to the lower corner of the picture as Francesca ogles. "However the sequence is incomplete."

"It was really a stash of treasures in the underground vault!"

"Whoever the model was, he had a great body and was well endowed! Do you know where I can find a time machine? I would like a ménage with this one and Raphael."

Anthony ignores Francesca's comment, "I am now looking for a copy of Lucretius's 'The Nature of Things.' I was told there is a sixteenth-century copy here at the shop."

Angelo calls one of his peers, Massimo, who has been working on the book's restoration. Massimo is proud that the book is ready to be sent back to the Secret Archives Library so while Anthony scrutinizes it, he explains that "The Nature of Things" was very popular in the late fifteenth and early sixteenth centuries. Massimo brags about the large number of scholars who have looked at the manuscript he has just repaired. He explains that this one seems to be a direct copy from the one made by Poggio Bracceloni, the humanist and book hunter who had discovered the lost Classical text in a Swiss monastery in 1456. With so many people handling the manuscript, it was no surprise that it needed restoration after some years of use.

Anthony has stopped listening a while ago. He is grimacing as his hands touch the slender leather covers. There is no space to hide a written confession. He might never learn the rest of Federigo Dottore's story.

"From your face, it seems this is not what you are looking for. I'm sorry, *Carissimo*." Francesca puts an empathic hand on his shoulder. Massimo recedes with brisk steps, irritated by the lack of praise to his work.

Angelo holds Anthony's arm for a moment. "Dr. Hibbert, I am evaluating some schools for my doctorate. Would you mind having a beer with me sometime so you can give me advice on American universities?"

Anthony's head is low. He gives a big sigh. "Sure, you can find me during the day at one of the Secret Archives study rooms. Happy to help."

• • •

Anthony climbs into Ellia Jones's limo, too submerged in analyzing the many avenues he can take to find a lost manuscript to notice that the car does not stop at Hotel Modigliani but continues until it reaches the American Embassy car entrance. The wrought iron doors open with elegance.

"The Ambassador needs to talk with you, Anthony." He responds with a shoulder shrug wondering if the Ambassador can be useful in his book quest. Ellia guides him to the Ambassador's office.

Ambassador Jonathan Bradbury is waiting. He is a slim, silver-haired man dressed in a light grey suit that matches the color of his eyes. "Please come in." He moves from behind his desk to point a chair out to his guests. His gestures exude the confidence of someone who has held power for many years. Yet there is a charming humbleness in the way he smiles.

"Mr. Hibbert, can I call you Anthony? Ellia has kept me up to date on the unfortunate misunderstanding with the Italian police regarding Avinash Sullivan's murder. She has talked highly of you and your credentials as a scholar but my Communication Director called my attention to the interview and social media responses from your press conference last week. It seems you are becoming quite a celebrity. The press liked the way you answered, and it seems the TV ratings in many places did, too." Anthony looks at his shoes wondering if he will need shoelaces soon. Since Ostia he has diminished the number of conversations with himself; now he is distracted by all his surroundings like a six year old on a field trip. "The Pope has called a council that he is calling the Catholic Transparency Conference."

Out of politeness, Anthony responds. "My research partner, Doctor Francesca Malatesta, has kept me in the loop on this. She believes the Pope was going to include me in it to apologize for my arrest." His eyes roam across the ceiling frescoes, darting at the cherubs hanging clouds around a sunset and on the branches of fruit trees.

"Would you like that? Twenty-five members have been invited to participate. Ellia is one of them. She represents the American government, but I think we also need someone who can embody the American people. Your research partner's instincts were right on. The Pope's secretaries and I discussed the candidates to represent the American people. Your name came to the top when we saw how you managed Friday's press conference. I want you to be part of the Catholic Transparency Commission. Your credentials as a respected American scholar and your involuntary involvement in Avinash's murder make you the perfect representative."

If there are no more surprises around the monk's confession to look forward to, maybe getting into a circus like the Conference can be an adequate distraction. "My university and I will be honored to represent the American public on this." Anthony's hands hold both armrests as if to keep himself seated.

"You will have to give periodic media roundtables. Do you mind doing this?" questions Ellia.

Why wouldn't Ellia do them herself? Probably she is too much of an official bulldog to be appealing. Also, her stern appearance is not welcoming. Anthony doubts reporters would feel comfortable talking to someone who looks like a stern high school principal lecturing on the horrors of detention. "I'll do whatever is needed from me. I promise." Anthony wonders if the American Embassy bathrooms have cherubs in them, or erotic frescos.

Ambassador Bradbury gets up and extends a grateful handshake. Anthony speculates on the methods the Ambassador employs to keep his suit perfectly pressed after a day in the office. The grey suit fabric has a drop as if it just arrived from the cleaners.

"Thank you. I know I can also speak for Ellia being very pleased. She enjoys your company."

Not that Anthony can say the same, but he shrugs politely and somewhat distractedly. His mind is now plotting on how to use the access UCLA gives him to all the major Classical literature and history libraries catalogues and databases in Europe, America, and Asia to search for a "Nature of Things" manuscript. His fingers quiver with anticipation. Laura had been right. While he hates it, technology might become handy once in a blue moon. She had always been trying to convince him, and he studiously made points about a simpler time when books and paper were the norm.

That night while the girls sleep, he goes onto the balcony of his hotel room and looks at screens in many languages. His web navigation is clumsy. He always had a bright intern to help him at UCLA. He reaches too many porn and social sites by mistake. For an instant, he considers waking up the girls so they can help him but reconsiders and forces himself to find the information. After a couple of hours, he has gathered data about libraries in and around Rome where he has a reasonable chance of success at finding his manuscript. His back and shoulders are stiff, and he has a headache. As Rome prepares for the next day, the sounds and smells reach him. He should go to bed and prepare himself for a busy day. He is eager to roam libraries in the city in search of non-digital card indexes with promise.

CHAPTER 9

THE DIGITAL WITCH

ngelo Simone works on his dream job in his dream city. He works intense and long hours during the day, and parties hard during the night. Some of his colleagues in the laboratory—heavy older bureaucrats—deride the time he invests in research and restoration, but to Angelo there is no other conceivable way to spend his days. The experience from his job adds to an already rare erudition. Despite being in his late twenties, he can go head-to-head against art and literature subject-matter specialists but he'd rather use his time growing his knowledge. At night, Angelo decants himself into his other passion: trance music. He works as a DJ four nights a week inside a rebuilt thirteenth-century monastery transformed into a techno club, Borgia's. Only a few walls of the original structure remain, the rest replaced by concrete slabs and arches. There, he jumps and dances while controlling the turntables, the beat, and music, a workout as intense as that of a professional athlete. When Angelo was growing up, his father trained him in the art of girl approaching and selecting. Nowadays, Angelo has no use for such skill. A large variety of women accost him every night, attracted by his curly dark hair, his slim body at peak fitness, and a contradictory combination of aloofness and friendliness in his demeanor. However, no woman fulfills the checklist to convince him to commit to a steady relationship after the one-night stands.

Despite the fun, Angelo knows he has to start preparing for a doctorate, so he goes looking for Anthony at the Secret Archives. What starts like an informational chat soon becomes a daily cold beer break for both. Anthony enjoys listening to both Angelo's deep knowledge of old text restoration and his adventures at the club while he provides perspective on American academia.

During one of those evenings, it hits Angelo that while advising Anthony on libraries and private book collections to search, Anthony has never shared the motivation behind his original quest. "Why is this specific Lucretius book so important? It seems the more you seek, the more riled up you get about broadening the search. When we first met, you mentioned that you did not want to share the topic with Francesca until you could better assess its value. It's been several days. You can tell me now. I'll keep your secret from Francesca. Anyway she seems so busy with the Vatican's internal politics that she has not time to visit. There is a very slim chance that she and I will even talk."

So eager is he to find this book, Anthony decides to trust him, and takes him back to the Secret Archives study room. He moves furtively to a bookshelf and—shifting two large, thick tomes—uncovers the nook where he keeps the thirteenth-century hymns book hidden so he can continue his research without revealing to the librarians the damage to the covers. Angelo and he go to one of the long tables and converse in whispers. He describes his discovery of the vellum confession. He pulls the pages from the inner cover and unfolds them, narrating the story of the monk from childhood to the time he accepts becoming an assassin for the Pope. He explains that based on the triads of numbers at the end of the document, he believes that the next part to the story is hidden inside a copy of "The Nature of Things."

Angelo's face perks up again. "You are talking about Pope Julius II's poisoner's confession! I know about him." His voice is intimate, like the one used with friends to share details of a torrid affair.

Anthony's voice trembles, his senses are heightened, "How?" the volume of his voice loud enough to make others turn to the two men with reproach. The study tables sit researchers too closely to allow any private space.

"Come, let's go to the lab."

"Let's go!" Anthony follows, feeling his pulse beat quickly. Once there, Angelo guides him to a computer terminal where he types a search on the keyboard pulling folders from a private shared drive.

"Remember the Secret Archives centralization dump on the underground files? It is there that we found Raphael Sanzio's sketches along with other documents that came from a sixteenth-century desk repaired at the Vatican's woodshop. Some Japanese researchers who were granted access to the subterranean storage brought the container with a pile of unsorted folios to our attention. They had discovered a fourth copy of "The Nature of Things" when exploring the dump's contents. They were very excited as they believed it might be Poggio's original. They brought it to me, and unfortunately I proved them wrong when analyzing it. Still I tried to restore it but the manuscript was much damaged. This copy is incomplete, only half of it remains, therefore I did not send it to the Archives library." Anthony cannot sit still, he moves like a boy waiting for the bell to call for recess so he can play with his toys.

"I have kept it in a climate-controlled vault in the lab. Several pages are burnt. It could have been damaged during the Sack of Rome by the French in 1527. Many items from the library burned or went missing then. Good coincidence, I also found a letter in a pouch in the inner cover. Nobody else in this room knows about the finding. Here, you can look at it." Anthony chuckles, excited. His eyes gleam looking at the computer screen.

Angelo reveals the image of a handwritten document. While the handwriting is very faded and difficult to read, it is familiar enough to make Anthony do a little victory dance in his place. "Anthony, I have been able to read parts of the text. I know it was written by a monk called Federigo Dottore who had been a poisoner for Pope Julius II at the break of the sixteenth century. He is certainly the same man from the letter you found. I have to bring those folios here. Take your manuscript out of hiding and back to the librarian. We will restore the torn inner cover of the hymns book, too." Anthony nods in agreement, somewhat embarrassed by his actions. "The part of the story at the lab is hard to follow not only on how much more faded the ink is in this folio than the one you found but you can see some words are missing from bookworms' scattered damage. Notice random holes on the surface." Angelo frowns at Anthony's horror-stricken face. "Don't panic. We have everything under control. There are others who enjoy reading first-hand accounts of the past. I digitized the letter because I know a person who could solve our problem. She is the head of Ghostwire, a digital company that supports the Vatican in cyber security and privacy matters. She is smoking hot but quirky." He leans closer to Anthony ensuring nobody else can listen while he murmurs in camaraderie. "Fortunately for us she has a passion for old documents and history. She is a regular visitor of the restoration lab whenever in Rome. I could even venture to say that we are friends, although with her you never know." Angelo shrugs. "She developed software that crawls documents and can read faded ink, repair and plug back missing words based on context and content. Yesterday, when she was here I shared my difficulty in deciphering this manuscript."

Anthony beams. He is holding a strong desire to scream, run, and whoop around the lab. Angelo continues, "This research is very private until I can publish a paper about it. I have only talked about the finding with you and her. I am delivering a thumb drive with the document's digitized images to her house tonight. I don't email these types of things from the Vatican shop. She confided lately she is too tired after having to deal with the Transparency Crusade. She is very involved in the Holy See's response and defense. So she finds working on things like this distracting and calming." Anthony walks impatiently around Angelo's twenty-something friendly demeanor. "You are welcome to come with me. She will be delighted to know you have found the beginning of the story."

"Of course I am coming with you!" The volume of his voice takes Anthony by surprise. "But shouldn't you digitize the other part of the letters so the software can have more context and the robots be smarter? We can get it from the library and scan it quickly! Forget the librarians. You have permission to remove books from the premises."

The challenge is to escape Ellia Jones's protective eyes. Anthony does not want an entourage when meeting the woman who can help him so he goes for a stroll in the Vatican gardens as if to clear his mind. He knows the Embassy limo will be waiting for him close to the *Porta Santa*. Ellia will be standing at the Swiss Guard booth. He is tired of Ellia's threats, so he decides to take the risk. Anthony navigates a circuitous path but gets to a parking area inside the Vatican wall. Angelo drives a green Vespa.

"Don't worry, Tony. I always carry two helmets in case I pick up a girl on my way home." Angelo departs accelerating enthusiastically. The wind hits their faces as they steer through people and cars filling the tight streets. Moving by Vespa in Rome is as normal as walking in New York City. The mopeds make their own rules, using pedestrian walkways or freeways as they please. The many Vespas charge like wolf packs assembling and splitting off as if bystanders were fat elks immobilized in fear of the predators. The vehicles and traffic signs are obstacles for the Vespa drivers to out-maneuver as if they were at the X-Games.

Faster than the subway on a good day, they arrive next to the church of *Trinitá dei Monti* above the Spanish steps. Angelo locks his Vespa next to a food truck. Adrenaline from the ride boosts their senses so the spectacle of *Piazza di Spagna* below glosses with enhanced colors and movement. Angelo rushes around languid tourists until he reaches a mansion's brown stone doorframe where he pulls a cord to toll a bell. The eyes of a sculpted angel light up when the cameras embedded in them come to life.

"Come in," calls a stern female voice as a buzzing sound unlocks the heavy wooden door. The house is crowded with antiques and artwork as if staged by Versace for an *Architectural Digest* photo shoot. There are no signs of real people spending time in the perfectly arranged room, no traces of daily life. The richly ornate shapes and colors inspired by Classical and baroque art are exuberant and reflect wealth. The abundance of antiquities, enamels, and mirrors sparkle as if they still inhabited an imaginary palace ballroom. What captures Anthony's attention are not the golden lacquers or the stunning velvets and silks but the many ancient books and manuscripts that populate the lower gold leaf vitrines and precious wood bookcases. The only thing out of place is what seems to be an authentic half unrolled Mexican pre-Hispanic codex next to an ukiyo-e Japanese woodblock print on the surface of a second-century Roman marble table. Anthony approaches them, hypnotized by their startling presence. He hovers next to the long stone slab eager to inspect them closely but looking around expecting a museum guard to stop him. His fingers crave contact with the centuries-old *amate* and paper but Angelo's voice breaks his trance. In the center of the vestibule is an elegant baroque spiral staircase winding to upper floors. Angelo ascends, taking two marble stairs at a time. Anthony strives to achieve three.

The corridor in the third floor is a major contrast with the ground floor. Minimalistic and postmodern, its fluid, curving white walls made of aerodynamic pliable materials are devoid of any decoration, as if one is entering a "Designed by Apple in California" spaceship. Small robots buzz around, scanning the visitors with their sensors like miniature geometrically shaped wolf guardians. "These are her companions. Not much of a social life. They are annoying but just ignore them," says Angelo.

Anthony peeks into an almost-barren bedroom where the mattress looks like an organic sleeping pod, and the furniture, protozoan wall extensions. Angelo stops in front of a double glass door that loses its white tint as it slides open.

The woman with the obsidian black hair is standing in the center of her sanctuary barefoot and scantily dressed in a tight white tank top and black skinny jeans. She is surrounded by several tall, extra thin vertical glass panels where data are shown as screens populate them, increasing and decreasing in size and moving into different locations on the surface, performing a liquefied dance. She is controlling the many screens with the movement of her body and with whispers from her desirable lips while catching murmurs in the air from a multitude of miniature speakers. She could invite them to approach and touch her but her incantations are for the web. Half of the screens at this instant are revealing data and graphs from Ghostwire's Social Media predictive tool. She is getting real time trends on the sentiments and collective subconscious reacting to the Transparency Crusade against the Catholic Church. Anthony hides his damp hands in his pockets to cover his crotch. The rest of his body is immobile as he becomes spellbound by the woman in front of him. One of the graph's symbols represent digital conversation posts and peaks in response to Avinash's murder as a visual constant against the forces of a troop of Ghostwire's social managers diminishing negativity by geography by posting altruistic stories about the Catholic Church. On another glass panel, someone is having a live conference call with participants from around the globe. The screen images enlarge or reduce in diameter based on the participation relevance or in response to unpredicted body language.

Anthony disregards the machines. He continues to be absorbed by the woman from the Pine Courtyard restaurant dancing with big data and numbers as if she were a sorceress in a clearing at a magical forest. She is one with technology, a complete alien to him—and that becomes her. A swirl of robots, the largest twelve-inches tall, dance in rhythm around her feet as if she were emerging from a whirlwind or a cold burning pyre of plastic wheels, transistors, mechanical claws, and spy lenses. Sometimes thin laser rays emerge from the woman's hands reaching a screen or a robot, light reflecting in the drops of moisture above her lips.

Angelo and Anthony wait a few minutes until the woman turns and nods at the young restorer. Her eyes widen a fraction when she recognizes Anthony inside her territory, her nipples seem to flash under the fabric of her top.

"Can you hear me?" The woman dims all the screens by extending her fingers and lowering her arms as if conducting the final notes of a cacophonic symphony. "Akemi, this is Anthony Hibbert. He came into a great finding that will help us complete the manuscript story we found in the Secret Archives underground vault. I brought what he found plus my digitized copy so you can use your software to complete it. Anthony, this is Akemi Morishima, owner and CEO of Ghostwire International." Incapable of blinking, Anthony can only keep an open mouth smile.

"I know this person. The stupid reporters thought he was Avinash's assassin." The three fidget in silence for a minute. Angelo studies his friends, Anthony radiates awe, and Akemi flares her nostrils at the American researcher.

"Hey, Akemi. Why don't we go sit on the balcony so we can talk about Tony's findings?"

"You know I don't have any food or drinks to offer and I am too busy to wait for delivery."

"Don't worry. I am not visiting you after a night of partying. I want us to be more comfortable for a moment.'

She walks pass them, leading the way. Anthony catches a breeze of her smell: lethargic citrus battling against the oxygen-rich ionized air that makes servers happy. The balcony opens to the *Piazza dei Spagna* over-looking a spectacular view of the city's rooftops. The tiles and shapes create a brick plain of undulating constructions.

Angelo describes to Akemi his earlier encounter and conversation with Anthony. She doesn't look at them, and Anthony doubts if she is listening but doesn't care. Her proximity is thrilling.

"Where are you from? Your name is Japanese but I heard you were Mexican-American?" asks Anthony trying to start a conversation.

She ignores him and stands up to grab a tablet, extending her open palm so Angelo can give her the thumb drive with the digitized foli-os. "These are magnificent!" she yells awkwardly to the images of the monk's letters. Her fingers enchant the screen's surface as she programs a sequence of commands for the robotic crawlers in her software to patch the text.

As a small pet robot jumps onto her lap, Akemi discusses timing for the repaired text availability with Angelo. Angelo lifts the tablet over his head with both hands to signal triumph as if he were lifting a soccer trophy. Anthony responds by raising his arms in a V and realizes how foolish he looks but for an instant Akemi scans his torso as if taking notes of every angle and hard place. She is explaining something with deep and meticulous technical terminology that makes it devoid of meaning. Anthony is a toddler sitting in an advanced quantum physics confer-ence. She then turns and stares at Anthony like a teacher who has just asked a question to the dumbest student in the classroom.

"Yes, my name is Akemi Morishima. My company specializes in pro-tecting the private digital information of companies or organizations. You could say I am one of the key players in many nations' silent cyber war and protect them against cyber terrorism. You probably have de-duced by now that my company also provides other digital services." Her arms are crossed tightly against her body pushing her large breasts up, her shoulders raised. "We do mundane but profitable activities like content reconstruction, emergency data recovery, and social media cri-sis management. We develop codes of all kind that touch the Internet with their digital fingers." She is enumerating as if she was repeating a sales pitch by memory. "Even Google and Amazon use my patents." Anthony nods like a teenager to his school principal. "I will have the monk's text reconstructed soon. I can't sleep tonight so I'll work on it. I can send a thumb drive to Angelo and I can easily get your email to share the file with you too."

Anthony hesitates, realizing she might be asking for his email. He stutters. She moves her hand in the air for some sensor to capture it.

She stands up and terminates the gathering by silently gliding back to her sterile control center as if hypnotized by the songs of faraway digital mermaids. Time is optimized by skipping the farewells. After a few fruitless minutes of waiting for her to return, Angelo signals to the confused Anthony to follow him. They walk back into the building. They are about to descend the staircase when Anthony feels a touch on his shoulder that makes his marathon-trained legs weak. Her touch makes all of the skin on his body flush.

"Are you available for a date?" Her tone is assertive, as if closing a business deal. Their eyes lock as the cameras of many robots converge and halt on them, too. "I know you are a widow and that you have not slept with other women since your wife died." She leans forward. He can see down her cleavage.

Anthony winces. How can she know that? He is breathless; however her lips make him talk: "Weekends are for my daughters." Better make it clear from the start. "Early next week is good. The girls can stay with their grandparents...y-y-yes...I would very much like to have dinner with you." Her black hair fans as she returns with no more words to her multiscreen room, leaving Anthony standing in the corridor. Angelo shrugs, entertained, and rushes down the marble banging his footsteps on the staircase, breaking the spell and signaling his friend to follow him back to the street.

"Do you need a ride, Tony? I have to go to work at the club but I can drop you at home."

Anthony is savoring the aftertaste of Akemi's words but he likes the young researcher. He is so different from what he was like when he was very young. At Angelo's age, Anthony was changing diapers. "Do you have DJ duties tonight? I should go visit you one day."

"Come with me tonight. Here is the address." Angelo hands Anthony a card with the name of the techno music club. "Remember there are lots of ladies looking for adventure. You just need to change your scholar-looking clothes and you'll pass for one of the crowd."

Anthony chuckles. "No thanks. My hotel is walking distance and I have a lot to think about."

"I have never seen her paying attention to men. There is always a first time," Angelo pulls his helmet on. "Dr. Malatesta is another story... She pays attention to every man!" He chuckles as the green Vespa rides away, leaving Anthony with confusion, guilt, and elation at having accepted a date invitation from Akemi.

"Laura would want me to keep on with my life..." he says to himself, unconvinced, "but I never dated anyone else but Laura. How am I going to go through with this?" The image of Akemi barefoot in her tight tank top and skinny jeans provides the answer.

CHAPTER 10

THE ART OF KILLING

On Friday night, Anthony checks his email. The girls read in their beds while pampering their stuffed animals. Mrs. Mouse is wearing glasses; Panda sits on a plate full of biscotti, and Gatito is used as a pillow. When the girls fall asleep and Anthony is about to turn off his laptop, an email pop-up catches his attention. It's from Akemi. He scratches his head with eager fingers and reads:

"Attached, reconstructed letters. Following our conversation for a date—Ducati Bistro at 8 pm on Tuesday. I've made reservation. Will be in the bar."

Anthony rubs his forehead. He then opens the attachment and, grabbing a jacket, goes out to the room's small terrace not to disturb the girls. The windows on the buildings around him are dark. He settles in and props his feet on another chair.

Day 2 - December 7, 1521

My name is Federigo Dottore. I have eleven days to live. This is the second part of my confession. I hid the initial part in an old hymns book that I placed in the Vatican Secret Library. Look for it if you find this first.

I became an assassin for His Holiness Pope Julius II. He valued my poisoning skills so I moved my quarters to the Belvedere building. I became part of the famiglia palatina, the permanent members of the Pope's household.

My place in the hierarchy was confusing to many. Some saw me as part of the lords and ministers with administrative tasks. Others saw me as one of the two hundred servants in court. Many considered me a threat—but whatever suspicions I might have generated dissipated quickly when the courtiers noticed I could not speak and gossiped about it as it made them feel superior. They pointed out the oddity that I worked at the libraries but did not report to the head librarian, a powerful courtier. This alone would have been enough to generate a rumor about how dangerous I could be, but not when the talk concerned the hole in my tongue. This fact relegated me to a miserable mute hound that the Pope would send on eccentric book hunts to rescue crumbling old manuscripts from monasteries and decaying aristocratic mansions.

Silence was a weapon. First it was defensive: an excuse not to partake in gossip and intrigue in the corridors and rooms of the palace. Second, it was a deadly instrument allowing me to become the perfect spy for the Pope. Many believed that being mute equaled being an idiot. They ignored me to the point that I was invisible, so they talked openly with others about clandestine matters.

Some saw my silence as a boon. People love to listen to themselves, so having someone who would not interrupt was a blessing. They caught me in the corridors to chat with an intensity that convinced themselves I cared. I refused to be anybody's friend even if a liked a few. I mistakenly believed that I had already experienced my share of grief for a lifetime. I refused to befriend men I might have to poison later on...I should have followed my instincts...

The only exception to all this was Callisto, the cook from Saint Benedictus Minor. I had to use him to get ingredients from the pantries to complement whatever I gathered on my field trips. Also I had to deliver the venom without raising any suspicions from the victims. Food was the ideal vehicle.

Callisto joined the Papal kitchens at my request to the Pope. There were so many principal cooks in the palace! Maybe twenty! Cooks, secretarial cooks, bakers, and sub-bakers working for two maître-d'hôtel, the chief butler, and the two kitchen stewards. Callisto became the cook for the secondary kitchen directing a crowd of helpers. As I had done in Saint Benedictus Minor, sometimes I would join him as a sub-cook so that my frequent presence at the palace kitchen would be normal and not raise suspicions when I was on a mission. Callisto always welcomed me with a big smile and two kisses on my gaunt, cleanly shaved cheeks. While my body became muscular from trekking to gather ingredients from faraway mountains and cities, Callisto's body became fat and soft from easy access to too many sweets. He enjoyed having me around to talk to as someone not involved in kitchen politics. Same as others, he considered my lack of speech a welcome sign for his long chatters. He would only interrupt his monologues to give orders here and there or to taste a sauce or dish. I learned every detail from Callisto's life: his childhood, his ailments, his love life, and his dreams.

Callisto served another purpose: He sent me sick people to cure. In the same manner I had become in charge of the infirmary in Saint Benedictus Minor, I became the physician to many of the servants. They had no money to get cured anywhere else. This work brought balance to my actions. Assassin by night; physician by day. It also allowed me to gather their stories about the courtiers they served. This proved to be a fantastic source of information. The Pope was so happy with my insights into everybody's life that, after the first few months, he allowed me to organize a fixed schedule for my work as physician. Every Monday, Wednesday, and Friday, when I was in Rome, I would tend to a long line of patients in an area close to my quarters, where the Pope had assigned me a private space for jars, cures, and unguents to administer to the sick. I also used this space to mix poisons.

The first three years at the Vatican were very good. I became very skilled in the arts of killing. Perhaps because of my nature, I was very methodical and detail oriented in my tasks. I transcribed and organized the poison formulas gathered from the clay tablets into a notebook. I improved my formulas through test and error. I would use different mix variants for a kill and observe which was more effective. I would then tweak a recipe, test again on some victims, and annotate the optimum results. I enjoyed precision. I learned to block any feeling that arose when I was on a mission. Death was always executed with accuracy. My knowledge as a physician allowed me to unlock the mysteries of many antique manuscripts in the Vatican library. My notebook grew every year with practical information. Exploring old books also allowed me to understand the origin of the clay tablets. By reading ancient historians, I came to the conclusion that that the underground palace was not Titus Baths, as my contemporaries believed. It was really the Domus Aurea, the magnificent golden palace that the Emperor Nero had built on the Palatine, an excess that had offended the people of his time. Where the Colosseum stands had been his private lake where he would stage nautical battles between gladiators and war prisoners. Next to the lake, he had built a colossal statue of himself, which remained, and gave the Colosseum his popular name: the amphitheater next to the colossus.

I must dwell now upon some historical details I learned that explain the origin of the poison tablets. Nero had been part of the Julio-Claudian dynasty. His great-great grandmother had been Livia, the wife to Emperor Octavius, the creator of the Roman Empire. Tacitus and Casius Dio, two Roman historians of the epoch, accuse Livia in their writings to have used ancient poisoning arts to control the succession to the throne. She murdered many members of her royal family. During his last days, Emperor Octavius was so afraid of her skills that he only ate apples that he picked directly from a certain tree in his orchard. However, some believe that Livia was able to poison even these and kill her elderly husband. I believe Livia handed her formulas down to other family members until they reached Nero. He was known as a ruthless man with no scruples. Being able to kill in secret through poison would have been an entertaining skill for him. The location where we discovered the tablets was probably Nero's private room for preparing the concoctions.

Julius II soon fixed the disastrous finances his predecessor, Pope Alexander VI, had left him. To my surprise, I received a salary for my services. I didn't drink, I didn't whore, I had access to any book I wanted in the city so I did not have to spend any money to create a library as my father had done. I used a fraction of my income for hygiene and personal appearance. I hired a barber to shave my head and pluck all my body hair. I bought eucalyptus oils to sanitize my skin and ash soap to scrub my body twice a day. I had three types of robes for my apparel. I did not belong to any monastic order any longer. My cause was to follow the Pope's orders. At the palace, I wore white robes—the color of white sheep's wool or cotton with no pigment. White was best for me because it allowed me to see any stain or dirt easily to maintain a spotless appearance. When traveling or doing errands in the city, I wore black robes—the blackest was best for hiding the filth that permeated everything outside of the palace. On many occasions after a trip, I would just burn the garments because soap and water did not suffice. The third color was a light purple, almost lavender, very different from any red or crimson that cardinals, nobles, and kings favored. This color was rare and expensive. I wore it when I had to kill. It was a way to link my physical presence to the poison and become an instrument of God's will, a tool for the Vicar of Christ to transform the Catholic Church.

During the first three years at the Papal court, I assassinated many. But two murders in particular are the most memorable for me:

Through his informants, his Holiness Julius II confirmed the rumor that his enemy, Pope Alexander VI, had been poisoned—not a surprise since the Borgia Pope had ruled the Catholic Church and its territories with unfettered nepotism and moral depravity.

Pope Julius II uttered almost to himself when he assigned me the mission: "If possible, I would have poisoned the pervert myself, but I was far removed from Rome exiled to the French Court. Fortunately, Alexander VI did not require my own hand to die. I only wish it had been sooner." He did not wish to punish the conspirators who had plotted the murder. He was displeased with the sloppiness of the assassin they had hired. A worse individual than the Borgia Pope had been his son Cesare—and the assassin had poisoned both during a party. Alexander VI died; his bloated body turned black and putrid a few hours after his demise—proof of his unnatural death. Cesare Borgia survived. He became extremely ill but lived. The time Cesare spent agonizing had allowed Julius II to manipulate the conclave so he could become Pope; however, the Borgia's residual power had induced the conclave to choose another Pope instead of Julius on the first conclave round. The same pope Julius II had killed using my lavender and honey venom. If Cesare had been in full health, history would be different. Cesare would have succeeded Alexander VI. After securing the papacy, Julius II set a plan in motion to wipe out Cesare and his cronies. I won't dwell on the details, as my role was just to eliminate the poisoner whose sloppiness had allowed Cesare to survive.

The Pope had reliable information that my target inhabited a dere-lict house next to the Church of San Clemente. I soon spotted the man. People in the region of Monti talked in hushed tones about him. They whispered that he was some unholy ascetic hermit. The man had grey hair and a beard—long, unkempt, and crawling with lice. He lived next to the church but never went into it. His house had a small stable where at times he kept one bull. Every now and then the hermit would disap-pear inside his abode for several days to kill the bull in his stable and emerge much later to sell the carcass, already drained of blood, to the butchers. I discovered this curiosity by studying him from a distance. When needing a respite, I would go into San Clemente, its frescoes and mosaics providing fresh energy to my spirit.

I followed the hermit on his occasional outing for bread at the bakery at the Roman Forum. It was the same bakery my mother had taken me to as a child. The hermit always looked at the freshly baked loaves but bought the stalest bread from the scarce leftovers from the previous day. I measured the time it took him to consume the bread and noticed he would return to the bakery every three days except when the bull disappeared from his stable to be slaughtered. He then would go to the bakery daily. With this information, I frequented the bakery myself. I counted how many loaves of bread were sold each morning. Tuesday was the slowest day for stale bread, and because of this they had only two or three available. When I noticed the bull disappearing on a Monday, I knew I had to act quickly. The hermit would be the first customer at the bakery on Tuesday and would buy the stale loaf of bread farthest from him on the display tray. I had been watching the baker, too. Lutti was his name, and he had two sons in his household that brought trouble day and night. They were young and querulous. One of them was already married, and his wife had produced two daughters that lived in the overcrowded baker's house. The other son preferred to spend his energy drinking and whoring at night. As a consequence, Old Lutti always left one of the bakery win-dows ajar after locking the door. That way, his son could crawl back into the house and not wake the rest of the family. I used this window to enter the bakery close to midnight on that Monday. I dipped a loaf of stale bread in arsenic and left it in the right position on the tray.

I waited all night behind a mound of ruble from which I could spy the bakery. To pass the time, I practiced vocalization. While I only spoke with the Pope, I did not wish to become a real mute. The hole in my tongue was smaller every day, and my speech more articulate.

As expected, early in the morning, surrounded by a swarm of flies, the hermit arrived to buy his bread. I walked into the store behind him to confirm that he was taking the intended loaf. What happened next adds to the uniqueness of this event. I experienced the contrast of the holy with the lowest of humans. The married son was at the counter hugging one of his daughters, an amazing young girl with clear white skin that glowed with the purity of innocence. Her large brown eyes had a trait I never had seen in such a young child: they were really look-ing at her surroundings. She was present and observant of the people around her in ways very few and wise adults are. Her hair flowed around her father's arms in graceful waves. She looked like one of the virgins I had seen in some of the new paintings in which the glow of innocence merged with ancient knowledge, erasing any darkness from the soul of sinners. The hermit ignored the man, as expected, but when the girl received the payment from him, her clean white hand touched for an instant the filthy cracked long nails of the poisoner. She looked at him, and he became conscious of his soiled condition. Still, she smiled, full of life, making him tremble. He could not help but grimace an involuntary smile back to her that quickly faded into darkness as soon as the girl turned her back to him.

I bought a warm loaf for myself. When paying, I asked the girl her name: Margharetta, and its sound resonated in my brain and my heart. She beamed at me and giggled while she stared at my hairless face with fascination when I asked for soap and water to wash the dust that dirtied my hands.

Returning to the hermit's derelict hut, and after checking the street's emptiness, I forced the door open and entered. I was surprised to find the one room place empty. From afar, I had seen him go inside. I was expecting the man to be dead after eating the bread; instead, a floor covered in muck surrounded me. The hermit could not have dis-appeared. I walked around, dodging cockroaches and maggots—as if I were walking inside a large coffin in which the body had rotted a long time ago. I had to inspect the floor despite my disgust, so I got on all fours. Only the shining image of the girl from the bakery kept me whole. Piles of dung revealed the hermit brought the bulls inside the house to kill them. I noticed hoof prints close to the sleeping cot and discovered sliding marks there. The hermit had pushed the cot around so I pushed it to follow the marks on the floor. I discovered a hidden entrance to an underground tunnel wide enough for a bull to walk down its inclined slope. I descended into the darkness, noticing a distant glow. The air was heavy with smoke and putrefaction making my throat gag and my eyes burn.

The tunnel opened to a square hall illuminated by four torches. The hermit lay sprawled next to the bull he had sacrificed a couple of days before. Both bodies were contorted. The hermit still held his half-eaten loaf of bread. It seems he had been dipping it in a bowl with the bull's blood to soften the dough. I then inspected the walls of the room. They seemed very ancient. The images on the temple walls revealed an ancient pagan religion: the Mithras cult, which had been very popular with soldiers during the later empire. In the center was an altar, a square engraved stone with the image of a man wearing a cap slaughtering a bull by slicing its neck with a sword. Around the room, on top of stone benches, were basins brimming with clotted bull's blood. My craving for knowledge and precision overtook the revulsion I felt. I did not understand the rite but I knew the technique the hermit used to produce its poisons. He would gather pus and infected tissues from the beggars and sick roaming the alleys of the city. He then would mix this with warm blood from the sacrificed bull so the evil spirits from the malady could multiply and develop. The serum that would separate from the blood clots was the poison. It was clear to me that his failure to kill Cesare Borgia was not the result of sloppiness but ignorance. Malady poisons are superior if the sick tissue is mixed with freshly collected pig or human blood instead of bull blood. The blood has to be kept warm. The cold underground temple was far from optimal. I wondered what was covering the underground pagan temple and realized with some surprise that the Church of Saint Clemente was built on top of it. I would have knelt and prayed as was my custom after a mission but the muck and maggots covering the floor convinced me to leave the place and go pray in the church where magnificent mosaics and frescoes would provide better surroundings for a spiritual communion.

The second murder that stands out in my memory during the first three years was the vengeance I had waited for. As part of the Pope's court family, I had access to most banquets and celebrations. Usually, I leaned on a wall observing and listening, taking mental notes of matters that could be of value to His Holiness. Other times I would sit at the long banquet table with visitors who, inspired by the wine and food, talked incessantly. On this occasion, I heard a vaguely familiar voice at one end of the table, its sound waking a subdued fury inside me. He was complaining that the majority of the inhabitants of Rome were no longer Romans but foreigners. He then told the story of a physician who was so interested in the city's ruins and history that he had moved in with his family from Florence. "The fool did not understand that Romans are more interested in discovering the cheapest wine shops in the city than unearthing their glorious past!" His remark was followed by a hoarse chorus of laughter. Glowing under the attention he was receiving, he proceeded. "Thanks the Lord for his imbecility because by brainwashing and swindling his wife, I got the land for my palace in Pigna. I tricked his wife to give me the property while he was on his deathbed, his mind still numb with pagan myths and history. She was so remorseful that her husband had strayed from the Catholic Church that she did not hesitate to sign the papers I needed and then she killed herself by burning the house to the ground. I did not have to demolish it afterwards to build my mansion! They had two young boys that I disposed of by sending to a monastery in the hope that the devout whip of an abbot would erase any interests they could have inherited from their father in ancient Roman ruins. I bet they are now model citizens."

What could be more model than to be in the Pope's inner circle? The man insulting me with his talk was my mother's confessor. With effort, I controlled a nausea attack as he bragged on about how he kept building his fortune on the "donations" he received from members of his congregation. He believed he would soon be able to buy a cardinal's hat. I forced myself to block my feelings and formulate a poisoner's mission.

I consulted with the Pope before putting my plan in motion. His mind was occupied with many events. He was plotting to recuperate the Papal States in the north; and he was scheming to stop the creation by France and Spain of a church council that would limit his power. Still, he listened intently to my petition and authorized me to carry on. In the end, my self-imposed mission would benefit the Holy See as my mother's confessor fortune would be absorbed by the Vatican.

With Callisto, I baked and confected a sumptuous basket of sweets and pastries the likes of which is only seen on a king's table. I had observed my mother's confessor all night. He had gorged on sweets with uncontrolled gluttony. I personally took the basket of goods to the palace in Pigna with a note from the Vatican's kitchen praising his pious work over the years and stating that the feast was intended as a reward just for him. I had mixed assorted venoms in the food in such a way that as he ate the different items the toxins would combine in his blood to give him a slow and terrible death. I hid in the foliage of the Mediterranean pine tree where my father had buried the tablets to observe his demise. In the course of a few days, his joints became terribly swollen so that even a minor movement would produce a stabbing pain. His intestines became inundated with worms and parasites that sucked his life as he had sucked my destiny away. God forgive me for the pleasure I obtained from seeing him as an invalid during the several months that it took him to die in violent pain and convulsions, his throat flooded with worms obstructing him from hollering in agony. I relished his pain, but once he was gone, I had only the empty destiny he had instigated for me.

There is no more text. Anthony closes the document on the screen and then closes his eyes while listening to the calm breathing of the night. He looks at the laptop again and notices another email from Akemi had popped up in his screen:

"There will be more soon. The ink is very faded in some parts but I can decipher it. Will send it when available. – Akemi"

CHAPTER 11

THE LINEBACKER

Saturday is a lazy day. They all wake up so late that they miss breakfast at Hotel Modigliani. Virginia wants to go shopping. She always does. Anthony negotiated with Ellia Jones not to have an escort from the American Embassy. Ellia had conceded, as long as Anthony consents to wearing a GPS bracelet so the secret service can track his whereabouts in case of an emergency. She assured him that the secret service would be close to them, just in case. The family joins the crowd roaming *Via Condotti* on Sundays. Anthony hopes to get something new and cool for his date with Akemi. He has not bought clothes for himself in a year. Even before that, Laura bought most of his wardrobe. *Via Condotti* is one of the main shopping arteries in the city. On weekends, it is as if all the people in Rome congregate to walk up and down it. Italians cherish window-shopping, ranging from top-end boutiques such as Versace to deals at Zara. The Hibberts finish at *Piazza del Poppolo* carrying more bags than expected. Anthony is glad he forced the girls to bring their backpacks. It facilitates moving around with their purchases and electronic gadgets. Although thinking about it, he realizes they always carry their backpacks. He relaxes sipping a Cinzano next to an art marketplace.

In the afternoon, they rejoin the crowd on their way down the street toward *Piazza de Spagna* and their hotel. However, something is pricking Anthony on the back of his neck. He feels watched. As one of the girls leans to tighten her shoelaces, Anthony looks around him. He inspects the masses, spotting a big man in the distance. The man could have been a professional football linebacker: taller than everyone else, stout, and muscular. He must be 6 feet, 8 inches tall. He doesn't look Italian. As if sensing Anthony's gaze, the man enters a shoe store. The girls advance. They want to enter the impossibly congested Disney store. Who cares—they never go to the ones in America. Anthony plays nervously with the GPS bracelet Ellia gave him, twisting it around his wrist. Where is the secret service when you need it? He has no foundation to feel threatened but keeps the girls at arm's length. The giant trails behind them again. Anthony reassures himself that there is nothing strange about that. There are hundreds of people behind them moving in the same direction. This man stands out because he is different from the multitude. Teenagers scantily dressed smoke on the stairs of a church. A couple argues as if they were in a stage. A boy is crying because his father would not buy him a toy. A baby is hungry, and the mother looks for a place to breast-feed. The linebacker lingers. He is not window shopping. His expression is one of annoyance. Trying to escape the churning of his stomach, and clutching the bags he is carrying, Anthony pushes the girls into the first store entrance. It is a men's underwear boutique. The orderly displays and bright illumination make him relax for an instant. He looks at the pictures on the walls and wonders. "How can anyone fit their junk into these things?"

Claudia is embarrassed. Briefs, trunks, jocks, thongs, bikinis, shape enhancers, and maximum exposure—no boxers—cover the walls and adorn explicit mannequins. Claudia pulls her father to the door while Virginia and Thalia giggle.

"I need some yoga underwear..." Words tumble one on top of another. They have to gain some time. Anthony examines the shelves. In response, Virginia points to a yellow thong with lace cherubs.

After convincing himself that he can use a "contour cut-away low rise" bikini in black for his upcoming date, and paying for it, they rejoin the crowd in the street. Anthony refrains from darting back. After a few paces, he cannot resist. The giant is behind them, same distance. He did not advance while they were inside the underwear store. Is he friend or foe? Is he a secret agent sent by the embassy or someone else? The eyes of Anthony and the man meet. Anthony dislikes his predator's stare. *Where is the secret service when you need them?* "Or do I need them? I should be able to protect my family!" He calls for the girls to run. They twist and turn around the passers-by. It is very hot. The girls ask why they are running. Sweat stings their eyes. They want gelato. Anthony urges them along, feeling increasingly thirsty.

A block away from *Piazza de Spagna*, the football linebacker is closing in on them. He is clearly after them, chasing them, hunting like an angry bear. His brawny and long arms reach out. The thrust is directed toward Thalia. Is he aiming to capture her? Anthony's years of yoga discipline pay off. With precise movements, he stops on his tracks. He intercepts the man's vector, shoving his knee into the man's groin. The giant's forward momentum makes for an agonizing and spectacular impact. The massive man bends over and crumbles to the ground. His fingertips brush Thalia's backpack as he collapses. The girls squeal and hurdle away to find the safety of their father. People are watching. Anthony feels the shot of adrenaline and relief rushing to his raised arms as he stands next to his vanquished foe. The man is in a fetal position trying to pull himself together. Anthony takes the girls' hands and sprints away into the square, ignoring the tightening in his chest. They race up the stairs of *Piazza de Spagna*. The four hold hands, snaking around tourists sitting on the steps. A panini spills cheese and salami down the stairs as Virginia knocks it away from the hands of a hungry backpacker in her rush. Don't look back. As if in a marathon, they keep a steady pace. They slow down when they reach *Via della Conzolazione* and the safety of Hotel Modigliani. They are all fit; while feeling the exerting, they still have breath. Thalia wants to do it again. Claudia is embarrassed by the scene and eludes her father's gaze. Virginia checks if all her shopping bags are accounted for, and Anthony looks back, down the empty street feeling every muscle in his body. He can't help but smile at having protected the girls. He is there for them when the secret service fails. All his life, he had played it safe—until now. In Rome he can take risks and succeed.

• • •

The girls have been up for a while. Anthony relaxes, aiming to get a few more minutes of sleep. Claudia reads on her Kindle. Virginia and Thalia watch cartoons in Italian while playing with their plush friends and an iPhone. The air is warm and the streets have a Saturday care-free bustle.

Anthony's father-in-law, while semi-retired, still works on entertainment deals. He has asked them to join them at a toy exhibit close to the hotel. Anthony and the girls stroll down the street to the museum next to Neptune's fountain—*the Palazzo Barberini.*

At the museum, Claudia uses her smart phone to tag the images and get information from Wikipedia. Thalia stops to admire the picture of a seated semi-naked woman. Her long raven hair is in a turban. Her eyes are optimistic, transparently hopeful, and match the playful smile. One of her hands is touching an uncovered naked breast.

"Who is this pretty lady?" Thalia stares at the picture with immense curiosity.

A snap from the phone camera, and Claudia provides the answer: "*La Fornarina* is a painting by Raphael Sanzio, a Renaissance artist in Rome in the early sixteenth century. *La Fornarina,* which means the baker's daughter, is believed to be the picture of his mistress, Margharetta Lutti. Raphael was working on this painting at the time of his death."

Anthony listens tilting his head toward his daughter. He is glad he does not have to be the one looking for data on his phone. He probably would not be able to do it. "It was finished by one of his disciples, Andrea Romano, who altered the original design. X-rays have shown a ruby wedding ring in *La Fornarina*'s hand and quince and myrtle bushes in the background that signify fidelity and fertility. The hypothesis scholars hold is that Raphael had secretly married Margharetta; however, because she was below his social status, his disciples covered the symbols of the union after he passed away, only a tiny pearl brooch on the turban—another marriage symbol— remained" Claudia shows her sisters a picture on her smart phone, "Look! Here is the image under the x-rays. That is a huge ruby ring on her finger!"

"Sweet!" exclaim Thalia and Virginia. Girls love sparkly accessories.

"I think it's stupid," grumbles Claudia. "Here is more. It seems Raphael had been engaged for many years to a Maria Bibbiena, the niece of a powerful cardinal and one of his most powerful patrons."

"I bet there is a wonderfully romantic secret story behind all of this," Thalia lingers in front of the picture, her young face aflame with imagination.

"Something like your story with Mama," adds Virginia.

"Well, we will never know girls. Our story was never secret. Maybe you can become art historians and uncover the saga behind this painting. Let's keep on moving."

They reach the temporary exhibit room. Antique miniature trains and porcelain dolls cover shelves and display cases. Some of the toys date back to the Middle Ages. Anthony sees his father-in-law talking with the show's sponsor, an elegant man in his sixties with silver white hair and deep blue eyes with a squint both sad and gentle.

"Let me introduce you to Adriano Giocatelli, he is working with my partners to bring a new toy line to life for one of the upcoming TV shows this fall." Elmer extends his arm to bring Anthony and the girls into the circle of people he is standing with. "He was just telling us about how his father had been a toy maker in Nuremberg before the Second World War. Giocatelli pats Thalia on the head. Elmer continues, "He came to work for the Vatican just before the war broke so he had to stay away from his craft for many years."

"Nuremberg was one of the most important cities for Hitler; did your grandfather attend any of the rallies there when he was young?" Claudia is really interested in coming face to face with someone who might have stories of Nazi Germany.

Giocatelli wrinkles his forehead, "My father did not like to talk about those times. His house was close to where Hitler built the parade grounds and zeppelin field. I am sure he saw many things that convinced him to move to Italy."

"Come on, girls. Come look at the exhibit with me," Melissa, Anthony's mother-in-law, gently pulls the girls away.

"Anthony, Elmer was telling me that you have been invited to participate at the Catholic Transparency Commission. I guess we will be seeing a lot of each other—I am also a member. Maybe you and the girls can come for dinner to my house one night. We would love to cook you a real Italian dinner." Giocatelli's voice is soft and inviting.

Anthony nods, feeling Virginia tugging on his shirt to go with her. She wants to go for gelato at *San Crispino*.

• • •

The next morning, Anthony goes to the American Embassy for a press conference. His role is to articulate the objectives of the Catholic Church Transparency Commission before its inauguration. He holds interviews with CNN and the main American TV stations. The press likes his boy-next-door good looks and family history. While you would expect an academic and aloof demeanor from a respected university scholar, he comes across with warmth and humbleness that lends credibility to his points of view. The public relations people have given Anthony all the talking points, and he delivers them as if conversing with a trusted friend at their favorite bar. He is then taken in a limo to the Vatican, where Commission representatives are gathering. The Pope will preside over its opening.

Akemi checks the screens in the palace control center while she communicates with the Swiss Guard and Italian police. Somewhat annoyed by the primitive monitors in the room, she creates content rules for her Google Glass to prioritize images projected to the corner of her eye. The meeting room for the Catholic Church Transparency Commission has been bugged with micro-cameras and microphones. The twenty-five selected delegates will be sitting on a round table facing a podium. In the control center, there are twenty-five screens—one for each commissioner close-up. Akemi will be able to zoom on their faces while software analyzes their facial expressions. A recording indicator will show if they are speaking in a low voice to themselves or their neighbors. There are other views of the room. Behind the round table is a small gathering area with refreshments where the council members can talk and drink espressos during breaks. The spying devices are hidden in the crystals of a seventeenth-century chandelier pointing to many angles in this portion of the room.

Alessandro scans his retina to get into the control center. He pulls Akemi to the side and murmurs in her ear: "Thanks for the council members' profiles. Very thorough. They are promising leads; however there is only one with a distant association to Nazi Germany. Mr. Adriano Giocatelli. He owns a toy and entertainment empire. His father was born in Nuremberg and came to Rome in 1933, supposedly to escape the deteriorating political environment as the Nazis gained power. He came to Rome to be a liaison between the Holy See and the German Catholic Party. Rumor has it he was a communications decoder. His skills allowed the Vatican to stay connected through encrypted messages with the allies. He also intercepted fascist messages between Italy and Germany. Just before World War II began, he was allowed to become a Vatican citizen. This is very suspicious as it is highly unusual for a secular person to be a Vatican citizen, and even more so during the war…"

Akemi peeks at the screen in her fashionable eyeglasses, "I know all this. Shut up. I have to pay attention. They are getting into the room. You can observe Mr. Giocatelli all you want. He has his own screen. He is the man in a blue Armani suit, a Missoni tie, and grey balding hair."

It is more rewarding to discover new books than to meet strange people. Anthony goes to the refreshment table for fruit. It feels like the first day of classes in a new school. Only this school has gilded frames, console tables, cabinets, and large objects ornamented with swags and drops of boldly scaled fruits and flowers. Everybody else is chatting with acquaintances after exchanging explosive greetings. He locates Gabriel Herrera accompanied by two other priests. Seeing him brings back un-answered questions. Anthony slides to his side.

"Gabriel, I've been meaning to talk to you."

The Bishop of Los Angeles Cathedral is not so welcoming. He pulls back a few inches from the friendly hand on his shoulder, and then scans his surroundings to check if anybody is observing them. He is unaware of the micro-cameras. "Oh, Anthony! Bless you, my son. I also wanted to reach out to you but I have been too busy working on this conference. It is very important for the Vicar of Christ. I apologize for the delay. I felt terrible the police thought you were Avinash's murderer. Francesca told me you kept our conversation from the previous night to yourself," his face invades Anthony's personal space with the eagerness of someone trying to hide a sin.

"I kept it to myself." Anthony maintains his position, refraining from acting on his natural instinct to retreat a couple of paces. His tone is smooth, "but I still want to know. How did you find Avinash's life was in jeopardy? Have you shared what you know with the police?"

Gabriel is pale; drops of perspiration cover his forehead. "This is not the place to talk about these matters." He cocks his head, and his hungry eyes follow the curves of a woman in a tight dress passing next to them. "The fate of Christendom will be affected by the outcome of this conference, and we need to focus on it. Forget everything else," but his eyes keep scrutinizing the room to find the woman in the tight dress.

"Then, give me a place and time. I spent a weekend in an Italian jail; my family was frightened and might even be in danger because of my involvement in this...situation. You have first-hand information...." Now it is Anthony who is invading Gabriel's personal space. His lips are almost brushing the Bishop's cheeks. Despite the violent beating of his heart, his voice is still smooth but has clear undertones of threat. "It's my family you have messed with. I am certain our American Ambassador would be interested in our conversation the night before the murder."

"Gabriel! Tony! *Ciao!*" Francesca wraps her arms around both men making their bodies clash. She kisses their cheeks in her euphoric manner. Gabriel jumps away from Anthony like a cornered deer who has found the escape route.

"*Bella! Qui piacere!*" he returns Francesca's kisses. After that, making the sign of the cross, he moves, almost runs, back to the group of priests he had been with before. Anthony is plotting his next action when someone at the podium invites the council members to take their places; name tags show where to sit, as His Holiness the Pope will arrive shortly for the inauguration ceremony.

Usually the papal seat has been occupied by elders, but the world has, for once, a younger Pope actively working to reconnect with his flock. When he arrives, everybody turns to him as his lack of wrinkles and energetic step never ceases to surprise those who have spent their life inside the Catholic Church. The Pope opens the session by giving a benediction to all present. He then talks about how the Vatican State— same as other countries in the world—deals with very delicate information affecting national and international security. This data, if misused or conveyed in the wrong context, could create a global conflict, even war.

"Transparency of information is not a matter to take lightly. The world will be watching this group, hand-picked by world leaders, to set the framework for a constructive conversation with the millions who are demanding it through petitions in social forums. May the Holy Spirit illuminate your thoughts and guide you in this journey. The actions you will recommend have implications beyond religion. The digital revolution has taken all of us by surprise. World leaders and institutions have to change their behaviors, but we do not know how. To provide some context I have asked my personal advisor in cyber security and cyber terrorism protection to provide some background. Some of you are aware of the data she will share; some will hear it for the first time. I leave you with Miss Akemi Morishima, CEO of Ghostwire."

Akemi is dressed in a grey Chanel business suit. She wears minimal jewelry and makeup.

Slides appear behind Akemi. She installed a movement sensor behind the podium to react to commands by her body. "Half of the people in the world are using social networks. These people are active not only on Facebook which has the largest membership, but also are engaged in LinkedIn for business, visit many forums for crowd-sourcing, learn on YouTube or get fresh ideas from Pinterest. Social media has proved to enhance connections with brands, improve productivity in the workplace, and even topple governments. Back in the 80s, a social movement could take years to be adopted around the planet. Now it takes minutes."

Ellia Jones's eyes wander away from Akemi as she studies the other members of the commission. Her jowls are tight with an angry fastidiousness.

"Avinash Sullivan was a genius in crafting technology to comprehend and harness the power of the digital social mesh. He had a younger brother who committed suicide after it became public that a Catholic priest had abused him sexually. When the media unveiled that the priest had committed similar acts in other parishes and that his superiors had chosen to move him around instead of punishing his actions, Avinash decided to apply his knowledge and skillset to enlisting communities around the world to demand transparency and justice. Avinash was one of those persons in Silicon Valley accustomed to changing the world with their actions. He never accepted conventions. He was always a believer of a new level of human moral consciousness, a new world order where hypocrisy would be obliterated and total transparency would be the norm." Gabriel fidgets with a rosary, looking away from Anthony and Akemi. He seems to be praying instead of listening. "In his mind, the best way to stop cyberwar was to transform mankind so that privacy would not be required. Everybody has flaws, and we would learn to accept the flaws of others. It would be like a city with wide-open windows to the street where anyone can see our actions, our finances, and our nakedness. No more secrets because secrecy only empowers the cowards and makes the natural seem unnatural or forbidden. The Catholic Church is an institution that has preached love and acceptance of others ever since its inception. *You shall love your neighbor as you love yourself.* But the Catholic Church is also the longest-existing, complexly organized institution in history. It is known for its humanitarian acts and mercy for others, but Avinash believed it is also plagued with hypocrisy and the politics of power."

Alessandro observes Giocatelli on the screens at the security center. The man seems like a very respectable business man, white hair neatly combed and eyes that reveal compassion and command. Could a man who makes toys be a murderer?

"Avinash believed in a no-privacy policy for the Catholic institution. Complete information, data, and procedures would eliminate future scandals inside the Vatican. He envisioned technology as the catalysts to expose injustice and to let the Catholic Church's great humanitarian work shine. No more hypocrisy to obstruct the True Light. To eradicate hypocrisy in all institutions and governments, we must commence with our souls."

Francesca crosses and uncrosses her legs. She wants the speech to be over. Herrera is sitting next to her but both lean away from each other.

"The crises in the recent decade have made humanity thirstier for spirituality. Avinash's social campaign caught force like fire on a dry grassland. Fast and furious messages in Twitter became instant prayers, viral posts in Facebook became pleas for change, videos on YouTube evolved from entertainment to education to indignation, and images in Pinterest reflected the human soul. When we pull the curtains back, the ugly, the petty, and the scandals are exposed. But through open windows, we allow the sun to enter. Usually our collective attention span is very short lived. But in this Transparency Crusade, bloggers have not stopped blogging. The news releases are not aging because the multitudes want to change the way the Vatican operates. They have waited hundreds of years to be heard."

"Still, when we look at our own lives, we don't want others to have access to our credit cards or know the passwords to all our sites. We don't want people to discover the sites we frequent. What would you say if I told you that I just hacked into your smartphones while I have been talking…which I have. I know everything there is to know about all of you. How does it make you feel?" Akemi gloats. "We don't want strangers spying on the pictures of our families. We want the errors we have all committed to be forgotten and transcended instead of showcased. Why are institutions different from individuals? What makes the Catholic Church different? You don't want me to post your information, do you? You don't want some of the texts we just hacked from your smartphones to hit the press. I won't do it. We are just performing background checks." The people in the room squirm in their seats with discomfort. Some force a tentative laugh, uncertain if Akemi is joking.

"It is your job to set the framework for this conversation. When is privacy common sense, and when hypocrisy? I repeat, whatever you produce will be a foundation for conversations within other institutions, corporations, and governments. We have very few digital natives as members in the conference. Millennials believe they are entitled to transform the world and change what older generations have believed. They are not asking for our permission. They are the customer and have been doing it for a while." Akemi smiles. She has spoken barely looking at her audience, yet everybody has listened intently. She seems to be smiling at some internal joke. It is very quick, like a sudden change of light when a cloud covers a bright sun, and just as quickly, she becomes aloof again, her features businesslike and practical, her mouth tight.

"I have created a shared folder on a secure drive to which you all have access. There, you have links to many articles, analyses, and sources. You can create digital forums to chat and discuss ideas. There is also a list of experts from many countries that you can call or Skype for advice and consultation. You already got blessings from the Pope. Now use the data. Good luck."

CHAPTER 12

THE SHACKLES OF A PROMISE

That night, Anthony lies awake in bed. He cannot stop thinking about Akemi's speech. After midnight he gets up and tries to browse the shared files Akemi created for the Transparency Commission but he can't figure out the navigation once inside the link. Unexpectedly, an email window pops up: "More. Akemi." She sent just the two words and an attachment.

Day 3 - December 8, 1521

Ten days left. Will I have time and strength to finish my confession? I feel weaker every day. My vision is blurry and I have nightmares even at daylight. The city transformed into a monster is back to haunt me. How many more sacrifices does it need? But I won't waste ink on that. I need to keep writing.

Pleasure from the agony of others is a sin. Even if I had the Pope's absolution, I felt empty after killing my mother's confessor. I desired to do penance for my transgression. Every twenty-five years, the city of Rome celebrates a jubilee. Thousands of pilgrims from all kingdoms and lands come seeking for penance for their sins. They visit sites where holy relics are kept. The route includes all the important temples. To purge my sin, I embarked on the circuit and implored forgiveness.

I joined the multitudes but it was not the prayers that enlightened me. The beauty of the holy sites lifted my spirit: the cloister of San Paolo fuori le Mura with its sublime use of marble and mosaic surpassed any creation the ancient Romans could have produced. The pink, red, and green wings of the angels surrounding the throne of Christ depicted as a fresco at Santa Cecilia in Trastevere. They were the vivid image and promise of a clean and hygienic heaven where trash and filth does not exist. Saint John Lateran where the pagan temples had transmutated into a Catholic cathedral. The bronze doors taken from the Roman Senate building and the golden columns from Jupiter's Temple surrounded the immutable mosaic images of Christ and his celestial court where no politics exist. Santa Maria Maggiore telling the life of Jesus with images. Christ crowning the Virgin with a power that no Pope on Earth can ever bestow on a king or emperor. Santa Prudenzia, Santa Sabina, and San Cosme and Damiano. Each place with art delivering shapes and hues that nourished my soul and made me stronger. God had poured into the world glimpses of His glory using artists as a conduit. But this also created a conflict in my intellect and heart from the split between pagan literature and art to these powerful expressions of the Bible and Catholicism. The roots were interwoven but the branches differed. What was the right cosmogony? A partial answer was provided by art inside the Vatican. Fra Angelico had decorated the chapel of Nicholas V with pigments and anatomical movement that celebrated the human side of the apostles. Their bodies had muscles and the robes revealed a celebration of our body similar to the exposed bodies in pagan sculptures. Even at the Pope's private apartment, which Julius II disliked immensely as it had been decorated for the Borgia Pope, I could not help but marvel at what Pinturiccio accomplished.

But in the year 1507, I also understood why His Holiness Julius II was nicknamed "Il terribile," the terrible one, as circumstances drove me to make an oath of obedience I have regretted, and which delivered dreadful outcomes that torture me in my final days. Yes, beauty was sprouting in the city driven by our powerful Pope. He was fulfilling his destiny to transform Rome into the center of the universe. His uncle had also been a Pope, Sixtus IV, and a notable one because he restored power to the Roman Curia after the center of Christianity had resided in France for many years. Sixtus IV had a vision to transform Saint Peter's Basilica, built in the third century under Emperor Constantine, into the most glorious and sacred center of prayer. But Sixtus IV did not live to accomplish his dream; instead he passed the challenge to Julius II. In 1506, Donato Bramante, an architect from the North of Italy, was hand-picked for the job of architect for the new Basilica. Julius II laid the first stone for the construction on top of Saint Peter's burial site during a grand ceremony. He then decreed that the old basilica would be razed to the ground so the new could emerge in its place. I personally loved the ruinous third-century building from Constantine even with its col-lapsed north wall. After more than a thousand years, so many saints and martyrs had been buried within its walls that every inch of the building was embedded with clandestine messages and stories from parishio-ners thanking and praising them for miracles. Every inch of the wood gates of the altars and benches was covered with engraved letters or in small silver tokens and perfumed candles and coins. This created an almost street market distribution for small chapels scattered within the five-columned aisles, and because the age and materials of the chapels differed from each other it created the atmosphere of a city inside the building with the taste of many generations and distant lands sticking to the tongues and noses of the visitors. It had been erected with scraps from the Classical temples; for example, its timber roof was covered by gilded bronze plates taken from Maxentius Basilica. Its bronze doors crafted by the top welders of its time. In the center was a huge solid gold cross over the tomb of Saint Peter that had shone for me and many other penitents in our times of need. Julius II saw only decay and ancient materials blocking his road to renewal. His closest bank-er, Agostino Chigi, managed the profits from the Vatican's alum and salt mines, magnificent sources of income, so he advanced funds for the project. The King of England sent copper for the new roof to re-place the bronze from melted Roman sculptures to create the old tiles. The best marble quarries in Italy sent their finest blocks. Many ancient constructions going back to the time of the Republic, including the temple of the Sacred Julius where Julius Caesar had been murdered, were demolished to provide materials. With all of these resources—plus the multiple Carrara marble blocks that Julius II had gathered so Michelangelo, a brilliant Florentine sculptor, could create his Holiness burial monument—the wide esplanade in front of the basilica became a stone labyrinth, a quarry in the metropolis.

The city was not as excited with the project. There was immense opposition. Saint Peter was sacred ground and the relics and chapel should be untouchable not only for their sanctity but also because they were the final destination for pilgrims coming to Rome. Pilgrims must not be upset; they were one of the largest sources of income for Rome's inhabitants.

On the day when Julius II gave me the mission, he reinforced how he wished for the new basilica to embody the glory of the present, but most of all, to showcase for eternity the power of the Catholic Church over this temporal world. I did not dislike the architect Bramante. After all, he had brought several of the new painters who were creating very exciting art decorating the Vatican palace. However, in April 1507, Bramante tore the roof atop Saint Peter's main altar, damaging beyond repair priceless mosaics, chapels, and relics. This infuriated the city dwellers and pilgrims who started calling him "Il ruinante," the destroyer. Angrier than most were the inhabitants of the Lateran quarter. The cathedral in that area had been the residence for the popes from the beginning until the seat was transported to France. When the popes finally returned to Rome, the Lateran palace had decayed so much that the Vatican had been selected as the new residence. Since that moment, the power elite at the Lateran quarter had plotted ways to bring the papal court back to its territory. The papal court was an important source of income for those who lived nearby.

After the roof in Saint Peter collapsed, Julius II had tried to diminish the city's discontent by continuing to officiate Sunday mass in the old basilica. This pretense only provoked the fury of the cardinals who now had to attend liturgy exposed to the weather. By August, Julius II was tired of the bickering and criticism. He had been organizing a military campaign against Umbria, so before he led his army to war he gave me the mission. He called me to a very private area within his personal chambers. He was going to teach the city a lesson not to oppose him. He ordered me to poison the consecration wine during Sunday mass at Saint John Lateran. The massacre would show anybody who defied his will that God was on his side and was displeased with the opposition to the new basilica. The poison had to create the illusion of a plague, not of venom. I listened with my eyes downcast, and when he lifted my face by the chin to confirm my understanding, my vision strayed on his white hair, evading his authoritative eyes.

In the following days, I would aimlessly journey through the Vatican palace delaying my mission. The palace was almost empty. Most of the three hundred administrators and two hundred servants had joined the war caravan. Even Callisto was gone. He had to cook for the six hundred Swiss mercenaries serving the Pope.

I spent hours staring at the paintings the new artists—Pietro Perugio, Pinturiccio, Luca Signoreli—had created for the palace or reading the Classical authors. With time, the bells of Rome became an inescapable presence. The city has hundreds of churches and bell towers that call for mass or indicate the time of day. After the Pope's army rode to battle, I ignored the bell tolls. As the weeks progressed, even the most distant bells would enter the empty rooms in the palace as messengers reminding me of my mission. With each peal, I was summoned to Saint John Lateran, and I accrued a burden that incrementally increased on my back, sinking me into nightmares where I was the beast devouring the inhabitants of Rome. I was the rabid monster crunching men and women with my distorted jaws. My father and brother pleaded me to stop. Another night, while the sound of bells flooded the midnight hour, I dreamt that the colorful angels from the frescoes in Santa Cecilia in Trastevere had become animated and tried to exorcise me, but as a beast I kept devouring lives until I discovered the body I was munching on was that of my grandfather, lost the night of the fire in our house.

Unable to bear this anymore, I commenced the operation. While crafting my plan, I observed the people at Sunday mass. There were mothers with their infants and elders misbehaving as much as their grandchildren. Men and women prayed to Christ Pantocrator in the Sancta Sanctorum chapel for miracles to solve their problems. I watched the lovers and the young, their faces brimming with hope and love for the future. The forces of everyday life kept distracting me from orchestrating the massacre. I was so engrossed in the mundane existence of the ones around me that I ignored the lice crawling in their hair. The smell of their unwashed bodies was dissipated by the choir and liturgy music, which was better than that of any other congregation in the city.

But I had a job to do, so instead of water I used my tears to mix the potion. Instead of using ingredients from the palace pantry, I made a point of buying them in the Lateran market. I wanted to capture the faces of those who went to mass in their daily routines laboring at their market stands.

One Saturday night I broke into Saint John and mixed the poisons with the water and wine for the communion the following day. Water and wine had been mixed by Jesus Christ during the Last Supper. Since then, this action was repeated in every mass by the officiating priest for the faithful to sip wine as part of the ceremony. My ingredients would become deadly when mixing the two liquids. Dressed in my lavender robe, I waited all night next to Constantine's sculpture at the entrance of the cathedral until the bells called for mass, the sound flowing like daggers through my veins. I then watched the faces of those entering the temple. Suddenly a very young girl ran away from her parents and hugged my legs. She was attracted by the lavender color of my robe, which she pulled with laughter as sweet as her honey-colored eyes and hair. Her mother came rushing to us and carried her away in her arms. "Hurry, hurry, the communion is waiting for us," she chanted into the girl's ears like a nurturing brook.

I was possessed by an energy I had never experienced. I did not care about the Pope's fury or if I was defying God's Will. I hurried down the central aisle, pushing aside anybody who tried to stop me, until I got to the main altar and grabbed the cruets, the two containers that hold the water and wine, and spilled them on the floor. Everybody was so stunned by my actions that I escaped before they could organize and chase me, exiting the cathedral and merging with a crowd of pilgrims on their way to the Scala Santa Church, which is next to Saint John.

That night the bell tolls prevented me from sleeping. I would vomit each time I heard their peal until my stomach hurt as much as my soul. During the following days, I poisoned the twelve most prominent men in the Lateran, the twelve who opposed Saint Peter's Basilica the most. They were men so adept at intrigue and greed that their demise meant nothing to me.

The Pope returned victorious at year's end. He marched on a triumphant parade with his court, his army and Swiss Guard celebrating the conquest of Urbino. I heard the spectacle had been magnificent, but I stayed in my room. I was waiting for the Pope's summon by the time he would discover I had not followed his instructions. Four days later he came to my room, something he had never done before. The guards emptied the whole building so His Holiness and I would have complete privacy.

After his military victory, he looked taller and stronger. Still, I gazed directly at him while on a kneeling position. He slammed my face with the back of his hand, making me collapse to the floor and then yelled, inquiring about my failed mission. From the floor I tried to explain to him the things I had seen when going to mass at Saint John. I described the innocents that would have died if I had followed his orders. I explained that I had still eliminated the most powerful leaders in the area, the problematic ones. He towered above me with disdain, putting his boot on my neck, and pronounced: "I exist to construct the glory of Christ. I am his emissary on Earth and my will is His Will. I don't hesitate to excommunicate a city or a kingdom if needed. If I am not concerned with the eternal souls of my enemies' women and children, much less about their temporal existence." He kicked me in the face; my lips covered his silk slippers with blood. The Pope called his guards and ordered them to take me to a dungeon in the Castel Saint Angelo. At that moment, I was certain my existence was going to end in a dank and dark hole infested by vermin.

During my imprisonment, the only satisfaction I had was to know that my whole body was devoid of hair, preventing insects from nesting. The cell was so deep underground that no sound from the outside penetrated. The only random noises were of mice stirring in the darkness and of my own scratching. The cell was so small I could not stand up straight. I had to bend my waist or crawl to move around. The total area of the cell was also unfit. I mapped the space in my mind to isolate a patch in which to pour my urine and excrement. I survived the degradation of those days by visualizing the paintings and mosaics I had admired throughout Rome in the recent weeks. The angels with green and blue wings smiled while I was delirious with hunger and thirst—I licked humidity from the walls covered in moss.

I spent close to a week in captivity, and then the Swiss Guards came to get me. The jailer washed me and gave me clean threadbare robes so I could be taken to the upper apartments in Castel Saint Angelo—the same apartments where the Pope could seek refuge in case of a city siege. The Vicar of Christ had come to this room expressively to meet with me. The guards dragged my weak body by the arms and dropped me on a couch. The Pope was standing next to an open window where you could see the Vatican with the Borgia tower jutting to the sky. The cold autumn air felt reinvigorating on my face, and I swallowed mouthfuls of it like someone drowning in the ocean. I was not rebellious anymore. When we were left alone, I slid off the couch to the floor, my head low. I had no energy left to stay seated. The Pope spoke with power strolling around the room as in a monologue. The death of the twelve leaders at the Lateran quarter had stopped the complaints in the city against Saint Peter's reconstruction. Julius II acknowledged that he had been impulsive in conceiving the mission. Impulsivity is a virtue when you are surrounded by bureaucrats and politicians. He had been surprised by my actions, as I had been his most loyal servant during his papacy. He wished to do the best for the Catholic Church and its flock. Still, he had been analyzing the causes of my rebellion. He realized I had been right in not killing all the people at the cathedral. Too many innocent would have died. He knelt next to me and embraced me, lifted my head and kissed me on both cheeks. He carried me back to the couch. Pulling a chair in front of me, he sat and thanked me for having done what was right and for having rebelled frontally instead of conniving behind his back. He recognized that very few of his men had that kind of courage. Maybe the banker Agostino Chigi was the only other one. He required moral men to follow his lead so he could deliver the undertaking God had conferred upon him, but he also needed people who would follow his commands without question. He made me a promise: in the future he would be more thorough when conceiving a mission—no more impulsivity for my missions. In exchange, he made me promise that I would never question him or doubt his orders...or, for that matter, the orders of any of his successors. The Pope was the Pope, and blind, silent obedience was required. I surrendered to being an instrument of the Pope's wishes. I became bound by the promise. He *made me swear on the sacred souls of my father, my brother, and my grandfather. If I rebelled against his Holiness, they would rot in hell. He had the spiritual power for that. Through the window, the church bells calling for afternoon prayers filled the room.*

I have to stop writing now. My head is exploding with pain, and my body soaked in sweat brings me to the present. The Vatican palace is empty now. Once again, servants and courtiers are gone after the Pope's death, having taken everything they could carry with them: money from the papal chambers, jewelry, fabric and tapestries, even the gold doorknobs. Meanwhile, the conclave gathers to choose the successor to the Pope I murdered. The consolation of the poison corroding my body is that I won't have to live through the proclamation of a new Pope ever again.

I have to rest. Some opium will do the trick. Hopefully, I'll dream of the happy times when I found love and friendship, when I was able to break my silence and talk with the two people I have treasured the most. I have to finish my story. Escape from the year 1521 and back in my memory to 1508, when the great artist Raphael Sanzio di Urbino was fetched to Rome by Bramante. Raphael was Bramante's protégée, but most important Raphael became my friend, and his wife the only woman I have ever loved.

The text ends too abruptly for Anthony. "This is the last fragment of text from Angelo. We need to find the other cover of 'The Nature of Things' book."

CHAPTER 13

AWKWARD DATING

kemi fears the night. Fears sleep. She searches for shelter working in her glass room surrounded by glass screens pulsating with the murmurs of millions of Internet users. There is always someone awake somewhere, working, browsing, or on a social network. Thousands of images and videos get loaded every second like layers of digital dust creating strata for future archeologists with infinite time to dissect our civilization. This life is the material that conceals her from the terrors in the physical world. The palpable is where death and pain reside. They become abstractions when they turn digital—abstractions that can be filtered, blocked, or deleted from existence. For the monsters that can slip through the cracks, she has the safeguard of her guardian robots and mini drones. She speaks on wireless microphones on a conference call with India, China, and Japan. When her body surrenders to exhaustion, she waves darkness into the screens and retreats into her sleeping pod next door.

Comforting fabrics envelop her body but her mind doesn't stop. She will have dinner with the pretty, tall American the following day and that unnerves her. She has played a video recording many times in her glass screens during the night. In it, she scrutinized his body and facial expression during the Catholic Transparency Conference. She likes the way his long, lean muscles move. She repeats the scene when he walks with expansive steps through the room to the Los Angeles Bishop before the start of the session. What did Gabriel tell Anthony the night before Avinash's murder? What is Anthony concealing with his handsome boy-next-door face and his startling blue eyes? What is the connection to Avinash?

• • •

For Anthony, the next Transparency conference session on Tuesday is slow torture. He cannot stop thinking about his date with Akemi while he repeatedly touches his wallet to feel the set of condoms he has slipped into it. Buying them had been an ordeal. He felt the humiliation of a teenager. He shifts in his chair and touches his wallet again, feeling the rounded contour of the preservatives through the leather as a reassurance that his attention should shift to the meeting room. He notices micro robots like the ones in Akemi's house at the end of the tables and at the corners of the room. He thinks it is some kind of security measure from the Italian police but they make her presence felt. Whatever anybody is saying at the podium become vacuous words. Like a boy trapped in elementary school, he moves nervously on his chair until he inventories the other members of the conference by giving them animal traits. The Bishop Gabriel Herrera is a zebra. Mr. Giocatelli is a grey fox. Francesca is a cockatoo. There are two more priests: one is fat and stooped, bald and with an overflowing belly. He is a hippopotamus. Another is very thin and tall, a cheetah. There are some renowned intellectuals. One is a woman with pomegranate hair, heavy cocoa butter makeup, and raspberry lips wearing a palm tree print blouse with a very revealing V-neck. She is a coral medusa under the Caribbean Sea. The IBM representative is a man from India. He has brown skin, dark circles under his eyes, and white hair and beard. He is in his early forties, tall and well built. Definitely a wise old panther. Ellia Jones is...somehow Anthony cannot relate an animal to her. A she-wolf? A hyena? A chameleon? There is something unnerving in the way her eyes glitter when she thinks nobody is looking. Maybe she is a mix of crow, hawk, and owl? Her body frame is too powerful for an office bureaucrat. Instead of breast she has powerful pectorals. She is a vulture.

• • •

The Ducatti Bistro building feels like an engine with Desmodromic valve control under a monocoque chassis. It is Italian design and engineering presented on a space built with glass, metal, and advanced ceramics in the middle of a park. Attached to its chrome pillars are motorcycles climbing up and then hanging upside down from the ceiling. At the entrance, the bar area has many couches with plush pillows. On one of the sofas sleeps a black-and-white Great Dane oblivious to techno music and the activity around him.

Akemi shares tequila shots with Alessandro Catzola.

"The traces are clear. The information keeps pointing us to Giocatelli as he is the only one with German connections in his past."

Akemi winces. "I am not comfortable with any of the lot. My suspects are: the Los Angeles Bishop—his career is too perfect. He is building his career to become a Pope in some years. Then the American lawyer, Ellia Jones: her information is unreal. She is a ghost. Her real life has been completely removed from any and all file, and this fictional character has taken its place."

"How do you know that?"

"The information layers are too thin. I have seen these cover-ups from the American Defense Department in the past. She hides something big."

"And you are still digging into Francesca Malatesta's information…"

"Too many jewels. Is her rich boyfriend trying to prove something? Plus, she has slept with half the men on the planet…"

"Not with me."

"Yet…Also, my three favorite suspects: Francesca, Ellia, and Gabriel all phoned a disposable mobile the day before the murder."

"How do you know that?"

"The commission members thought I was joking when I said I had hacked their smartphones while giving my presentation during the opening ceremony. It was no joke. I got a list of the phone numbers they had called in the last month. I ran a cross-reference search and found who called whom within the group. The calls to this unidentifiable number popped out. I checked in the phone company database. The phone number was disposable, pay with a card bought at a supermarket kind. Was Giocatelli the one with the disposable phone? My team found where the disposable phone was sold: a Carrefour store close to where Giocatelli works."

"Too many coincidences, yet not enough for us to arrest any one of them. I respect your list of favorites but I don't get how any of them will be connected with bullets and a gun from Nazi Germany."

"Who says they have to be connected?"

Alessandro rolls his eyes. "Have you found anything more on Avinash? Do we know what he was going to share with the Pope on his private audience?"

"We have general information, no details. I've talk with the new Transparency Crusade leaders. No help there yet."

"They were friendly with you? Why have they not cooperated with us?"

"We have a past..."

• • •

Anthony enters the bistro and is immediately surprised to see Akemi standing next to Catzola at the bar. "I thought it was only two of us on this date." The side of his mouth whispers to the Great Dane on the couch, "Want to join us, too?"

The lieutenant checks him out as he approaches, but Anthony is too interested in Akemi to return more than a frown to the policeman. Getting close to Akemi is like entering a tropical forest where all of the animals are in heat. Akemi is wearing very high-heeled Louboutins and a long tight dress. It covers her body like black lacquer and enhances her bosom and hips. Her black hair is pulled back, making her cheeks and lips more pronounced. She is wearing her one-of-a-kind web-connected eyeglasses. She reminds him of the heroines he has seen in posters when taking Virginia to the videogame store.

"Mr. Catzola was just leaving." She kisses Anthony on the cheek. Her orange blossom perfume invites Anthony to lick her neck and find a vein to cling to, but he refrains.

Alessandro curls his lips, forming a smirk in a failed attempt to be friendly and retreats with an offended attitude rolling his shoulders inside his crumbled shirt and jacket as if the movement would allow his body to fold and fit better into the crevices of his clothes. The waiter takes Anthony and Akemi to their table next to a self-standing crystal chandelier whose many lights sparkle as if illuminating a ballroom in a spaceship. Anthony clears his throat and controls his voice to sound casual: "What were you doing with Detective Catzola?"

Akemi is looking at something in the display in her glasses so she answers without looking at her date: "I am part of the Vatican's security team. He and I are collaborating on the investigation of Avinash's murder."

Anthony concentrates on her lips to ignore the annoyance of having Avinash's case touching everything in his life. Akemi keeps talking, "Did you know that the American Embasy took all the surveillance tapes from the Excelsior Hotel? They told the media they are working with us but they are not part of the core cell for the investigation. I might have to hack their system soon."

"You can share the tapes with me after the hacking," Anthony narrows his eyes as if weighing with his eyelids how much he can share. "Ellia Jones, the lawyer from the American Embassy believes my daughters might have seen the killer the night of the murder."

"I know who Jones is," she sounds annoyed, her tone saying—never assume I know less than you do. "Children are difficult witnesses in court. I would not pay attention to this."

"It is my family—"

"I'm trying to solve the case," she cuts him off, uninterested.

While Anthony searches for a reply, the waiter brings him a beer and he drinks it eagerly. Akemi types on her iPhone. He orders a vegetarian antipasto, and she orders breaded veal cutlet after a raw beef Carpaccio appetizer.

"Your English is perfect. Where are you from?"

Akemi scoffs, "I am American. You don't need to stereotype me because of my looks. My father was Japanese-American and my mother Mexican."

"So you come frequently to Rome?" Anthony tries to break a long silence while picking at an eggplant slice.

"Uhuh." She types on her phone.

He looks around at the hip young Italians dressed in tailored suits next to thin, glittering women. They seem to be doing well with their conversations. On the table, some buffalo mozzarella on toast. She pushes several slices of prosciutto in her mouth with one hand while pinching some screen on her wrist with the other.

Anthony wonders if all first dates are this awkward. His Italian underwear is tight. The "contour cut-away and low rise" made him look like the guy on the underwear box when he checked himself in the bathroom mirror, but he wishes he could push his hand down the underwear and re-arrange his balls. At least the food is good. After three olives, he ventures again. "I have to thank you for rebuilding the text about the assassin working for the Pope. It is fascinating to read a first-hand narrative of the time. It makes you realize how much the world has changed."

"Has it?" She raises her face away from the iPhone for the first time. Her black eyes soften, and the ice in them seems to glow with the promise of melting someday.

"The monk is writing from his experience." His tongue plays with an olive pit inside his cheek.

"I have fact-checked the letters. The monk's descriptions of Rome match the primary sources. On the Vatican, there are not many files of the time but the few I found match Federigo's description of Constantine's Basilica." She tilts her head and lightly plays with her hair like a girl talking to a boy on the playground for the first time.

"Bramante's destruction of the old basilica is a required story for anyone who studies art history." Anthony stops picking on the food. "I wish they had been more careful."

"Reading about art and history has been my only distraction. The monk's story merges both, making it very satisfactory." Her long fingernails distractedly caress the glass surface of her iPhone as her interest shifts away from the gadget.

"Did Angelo tell you that we are looking for the next section of the monk's story?" He leans toward her across the table and inadvertently their hands slide on top of the tablecloth almost touching.

"He did. It *has* to be in the underground vault of the Secret Archives along with the rest of the book. We *must* find it," she enunciates each syllable with an intensity that reflects his own. "All books should be electronic. Where I grew up we did not have public libraries. Whenever we could get a book, we would acquire it for our family bookshelves. I read anything available there. Later, the boarding school had a well-stocked library with books in Latin and Greek. I had to self-teach the languages to decipher the texts which led me to find electronic books by hacking on college digital libraries. It proved to be a very useful skill for breaking codes."

Anthony is sitting very straight. He takes a piece of bread, and Akemi looks at his long and graceful fingers as he breaks it. "Where was you boarding school located?"

"It does not matter. I try not to remember anything about those years beyond deciphering books and digital codes," declares Akemi looking down at him.

"How could your childhood and teen years not be important? Those are the years that make us who we are." He instinctively reaches for an olive.

"Maybe I don't like who I am." An uncomfortable silence surrounds them. All the intimacy is gone, as if the oxygen between them had frozen from the chill returned to her dark eyes. Anthony nibbles on the olive. Akemi recedes to typing in her wrist screen. The waiter brings their plates.

"I am not a hired assassin but I don't want friends. I don't enjoy interacting with people. It's hard for me. He was a poisoner and a spy for the Pope. I am also a spy for the Pope, a cybernetic one, and information can be deadly. I protect the Vatican's privacy from hackers and terrorists like me."

She is now engaged in the conversation, directing her words to him as a college professor would while giving a lecture in a crowded college hall. "The Vatican is a country. They have state secrets. They deal with many other countries and their nature as the leading religion in the world makes their information exchanges as dangerous as military secrets." Anthony reads a spark of fear in her eyes like a chip off the ice. What is she afraid of? "The information in those Secret Archives could cause wars. Have you forgotten the death toll of all the religious wars through the centuries? While you care about your little research, others want to hack the data to propagate hate and conflict."

There is something very profound in her eyes, like staring into a deep ocean trench where shadows of crushing destruction and death hover worse than the memory of shark attacks. "Only a fool like Avinash

Sullivan could come up with the stupid idea of asking the Holy See for complete transparency. The planet is not pampered and spoiled like Silicon Valley, where everybody is a millionaire. Even the homeless wear North Face hand-me-down duck feather jackets there. Let's see how Google, Facebook, Apple, and Amazon feel about opening their servers to the world and becoming transparent. Those guys know more about ourselves than we do! However opening their servers..." She nods as if hearing the list of casualties in a natural disaster. "Their intellectual property and big data would create carnage and chaos. Other nations would use their data for their benefit. The world is not made of idealistic start-ups! If anything, it is made of sclerotic and arthritic governments and corporations...and spies and bad shit people. While the Catholic Church is the most senior of these institutions—and maybe should be interned in a retirement home, many demons would use her data for bad shit."

Her lips tremble with apprehension. The monologue makes Akemi even more alluring. Her cheeks are flushed; her eyes radiate intelligent iridescence. He feels his hard on pushing against his tight underwear.

The food plates are now untouched in front of them. Akemi's gaze wanders in a silence so dense that it submerges the electronic music and cheerful conversations around them as if she had taken the restaurant with her deep down a trench in the Pacific Ocean. Picking up his fork, Anthony wavers between his food and resuming the conversation. "My motives are simpler. I like Classical texts because they deliver beauty and truth. I find truth in the voice of the monk's letters."

She has sliced her veal, revealing a very pink center. "Don't fool yourself. We all are like him. We all are servants of a bigger power, a bigger corporation, a bigger country. And when you hack your way to the top and distil the truth, it is always about greed, lust, envy...there is always a mastermind on top of those who think themselves to be the most powerful..." Her voice trails off as she gets distracted by an image in the monitor inside her glasses. She moves her veal to the side and pulls her iPhone in its place.

Anthony's eyes wander around the glass restaurant while his fingers circle the rim of his beer glass. Is this the end of the monologue? Yes, it had been very academic, more of a dissertation, but has he offended her? He asks if she would like a dessert but she ignores him. She is absorbed in typing as if the glow coming from the electronic screen immersed her in a submarine's isolation chamber. Anthony squints to study the dessert menu until he memorizes the name and description of the items while biting his upper lip. "*Amaretti panna cotta, limoncello gelato*, green tea and coffee *tiramisu*, three chocolate covered berry tart..." He rubs his neck and checks if the Great Dane has shifted from one couch to another.

Finally, he takes a deep breath and demands attention bearing his teeth in a forceful smile, "Can you stop looking at your videogame or whatever toy you are looking at? Or at least can you text me a message so I can confirm you are still here?" Blood throbs in his temples. He feels humiliated. The heat has migrated from his groin to his skull.

Without moving, she describes her actions: "I am reviewing your medical records. You are a very healthy man; still you have to be careful with your liver after that infection..."

He thinks about her words for a minute, repeating each word to himself and then covers her iPhone screen with his extended palms. That forces her to raise her head. "Are you kidding?" He bends his neck forward. "Are you hacking my medical records while I am sitting in front of you?"

"Your financial history is rather boring. Don't take it personally. I had to review the information of the twenty-five conference members. We had to do extensive background checks on all of you—" He stops her new monologue and any further typing by grabbing her wrist. Her pulse travels through his fingertips filling his lungs with its tempo. Anthony is furious by the privacy invasion but he is also aroused by her contact. She ignores how tightly his hand is crushing hers. "Watch out for those two friends of yours: your research partner and the Bishop from Los Angeles. Don't trust them," her narrowing eyes reveal a glint of care.

"And I should trust *you*?" Smiling, he increases his grip on her wrist until she winces. "After all, for *you* my daughters are not relevant because they are not valuable for court testimony."

"I never said *that*." Her bracelet is a mini-robot that starts unfolding, animating like a wide band of animalistic living metal. "Don't trust anybody." A touch from her free hand stops the object's movement.

He releases his grip and wraps his arms around himself. "Then...why are we here?"

"I want to have sex with you," she declares matter of fact as if she were ordering coffee.

The direct statement hits Anthony's face like a rain of pebbles making him shut his eyes. This is not how he had planned to seduce her. He wants her. Actually, he did not know how he was going to seduce her, but is certain that this is not how he likes it.

"I-I..." Why the stuttering? "I am not ready for a relationship." He crosses his legs under the table covering himself and turns toward the sleeping dog.

"I don't want a relationship, pretty boy." Her eyes are mathematical. "I have not fucked for a year. My research shows you have not fucked either since your wife died about a year ago. That was around the time I terminated my boyfriend." She forms her hands into a steeple – or a building to host servers - while raising her chin to expose her neck. "I figured, if I am ready for a fuck, so are you!" He does not respond. He wonders if the Great Dane will obey him if he commands him to attack. "Aren't men supposed to be in this just for the sex? No feelings?"

"I'm not..." Anthony acts like a high school sophomore girl, still innocent but flushed with the confusion of anger and craving. He would like to take her on top of the restaurant table, rip her dress and just hump her, but he is confused by her logic and analytics. "You know? This date was a mistake." His shirt is sticking to his back as if he had been jogging at noon. "Let me get the check." He pulls the napkin from his thighs and, folding it, places it on top of the table.

"Did I offend you?" She laughs out loud, pulling her head back. The burst of laughter fills the glass vaulted ceilings like a flock of flying stingrays. "Don't worry about the check. I'll pay." She sneers, blowing air forcefully through her nostrils. "I make a lot more than you do."

"I couldn't care less about you or your money." He stands up, thrusting his chest out.

"Well, you should. The people you are dealing with are the wealthy and the powerful of Rome. Only those with a significant net worth can pull strings inside the Vatican. Only those with power can be threatened by the truth in facts." She uses the college professor tone in her voice.

Anthony's neck becomes corded with protruding arteries that pound blood through his eardrums and cloud his vision. He crumples and piles every single Euro bill from his wallet on the table with swift motions. The curled Euros bounce around the tablecloth. He then stomps away shaking with frustration using all his yoga training not to kick things on his way out. Behind, she tilts her head and frees her black hair from the brooch that has kept it in order all night.

CHAPTER 14

THE SECRET ARCHIVES ABOVE THE GROUND

Dissatisfaction and blue balls are great fuel for a night of tossing and turning. Covered in sweat, Anthony swims in his bed, gyrating, flapping his arms and legs as if that could restore the chance of exploring Akemi's body. At two o'clock in the morning, he opens his eyes because Akemi is also the person who can help him access the balance of the monk's confession, and she might not be willing to help anymore. Should they return to America? Has he been lying to himself that he can rebuild their life in Italy? Things don't make sense. Haggard and dehydrated by sunrise, he jogs and has breakfast in a hurry. Off the subway, instead of going to the Secret Archives library, he goes to the restoration laboratory to look for Angelo. He could finish his paper on *Catullus* in the US but if he could only find out more about the monk's story he could justify dealing with the chaos. He finds Angelo wearing his white laboratory robe and latex gloves working on the erotic Raphael drawing.

"*Ciao!* It seems you need a double espresso! I hear your date might not have gone as expected."

"She told you about it? When?" Anthony grabs the border of the worktable to keep his peevishness check.

"She is hostile but once you get to know her she is one of the most loyal friends you can ever get. She growled about it when I left her some folios on my way to the office at 6 a.m. She seemed as unrested as you do. She does not sleep much anyway but today she had fatigue written all over her. I think she was standing up propped by a robot on her back."

"Growled?"

"She was very angry with the world, but did not get into details. I could see she considered attacking me with a horde of her cyber minions when I asked about the date. She was not happy with whatever happened between you two."

Anthony is sweating without sweat. The air-conditioned laboratory does not keep enough of the Roman summer at bay for him. He holds his forehead with one hand. "How long have you known her?"

"Since I've worked here. She was a regular before my time at the restoration lab and on the main Vatican library labs, too. She prefers to chat with crumbling manuscripts than with humans. So you can tell me the details. How was the date? Do you need me to put you in contact with a 'girlfriend' who can improve your technique in bed? "

"There is nothing wrong with my technique in bed." Anthony's chin juts forward like an angry viking as he takes a stance with his feet firmly planted and his hands on his hips. He does not want to get into a discussion in which he will have to admit that his technique was perfectly adapted for Laura's needs—the one and only sexual partner in his life. "Great restaurant: amazing decoration with the motorcycles everywhere, delicious food. That is as good as it got. She and I could not be more different."

"As I was saying, she can be very unkind, even plain rude. My brother is like her. He is a genius and my best friend. He is now a programmer in Silicon Valley. They paid him a fortune to move over there. Some of her behaviors remind me of him when we were growing up. I know not to get offended by their caustic remarks and just to focus on the good. People like them see the world differently."

Angelo's conversation relaxes Anthony's back muscles in a way that not even his morning yoga routine has since the previous night. "We had a good talk about the monk's confession."

He continues, "She is passionate about it, but greedy about the information. This morning she turned back into a human being when I told her the latest. I went to speak with the woodshop guys to find out more about the damaged copy of 'The Nature of Things.' The sixteenth-century desk they repaired had two secret compartments. Their first finding came from a double bottom drawer. In line with protocol, they sent this to Monsignor José Dosal, the Secret Archives Prefect. I don't think there was much in that lot. The damaged book and the erotic drawings came from the second compartment. They sent it to José but he was on vacation. Because the Vice-Prefect was too busy, it ended up in the area where they aggregate documents for future sorting. This is where the Japanese researchers found the drawings and the damaged book with the confession. I am having coffee with the Prefect to see what I can find about the first batch. Do you want to come? I have to warn you," he lowers his voice, "it will be very tricky because…" Angelo weighs his words, "I don't want him to know about the findings on the second batch."

José Dosal's office door is partially hidden by a column at the entrance of the Secret Files Archive. His name is engraved in a long bronze plaque: "H. Exc. Most Rev. Mons. José Dosal O." His position is a powerful one, as the more than sixty people that labor in the files report to him. It is also a coveted one only reached after years of study, a PhD, and hundreds of articles and publications.

Before entering, Angelo cautions his friend in a low voice: "José is VERY territorial so share as little as you can. He is a control freak and does not like anybody doing independent research without his knowledge, which we all do because we don't want him to steal our papers and publish them under his name. He has done this to many of my colleagues. He also loves to showcase his knowledge. He is one of the most informed persons about documents, art, and books in the Holy See but you know a lot, too. Let him talk. Akemi and he hate each other. I think this is because both like to indulge in long monologues. He prefers if those around him appear to have the culture of a five year old. Don't contradict him and laugh at his jokes. He is temperamental and very well connected with everyone that matters in the Vatican. You don't want to be on his bad side."

The man Anthony encounters appears to be very different from what he is expecting after Angelo's advice. Monsignor José Dosal is an affable priest in his fifties. A heavy set Spaniard from Asturias with a jovial face, he speaks English with a thick Northern Spain accent. His tone is playful and approachable.

"Dr. Hibbert, what a surprise! The Pope himself has sent instructions to treat you or any of the twenty-five members in the Transparency Commission as VIPs. For this appointment, I was intending to spend just a few minutes with young Angelo but you deserve more of my time." The Prefect shakes his visitor's hand with a strong self-assured grip. Angelo has picked breakfast for his boss on their way. With a double espresso in one hand and a croissant in another, José lectures on the Secret Archives and how they have become a myth through literature and pop culture.

"But their name does not come from secret. It comes from *secretarial,* the secretary in charge of the archives. No one else but the popes' private secretaries could manage the files. As we say on our website, the Secret Archives have two goals: 'One is to protect its documentary heritage ensuring its preservation, while the other is to provide scholars with research tools to enhance access to this treasure trove of the Church's activity in documents spanning thousands of years.'" He smiles proudly and raises a pair of unkempt brows. "You should be happy about this second goal, Dr. Hibbert, that's why you are in Rome. And you should be happier to know that in the past we only opened the Archives from October to June. This is the first time we will open year round and in the afternoons." He gesticulates like a Roman emperor offering a feast to the hungry crowd. "Your research partner is an old friend and did a great job of lobbying to be in the first group to enjoy these benefits. Still, going back to the Secret Archives, there are many inconvenient stories for the Church contained here, many uncomfortable truths."

He chuckles to himself and then winks at his visitors. Anthony and Angelo smile complicitly. "You know, the ladies and stuff," and laughs again. "Many popes had mistresses they had to hide. We have the files from many religious Congregations. You don't have to possess an overactive imagination to grasp the kind of scandals in monasteries and convents we have documented through the centuries. There were also many amorous scandals pertaining cardinals and bishops where the pope had to intervene, and these are recorded in the meeting notes kept here."

With gusto, José crams a piece of the croissant in a small coffee cup. "Yes, it also contains copies of the books in the index, the list of forbidden books created in the late sixteenth century as part of the Counter-Reform Movement. They did not want people to read them, but I am sure many came here to consult them." More chuckles and more winks of collusion. "Some salacious titles there." Anthony wonders how long he will have to act amused before they can get to the matters he cares about. The Prefect disposes of the empty cup into a trashcan with a nonchalant throw.

"But the index has kept adding titles, hasn't it?"

"Yes, but nobody cares to consult them anymore when you can download anything you wish from the Internet. And then..." he gestures with theatrical intonation. "We have the documents that changed the world."

He leaves his chair, guiding them to the corridor outside his office where documents are displayed in glass cases. The pieces selected for the area have immense historical meaning: the Trial of the Templars, Henry VIII's letter to the Pope asking for a divorce, a letter from Mary Queen of Scots to Pope *Sixtus* V, the Bulls Condemning and Excommunicating Martin Luther—June 1520 and January 1521. "These pieces of paper represent turning points in history. Come, follow me. To the right are the study rooms. You don't want to go to that metallic door. It leads to the underground depository and is locked at all times."

From the looks he get from the librarians, touring with the boss gives Anthony enhanced status with the Reading Rooms and Index Managers. "These are my favorites," he points possessively toward a group of letters. "I really don't care much about Lucrezia Borgia's letters to the Pope Alexander VI, or the Enrollment of the First Contingent of the Swiss Guard in 1505. I am passionate about the ones like this one here." Anthony reads the inscription: "Nomination of Raphael Sanzio as Scriptor of Apostolic Briefs and his Contribution to the Plans for *Piazza del Popolo*."

"This is art history in the making. By naming Raphael a scriptor, Pope Leo X ensured that the artist remained on the payroll to finish decorating the four apartments in the Papal Palace. There are so many documents related to art, it is a joy to dig deep! There! This is correspondence between Michelangelo Buanarroti and Paul III; here is a notice of payment to Gian Lorenzo Bernini. This one is just one of a large file about Tintoretto. Let others gawk at the Process against Galileo Galilei, give me art or sexual scandals any day!"

He opens his arms as if he were a preacher on a mountain summit, as he stood illuminated by the light streaming from the tall windows under the vaulted roofs of the Index Room. Anthony and Angelo nod in agreement pausing to examine the documents in front of them.

They walk to the cordoned entrance to the Tower of the Winds. José Dosal launches into a dissertation on the murals decorating the two stories and dividing mezzanine.

"Are you coming?" The Prefect calls looking down the staircase with superiority.

Anthony swiftly climbs the tight concrete stairs of the steep circular staircase that winds up to the first Vatican Observatory, built for astronomical studies. Thanks to the findings there, the Julian calendar was replaced by the one dictated by Gregory XIII in 1587—the calendar used today. Anthony slips and stumbles. Climbing two steps at a time was not a good idea. He prevents his fall by grabbing an iron rod around which the stairs revolve. He is satisfied with his quick reflexes as the fall would have been fatal.

When they return to the Prefect's office, José stows the keys to the Archives on his desk, Anthony notices an automatic handgun in the drawer and gives the priest an inquisitive look. José squints and gives him a hard smile. "The items in the Secret Archives are priceless. Other items are so confidential that they could create unwanted controversy for the Holy See or produce world conflicts if they fell into the wrong hands. Thieves have tried to enter in the past, many times. The Swiss Guard is too busy with other matters for my personal taste especially when you think of the fifty kilometers of shelves in the underground vault, the subterranean depository. It can be long and lonely down there. I need to be able to stop intruders by myself. I might wear a long robe that looks like a skirt but I have big balls. Bull's balls." He horselaughs again while caressing the weapon in his hands. Noticing the surprise in his visitors' faces, he adds: "But don't worry. I am very careful when I use this baby—the bullets can damage the books."

To change the topic, Angelo tells José Dosal about their interest in the first group of documents. "We are looking for the other half of a damaged book from Lucretius that some Japanese researchers brought to our attention."

José hesitates before answering. "You mean a bunch of garbage that came from a sixteenth-century desk repaired at the woodshop?"

"I don't know what you got on the first batch but on the second we have half a copy of 'The Nature of Things.'"

José talks over Angelo. He likes to have control of the conversation. "The contents are being sorted as far as I know. They should have been sent to the underground vault in the first place, not to me. I sent them back there." José does not look so jovial anymore. He creases his forehead, and his bushy eyebrows show that something is bothering him. "We have spent quite some time together this morning. I had to honor Dr. Hibbert as he is part of the Transparency Commission. Now I need to get back to work, so I apologize to ask you to leave... Is there anything else you might be looking for or that you might have found in the second batch that I might need to know about?" He leans and stares at Angelo.

"Nothing to report yet, but I'll reach out to you as soon as—and if—I have news."

"I'm very busy but I will make time for any discoveries. How come no one informed me there was a second batch and that you were perusing it? It is my job to allocate the resources in the Archives."

Angelo is cautious. "The paperwork was submitted and approved by the Vice-Prefect while you were on vacation. I hope we don't have to stop the work. This is one of the oldest copies of Lucretius we have encountered."

"Hmmm. No, no. Keep on working." He opens the door for his visitors, deep in thought. "Did you find any drawings? I know the Vatican Museum's curator would be interested."

Angelo stops in his tracks. "I'll check with my companions. There might be something...What makes you think this? Were there any drawings on the first batch?" He enunciates his words carefully.

"As we say in Spain, the devil knows better because he is very old. The sixteenth century was the climax of the Renaissance. It is not uncommon to discover sketches by famous artists when we find a trove of papers from the time. Unfortunately, they don't stay in the Secret Archives." José sounds aggravated.

"You should visit the restoration lab and see our findings for yourself," Angelo forces a smile. He knows he is taking a big risk. The Prefect will appropriate the right to a research paper if he sees the erotic drawings before Angelo advances his investigation and disseminates it. That invitation seems to dissuade the Spaniard.

"I'm very busy right now with this Transparency Conference. The Pope's bureaucrats request information every other hour. You understand the Secret Archives are the eye of the storm in the matters related to the Transparency Crusade. I trust your supervisor is keeping you busy and optimizing your time." The Prefect briskly shuts his door.

"That was odd," remarks Anthony on their way back to the laboratory.

"He is an interesting one. I am sure you are familiar with the politics within intellectual institutions."

"Do you think we will find more of the monk's story?" Anthony's lack of sleep is dragging him down. "I am worried that after yesterday night Akemi won't share any more with me."

"She will share it if we can find more text. She is as concerned as you are about their location. We need to get it. On a separate note, come see me later, and I'll guide you to a place under a tree where you can take a nap. It is very secluded so nobody will bother you. I use it if I need a respite after a night of partying…so almost every day."

Anthony appreciates the offer and nods. "Thank you, Angelo. I have to see Francesca now but be sure I will come back later. I need to recharge or I won't make it through the day." He starts moving away but stops to dissipate his worry. "Keep me in the loop on the monk's letters. I'm certain Akemi won't." Anthony walks away toward the garden cafeteria to find his research partner.

Francesca hugs Anthony tightly. "You survived a night with that horrible woman!"

Anthony shrugs and powers his laptop as he sits in the open air cafeteria. "You won't have to worry about her anymore."

"So I guess dating Avinash Sullivan's ex-girlfriend was not such a great experience as her pointy breasts and long legs would seem to promise," Francesca teases but Anthony stares at her with disbelief.

"What did you say?" The summer air is not enough to cool the furnace that fills his bloodstream. "Akemi Morishima was Avinash Sullivan's girlfriend?" Anthony raises his voice to the levels of an Italian taxi driver caught in traffic. "Why didn't you tell me that! Why didn't anybody tell me that?"

"It is common knowledge!" Francesca waves her hands simulating the movement of a tsunami.

"I despise this Avinash character! What did I do to him to have him haunt me after his death? Why is everything I now do connected to him? This does not make any sense." Anthony gestures with his hands and arms.

"They broke up when he decided to start his social media Transparency Crusade against the Vatican. Her job is cyber security. Let's say their relationship became a conflict of interests." Anthony feels nauseated. The lack of sleep and the excess of caffeine in his system block his normally civilized reactions. "Why do you think she was staring at you the other day when we were at the museum's restaurant? She wanted to see firsthand the man the world believed had shot her boyfriend."

The logic is crushing. "So you think yesterday's date was out of curiosity?"

"*Caro*, that and…well, you are hot! You are better looking than you realize. If you were Italian, you would be sleeping with a multitude of different women every week—like I used to do with men. I cannot blame the Ghostwire bitch. She wanted a good fuck while satisfying her curiosity about you. This only speaks highly of her intellect."

Anthony slams his laptop shut. "I must take a nap. I cannot think with clarity right now. Besides, everything is so absurd, I might not be able to think with clarity even then! Good luck working on *Catullus* today. I can't." He rises to his feet evaluating the fastest escape route.

Francesca chuckles and leans her head backward in a joyous realization of how Rome is transforming her research partner.

CHAPTER 15

THE SECRET ARCHIVES UNDER GROUND

Anthony is certain the next section of the monk's letters is hidden inside the missing half of the damaged copy of "The Nature of Things." He visits all the libraries in Rome in search of antique copies of Lucretius's book, but mostly spends many hours of the day in the Secret Archives study room wondering how he can infiltrate the subterranean bunker.

When the archives close, he carries his thoughts to the Swiss Guard *Porta Santa* checkpoint and then down the street to the subway station. He is blind to the tourists and street vendors. At the corner, someone grasps him with strength by the shoulder. He is surprised to find Melissa, his mother-in-law, standing next to a short, thin nun.

"Anthony. I calculated correctly. We have been waiting here for you for a few minutes." She pulls him to a coffee shop, the nun trailing behind them. "You know how much I disapprove of this Transparency nonsense. The Catholic Church has done many good things that the tabloids choose to ignore. They just center on the scandals."

The three sit and order coffee with brisk gestures.

"What is so important that you could not wait for us to be back at the hotel?"

"I wanted you to meet Sor Alegría. She is a nun from Peru who recently joined the order founded by Mother Theresa." The small nun shuffles her feet while sitting. "There is a kitchen for the needy close by the Vatican museum. I have been volunteering since we arrived whenever I can get some spare time. You know how the Catholic Church gave me strength during Laura's sickness and after she died. I have a lot to thank God for and a lot of good deeds to accomplish in gratitude for the strength He gave me."

"You never mentioned this volunteer—"

"You know Elmer! He thinks I am taking art classes. He would not like the wife of a fancy Hollywood producer to spend part of her days in Rome serving soup to the hungry."

"Yet you have always worked on charity." Anthony extends his hand to the nun, getting a weak response. "Nice to meet you." The nun's hand is sweaty and hardly clasps his; she just cups his fingers while holding her head down.

"I met Sor Alegría at the kitchen. She is a very hard worker. A silent one. I chat with her every day sharing my thoughts on this Transparency Crusade absurdity. She listened to me and nodded but recently she pulled me aside." Melissa looks at the nun requesting consent to proceed. The woman curves her back and nods. She is fidgeting with the hem of her sleeve. "I don't know everybody, but some of the people inside that Catholic Transparency Commission are not good."

"Hmmm. I've heard similar warnings."

"Watch out for Gabriel Herrera, the Los Angeles Bishop. He has done very bad things." She looks again at the nun who nods in response.

"While he was in charge of many convents across Latin America, he did horrible things. Sor Alegría was in one of the places he chose to transform into a whore house for traveling priests." Now Anthony leans closer to Melissa incapable of uttering a word. "Gabriel Herrera selected a few convents and forced the nuns in them to give sexual services to the priests he sent there." The nun grimaces and squirms in her chair trying to take less space in the room as if becoming smaller would let her escape the memories. "That lasted for a few years until the scandal reached Rome. By then, his actions had acquired him so many allies that instead of being punished, he was sent to Los Angeles as Bishop." Anthony's eyes are wide; he looks down and away from the nun so as not to embarrass her further. "The monasteries closed and the nuns were relocated and forced to take a vow of silence."

Sor Alegría cries without a sound. Heavy teardrops fall on the table top next to her untouched espresso. Melissa is shaking and covers her mouth. Anthony remains quiet. He extends his arm and touches the nun in the shoulder. She winces. "Sor Alegría told me this when she heard you were part of the commission. She broke her vow to warn me that you could be in great danger. If the other members are like Gabriel Herrera, then they have personal agendas that will further damage the Church."

The nun raises her head. She has brown skin and the proud features of a Peruvian descending from the Incas. Her forehead is wide and beautiful, revealing a devoted soul. She stutters with her chin trembling and speaks with a murmur. "I have forgiven. Christ told us to forgive. I had to break my vow of silence and warn you because I heard you care about your family and you are driven by good. Don't listen to others in these arguments about what is good for the Vatican. Listen to your heart, and Christ will show you the way. Only in you can I see burning the light of His Hope and His Justice."

• • •

The beat of the electronic music is in his head even when he dwells in silence. Angelo will DJ a rave tonight. His eyes hurt after looking all day through magnifying glasses at diminutive fragments of paper pieced together. He is proud that he has almost completed Raphael's erotic drawing restoration but his back hurts and his arms feel as if he had been carrying bundles in a warehouse instead of holding paper particles with pincers. Just one more slice, and he will go home, take a shower, and go to the club. He puts the minuscule fragment in place and exhales a satisfied sigh. He is ready to leave when he feels a presence behind him.

"It's a very beautiful picture, although it seems a little overt for the time," Akemi inspects the naked torso and the sketches of a penis in different stages of arousal under it.

"Raphael knew what he was doing," Angelo answers without turning, "I wonder why he did not use this image for the *stuffetta*."

"Well the big penis seems to match the one of the satyr in the wall." Akemi is wearing business attire. Her hair is clipped in a ponytail.

Angelo is about to remove his gloves and wash his hands but refrains as he wants to archive the finished drawing with the others they found in the underground depository. "It is hard to tell if it matches the *stuffetta* since the satyr's penis it is now covered with plaster. We only have some old pictures and drawings of how it used to be." He turns. "It's good to see you."

"Have you found the next section of the Pope's poisoner confession? It is the only thing that can relax me right now. Everything is very screwed up." She holds her extended arms against her body.

"I don't have it. I have asked José Dosal to give me access to the underground vault several times. He says he is working on it but he takes extreme precautions and grants limited all-access nowadays because of the Transparency Crusade."

"You should know better than to waste your time with him. I have access, and I can take you with me. My security clearance allows me to go anywhere in the Vatican. We can go tonight, I just have to review some data but I will be available in a couple of hours."

Angelo thinks of the party waiting for him. "Tonight is not good for me. I can tell you where the gathering area for sorting documents is and you can look for the missing half of the book. Here, let me draw you a map." Angelo tears a piece of paper and sketches on it. "You and Dr. Hibbert both seem to be obsessed with this. I like that. I don't understand why your date with him did not turn out well."

Akemi frowns, moving away from him. She wanders around looking at objects on the different shelves. The rest of people in the laboratory ignore her. "I guess men don't like to be approached directly when it comes to sex." Now the restoration experts raise their heads to look at her.

"I have no problem with it!" Angelo smiles raising his head with relish, "and it has worked very well for Dr. Malatesta." A couple of men in white robes agree with an involuntary head movement.

Akemi closes her fists. "Don't compare me with her! She has slept with half of Italy and all the Holy See. I was looking for a very rare one-night stand." The eldest lab worker raises an eyebrow. He is ready to volunteer.

Angelo keeps smiling. He has white teeth and a complete lack of malice. "I know you don't have a little notebook where you write the names of all your lovers. Francesca has one, and it is crammed to the margins."

"Mine would be a very empty book. Did you sleep with her?"

"It was fun." He shrugs. "Just one time. We had great sex, and then in the morning she wrote my name with pink ink in her notebook. She carries the notebook in her purse everywhere she goes, just in case." Wink. "It would be very informative to browse through it. I am certain many famous names are there."

"It would definitely help my background checks to take a look at it."

Angelo shakes his head. "Don't get me in trouble."

"We have to go now. We both have things to do, and I need to hurry if I want to visit the underground vault. I also want to do some hacking; maybe she transfers the information to some electronic depository."

She leaves while Angelo rolls his eyes. For the first time, he fully turns the restored drawing around in front of him to ensure that all of the fragments stay in place. What he sees drains the blood from his body. He puts the folio back on the lighted table and sprints for his laptop with the digitized images of the monk's letters. "Where are the other Raphael drawings? I must look at them!" He shouts as he crosses the conservation laboratory.

• • •

Francesca's breath has an alcoholic aftertaste that lingers in the air despite being in the open cafeteria. Her face is close to Anthony as they review an analysis of their recently discovered *Catullus* poems. Both have to submit a research paper draft to their deans.

"Did you only have cocktails for lunch? You smell as if you had a very long and happy hour. It's almost time for the archives to close."

Francesca's hoarse laugh is contagious. "These Commission meetings are a drag. I have to find some entertainment after them."

"I know. I sit there with you, remember? I also listen to everybody's long-winded statements."

"You don't get it. Between that and our research, I hardly have time for my boyfriend. There is nothing wrong with some cocktails when he and I can escape for a bite together."

"Nothing wrong, just don't talk to my face. I am getting dizzy."

Francesca waves her hands disapprovingly. "The protest marches are growing worldwide. More people are requesting that the archives be completely open."

"Yes, but other groups are marching, too, asking the protesters to leave the Catholic Church alone. It's messy."

"Do you follow the conversations on Twitter?"

Anthony shakes his head. "Of course not. I hate all social media sites. It's me you are talking about, remember?" He points to himself. "I hate technology. Twitter and Pinterest are the kind of things that Virginia does." They keep on working but Anthony gathers courage to discuss the topic that bothers him. "How well do you know Gabriel Herrera? What kind of person is he?"

"Well, well. I've known him for some years now. He is a rising star inside the Curia." She speaks quickly as if trying to go over the sentences in a hurry.

"I mean do you know him well? What do you know about his past?"

"What everybody knows." Francesca fakes boredom. "He oversaw several convents and monasteries in the Americas. He is well known for his crusade against urban violence. In Los Angeles, he has obtained funds and opened activity centers in underprivileged areas. This project has expanded to other cities with gang problems."

"Why is he so interested in the transparency controversy?" Anthony senses there is a lot more his partner is not talking about. His voice is assertive.

"I guess he likes to be close to the hot topics." She rolls her eyes. "It puts him in the spotlight and gives him the right exposure with the body of cardinals." She suddenly reaches for her purse. "Sorry. My phone is vibrating." Anthony did not hear a sound. "It must be a reminder from my calendar. I just remembered I have to see my hairdresser in fifteen minutes. These beautiful colors fade too quickly." Francesca grabs her Hermes bag, kisses Anthony on both cheeks, and escapes.

Anthony's eyes wander around the gardens surrounding him while analyzing Francesca's behavior. He is about to get back to his computer when he sees Angelo hurrying toward him, his face radiant with excitement.

"I have found a lot more! It was in front of us all the time." Angelo is so excited that he does not care to be late for the rave.

Anthony jumps up and holds Angelo by the shoulders unable to control his happiness. "Did you find the missing cover of 'The Nature of Things' and the next part of the confession?"

"I am still working on that. I spoke briefly with José Dosal again today but no progress. The good news is that I have found another part of the narrative. Akemi missed the discovery by minutes. She is going to be so jealous if you see this first. Come to the laboratory with me!"

Anthony folds his heavy laptop and follows his friend. The laboratory is almost empty as it is late in the day. Angelo invites him into a private meeting room carrying a large cardboard folder. Angelo is wearing gloves again, and as he turns on lamps on a worktable he hands a pair to Anthony.

"You have seen me working on Raphael's erotic drawing since you met me. Here is the irony: I had been so focused on the drawing that I ignored the reverse of the folio. Today when I finished the restoration—half an hour ago—I turned the picture from the lighted table and discovered that the back is covered in small writing. It is the same handwriting as the vellum pages found in the thirteenth-century hymns book and the Lucretius book. It all makes sense. They all came from the trove of findings inside the sixteenth-century desk! They were all Federigo Dottore's property. Why would he have an erotic drawing from Raphael?"

Anthony does his little triumphant dance shaking his hips and waving his arms. He looks ridiculous. "Is this the next part of the story?" He caresses the restored paper as if he were touching a newborn's forehead.

"From what I could read, we are still missing a portion. There has to be more on the other cover of 'The Nature of Things.' Have you noticed how the monk dates every narrative? The date on this drawing is a couple of days later than the last date we read. Also, a portion of the drawing is missing. It seems it was torn in half. But I have more good news..." Angelo holds his breath and beams with operatic splendor. Anthony's hands tremble. "You remember there were more drawings found in the trove...?"

Angelo opens the large cardboard folder revealing delicate erotic images. The first one pictures a man on top of woman penetrating her while she raises her stretched legs against his shoulders making a V-shape. Anthony did not expect to be aroused by the pen-and-ink traces as they fan across the table but the illustrations exude sexuality. "We have five more drawings. Six in total with the one I had been restoring." Angelo notices Anthony's blushed face as he studies a red chalk over stylus study in which the man takes her from behind while she bends for her palms to be extended and flat on the floor. "I know. They are hot! But reverse them and take a close look." He moves the lamp so the light shines directly on them. Anthony can see the texture in the paper and the marks left by the metal point. Although very faded, the reverse shows a handwriting he recognizes immediately. He scrutinizes the paper for damage. "They are in fairly good condition. Not many words missing. I won't have to spend days repairing them as I did with the first one. I can organize the portions according to the dates. Scan them and take the digital images to our *bella* Ms. Morishima. She can solve the faded ink issues. I looked at the dates in all. We are still missing the bridge between where we are and where the story picks up in the drawings. Why Raphael?"

"He mentions that they were friends at the end of the last fragment. This gets better by the minute! We need to get all the parts!" Anthony is beaming. "We should get beers!" The pieces of his life are falling back into place.

Angelo looks at his watch. "You'll have to save that beer for another time. I am already late but I had to get you as soon as I made the discoveries."

Anthony embraces the young researcher. "You made my day!"

"You can go celebrate with Ms. Morishima if you give her the good news," Angelo teases. Anthony huffs and steps back, making a protective cross in the air with his arms.

● ● ●

Anthony returns to the Secret Archives library to get his briefcase from a locker. Security in the study rooms allows only laptops—no bags, pens, or sharp objects—so all the researchers have to leave their personal belongings in lockers close to the entrance. Anthony takes the long way back. He paces around the Secret Archives corridors following the route to José Dosal's office. He ponders whether there is an easier route to the underground depository. It is late in the day so the researchers and librarians have left the study rooms. The corridors are empty. The heavy metallic door that leads to the underground vault mocks him. With dismay, he notices a sophisticated retina scanner, the best security system to prevent entry to unauthorized visitors. There must be other entrances in the Vatican. He leans against the metallic door and slouches, disappointed. Under the weight of his body, the door slides open. Anthony tumbles in. The door had been left ajar! He regains control of his muscles and pushes the door wide open. The scent of paper and dust fills his nostrils, the smell of a forest of human intellect. He walks down an iron staircase that leads to a very long tunnel 31,000 cubic feet and 43,000 linear meters of metallic shelves cramming yellowing documents in two floors of steel and concrete under the *Cortille della Pigna* outside the Vatican Museum. He has seen layouts of the place and has a general idea of its overall distribution. Its colossal magnitude is breathtaking. He is ignorant about where to find the area where they gather documents to queue for sorting and filing. The soulless lights hanging from the ceiling give a very flat illumination as if entering a badly lit subway tunnel.

One third of the way into the tunnel, he remembers it is past the library closing time. Will there be a lockdown in the vault? Will even the weak illumination go off? Will he find himself trapped in darkness for the night? He checks his phone screen. No signal, but he realizes he can use the glow of the screen as a primitive flashlight if needed. He considers turning back. His family will be desperate if he does not return at night—especially if he cannot call them. He has been wishing to enter the vault so much that he takes the gamble and moves forward. Bundles of documents are tied together with ribbons and neatly organized by year. The First and Second Vatican Council meeting transcripts are next to documents of the many pontifical representations pouring from every country. The sexual scandals bound in handwritten folders wait for a cardboard eternity to end so they can release their ugly secrets. The main lanes have side alleys. With each step, the dust gets thicker and the silence louder. The labyrinth makes him feel like a lost soul astray in purgatory. He keeps walking in the hopes of finding an area with a sign to indicate a gathering center for documents to be classified, but instead finds a flat prairie of grey metallic card files. He speeds his pace while stumbling over random objects. His forehead is covered in a fine mud from sweat and millenary paper dust.

He turns a corner to discover a larger area opening like a grotto where four tubular staircases climb to the second level in an X shaped crossroad. He rests for a moment as if he had reached the center of the Earth until he hears a voice in the distance: "*Qui*? Who is here?" It is the Prefect José Dosal. He has not seen Anthony but knows there is some-one else in the tunnel. Anthony slides into one of the side corridors and sits on the floor leaning against a towering bookcase. His mind is rac-ing, should he reveal himself or stay hidden? The Prefect could rescind his researcher pass to the Secret Archives. Trespassing in this area is a felony. The scandal in studious circles would be major. Anthony joins his palms and closes his eyes to meditate and slow his heart beats while listening to movement.

"I have a gun. Show yourself!"

The steps are approaching. Anthony lies on his belly, with his fore-arms flat on the floor, elbows under the shoulders, chin on the floor and legs together as if to start a yoga pose. When accommodating, his foot inadvertently pushes a misplaced package from a shelf. He cannot ex-amine it but feels like a brick of soft clay that makes a loud thud hitting the ground. The sound is followed by a gunshot. José is firing his gun, and the echo resonates like a cannon.

"Show yourself!" Two more discharges explode, permeating the si-lence of words held back for centuries. One bullet shatters a lamp. José knows darkness will give him an advantage in the kill as he knows every inch of the underground depository with eyes closed.

Anthony realizes he will have to come out of hiding. This is not go-ing to look good on his resume.

CHAPTER 16

SECOND DATE, SECOND MURDER

A small toy-like vehicle spins in the corridor. Another one turns into the crevice in which Anthony is hiding and stops in front of him—thick rubber wheels, folded aluminum arms, and a camera eye that stares at him. These are *her* heralds. "*Ya*, Pepe, *ya. Soy yo*, Akemi. I needed to do errands down here. The guards have complained of receiving a weak signal in their communication devices when patrolling this area. We need to be perfectly connected at all times." She is approaching Anthony's hiding spot, where he is shoving the package he kicked back to its shelf. "Chill out, Pepe. I've told you many times not to use that gun." She sounds angry.

"*Mierda* Akemi! *No podéis venir aquí cuando os plazca!*"

She is next to Anthony and pulls him up by the hair. The micro-robots swirl away leaving the two humans alone. She looks at his surprised face with a mocking grin. "I had also promised Mr. Hibbert to give him a tour of the underground vault. *Dos pájaros con el mismo tiro.*" The fragrance of orange blossoms replaces yellowing paper. The Prefect has reached them now. The dim light hides the layer of thick dust covering the front of Anthony's clothes and his disconcerted expression. Akemi still has her hand on the nape of his head and keeps pulling his hair, making him lean backward.

"You are not respecting the protocol—again! Before coming here, you *must* inform me. I will have to complain about you—again! Are you going to be here much longer? I have things to do! I had to be out on an errand all afternoon and just came back."

"*Vete a hacer tus cosas y deja me jalo a este tío a un rincón apartado para ver si está tan bueno bajo la ropa como aparenta.*" Akemi's Spanish is flawless. Her accent is clear with a sensual cadence. Anthony makes an effort to assent with his head without understanding her words.

"No sinning at the Vatican." José transitions from anger to amusement.

"I doubt many popes have read that warning."

José laughs at the joke. "You two have to come with me and leave." With a gesture, he signals them the way to the exit and escorts them out. He despises intruders in his territory.

"You have to be careful with that gun, *cielo.*" Akemi pats his shoulder. It appears her social skills turn on when in danger.

"Sure, and let any *cabrón* strangle me in the darkness," Gabriel huffs with his caterpillar eyebrows covered in dust, "Security has to be a lot better for me not to carry my gun when I go down those corridors."

As they walk, Anthony still strives to read the many signs and labels around him. He stops short in front of a spot and questions: "What are these?"

"Can't you read? It has a big sign in front of you. In 1965, the documents from 'the Vatican Information Office for Prisoners of War' were brought here." Anthony dreads that José or Akemi will start one of their college-like orations. However he is interested in this one. He just wants to get the information quickly. "After World War II started, requests began to arrive to the secretariat of state for information about prisoners of war and persons displaced in the affected territories. The requests were sorted and then the Vatican activated its dense network of connections, like bishops around the world and their diocesan offices to gather data. For those busy criticizing the Catholic Church right now, we did this free of charge and without partiality to any political adherence, religious affinity, or geographical location." Anthony corroborates. José loves to lecture as he keeps on talking instead of pushing them out. "These archives contain the names of the persons who died in hospitals and concentration camps. They have detailed information about the ransacking of the Roman ghetto in October 1943, the bombing of Rome in July 1943, and the cruelty practiced in concentration camps as well as testimonies of those who survived. Reading them is not for the faint of heart, but they inventory the charitable work that the Catholic institution can deliver even in the darkest hours." José catches his breath, and realizes he is wasting time. "*Coño*! Let's go. It's late."

Back in the upper corridor, the Prefect locks the metallic door. Akemi holds Anthony's forearm and drives him to a chair next to a framed letter from Abraham Lincoln to Pius IX. "*Adios*, Pepe. I need to talk with Dr. Hibbert."

"And you cannot chat with him somewhere else?"

"No, I want to chat with him here."

"Mira *Cielo*, I know you have unrestricted access everywhere in this City Estate. For all I care you can go to the Pope's bathroom while he is showering, but my files are my files! Don't go to my private vaults without my permission. I am The One responsible for every document and book filed here."

"You and I, *corazón*, you and I, both. Remember I am part of the security systems here?" She turns her back to the Prefect who leaves in a hurry, talking to himself. She forces herself to connect her eyes to Anthony's but his gaze is unsettled by her long legs in tight black trousers.

He forces himself to utter the words, "Thank you, Akemi. I was in a lot of trouble. Why did you help me? Wouldn't it have been more entertaining to watch José Dosal kill me?"

"I was not there to spy on you." She pulls a half torn book from her jacket. "I found what we are looking for. Angelo gave me a sketch to guide me to the consolidating and sorting area. I found it! The monk hid a vellum confession in this cover, too!" Her joy is minimalistic: direct and enhanced by not having hidden undertones, only satisfaction coming from the discovery. "We can keep on reading now." Anthony makes an effort to continue disliking her but the missing cover of "The Nature of Things" in her long, well-manicured fingers makes him share the joy. "I am not wasting resources anymore spying on you. You are boring. You are the only one on this commission who does not seem to have a secret agenda."

Anthony wonders why she did not stay with sharing the news about the discovery. Her lack of tact brings back his anger. "Why did you not tell me about your relationship with Avinash during our dinner?"

"Everybody knows. Only idiots don't know about it."

"Well, I am an idiot, and I am annoyed that Avinash is getting involved in every aspect of my life." He leans toward her, defiant.

"Avinash and I lived together for some years. He was a wonderful person but the death of his brother resulting from the sexual abuse from a priest drove him insane. He could not accept that the Church had just kept relocating the child molester from one parish to another. He believed his destiny was to lead this Transparency Crusade. That tore us apart... Yes, I have my own personal agenda in this case. I want to bust the balls of whoever killed him with my bare hands."

She speaks with the assurance of someone used to being powerful. Akemi's perfume engulfs him. Despite his anger, the attraction has not diminished. "So you wanted to talk with me..."

She shifts uncomfortably. She wishes to say something nice but knows she is not good at that. Better to rely on usual behaviors. "No, I did not. That was just to make José go away. Although, I did want to show you my find..."

They are standing side by side, surrounded by documents behind glass frames. They are indifferent to a letter from the American Indians to the Pope or the letter of Hirohito to Pius XII, their arms are slightly touching and when she averts his gaze, he can see more. She is shaking. Involuntarily, they make the sides of their legs come into contact as they feign interest in the walls. He is now trembling, too. The silence is awkward. The stillness around them creates a void in time. His palms are sweating. He feels a vein throbbing in his temple, and another between his legs. Inhaling deeply, he gathers courage. He turns to her in the same instant that she turns to him and holds her head with both his hands forcing their eyes to come together. They gasp. He kisses her on the mouth pushing her lips open with his tongue. She responds with wolf-like intensity. He kisses her with his eyes closed; she keeps her eyes open. Both squirm against each other eliminating any remaining space between them. With her back against the wall, he pushes his knee between her legs rubbing her softly while their tongues entwine. Their bodies knock down a letter replica from the wall.

Akemi's phone rings with the insulting outcry of a fire alarm. She pushes him away and reaches into her jacket. She pulls out her Google

Glass. They have integrated speakers that transmit sound through her temples and a hands-free microphone.

"Akemi here."

"This is Alessandro. We have two pieces of data that confirm our suspicions on the murderer identity. Recall our disposable phone lead? We traced the credit card that purchased the disposable mobile phone that communicated with Francesca, Ellia Jones, and Gabriel Herrera a day before Avinash's death. The phone was not only purchased close to Mr. Giocatelli's offices but also we got confirmation that the credit card belonged to Mr. Giocatelli. I also got more information about his family. We have traced a reporter who made an investigation into Giocatelli's father in the 60s. We talked to him, and he revealed that he had uncovered evidence proving that Giocatelli's father was a member of the Nazi Party in his youth. Our informant gathered testimonies from key Vatican insiders who confirmed that Giocatelli senior had been an agent for Hitler during the war. The investigation took place when the Vatican-Holocaust connection scandal was going on. During those days, it was discovered that the KGB had insinuated false documents into the Secret Archives and then leaked them to the press. The reporter's editor censored the story, then confiscated and destroyed the evidence, claiming that the Pope's Communication Secretary himself had called him directly to stop the investigation from going to print."

"This is good data. Is it enough to send him to jail?"

"I have an arrest warrant from a judge. After the scandal with the pretty American, he has asked me to do this arrest discreetly. We don't want the media to find out until we are certain. My car is parked close to Saint Peter's square. I want you to come with me. It will attract less attention than if I go with some other police officials."

"I'll be there in ten minutes. By the way, the pretty American is coming with us."

"What? No, please don't do that."

"Pretty American?" questions Anthony who can hear Alessandro's voice though Akemi's device. Realizing the moment is lost, Anthony covers his crotch with both hands to cover his frustration.

• • •

"After the war, his father changed his name from Weiss to Giocatelli. He started a toy company that grew into a multinational success. Our Mr. Giocatelli inherited the enterprise, which has become a conglomerate that operates in many industries." Alessandro explains while he speeds through the streets of Rome in his small, angry Fiat as if he were on an obstacle course.

"We did not find anything particularly scandalous when my people rummaged his digital footprints. He has children with a couple of his mistresses but that can be normal in Italy for someone of his status."

"Mr. Giocatelli, the grey fox." Anthony listens to his inner thoughts. "Finally, this Avinash murder will be solved, and I will be able to focus on other matters in my life."

"Have you been able to...*investigate*..." Alessandro does not want to use the word hack, "the American Embassy files?"

"To access the surveillance tapes they took from the Hotel Excelsior from the night of the crime? No. I work with the US government so I can't. I've been using my contacts in the Pentagon and CIA to get permissions but I am still working on it. However, we were able to get the video from the ATM machines around the hotel. We used face recognition software on the passers-by behind people using the machines. One match comes very close to Giocatelli. He was the only image captured from our twenty-five commission suspects around the time of the murder."

Anthony presses: "So we all are suspects in that commission? You had mentioned background checks not suspected criminals." His temples throb.

"I imagine this one," Alessandro points to Anthony, "appeared also."

"The time he passed next to the ATMs matches his story about the time he arrived to pick up his daughters. The crime had been committed by then."

"You know I am here, right?" Anthony contorts his body forward between the diminutive space of the two front seats. Alessandro lights a cigarette, burning Anthony's eyelashes.

"Giocatelli's family is on vacation at their villa in Bari. He plans to join them tomorrow so he will be by himself tonight. He gave the household servants the day off. He left his office at noon to shop and pack for the trip. He has been by himself all afternoon. This will be the right setting for the arrest. It would have been impossible at his office. Too many people."

"Can you open your window? I'm going to puke here." The Fiat's back windows cannot be lowered. Smoking with the car windows closed is making Anthony nauseated. Alessandro speeds his Fiat Cinquecento through the streets but traffic is bad everywhere. He tries several short cuts but each short cut makes the transit worse until they are detained for twenty minutes in a small alley.

"I should have brought a police car! Merda! He will be asleep by the time we get there!" Anthony is too sick with the cigarette smoke to venture into any conversation. Akemi, who has been using her eyeglass computer to direct Alessandro around the traffic jams, fumes on her seat at the unreliable traffic maps she has been looking at.

Finally, the little car is able to advance again, and Alessandro pushes the accelerator crossing the now-fluid freeways out of the city and onto the *Via Appia*. He parks in front of a seigniorial mansion close to the entrance of one of the early Christian Catacombs. Opening the car door, he points again to Anthony and sticks his tongue out. "So one more time, can you explain to me, what is the American doing here?"

"We need him to trust us. He is the only clean one of the bunch. We just talked about this in the car." She analyzes the fence around the mansion.

"I don't listen when caught in traffic."

"We might need someone on our side within the commission once the scandal explodes after the news of Giocatelli's arrest hits the media." Anthony remains in the cramped car regaining his breath.

"I hope that is the reason and not that you wished to bring your boy-toy for a drive." Alessandro squashes the cigarette butt with his foot. He lowers his chin to look down at Anthony as a Roman soldier would look at a barbarian.

Akemi plants herself in front of him, her body tense, and her hands on her hips. "You want me to be your collaborative partner, you play by my rules. I did not need the fucking Italian police to find Avinash's murderer. Having the Italian police is convenient in case I bust the bastard's balls by kicking them, as he deserves, but in this instance I don't care if I have to go back to jail when I finally deliver justice…not that your government or mine would be happy with me going to jail again as I have become indispensable to their national security against cyber-terrorism."

Anthony promises to himself never to kiss the woman again.

"Come on pretty boy," she signals to Anthony to get off the car and follow them, "you are coming with us."

Anthony inhales the cool night air. Mediterranean pine trees like inverted umbrellas mixed with Roman ruins surround them. *Caecilia Mettela's* tomb must be nearby.

Alessandro pushes the intercommunication button on the gate of the eighteenth-century mansion encircled by an aristocratic garden. The old stonewall facing the street is high enough to prevent tourists and intruders from entering but has an iron stockade that allows spectators to see portions of the property. The lights of the upper floor are on. Alessandro insists on calling on the intercom but gets no response.

"I had an officer follow him to ensure he would be home. Giocatelli did not leave. As I mentioned, the household service is gone since the family is away." Alessandro is thinking out loud.

"Maybe he is in the bathroom," Anthony remarks casually. Alessandro and Akemi stare him down, their eyes claiming to have superior intellects. She clenches her fists and tightens her arms. Alessandro walks in circles, chain smoking and pressing the intercom button every few seconds. Anthony leans on the Fiat and delights in his surroundings. The constellations he sees are the same that shone on the Romans when they traveled on the exact same road centuries before.

"My officer stayed and watched the house. No one came in or left after Giocatelli arrived from work." Alessandro puzzles, and the cigarette smoke seems to be coming out of his ears, too.

"Could there be a service side door that your people did not watch? You know, the kind used for the gardener and servants on these rich mansions," volunteers Anthony in a casual manner while leaning on the cold car metal. Akemi twists her mouth deprecating herself for not having thought of the possibility herself. Alessandro's mouth explodes with such an onslaught of curses that the words clog, and he remains silent. His scarlet face illuminates as he lights a new cigarette without letting go of a half burnt second one already in his lips as if doubling the nicotine, tar, and smoke could transform him into a dragon so he could devour Anthony in one bite.

Anthony smooths his trousers and signals, "Let's go." He strolls around the wall. The mansion borders a park where the foundations of ancient buildings protrude from the grass. Akemi and Alessandro follow.

In the back corner, deep in the darkest part of the park half hidden by shrubs is a metallic door that connects with the mansion's garden. The door is ajar, allowing for passage. The mansion's landscape has carefully orchestrated ponds, wild flowers, trees, Corinthian columns, and sculptures of naked gods and heroes in patches of light and inviting shadow. They walk to the main entrance. There are no signs of violence as they approach the carved front double door, also ajar.

"*Pronto! Polizia!*" shouts Alessandro. Ducks that had been asleep with their heads under their wings near a pond ruffle their feathers and answer to Alessandro. "Mr. Giocatelli, this is Alessandro Catzola with the Roman Police. Are you alright?"

Akemi pushes the doors open as if making a grand entrance to a ballroom, her long legs crossing into the reception area, as a fashion model would stroll on a catwalk. Everything seems in order in the spacious vestibule. A double staircase winds up to a second floor. Akemi and Alessandro take the left side, Anthony climbs to the right. He stops midway. On the wide, white marble stairs with carpet on the center lie five large photographs, digital erotic reproductions of human body drawings in motion with a Christie's seal in the lower corner to indicate they come from that auction house. Anthony picks them up. They remind him of the drawings by Raphael. These are also traced with lead point. One is of a naked woman graciously combing her hair with her hands, her breasts plump and nipples erect, her genitals exposed as she sits with one of her legs raised. The second is of a satyr with an oversized erect penis, his torso twitching in countermotion to his thighs; his arms raised celebrating music with a dance. The third is a man and a woman. One of his arms is cradling her head as she lies on her back with the man crouching between her legs. She has one of her legs resting on his right shoulder. Rejoicing, the woman holds his swollen member in her hand.

Before he can look at the rest of the images, Anthony hears Alessandro's loud swearing. "*Porca miseria!*" He follows the racket. "*La puttana de Eva!* We are late!"

In the main bedroom, Akemi is standing very straight, her shoulders raised and her arms tight against her sides with her fists clenched in fury. She looks like a little girl frozen mid-tantrum. Alessandro is pacing around the room like a maniac waving his hands high above his head and cursing to himself. Anthony had never heard so varied and creative swearing in any language.

Between the bed and the open doors of the balcony lies Mr. Giocatelli in his perfectly tailored light grey business suit. He is sprawled face down with his legs contorted revealing he had experienced violent death spasms. His eyelids, half parted, reveal a white blank stare. A black swollen tongue protrudes from his foam-covered parched lips. His left hand is clutching an almost-eaten red apple like a modern Snow White. His right hand is folded under his torso.

Anthony plants himself in front of Alessandro and holds him by the shoulders. "Calm down. Will you? Can you call for reinforcements? The assassin might still be close by." Alessandro pulls out his phone and walks out to the balcony. Akemi, as if coming from a spell, marches to the death corpse and kicks it in the crotch repeatedly until Anthony pulls her away. She is shaking. Her eyes are red, and she can barely hold her tears. However, her last kick has moved the death body revealing the right hand. Anthony pushes the body some more with his foot; they can see that the right hand is holding a Luger pistol. Akemi stares at the Nazi weapon. From the way he is gripping the pistol, it seems Giocatelli was showing the gun to someone when he ate the poisoned apple.

Anthony looks around the room. The assassin knew what he was doing. There are no signs of struggle. Whoever gave him the poisoned fruit was a friend. Anthony is enumerating his observations out loud. Having read mystery novels all his life helps. "He must have died a few hours ago as the body is just entering rigor mortis…" Alessandro joins Akemi in listening to him. They accept that this is also Anthony's war. He has been in jail; his family has been bullied and threatened. He now is with them on a new murder scene, the murder of one of the Catholic Transparency Commission members—and Avinash's executioner.

"There is more, my friends." Anthony carried the Christie's pictures with him, so he hands them to Akemi and Alessandro. "These were on the stairs. Whoever killed Giocatelli dropped the package on the way out. Look at them, Akemi, they are like the erotic drawing Angelo has been working on."

Akemi holds one of the pictures Anthony did not get to look at. Analyzing the images has calmed her down. She returns them to him, "These are part of the same series. Look at this one." It is smaller than the rest. The main image is of a woman lying on her shoulder with her hips raised up high as a standing man penetrates her. On the bottom of the image is a sequence revealing an erection in its different phases. This is the sequence that starts in the drawing Angelo has been restoring. "These are erotic drawings from Raphael. The woman combing her hair and the satyr are studies for Bibbiena's *stuffeta* in the Vatican. They perfectly match the pictures I've seen of the place. Why are these pictures here? Where are the originals?"

Sirens blare in the distance.

PART 2

A Chapel for the Unholy Pope

CHAPTER 17

WHAT IF...

Awake. This is not insomnia. He can sleep well if he is given the option. Nights of police work and investigations are becoming frequent. Anthony realizes sleeplessness can be the norm in a city more comfortable when the nights are spent partying inside clubs that close at 5 a.m. He has no regrets of tagging along for the ride with Akemi. The brief time spent kissing in the corridor in the Secret Archives animates his skin with adrenaline, as he wonders, "What if they had not been interrupted...?"

Anthony goes to bed close to sunrise and sleeps only three hours. Not being able to exercise, breakfast is harder than he had anticipated. He drinks espresso after espresso with an eagerness which imitates the locals. His daughters are chirpy and full of energy. He cannot help but admire their courage. When coming to Rome, he was afraid that taking them away from California and their friends would make them hostile and resentful. Their movements are self-assured and their laughter true joy. In the depth of their eyes, sadness for the loss of their mother remains, will always remain, but they are moving forward. They are now strong young girls absorbing the marvels of Rome. One of those marvels today is being able to tease their father's lack of sleep.

"Where were you last night, Papa? You look terrible." Virginia munches on her toast.

"I had to work until very late."

Maria, the cook at Hotel Modigliani, made sweet-cream pound cake. Thalia sits with her stuffed bear sharing a slice. "Papa, Panda is on a diet. He has not been able to gain the twenty pounds that are his goal for Rome. He says food is so delicious here, he desires to get the body of a sumo wrestler so I am feeding him more than normal." Thalia is about to smudge cake on Panda's face when Anthony holds her hand.

"Thalia, remember this is make believe. Don't make Panda any dirtier. If we wash him now, the fabric is so old it might dissolve and vanish."

"But he is truly gaining weight. Not as much as he wishes for, but here, hold him." He weighs the stuffed animal in his hand and notices it is actually heavier. Thalia points to a little hole on its neck. "See? He can really eat."

"Just be sure that whatever he eats is not real food. It would spoil inside him, and we would have a big stinky problem on our hands."

"Don't worry, only paper and erasers," Claudia intervenes. "Dad, do you think I should read Nietzsche?" Anthony gulps more espresso. "I was talking with Grandma yesterday about good and evil, and I think she needs to read it, too."

Anthony's neck hurts, the pain going down his shoulder and back since he sat uncomfortably most of the night at the police station. He has a meeting with Akemi, the Italian Police, the head of the Swiss Guard, and the Vatican Central Security Corps in an hour. "Grandma says that now that Mama is gone, she will take us to church on Sundays but I believe we can achieve spirituality without religion. Morals are embedded in our genetic code. We would not have survived otherwise. Maybe technology in the future will help us boost some areas of our DNA that will enhance the virtues of mankind. Do you think cybernetic implants could enhance us not only physically but also in spiritual ways? Maybe we can have a microchip implanted next to the brain center where our perception of God resides. We could be spiritual beings all the time, perceiving the 99% of intangibles. We might become a new race symbiotic with technology because information and accelerated analysis of big data is another area that is converging on us. Our senses would be altered. I wonder if we would develop an organ to perceive spirituality or if we have the equipment to do it but we just need to upgrade it to another version?" Anthony takes a slice of pound cake from Thalia's plate and gobbles realizing *his* brain is processing the day's information sluggishly, with the clumsiness that lack of sleep can bring. His stomach is protesting from too much coffee. Food might stabilize his system.

"Do you think reading Nietzsche will help me understand this or should I download this new book from an Indian investigator that used cloud servers to prove reincarnation is real?"

Before Anthony can answer, Virginia volunteers a question, "Papa, are you going to get a girlfriend? I see all these fab Italian women and wonder if you are falling for one. They have great shoes, and I have been wondering if you need a new wardrobe to match them. You look a little boring, maybe too academic. Maybe we should go shopping for you, if you are too busy."

"Why do I need a girlfriend?" More pound cake and coffee! The girls are selecting the worst topics for a morning like this one. His hands are shaking with caffeine.

"It is biology, both mating and spirituality. Can organic microchips and genetic modifications enhance our perceptions in both areas?" remarks Claudia trying to steer the conversation back to her topic.

"Panda will never get married; he is too fat and indolent, but you are not, Papa," adds Thalia.

"You are fit, just badly dressed," concludes Virginia.

· · ·

Hot water runs on Akemi's body. Her sleeping habits are minimalistic. As part of her daily routine, she lets the hot shower run on her skin for several minutes. She analyzes facts at a fast pace while the shower stimulates blood circulation and relaxes her muscles. Preliminary analysis showed that the gun in Giocatelli's hand matched the bullets that killed Avinash. Italian bureaucracy dissolved when a case related to a wealthy and powerful national occurred. The police forensic lab personnel had been pulled out of bed and sent to work before sunrise. They had provided good data to solve Avinash's murder. But the new important question was who had assassinated Giocatelli with a poisoned apple, and why? The autopsy had only confirmed the obvious.

She shampoos her long dark hair for a third time…soft foam and fragrance while her mind races on. The assassin had taken the original erotic drawings but ignored the photographic facsimiles he dropped on the staircase. A small oil Modigliani and two Franz Marcs were also missing. Were they dealing with an art thief? The assassin had left behind the most valuable pieces: a Picasso, a larger Modigliani, and a rare Giorgio de Chirico. It seemed he had chosen what he liked and could easily carry. An art-loving assassin...During the night she had called her contacts at Christie's leveraging the time difference between New York and Rome, and they had confirmed the erotic drawings were Raphael's and were studies for Bibbiena's steam bath inside the Vatican. The collection of drawings had come onto the market recently from a global 500 company. Its new CEO believed erotic art did not match the company's image. The Christie's people had sent her front and back digital images of the drawings revealing the familiar handwriting on the reverse: the sixteenth-century monk's story.

Her mind is vibrant with the discoveries and questions. She switches from hot to ice cold water. This is her daily routine. She knows if she relaxes she might get depressed because in her emotional clumsiness she doubts if she ever showed Avinash how much she loved him. He had rescued her from jail, recruiting her for one of his companies. Developers are a very rare commodity in the US job market. Add to that her qualifications hacking drug cartels, working for the US government, and managing crises. She had already been cooperating with the CIA and DEA breaking into the data centers of several terrorist cells with uncanny success. While highly classified and completely undercover, her work from jail with these groups had made her a legend within anti-terrorist and cyber-defense circles. Avinash was a contractor for the CIA and FBI working on national security projects. She was unique, and he needed her for several products in the development stage. Her dysfunctional social skills were no deterrent to offering her a job. When he met her, he also got tangled in her eyes as they moved from one point to another in the room; she rarely fixed them on the person she was talking to.

Akemi dries her body with a lush white towel as big as a queen-sized blanket. As she stands at her window looking down at tourists at the *Piazza de Spagna,* she muses on the approach taken regarding sharing the news from Giocatelli's death with the media. They had decided to withhold all details of the event. Not only was Mr. Giocatelli a very important member of Italian society but also they were developing a plan to catch the assassin.

She crosses the room surrounded by thin glass panels, LED screens. Her cyber-pets and helpers scurry around her bare feet. She gets to her room and lets the towel fall. Once she lacked any luxury. She had lived in a Catholic boarding school in the desert. The furnishings had been sparse: frugal metallic beds with bare thread sheets. Towels thin after decades of use. The windows she had gazed through overlooked desolate, arid plains. Barren landscape with undulating striped mountains in the background and nowhere to run. Unforgiving sun, unforgiving insects—giant scorpions, centipedes, tarantulas—unforgiving plants covered in thorns too busy with survival had made her unforgiving to her parents for having sent her to such place. She was thankful to a priest who taught classes there. He had brought computers to the school. She remembered her primitive PC desktop with the fondness of a best friend. Through it she had been able to escape to other countries and communicate with people who lived in forests and never judged how she interacted with them. People who then became her friends, trapped as she was in their own geographies. Hacking was their preferred sport.

She selects her clothes carefully from a walk-in closet full with high-end fashion. She wants to look especially attractive. She wants Anthony to take Avinash's place in her mind. She commands the safe box where she keeps her jewelry to open. Layers of metal slide in a wall area and reveal the shelves for her valuables. In a corner lies the last present that Avinash gave her, stupid and silly as he had been. Somewhere he had found a jewelry store for music rappers. He had been presented with an assortment of obscene gold and diamond–encrusted letters, cartoon characters and objects such as the ones performers wore with thick gold chains on their naked chests while gulping the most expensive cognac. Avinash confided that he had invested two hours exploring all the possibilities of the jewelry in front of him until he found the perfect gift: A gigantic 20-karat diamond–encrusted hot dog, his favorite food. A hot dog. Akemi favored her meat unprocessed: steaks thick and juicy with blood in their center, pork chops with a delicate char on the outside, lamb chops with a bone to nibble on. That night she and Avinash had made love while she wore the hot dog on a heavy platinum chain around her neck, and they had remained naked during the following week working from home while the dangling diamond-encrusted hot dog overturned glasses and knocked down vases as she moved from her laptop to the kitchen and back to bed where they would make love again.

• • •

Alessandro slept in his car. His body feels as crumpled as his suit. He drinks his espresso while talking on the phone to his son. The boy giggles as his father tells fragments of the story he has been writing for him whenever he gets a minute to jot in a little notebook he carries in his jacket.

"Papa, this could be a great TV show!"

"Get me the TV producer and I can start taking you to school in the mornings instead of working long nights to catch the bad people."

• • •

Akemi's image pulls Anthony's mind and groin through the Vatican gardens and to the *Palazzo del Governatorato*. He tries to stop thinking about Akemi by repeating to himself fragments of the newly discovered *Catullus* poetry but the erotic content in them makes it counterproductive. He then tries to empty his mind by looking at the manicured greenery around him. It is a hot summer day so he is sweating, but the heat of the day is not the reason that his hands and legs are trembling with anticipation. He crosses the square in front of the building where the Vatican's day-to-day government operates. He crosses a long corridor and stops in front of a meeting room. The cold bronze doorknob on the palm of his hand feels like an ice bag. He rearranges his crotch and pauses for a couple of minutes inhaling oxygen in a controlled manner in front of the closed door. He is waiting to recuperate total self-control before pushing the door open when he is startled by a snarl behind him.

"Anthony, are you going in or are you going to spend all day blocking the entrance?" It's Akemi. "The meeting cannot start without you, Alessandro and me, and the three of us are standing here right now." The surprise dissipates Anthony's horniness as he turns to find Akemi and Alessandro staring at him. He mumbles something with his eyes downcast in humiliation. Alessandro ignores him, and Akemi pushes past him into the room full of men.

Anthony sits down. His eyes wander to the view of the Vatican gardens from the meeting room. What if they had not been interrupted the previous night? Would Akemi and he have gone all the way? Would they be now talking about ancient manuscripts while having breakfast in bed? With a jolt, he realizes he has missed the introductions around the table. An awkward silence hangs around him. People are waiting for him to introduce himself.

The session starts with an autopsy conclusions reading from the coroner's office. Mr. Giocatelli had died from the substances covering the apple he ate four hours before the body had been found. Among the many toxic ingredients they had found was arsenic. Whoever killed him had entered the property through the side door connecting to the park since the police surveying the property had not seen anyone coming in through the main gate. It had to be someone whom Mr. Giocatelli knew as there were no signs of forced entry into the mansion and only someone close to the family would know of the side door. The visitor had brought a basket of fruit. The rest of the fruit was found on a kitchen table, all was poisoned. The apples were not commercial grade but of the kind grown in private orchards in Tuscany. Mr. Giocatelli seemed to have eaten the apple while talking with his visitor. They had been in the living room at that time. The investigators found an open bottle of port with two glasses next to it. Giocatelli and the visitor did not have time to drink from them. Feeling sick from the venom, Giocatelli had gone upstairs to his bedroom looking for some remedy. He died there. The assassin knew Giocatelli's house well as he forced the armory open, extracted the Luger, and squeezed it into Giocatelli's tight, dead fist to signal that his victim had been Avinash's murderer.

"We found a box with bullets similar to the ones used on Avinash locked in a drawer on the master bedroom night table. Five bullets were missing from the box; Avinash was shot five times in the chest. No jewelry, money, or financial papers were removed from the house. One small Modigliani and two Franz Marcs were taken. They were not the best or the most valuable artwork on the property. The theft appears to have been more of a whim than a murder motive. We have alerted Interpol, and they are now on the look out for art dealers who might try to sell the pieces on the black market." The coroner's representative sits down.

Alessandro stands up to continue exposing information to the group. For the first time, Anthony notices that the only pieces in his whole attire that are not wrinkled are his shoes. The smooth, hand-made loafers contrast with what could be mistaken for a human crumpled piece of paper on a traveling carnival menagerie. "We have Avinash's murderer but we don't have the motive yet. We know Avinash was going to give something to the Pope related to the Transparency Crusade. We don't know his relationship with Giocatelli or how this incident is related to granting full access to the Vatican's Secret Archives. The hypothesis is that Avinash found something in the Secret Archives about the Giocatelli family he was going to share with the Pope."

A female voice crawls from Anthony's ears into his bloodstream. "We know Avinash had set a trap for some powerful people to make his case. Clearly, Mr. Giocatelli was one of these persons. We are assuming that there were more and that last night's crime was perpetrated by one of them." Akemi lowers a screen and pulls a micro projector from her handbag.

What would he tell her if they were alone in the room? Would he invite her to a more interesting part of the Apostolic palace? Would he be selective about what area to go to so they could make love surrounded by the best artwork in the Vatican Museum, or would he just seize the moment even if he had to pull her into a broom closet? Would she go with him? The Vatican gardens have a little villa in them, *la Casina* of Pius IV, with a barrel-vault vestibule portraying Adam and Eve as a superb example of Christian art symbiosis with pagan iconography that would make a perfect spot for them.

"Miss. Morishima has her list of favorite suspects and we can talk about them in a minute. Let's finish with Giocatelli's murder and the artwork taken from his house. The coroner's representative did not cover all the missing items," the head of the Swiss Guards interrupts.

"You are right." Alessandro explains. "Five erotic drawings from Raphael were taken from the mansion. We found facsimiles of them scattered on the staircase."

"This is what we know about those drawings," Akemi takes control of the meeting again. "Christie's has sent us a complete set of pictures of the missing drawings. We are certain Mr. Giocatelli had them with him last night. They were not in the mansion when the police arrived. Interestingly, while in most transactions the Giocatelli family used a broker and a curator on their payroll, for this transaction Giocatelli dealt with Christie's directly and in secrecy. Not even his administrative assistant, a woman who, for all practical matters, has run his life for the last twenty years by managing all his appointments and calls, knew about this."

"We have done some interrogations but have kept the matter away from the public," adds Alessandro. "We have also told the press that Mr. Giocatelli died of natural causes. We don't want them to know about the poisoning, or that he was Avinash's murderer."

"Is that the right thing to do?" Suddenly Anthony does not like being part of the investigation's inner circle. Alessandro's statements have disrupted his fantasies. "We are discussing transparency and honesty with the world. We should not be lying about Mr. Giocatelli's death and his crime."

"I told you we should not have invited him," Alessandro addresses Akemi.

"We have to trust him. We need him."

"You might need him. This is a very delicate matter."

"No more secrets." She moves around the tables and stands behind Anthony. "No more secrets with him...and you know, he is right. No more secrets outside these walls. I am the last supporter of complete transparency but Avinash wasn't and this is his murder we are talking about. No hypocrisy here. We should be forthcoming with the press."

While the perfume of orange blossoms surrounds Anthony, the gathering bursts into many conversations and arguments. All people present are talking at the same time. The opinions are divided between Anthony's push back and the Italian police's approach to managing information regarding Giocatelli's death.

A frowning Alessandro circles the table and stands next to Akemi. He is red with fury as he murmurs in her ear loud enough for Anthony to catch his words: "Don't let your crush on him affect you!"

"Crush on me!" Surprising himself, Anthony stands up and pulls Akemi's arm demanding an investigation. Her contact blurs his reasoning for an instant with many *what ifs*.

"We need to talk with the Press Office. I cannot make the decision about communicating everything!" exclaims the head of the Swiss Guard while pulling his mobile from a pocket.

"This is a matter of security for the Vatican. We should keep the facts from the public!" The head of the Central Security Corps makes his chair topple as he violently moves away from the table.

Akemi adds, "Gentlemen, talk with your superiors and let's meet here in a couple of hours. Just one thing: if they decide not to share the facts with the public, make them aware that the information will probably leak. We have hundreds of hackers who support Avinash's crusade spying on all of us. They will find the truth. I can protect the Vatican's digital information but your organizations have feeble firewalls. They are not strong enough to even stop a teenage hacker." Akemi walks to the door and stops to stare at Anthony for an instant and look around the room as if inspecting the artwork while stating: "You don't need to be in the afternoon session, Anthony. We will summon you when we reconvene on the investigation." She speaks loud enough for everybody to hear. "Your superior is the American Ambassador, talk to him if the facts are released to the news. He is not part of the decision makers on this case so you should not be present." Her black eyes zoom to a cherub painted next to a window.

Infuriated, Anthony calls back, "Akemi, look at me when you talk! If you want my help, you have to respect me," he demands. "Don't just walk away, look at me! Didn't anybody teach you manners?" The volume of his voice is loud, commanding.

Alessandro holds Anthony by the shoulder and adds with a smug sarcastic smile, "She never talks to the eye. She never looks at the person she is talking to. I thought you had already noticed. You better get used to that." Anthony pushes Alessandro's hand away to go to the outside corridor. Akemi is gone, and all the men in the meeting room are busy calling their command centers.

"What if I never see or speak to her again?" whispers Anthony in furious breath.

CHAPTER 18

RAPHAEL SANZIO

That night, the girls go to bed early, and Anthony stands on the balcony of his hotel room, ruminating about the events of the last couple of days. He misses the stability of his life with Laura. It was a time when he believed things would never change. He and she would get old while the girls grew up, went to college, got married, had a successful career, and gave them grandchildren. Laura and he would be together—always. How and when did he fall into a time warp? He still has a clear awareness of what it felt to live next to his wife away from all technology, letting her manage the electronics at home while he read printed paper and hard cover books. It is an ugly realization how ephemeral each moment can be. His life in Rome is the opposite of that stability. Everyone seems to be speaking at the same time, gesturing, and saying more things than he can comprehend. Everyone is so intense. The safety and security of Redondo Beach has been replaced by murders and danger. The sounds of the ocean by the rumble of traffic. Instead of serene nurturing love from Laura, he is unsettled by everything from Akemi. Now technology has become very important in what he does and in his relationships. To confirm these thoughts, his iPhone pings, signaling he has received a text message.

He reads the bright screen in the dark: "The manuscript hidden on the inside book cover we recuperated from the underground vault continues the story. I just emailed you the text from it. A."

Holding the phone in his grip, he closes his eyes, furious and offended at how matter of fact she can be, yet exhilarated that she sent him the story as soon as she got a new update.

Day 4 - December 9, 1521

My name is Federigo Dottore. I have eight days to live after today. The poison I chose to drink has given me time to write the confession of my sins. It is also the poison I used for my friend. I wanted to experience the pain and sickness he went through. He used to say that he and I were two sides of humanity. Now my flesh is going through the same decaying process that corrupted his body.

However, the nightmares from the opium-induced dreams are only mine. Chasing me as they have done all my life, approaching my death time, the nightmares are the cruelest. They know I have nothing left to hide. Death is portrayed as a skeleton because that is the ultimate form of nudity, because bones are the foundation to our bodies—what remains when blood and tissue has been stripped away. The empty orbs of a skull reflect the darkness we might plummet into when we have forsaken our holy soul during life.

I have locked myself in my private chambers where I write at my favorite desk. I have twin desks but I use the other to write formulas in my book of poisons. Callisto the cook brings me food. Sometimes I open the door to him. His face cannot hide his pain as he sees my head and face covered in hair for the first time. He knows I have poisoned myself and keeps pleading for me to drink the antidote. He states that the court servants need me. Who will cure them and their families when I am gone?

Callisto now has a wife as fat as him and two chubby children. Who will cure them if a pest punishes the city? Maybe he knows I am an assassin. He has been close to me since Saint Benedictus Minor. I was a teenage boy then. He saved my life. He nurtured me until I regained my strength.

Callisto is worried about the Pope's successor. What kind of people will he bring to court? Will Callisto keep his job?

I do not mind the pain as the venom corrodes me. I've come to enjoy it as penance for the sins I cannot confess in church. I abhor filth, and dying is an untidy business. I vomit frequently. My breath and sweat are rotten. My urine…

For life lived in the grandest city of all times surrounded by the most gifted artists that have ever existed, death is a formality, a bureaucratic process if your existence has been illuminated by atemporal creatures whose genius could only emanate from the eternal Light of our Creator.

In 1508, Bramante brought young Raphael Sanzio da Urbino to Rome. To me, at the time, he was just one of the many artists Bramante had been enlisting for court from the North to break the dominance of the Florentine group that had previously controlled the art scene. I had heard Pope Julius II complain about the decoration of his living quarters as it had been created to please the Borgia Pope. Julius II had moved there after his victory in the Umbria war. The imagery contained pictures of Alexander Borgia's mistress among other elements that made his Holiness furious. Julius II wanted the best talent to decorate his new apartments, located in the second floor of the palace. Raphael was one of the chosen.

I have no strong recollection of Raphael until 1509. Let me give some perspective of what absorbed my interest at that moment. Since settling into the Vatican court, I had spent a portion of my time and money searching for my lost grandfather, who had ran away the night my father died. I still had a glimmer of hope that I would find him, even if he had run away naked and insane into the night before my brother and I were sent to a monastery. I wished to discover his destiny even if it had not been good. I believed that knowing this would help me escape the nightmares that plagued my dreams. I had searched many of the sanitariums in Rome. I had talked with inhabitants in the area around our old house. I had written letters to his friends in other cities, especially in Florence. Nobody had given me hope until I received a letter from one of the merchants that had traveled with my grandfather in his commerce excursions to distant lands. He had been away from Florence for a long period but he remembered having seen my grandfather when he was on a trip to the northern states belonging to the Holy Roman Empire.

My grandfather had been the first one in the family in love with Classical art and literature. As many other Florentine men of his generation, he believed we would find meaning in the Classical heritage from the Greeks, and the Roman Republic and Empire. This legacy, he believed, was vital to pulling us out from the dark ages into a new era for mankind in which the educated mind would prevail over superstition.

My grandfather met with other advanced thinkers while traveling his commercial routes. His best friend became a bishop from the German States. I remember him telling us stories about his friend and how they would engage in magnificent arguments about philosophy and art that would last for days. He was particularly intrigued by how his friend looked for meaning in the roots of Christianity instead of pagan culture. The bishop studied Saint Augustine and learned Greek, Hebrew, and Aramaic to read the Bible in its original languages. Their conversations had been so rewarding that the bishop gave my grandfather a beautiful ring with an engraved stone embossed with his parish coat of arms. I know my grandfather mentioned the city where his friend lived many times but I had forgotten the name. The Florentine merchant who had sent me the letter and believed he had seen my grandfather in the northern states did not know the city either as he had not been part of the intellectual gatherings. But he remembered my grandfather's ring. Closing my eyes, I could visualize the ring. The red stone would open to reveal a secret compartment that my father would fill with honey for my brother and me. I remembered the coat of arms engraved in the ring's red stone. Even then I could vividly envison two cart wheels joined by a cross—almost as if the huge ring sat before my eyes. This was the only clue I had in 1509 to guide me to a city where my grandfather could have retreated in his final days. The challenge was that the Holy Roman Empire was made of three hundred states. I had support and funds from the Pope to go on a trip there as I had convinced his Holiness to send me to those lands to hunt for ancient manuscripts. Since Julius II at the time was enjoying killing his enemies directly with his sword instead of using his poisoner, he allocated money and people to me. Finding old manuscripts was high on his agenda as he wanted to surpass the size of the library of the King of France, famous across Europe for its vastness.

So on that evening, I was immersed in a coat of arms treaty in a reading room at the Vatican Library when I was distracted by loud voices coming from an approaching group of men. There were three in the party: Tommaso Inghirami, Agostino Chigi, and Raphael Sanzio.

Tommaso was the head Papal librarian. One of the most brilliant courtiers I ever met, but who unfortunately disliked me as I answered directly to the Pope instead of him. He always regarded me with suspicion, but after years of supplying new texts to his collections without engaging in politics, he left me alone. He even chose to ignore me after having failed in his intrigues against me, noticing how Julius II halted any rumors without allowing any room for doubt or negotiation. Tommaso realized with time that I was mute and that I did not participate in any conspiracy to advance my position or wealth, an oddity in a conniving environment. Tommaso was heavy and dressed lavishly in scarlet robes in line with his court status. His face was round and clean shaven with an intelligent left eye over pudgy cheeks and a permanent squint in his right eye.

The second person was Agostino Chigi, the wealthiest man in the world. Originally from Sienna, he had been one of the many bankers serving the Popes, starting with Alexander VI, and had swiftly moved from being one of the many to the preferred one. He became the Vatican's assigned trader of the alum extracted from mines around Rome. This monopoly had become a vital source of income for the Catholic Church since the fall of Constantinople had severed trade with the East. He was so well liked that Julius II adopted him as a son in 1507. He was a strongly built middle-aged man with handsome, noble features dominated by carnal lips. His voice had an aristocratic tone and an undercurrent of the joy that only power and wealth can deliver.

The third man was Raphael Sanzio, a painter. He was very close to Bramante, who admired his talent. Raphael had amazed the world at a very young age. While I had seen him from afar in parties and the corridors of the palace, I had not paid a lot of attention to him. He was dressed in ornate black clothes that highlighted his fair brown hair. A newcomer, he seemed to be relishing the company of the two other powerful men in his company. He was in his mid-twenties and his face could have been considered pretty, almost feminine, if not for the masculine expressions, the manner in his movements, and eyes that exuded the virility of a young man exploring his sexuality. Many stories about his sexual exploits circulated.

I noticed that Agostino wanted to become a good friend to Raphael. A forward-thinking man, he was recruiting Raphael for his payroll as soon as the artist finished his work for the Pope. Raphael was the rising star on the Pope's roster of carefully hand-picked artists. His only true contender was the hermetic Michelangelo Buonarroti, who had secluded himself in the Vatican palace chapel built by Sixtus IV and was decorating its ceiling with Biblical frescoes.

The loud conversation was centered on a story Agostino was narrating. He was describing in explicit detail a racy encounter with Imperia, the most expensive and desired courtesan in Rome, mistress to the richest men and the most influential cardinals. Tommaso, who had also slept with her, laughed like a growling circus bear as Agostino described the expert gyrations of her hips. Raphael was entranced, listening with wonder.

"Maybe one day I will pay her to frolic with you!" Agostino winked at the young painter while Tommaso slapped him on the buttocks. In that moment, they discovered me in one of the library desks.

"Don't pay attention to him," derided the Papal librarian, "he is mute so he will never repeat anything he hears."

Raphael studied me for a moment, his curious spirit stimulated by every new discovery at the Papal court. His eyes roved over my clean-shaved scalp and hairless face. He also had a clean-shaved face but had never seen anyone who plucked his eyebrows and eyelashes. He also noticed my white robes, a bold contrast with the black fabrics he favored. To get the black color in a cloth, many types of inks and pigments had to be used, but he realized that to have a robe as clean as mine, a high expense would come from the careful fiber selection and delicate bleaching process.

Tommaso kept on talking as if I were not present, "I don't comprehend his connection with the Pope. He has obtained some good manuscripts for the library, but other book hunters who have similar accomplishments never get close to His Holiness. This shows you, young Raphael, that no matter how much time you invest in this court, its secrets are created faster than the time you have to live." He led his guests into the Greek and Roman literature room, opening the pews where the manuscripts were kept. "Here you can find anything you can dream up to research your painting at the stanza." He spread his arms wide with open palms facing up in a magnanimous pose.

"I hear you are painting a dissertation between Philosophy, Astrology, and Theology." Agostino's knowledge of the project evidenced his closeness to the Pope.

"I want to have a section where the best poets in history are at Mount Parnassus under the shade of Apollo," declared Raphael with a soft musical voice.

"That is a great idea!" roared Agostino. "Our Dante, Petrarch, and Boccaccio!"

"I enjoy reading very much," Raphael's voice sounded bristling with life but somewhat intimidated by the banker's exuberance.

"We have splendid manuscripts from Virgil and Homer. They were copied directly from Greek to Latin. We even have Catullus, although I keep him and Ovid in the Secret Archives room. I don't want our clerics to become more licentious than they already are!" Tommaso's laughter boomed in the library vaults and I could hear him slapping Raphael on the back. Although I was in another room, I could see them through the archways connecting the library. I peeked over the thick volume I was reading and noticed Raphael was struggling to say something. He had the delicate and deliberate manners of a courtier but I discovered an authenticity in him that I immediately liked.

"I've read adaptations from Homer and Virgil, but never a direct translation," Raphael succeeded in wording the phrase.

"You can stay away from those corrupted versions. You can read them in Latin directly here!" Tommaso caressed one of the wood pews where the manuscripts were kept.

"I can read very little Latin." Raphael lowered his head and looked around, ashamed of his confession.

Agostino and Tommaso roared with mocking laughter. "Same as Bramante! The Northern education is clearly inferior to the Florentine! We are lucky your lot can read at all," chuckled Tommaso. "You are at a great disadvantage against Michelangelo."

"You can visit me. I have translations of Ovid's works although I think the transcribers have added a lot from their imagination when funneling the words through their pens into our corrupt language," invited Agostino.

"What about Catullus and Epicurus?" Raphael probed shyly.

Both men look at each other. "There is no Epicurus left for any-one to read. We know about his philosophy from a poem written by Lucretius called 'The Nature of Things.' Scholars in Florence study it but I believe it will be impossible to find a translation. Catullus is also very hard to find. His poetry is sultry."

"We don't need to translate the Classics for eroticism. You can go chat with Imperia for that! She gets filthy poetry from her admirers every day in the language of Dante." Despite Agostino's friendly demeanor, Raphael's face denoted internal struggle. "The frescoes you are work-ing on are fantastic. His Holiness showed me some of the drawings of how they will look. They will celebrate the high intellect of Julius II's court and showcase it to kings and ambassadors that come to Rome from other lands."

A distant bell surprised the group with the time of day. The librarian and the banker were late to other appointments in their busy sched-ule. Raphael looked at them hurrying away but decided to stay. His eyes wandered with hunger around the manuscripts hanging on chains by their pews. With his fingertips, he touched some folios stacked on shelves on the wall. He sat in front of the Ennead in Latin, and his sensi-tive fingers traced the handwriting on the vellum with awe.

From a recent book hunt, I had brought back a book with translated poems from Catullus. Without Raphael noticing my stealth movements, I pulled it from a cupboard and walked up, placing the folios in front of him. Startled, he stood up, having forgotten about my presence. I sig-naled to the sentences in modern language so he would start reading. His face brightened when he realized what I was giving him. He smiled at me with a gentleness that revealed an exquisite soul. A soul that had not been corrupted by pain and torture as mine had. We stood in front of each other, he dressed in black and I in white like opposite reflections in a dark mirror. We both loved human thought and creation. For him it was inspiration and guidance, for me it was the rope I clung to not to fall into an obscure abyss. His body was lean and sensual, open to all the pleasures Rome could provide. Mine was tight knotted muscle and scars that created a wall against any intimacy. Quietly, he thanked me with gestures that acknowledged my muteness and respected my silence.

I turned around, unwilling to connect more with him. I liked him, which meant I should keep a distance. I wished to remain faithful to my principle of not having friends in case Julius II ordered me to poison the painter in the future; but as I moved away, the image of his warm smile revealed the chill of my isolation and loneliness. I accelerated my pace to move away from him. I forced myself to think about making arrangements for my trip to the Northern Countries to continue the search for my grandfather.

"Hope this makes you happy. I will keep sending you more. Let's try to be friends. A." Anthony stared at the screen of his laptop until the night cold air forced him to go to bed.

CHAPTER 19

SOMEONE ELSE IN CONTROL

Akemi jogs in the *Borghese* Gardens early in the morning. The summer air is still cool and clean. Her black spandex top and pants are soaked in sweat and so is the band holding her black mane in place. She craves her exercise every morning to keep her controlled during the day. If she burns a significant amount of energy and exhausts her muscles, she is less inclined to bouts of anger. It also releases the knots on her back, neck, and calves that form from the memories and suppressed terrors that surface at night. Sweat from the morning exercise washes them away, makes them rise to the surface of her skin and evaporate like toxic gases.

She also loves to jog in the *Borghese* Gardens because she gets to see Anthony from a distance on a ledge overlooking the *Piazza del Popolo*. His glistening body twisting in yoga postures after having raced across the pathways. Today, he is sitting in a lotus position wearing his skimpy running shorts. His bare, smooth chest and back are heaving with controlled breathing.

She continues in her direction, choosing not to approach him. The recent days have brought them closer than she wanted. Today, the news from Giocatelli's poisoning will surely force them together again.

The previous afternoon, the Italian police and Vatican authorities agreed to announce the real causes of Giocatelli's death. But they had agreed also to withhold that Giocatelli had been Avinash's murderer. That part of the story had been expurgated from all and any system to prevent hackers from finding it. They had only verbally shared that portion with the American Ambassador when asking for his help in recruiting Anthony as a spokesperson. It was going to be a PR nightmare anyway. The American researcher had proven so good with the international press that the group had designated him to talk to the media. Jonathan Bradbury, the American Ambassador, had phoned Anthony the night before.

The Council of Social Communication had released the blurbs earlier from the *Palazzo dei Propelei* facing Saint Peter's Square. Akemi's social media teams had worked all night preparing to respond to the onslaught of postings around the world. Her social media feelings tracking systems had shown that the release had been just in time. The followers of Avinash's Transparency Crusade had hacked into the Italian Police system during the night and would have released the news anyway. She was glad that every word linking Giocatelli to Avinash had been expunged from all servers except hers.

Anthony goes to the American Embassy after breakfast. The Ambassador is eager to get all the details about Giocatelli's death from him. Ellia Jones sits on a couch next to the Ambassador's desk. Her lack of make-up emphasizes her frowning face. She would have liked to have known about the events before the press had. Anthony describes the discovery of the murdered businessman, and Akemi and Alessandro's frustration. Ellia listens without moving any muscle from her body but an artery in her forehead appears to bulge and pulsate with fury. Later, the Head of Public Relations preps Anthony for the upcoming press conference, and soon Anthony is the one wearing make-up while rehearsing his speech.

The press conference is in a large ballroom inside the embassy. Murals on the walls and ceiling displaying pastoral scenes frame the room, packed with cameras and reporters. Reuters, CNN, NBC, Fox, Al-Jazeera—all are eager to get the event's perspective from an American. Anthony delivers the agreed messages with grace and clarity. He answers questions with efficiency. The press conference would have been flawless but then a very tall man stands up at the doorway. Anthony's body tenses as he recognizes the muscular man. It's the linebacker, the predator who scared him and his daughters in *Via Condotti*, the one who had tried to grab Thalia's backpack. Anthony's palms become sticky with perspiration.

"What is he doing here? Who is he?" Anthony questions himself, unable to look anywhere else in the room. The woman handling the microphone for the reporters follows Anthony's gaze and hands the microphone to the large man, who grabs it and, turning to the room, declares: "Dr. Hibbert, you say you still don't have the motivation for the murder. Why are you hiding the rest?" The room delivers a collective gasp. The cameras turn to the man while Anthony's mind races with possible answers. The giant continues in a louder voice. People around him take a step back. "I have information here that shows that Mr. Adriano Giocatelli was responsible for the death of Avinash Sullivan, another murder scandal about which the Italian authorities have kept the public in the dark. Giocatelli killed Avinash Sullivan because Mr. Sullivan was going to expose information that would harm the Giocatelli family name." Murmurs fill the room. The Embassy guards are ready to intercede but Ellia Jones signals for them to be still. She also tightens her grip around the arm of the PR agent so she cannot redirect the conference back to Anthony. "What my sources revealed is that Mr. Adriano Giocatelli's father was a Nazi spy inside the Vatican during World War II. He collaborated with Fascist sympathizers to advance the Holocaust agenda and was one of the main contacts with the Gestapo to develop a plan to kidnap and eliminate the Pope. I have thumb drives containing scanned images of documents for anyone interested." He pushes a hand in his coat pocket and extracts a handful of thumb drives he raises in the air for the cameras to capture. Some reporters extend their hands trying to get one of the tiny objects. He continues: "In the 90s, the KGB planted false documents inside the Secret Archives to be used as testimony that the Pope had been in coalition with the Nazis. This conspiracy was organized in retaliation against the Vatican for supporting Eastern Europe's efforts to separate from the Soviet Union. Mr. Giocatelli's father had realized his error in helping the Nazis. When he saw the Church in danger, he helped the Vatican clear its name by exposing the spy network inside the Vatican during the war. This effort revealed true documents evidencing that the Pope and Hitler had been no allies and that, in fact, Hitler had a plan to get rid of the Pope. The KGB conspiracy was revealed, and the Church's name cleared. Mr. Giocatelli's father did this work in exchange for total anonymity to protect his family, however the minutes of his meetings with the Holy See and his declarations were captured in documents stored inside the Secret Archives. Those documents are also on the thumb drives." Grasping hands reach through the air. "Avinash Sullivan's transparency crusade would have made these documents available to the public. Mr. Giocatelli had to stop him so he got his father's Nazi gun and shot him five times in his hotel room!"

The reporters crowd around the muscular man while he hands out the USB drives. He is so tall he seems like a man handing away multicolored caramels to children. The reporters demand to know how he got the evidence he is handing out. They also want to know his identity.

Ellia Jones cups her hands around her mouth and calls for order: "Please, everybody refrain from further questions or I will have to call the press conference off." The reporters ignore her, so she signals to the ready guards arranged around the room to intervene. One of them blows a loud whistle that startles everyone and allows the linebacker to rush out of the room. He had been at the threshold all this time. Another guard turns the lights on and off signaling the event is over. Someone pulls Anthony by the elbow, guiding him down from the podium. The reporters are rushing out to chase the man who has given the unexpected testimony but find themselves halted by locked doors and restricted areas inside the Embassy. The linebacker, despite his extreme height and muscles, has vanished into thin air.

"For God's sake, who was that?" asks Ambassador Bradbury to an amazed Anthony and a smug Ellia Jones.

"I don't have his identity, yet. He must be one of the Transparency Crusaders. I don't understand how he could infiltrate the press conference," Ellia sounds apologetic.

"That would explain a lot. He could have hacked the information from some system, even from the Secret Archives themselves," deduces the Ambassador.

"Or he could have received Giocatelli's information from Avinash himself," adds Ellia.

"But how did he find out that Giocatelli was a murderer? It is a disgrace for all of us involved in this case and certainly for my Embassy not to have matters under control!"

"A hacker of that caliber could have gotten fake press credentials easily," ads the PR agent.

Anthony observed the events from the height of the speaker podium. He saw Ellia stopping the guards from acting earlier. He realizes he cannot trust anyone around him; even the elegant Ambassador with his soft grey eyes and suit might have secrets of his own related to the case. However orchestrated, the linebacker had not only access to the Secret Files but also to the Italian Police coroner's office documents. While the Ambassador speaks with his team, Anthony walks to the entrance archway and picks a green thumb drive lying on the floor. He now has a gift for Akemi. He knows he will spend the rest of the morning at the Embassy but is able to get a courier to deliver an envelope to the *Palazzo del Governatorato.*

• • •

"Mike, tell me if it was one of yours!" Akemi speaks to the microphone embedded in her computer glasses. She has the person who took over Avinash as leader of the Transparency Crusade on the line.

"It is also a pleasure to talk with you again."

"Don't fuck with me! How did the man at the American press conference get the information about Giocatelli's father? The archives in the thumb drive are scanned copies of meeting transcripts from the Secret Archives. I purged all references to Giocatelli's guilt from the Italian Police servers. Whoever got them is copying the coroner files in real time! Was it you and your team, or do we have to be wary of yet another group involved in this?"

"I wish it had been us. This was brilliant! Unfortunately, it did not come from us. You know that you had already sanitized the files when we hacked the Italian Police servers. You were ahead of us and had already released news of Giocatelli's murder to the press. Why are you asking me these questions? It had to be some institution with a more powerful net of spies than the Transparency Crusade. I am certain you are wondering why the big reveal was done at the American Embassy. The US government has more resources than God."

"Damn you! I will cut your balls and fry them if you are lying to me!"

"You are sweeter every day, Akemi. In the old days you would have fried my balls before cutting them. For all we know it might have been Giocatelli's poisoner who revealed the news in that room. Have you done any face matching on the giant at the press conference?"

"I get nothing! He doesn't exist. That is why I suspect you. Only the Pentagon and you have this kind of stealth!"

"What has to happen will happen. If transparency within the Catholic Church is what is to be, nothing will stop destiny."

"Fuck off!"

• • •

Anthony has a meeting with Francesca scheduled in his calendar. He would rather see the others but realizes he would not know where to look at the *Palazzo del Governatorato*. It will be easier to send an email to Akemi and arrange a rendezvous.

Holding his briefcase close to his body, he walks to the Secret Archives library. Francesca is sitting in the outdoor café with the Secret Archives Prefect, Monsignor José Dosal. They are engaged in an intense conversation, both gesticulating and alternating between hushed murmurs and exalted shouts. One part of Anthony wants to scurry to the study room to email Akemi, another pushes him to greet and sit with them at the table. They are startled by his presence. José grabs the table with terror as if he were an altar boy caught stealing donations. Francesca crosses her arms tightly in front of her chest as if caught naked leaving the bed of a lover.

"*Caro*, I had forgotten about our meeting." She pushes her knees together in a gesture of self-conscious protection.

"*Vaya con el Tío!*" José exclaims in a voice too loud even for him as he opens his arms to the heavens. "You have heard the news right? Am I stupid?" His face contorts as if each word created a tidal wave across his cheeks and forehead. "Of course you have heard the news! You were there! I guess your friend Akemi has gotten you into a lot of trouble! She is not informing me about matters. All of this has to do with my territory! I am the Prefect of the Secret Archives! I should have shot you both that night in the underground vault!"

Anthony listens. Francesca and José seem to be actors in a performance to hide their guilt. Francesca floods Anthony with questions. "Were you there when they found the body? Why did it take a day to release the information to the press? Do they know who the assassin was? Who are the suspects? What did the American Ambassador have to say about the scandal at the press conference?" Anthony looks at her, realizing she is one of the suspects. He cannot trust her. In his silence, he observes José and Francesca as if he were watching them sitting far away from the stage, pushing himself away from the brash voices, focusing his body's center of gravity and managing to block the sound and the words in order to interpret their body language. The now becomes the view of a magnificent building that houses the Vatican Museum with its knowledge and centuries of intrigue and passions. Anthony realizes that in very few years his now will be part of the memory within those walls and new men and women will replace him amid new conspiracies and plots.

Anthony is pulled back to the moment when he realizes that their mouths have stopped moving, Francesca's diamond earrings have stop twinkling, and their hands lay expectant on the table. They have asked him something and are waiting for his answer so he just blurts whatever crosses his mind: "Akemi promised to show me the underground vault again. I only care about my research, and I am very tired of these murders." Francesca's and José's eyes meet in silence, jolting Anthony. He has read a deeper and unexpected connection between the two of them as if they were members of a secret society or clandestine lovers.

Pause. Francesca playfully slaps Anthony in the cheek. "*Bastardo*, so it is your girlfriend who has the information. Can you let me to talk to her before you go frolicking around? I am so glad you are back in action.

José snorts laughter. "*Por Dios*, Francesca, you are inside the Vatican City! Next thing you will ask for the details of their copulation."

"Says the man who never has vulgar jokes…" Francesca and José laugh together but the laughter is forced.

"I'll ask her to meet with us," volunteers Anthony.

"Look, Anthony, if it is true that the documents shared at the press conference came from the Secret Archives, this would be serious business." José continues, "It would mean someone is taking files right underneath my nose. That is why I got so upset when you and Akemi were in the underground vault. I had just returned from a reunion with the President of the Pontifical Commission of Cardinals for the Vatican City, the Treasury Curator, and the Vatican Information Office. They want to accelerate the digitization of the Secret Archives so they can understand what we have. We cannot open everything after 1939 and hope for no surprises. You noticed that despite all our well-meaning efforts, the place is not as organized as it should be. There is a lot of work to be done. Not counting the work that has to be done at the main library."

José sips on his coffee and stands up. "This has been a delightful encounter but I have work to do." He beams first at Anthony and then Francesca, a hint of recrimination directed at her.

As José retires, Anthony leans toward Francesca: "Why the intensity?"

"He is a micromanager. He wants to control everything related to his area. He was very irritated by your and Akemi's escapade, and the news from today just made matters worse. It is impossible for him to have full control. Just think about it, the digitized documents in electronic format are housed in five secret locations around the world. He doesn't have complete visibility of that. Your friend has more information—and that makes matters worse." Still uncomfortable with the whole exchange, Francesca redirects the conversation. "Now, let's go to work. *Catullus* is waiting for us to rescue his poems."

CHAPTER 20

FORSAKEN BY THE CHURCH

"You did not answer my messages during the day," Anthony texts to Akemi in the calm of his room after the girls are asleep. He likes this new communication routine.

The phone buzzes with the instant message answer. "I know Francesca wants to talk with me, I also want time with her. Can you get her boyfriend to be there?"

"Who was the man in the press conference? How did he get the information? You are the hacker."

"He left no trail behind."

"I had seen the man before. I don't like him. He is dangerous."

"Tell your Francesca we should get dinner after the Catholic Transparency Conference tomorrow. She should bring her boyfriend. You and I can find a moment to talk then."

"I'll do that."

"Can you invite the bishop from LA, too?"

"If he has something to hide, will he want to talk with you?"

"They are all hiding stuff."

"Are you?"

"Check your mail. I am sending you more content from the monk."

"Thx."

Anthony listens to the serene breathing of his daughters. Sitting in bed, he opens his laptop.

(Continued) Day 4 - December 9, 1521

His Holiness invested generously in my trip. I traveled with soldiers for protection, a covered wagon to store a small pantry and tents but mostly empty as we needed space to transport the manuscripts we recover from the many monasteries on our journey. I had servants who prepared my baths in the morning and at the end of the day's march. They also washed my clothes daily. A barber accompanied us to shave my face, head, and body. Lastly, but very important, I traveled with a translator so we could communicate in the many dialects of the Holy Roman Empire.

During the trip, we were surrounded by filth and vermin. I would lie on my cot at night scratching, disgusted by the miserable conditions peasants lived in. There was dirt everywhere, stuck on the wheels of our wagon, on the hoofs of our horses, on our clothes, and on every inch of the peasants' skins, even on their newborn babies.

When stopping at monasteries, I would use the afternoon to set up a makeshift infirmary for the inhabitants of the area. The desolation was overwhelming. The farmers' pleas for help were loud enough just by looking at the rags they wore and the condition of their bodies. I should not have been surprised, but still I was struck by the aloofness and indifference of the monks and priests. Instead of concern for their parish, they maximized the price of the sacraments to squeeze the most money from the poor.

One day we arrived at a church that had wheels on its coat of arms. It was not identical to the one I remembered on the ring but still my hopes to find my grandfather's archbishop were high. It was Sunday, so I signaled my entourage to stop so we could attend mass. I could recall my grandfather repeating the dissertations with his friend about religion. They were passionate about how to gain entrance to heaven. Would it be through pure faith, good deeds, and penitence, or ethics and moral behavior? I prepared myself for a brilliant sermon.

The church was crammed with people standing in overcrowded quarters. The choir blocked the view to the altar so the congregation would only be able to listen to the priest's words but not see him. I struggled to find an area where the bodies of others would not touch me, but I failed and could sense fleas and lice jumping from the un-washed bodies onto my limbs. When the ceremony began all I could hear were grunts and grumbles. I wondered if the priest had decided to give the liturgy in the local dialect instead of Latin, a violation of the Church ordinances. The translator nodded his head and explained that many of the rural priests did not speak Latin. They came from peas-ant families and did not know how to read. They might carry the Bible around but could not share the Word. What we were listening to was an invented nonsensical language to deceive the villagers into believing they were listening to the Gospel in Latin.

I looked around. The faces were tired and spent. People were there because religion kept the community together. However, they would invent myths from bits and stories from the lives of saints and forward these stories on to their children. They had not been evangelized; they had not been instructed in the true Word of Christ. I heard a woman entertaining her son by telling him the legend of the wandering Jews, and how that race had been cursed for having crucified the Savior. A grandmother explained how the priest was using magical powers to transform bread to human flesh. The children doubted her but were so hungry that even a story about food was itself nutritious.

The priest did not offer any sermon. He wished to finish the cere-mony as quickly as possible, to run to us, as he had been alerted that an elegant monk from Rome was in his parish. I signaled to him that I was mute, but he pulled me with his unwashed hands, his fingernails long and cracked—green and brown muck stuck under them. He guided me to his house as he wanted to honor us. The vision of the place stopped me. Two half-dressed women were inside, one with an advanced preg-nancy and the other carrying a boy whose stained face was identical to the priest's. A pig lay in a corner. Two hens nested on the only cot in the room where everybody must have slept.

That night in my sleep I remembered I had promised my grand-father and my brother to take care of them. I had failed, I had lied to them. My brother was dead, and my grandfather might be sunken in this sewage. In dreams I could hear the voice of my grandfather talking about the ring his friend the bishop had given him to ensure they would meet again. My grandfather had promised to visit him again to return the jewel. What if my grandfather had recovered reason the night of the fire and had gone to look for his friend? I had to find him if I ever wished to rest again.

During the two years that the trip lasted, we were able to gather many manuscripts but I did not find what I was searching for. I initiated the journey, certain that the Catholic Church network would aid in my quest, but I found too many empty bishop seats. Their owners had bought them for business. One bishop had not given mass in his parish for last twenty-seven years. When I met with some they were wary of me, certain I was a spy from Rome sent to obstruct their mundane ventures. They sent me away as fast as they could.

When I turned to the aristocrats, I did not get help either. They resented the Vatican. The kings of France and Spain had strong influence on the Church posts in their lands. They had power to place or remove bishops. Not in the Holy Roman Empire. Rome appointed, and sold the posts directly, and as part of this arrangement owned a quarter of the land in every state. The Pope syphoned riches from these lands without its rulers getting a cut in the profits.

At night I slept away from my entourage. I did not wish to socialize. I sat and meditated about how the inhabitants of the Empire were desperate for spiritual guidance after years of famine and plague. They needed comfort and meaning but the Catholic Church failed to provide it. What was the value of the new thinking? Where were the new thinkers? What good was it to rescue the ideas of the Classical philosophers or the founders of Christianity if there was no action? I struggled to reconcile the beauty I had seen in churches and Roman temples, the music I had learned to love, and the elevated science with the filth and despair I encountered on my journey.

I had great books for the Pope, even dissertations believed to have been handwritten by Saint Augustine. Would they make a difference to the misery of so many?

It was late in the year 1511 when, one night, I ordered the convoy to turn around. I wished to be in Rome as soon as possible, so we hired a boat from the North Sea to Ostia. The city greeted us with more activity than I had seen ever before. There were construction crews everywhere raising magnificent palaces and temples. The forest inside the city wall had shrunk, making way for more development to house the large number of immigrants into the city.

While the Vatican palace was humming with labor—especially on the new Basilica for Saint Peter where Bramante had almost completed the central walls—the Court was empty. Julius II had gone to war again, this time against France and the Duke of Ferrara to regain some of the Italian lands in the north. He had taken most of his courtiers, and those left behind were in a foul mood as news from the battlefront was bad. Victory had not been swift. Julius II was stuck holding a siege in the city of Ravenna. There was a rumor that His Holiness had been very sick during the military campaign.

Callisto had stayed this time. He prepared a small feast upon my return, which I ate, relishing the cleanliness of its preparation and presentation. My small quarters felt like a mansion. While away, the court woodshop made two twin desks for me to express their gratitude, for I had treated their families during a plague. Other servants had contributed to the gift so the carpenters could buy the finest woods. Calisto had told them that I spent many hours studying ancient texts and manuscripts from the Secret Archives so they created hidden areas and double bottom drawers on both pieces of furniture for me to hide documents. It was impossible for anyone to detect the presence of these compartments. This became very helpful for hiding my poisoner's notebook from prying eyes. Calisto had suggested two identical desks as he saw me working on more than one thing at a time.

The unexpected marvelous gift inspired me to dedicate myself during the next weeks to treat and cure the servants left at court. My absence allowed many ailments to accrue, so I had many people to treat and very little time to wander the corridors. Still, I soon found out that in my absence, Raphael Sanzio had become Julius II's favorite painter. The Pope had sent many of the other artists away, and even tore down the new frescoes they had recently painted so Raphael could be the main artist decorating his second floor apartments. The gossip I soon heard from many sources was that Raphael and Michelangelo hated each other, and I believed it as both were very competitive. Michelangelo had locked himself in Sixtus Chapel sick with jealousy and determined to keep everyone out of his way until he could finish his work. He had fired almost all the apprentices that had worked for him. In contrast, during this time, Raphael had created a group that allowed him to do more projects, thus he was always surrounded by his entourage and courtiers. The banker Agostino Chigi had finally managed to get him to work for him. Raphael had been painting the Chigi family chapel at Santa Maria del Popolo.

During my trip, I had been able to collect several texts well translated from Latin to Dante's language. I remembered fondly Raphael's eagerness to learn, so I sent the manuscripts to him upon my arrival. To thank me, he sent me a luminous drawing of a mother and her baby that he had done as a study for a Madonna. I was amazed by the tender expression he was able to capture on the mother and the realistic proportions of the baby's body. Instantly, it became one of my most cherished possessions.

But my soul was still in turmoil, unable as it was to reconcile the beauty of the past with the spirituality of the Church and the misery of man. Whenever I was finished with the infirmary for the day, I would walk around the city looking for a sign from God to help me find an answer and to illuminate my darkness. I would stroll to the Roman Forum and lay in the lavender fields gazing at the sky for an omen. I also went to the bakery where my mother took me as a child, only to discover that the owner had died. The roof built on top of a pagan temple had collapsed, breaking the bread oven. One passerby informed me that the baker's son, Francesco, had opened a new shop in the Street of Santa Dorotea. Craving the comfort of the bread, I went to the new address and to my delight discovered that, if anything, the old flavor had been perfected and enhanced by the new ovens. Here, I discovered how beautiful the baker's daughter had become. She was no longer the skinny girl I had seen the morning I had poisoned Alexander VI's assassin. Her body was taking the shape of a woman and her dark long hair curled with a command of its own. What struck me the most was her laughter. There was so much joy in it that it was like an incomprehensive language to my desolation. Her laughter was as beautiful as the art that covered the temples of Rome. People loved to be around her. It seemed even the most downcast patrons came alive when in contact with her. Was it that her eyes expressed true interest and warmth for others? Was it the young energy of her voice?

I returned to the bakery almost every morning after that day. Fresh warm bread handed to me by this young woman with white perfect skin and brown alert eyes brimming with desire to live sustained me. I could not speak to her, but she enjoyed chatting with me happily, like a little chirping bird. She would tell me about everything good and magical she was discovering in the world. She smiled all the time with a deep tenderness that reminded me of Raphael's drawing of a Virgin. Her mood was contagious, so seeing her will allow me to carry on even on my gloomiest moments—which matched the city's mood—as rumor had it that the French troops had defeated the Pope and were marching toward Rome.

The Pope returned from war in late spring 1512. His army had been defeated at Ravenna but luckily they had killed the French commander. Without leadership, the French troops had fallen into disarray on their way to the city and never reached us. His Holiness did not summon me to his presence for several weeks. I had given most of the books and manuscripts from my trip to Tommaso Inghirami and his clerks. I saved very few to hand directly to him. With the return of the troops, the court filled with more courtiers than I had ever seen and their servants. This kept me busy in my medical practice.

Finally, one morning, the Pope invited me into his presence. As we usually did, we met at the Secret Archives room in the Sixtus Library. I was glad to receive the summon, as the previous night I had experienced particularly tormenting nightmares. I was hoping that the Pope's presence and blessings would pacify my spirit and fill me with Holy Grace.

The man I met this time was a stranger. The Vicar of Christ had aged significantly—much more than the two years I had not seen him. He still had the handsome and powerful poise that I remembered from our first encounter, but his face was haggard. He had grown a long white beard. Although in his sixties, he looked as if he had lived for a century. His back was slouched. For the first time, I detected hints of doubt in the depth of his eyes under an unusually furrowed brow.

He smiled at me without getting up from his comfortable chair but still extended his arms for an embrace instead of allowing me to kiss his feet and hands. Through his robe, I felt the sharp angles of his bone structure. Sickness, age, and defeat had embedded in his spine.

At the beginning, I entertained him with stories from my trip and the manuscripts I had discovered. But later, he closed his eyes, dismayed with the tale of the mumbling and grunting peasant priest. He then looked down, and while he was staring at the mosaics covering the floor, it seemed to me that he was staring at his soul. He had been a warrior for the Catholic Church, leading armies and keeping kings abreast. He had given his all to bring order and clean the decadent legacy he had inherited from the Borgias. He had attracted the most talented artists in the world, and made Rome the center of the universe one more time. Yet, the confused movements of his jeweled fingers and his trembling chin revealed that he might have overlooked the fundamental missions of the Church. Only to me, the mute, could he show this weakness. I had helped him rise to power and now my narrative of the misery I had encountered made me his conscience. In spite of being the representative of God on Earth, he had lost His Divine guidance. He was the Pastor of Christ, and had allowed his flock to be unprotected. Maybe he had spent too much time listening to the Classical Roman pagan thinkers who could not co-exist with Catholicism.

To lighten his mood, I returned to the topic of the manuscripts I had rescued and mentioned the books that I had separated for his personal use, for his private library. I heard the distant bells. Our reunion had lasted longer than usual. He needed time to be himself with someone who would not judge him or jockey for his favor. Crowds were a lonely place, his private chamber too dark.

"Federigo you are a good man." I knelt, and he blessed me. Finally, resting his hand on my shoulder, he pronounced: "I absolve you of your sins and failures...pray the Good Lord forgives mine." His eyes wandered around.

"Your Holiness, I pray that one day people will see what Christ Our Lord allowed you to build: a Church whose sovereign is not the puppet of foreign nations, a magnificent basilica for Saint Peter, a divinely decorated chapel, a Vatican palace with walls resembling heaven, a city resurrected from its ruins, a new race of men able to reason by them-selves…," My voice broke as he closed his eyes in silence.

"Mankind requires beauty to transcend. I've harnessed it to tran-scend me. But have I forgotten Him in my pursuit of glory? Did I be-come another Borgia? Did I expect art to evangelize for me?"

I pulled my robes over my head so he could see my naked chest and back crisscrossed with scars from the whipping and tortures I had re-ceived during my youth. "Look at my skin. This is what the Borgias gave the Catholic Church. You have been a good man. You have created the most sacred spaces for retreat and prayer." The old Pope extended his right hand, and with the tip of his index finger traced a deep scar from a cut in my collarbone down to my heart. He then recoiled.

"Thank you, Federigo. Christ put you in my path as a true friend. Now…please leave me…I want to meditate and pray. Go to my private library and place the books you brought for me in a visible place so I can go over them later. They will be a constant reminder that my mission is not complete. A military defeat is not the end of it all. I am a fighter. I am a warrior. I will keep on…there are many things that we are not equipped to comprehend. God sent me on this path with my defects and virtues. I won't stop now. I don't want to leave a cracked foundation for the Church. I have worked so my life would become the stone upon which the new Church is built."

I knelt in front of him and kissed his open palms. "Thank you Father."

"Return to your silence, Federigo. Let me linger in mine a little longer."

I left the library rooms, signaling the guards posted at the entrance not to disturb the Pope.

CHAPTER 21

STANZA DELLA SIGNATURA TWENTY-FIRST CENTURY

Breakfast has become a welcome interlude amid Anthony's new routine of chaos. Sitting with the girls is always a good way to start the day before facing the roster of maniacs he was encountering each day. The girls are in very high spirits. Elmer is taking them to a film animation studio in the city. His business partner has prepared a tour for them, promising to reveal how they create fashionable fairies with intergalactic magic powers for a theatrical movie release. Thalia is especially sparkly, glitter on the hair, glitter on her t-shirt, and glitter on her shoes. She plays with her cantaloupe. Suddenly her face becomes distracted by something else.

"When I grow up I hope to be as pretty as that girl." Anthony follows her gaze and discovers Akemi at the entrance of the breakfast room, a micro-robot at her feet like a lap dog. She is dressed in a black knee-length skirt suit with bright pink accents on the sleeves, lapels, and down the sides of the skirt. Her dark hair is half coiffed with a string of fuchsia crystals that matches her necklace and rings. Alessandro, wearing a surprisingly clean, ironed suit is with her. He is wearing a light wood rosary around his neck on top of his tie. He sees Anthony and approaches.

"Sorry to interrupt, but we got a call from the Pope's secretary this morning," his tone has lost sarcasm and shows a hint of respect driven by the humbling events of the last couple of days.

"The Pope? You should take me with you. I can give him a young girl's perspective on everything they are doing wrong to acquire and retain parishioners. That's the problem with old institutions; they don't listen to minors." Claudia puts her book down, eyeing Alessandro with heightened interest.

"Papa, do you know the pretty girl?" Anthony caresses Thalia's hair while she continues scrutinizing Akemi.

"The Pope wants to have a conversation with Akemi and me...he also requested your presence."

Anthony gets up, "Sorry girls, I need to attend this. Your grand-parents will be here any moment. Can you stay with Luca and Maria meanwhile? Alessandro, are there any new serious events I need to be aware of?"

"You mean more serious that the carnival we have been going through with the murders and revelations? We will brief you in the car." Alessandro checks Anthony from feet to head. Anthony is wearing a sports jacket, khakis, and no tie with his light blue button down shirt. An Italian would never go to a papal audience dressed like that. "I think you need to change into a dark suit and a tie."

Anthony runs upstairs and changes clothes. When he returns to the breakfast area, Melissa and Elmer arrive. Melissa's face is bright as she hugs her son-in-law. "Make Laura proud. She was a good Catholic." She blesses Anthony, making the sign of the cross start-ing with his forehead and swooping over his chest and shoulders. "Remember, there are not only bad people in the Church. Most are good. This Pope is one of the very, very good ones." Melissa is a short woman but she stands on her toes and kisses Anthony on the cheek.

Anthony grabs his briefcase after kissing the girls. The cook and the waiter have gathered around him. He has achieved a new celebrity status—again.

This time they are riding Akemi's car, a driverless red Lamborghini prototype that will never make it to the market. The Aventador four-seater is no more comfortable for Anthony than Alessandro's Fiat *Cinquecento*, as he has to sit sideways in the small rear jump seats. Akemi turns off the driverless mechanism and holds the steering wheel.

She drives fast but her moves are smooth, almost as if her mind were connected to the engine through the gears.

For a moment, they are all immersed in their thoughts. Alessandro has met with the Pope on other occasions, but he still feels awe and pride at meeting with the Pontificate. This will fuel long hours of conversation with his mother and relatives as they relish descriptions of everything involving a Papal audience—down to minute details in the furniture. Akemi's mother was Mexican. Akemi remembers her childhood, the happy years, when she lived in a small town in Mexico's northwest region. Everyone was Catholic, and Sunday mass meant seeing all her neighbors and relatives who accepted her as she was. The Pope had been the top celebrity for all those people. For Anthony, it is like jumping into a time machine. Fascinated by history and Classical literature, he realizes that being in an audience with the Pope can provide enough material to give an account of the evolution of Western culture through the centuries.

"I don't know how much you have followed the career of this Pope but it won't hurt to provide you some background. The average age for a Pope has been in the early to mid-sixties. His Holiness began his papacy in his early fifties. His twin brother is an advertising executive who lives in New York and runs one of the most prestigious digital advertising agencies focused on branding. This Pope was elected to revolutionize the Catholic Church, to bring it closer to its 1.2 billion members. From the outside, the Vatican is perceived as a modern corporation. Literary fiction and media have cultivated its image as a tightly controlled institution; the reality is that it runs like a medieval court. If you talk with insiders, they will say that all official communications are well orchestrated yet everybody loves to talk behind closed doors, spawning rumors and intrigues every hour of the day. The different offices are not coordinated, so many times information from one contradicts information from another, and chaos ensues."

"Not anymore!" Akemi snaps back.

"It still happens." Alessandro retorts firmly to Akemi. "The new Pope brought Akemi and her company to revamp the digital infrastructure for the Holy See. She has done a very good job creating an ecosystem of platforms that speak to each other and allow for more internal transparency. The problem is not the systems anymore but the people who use them. The Church is divided into reformers and traditionalists. The traditionalists could get a computer implanted in their butt and they will still protect their fiefdoms and deride anything that deviates from centuries of tradition and ceremony. The Pope knows this, and his inner circle invests too much time balancing internal struggles between the different ideologies. This Catholic Transparency Commission is more than it seems, it is a vital part of the Church's transformation."

Anthony nods. "Reinvent or die."

"Of all the bastards in the world, it had to be Avinash who started it!" remarks Akemi to herself. She was one of the architects of the new twenty-first century church, and her man had been the one to ignite the biggest attack on it—not allowing time for change to settle.

"This Pope has a better understanding of his organization than many chief executive officers of multinational companies. He understands that the Catholic Church needs to be remodeled and rebranded, which has to be evidenced through actions posted on digital channels. Right now, the other Christian churches have Sunday mass in multi-player digital platforms like Second Life and World of Warcraft. Others stream videos on YouTube and Facebook and have a plethora of Bible apps."

"He has all the tools and widgets now! They just need to use them," snaps back Akemi while negotiating a sharp swerve not to hit a bicycle, "I have presented solutions and options to him and his inner circle numerous times. It just takes them too long!" she grips the steering wheel with ferocity.

"This is not Silicon Valley," patronizes Alessandro.

Looking out to the bridge they are crossing, Anthony asks, "Why did he call us today?"

"He feels the fucking crusade for transparency and the murder investigations are out of control," barks Akemi.

Alessandro blushes with shame. "He also lacks people in his inside circle who can talk technology and branding, so he tries to see Akemi as frequently as possible, sometimes three times a month. He knows me from previous scandal investigations. Now, while he is a very progressive Pope, remember that in the Vatican, protocol is very important. Never cross your legs in front of him…"

"Go ahead, bore him with details for the greeting ceremony. At least he doesn't have to wear a veil on his hair like I have to."

• • •

Anthony expected the Pope's private meeting room to be more sumptuous but he finds it with frugal furniture. It seems all the museum-worthy artifacts have been removed and utilitarian budget-conscious items have moved in to occupy the vacated spaces. Still some of the previous luxuries cling to the room—like the ceiling decoration and the millenary carpets.

The Pope, a middle-aged man in an impeccable white robe welcomes them. He has a supersized smartphone on his lap and an 80-inch LED monitor on one of the walls. Anthony kneels and kisses the papal ring, so do Alessandro and Akemi (now wearing a wide black lace veil on her hair). After the welcoming ceremonies, the conversation jumps to a brisk start with Akemi downloading facts on the screen: Mr. Adriano Giocatelli had murdered Avinash. They knew the motive and had the weapon. They lacked the information of who the burly man at the press conference was or where he had acquired the information.

"It must have come from an insider in the Vatican," the Pope nods his head. "Someone against allowing for more transparency must have given it to him."

Anthony, fascinated with the oversimplified pattern on a millenary carpet, comments distractedly, "Could someone hack one of the five information centers that host Vatican information?"

Akemi's face turns red with rage, "No way! Those are under my contract."

"Let it go, Akemi, you have been over-stretching yourself with all of this," the pontiff holds her hand and pats it in a reassuring way. "What do we know about Mr. Giocatelli's assassin?"

"We have three suspects, your Holiness," explains Alessandro, his body stiff as a boy during his first communion. "Giocatelli bought a disposable mobile phone and made three calls with it in the hours before killing Avinash. The three persons are members of the Catholic Transparency Commission and might have similar reasons to support

Giocatelli's intent to stop the Transparency Crusade." The Pope nods and encourages Alessandro to proceed. "One is a lawyer in the American Embassy, Ellia Jones. She has been very close to the case but the background checks reveal that she is a ghost—a CIA agent who has a made-up background to erase her from any involvement in global events. The second one is a researcher from the University of Milan, Doctor Francesca Malatesta. She is Dr. Hibbert's research partner. She has come into significant wealth in the recent year through her relationship with a Saudi prince. The third suspect, and it pains me to mention this, is the Bishop for Los Angeles, Gabriel Herrera. We do not know why he would be linked to this," Anthony bites his tongue not to repeat what Sor Alegría confessed to him. "Still, he knew that Mr. Sullivan's life was in danger. He told Dr. Hibbert the night of the murder."

The Pope joins his hand as if in prayer placing his chin on his knuckles. "Anything else?"

Akemi and Alessandro nod but Anthony raises his head and ads: "There are the erotic drawings by Raphael." He gets side looks from his partners.

"I did not want to mention this since we don't have enough to conclude it is connected," Alessandro loosens his tie while the fibers of his jacket start their inevitable crumpling.

Akemi's body tightens again. She is again furious with herself. She pulls her Google Glass from her handbag and asks the device to connect with the monitor in the room. Images of the drawings found at Giocatelli's house fill the screen. She grunts with clenched teeth, cursing to herself about her lack of sleep. "We found facsimiles of erotic drawings by Raphael on the stairs of Giocatelli's mansion the night of the murder. They had recently been acquired from Christie's. The assassin took the originals with him or her."

Anthony decides to keep his mouth shut and not forward the question about the assassin's story written on the back of the drawings or their connection with recent findings inside the Secret Archives.

"I am really concerned with all that is going on. The marches around the world calling for us to open our archives are growing and becoming more frequent. I worry that I am doing too little too late. Where does transformation begin? Priests' celibacy, abortion, inside corruption, wealth inequality? The inner opponents of my Church reforms are becoming stronger," the Pope covers his face with his hands for a minute. "I can see you are doing as much as you can. Akemi, you have to rest a little bit. You have an army working for you. I am praying to God to show us the way. Let this not be the century when the Catholic Church collapses, weakened from the cracks in its foundations. Let this be the era in which the storm washes the filth and clears the path to new horizons." The Pope meditates for a moment and then looks straight at Anthony. "Be honest. What do you think of the members we assembled for the Catholic Transparency Conference?"

Anthony takes a minute before answering. "It feels like one of the many scholar conferences I have attended around the world: lots of words going nowhere. Some of the presenters are brilliant; others have no clue what they are talking about. Everybody has his or her own agenda. Still, it's a good thing that the Conference exists. The Transparency topic is being discussed; the media and public feel the Vatican is doing something to answer their questions and demands. I worry we might be trivializing some of the tragedies stemming from the many Church scandals. It is civilized and rational to discuss horrible Church failures in the context of Transparency, but I would be a very different person if a priest abused one of my daughters. I am not a religious person. My late wife was, so I respect the Catholic Church, and I want it to get past this moment."

"Saint Augustine said: 'This is the very perfection of man, to find out his own imperfections.' The Church is a living thing, and may God allow me to find and fix many of its imperfections during my pontificate. I rarely sleep well at night. The ship has been floundering for years, and we have not been quick enough to repair the leaks."

"As I said, I am not a religious man, but if you don't find and fix them, the Catholic Church will become totally irrelevant to the new generations."

"Why would that be a problem if you don't believe in us?"

"I believe in the Church legacy. Just because religion can fail doesn't mean we don't need spirituality. When my wife was dying, I called to God. I prayed. I looked for answers in old Greek and Roman philosophers and literature. I lit candles to saints in my house because it gave me something to do besides wait for the inevitable. The global economy, the corrupt governments, greed and hypocrisy ambushing the weak, the naïve...human nature wants us to be part of a bigger plan that makes some sense of the pain and suffering. You have 1.2 billion people with their souls looking to you for guidance. You have the gravitas to invoke the major spiritual questions of our time. The media apparatus listens to you. I am willing to participate in as many Transparency Conferences as needed if you bring hope and sense to your flock." Silence tangled with dust particles illuminated by a stream of light from a roof window hangs around them. Anthony lowers his head. "I have probably said too much and out of protocol, but you asked for the truth."

The Pope closes his eyes for a moment. "It is more complex than that, but you are correct. Being Pope will deplete every cell in my body. I will age and become sick in a crusade to change what has been the same for two thousand years. I give thanks to Christ every day for this honor. I bless the three of you because you are honest about what you are doing. No secret ulterior motive. You will do it regardless of the politics around you. I bless you." His extended arm makes the sign of the cross, stirring the air so the dust particles floating in the stream of light come alive, swirling like miniature hurricanes.

• • •

Immersed in silence, the three walk through the Vatican gardens.

"I have to share some things I have learned about Gabriel Herrera," Anthony's voice is low. Akemi and Alessandro nod.

"We should also ensure that you have complete access to the files for Ellia Jones and Francesca Malatesta." Alessandro talks to Anthony as an equal.

"Are we still having dinner with your research partner tonight?" Akemi hopes for the plan to be canceled so she can sleep, but she knows that she has to interrogate Francesca and her boyfriend. Anthony assents.

"Let's go to a meeting room through the museum, it will be a shortcut." Everybody agrees with Alessandro's plan.

They go up an external staircase and open a door into a small corridor. Anthony notices that the room next to them is the *Sala della Signatura,* where Raphael Sanzio painted *School of Athens,* the fresco that assured his ascent to fame. He pulls them into the room that earned its name from having been used as the Pope's private library in the sixteenth century—the room where he would sign letters and documents. The room is empty; tourists will soon storm in, crowding its space. They look at the murals, the artists, and court celebrities of Raphael's time embodying saints, Biblical figures and philosophers, mathematicians and artists of the Classical era. Saints are located next to pagan gods. Alessandro smiles proudly as the images and colors of Italian culture unite the three of them, wrapping around their minds. It seems each color has a voice. The air becomes thick with light as if the lines around the contours of Aristotle and Socrates deconstruct and extend to bind the three twenty-first-century bodies together in an intangible form. Raphael's images are not representing a scene different from that of the twenty-first century. Human kind is still looking for answers. Absorbed by the murals, the light sepias remind Anthony of the sand in Redondo Beach at sunrise. His back touches Akemi's, and he feels her heat twisting around his spine. They turn, and he gets lost in her eyes. She is gazing directly at him.

CHAPTER 22

STANZA DELLA SIGNATURA
SIXTEENTH CENTURY

Day 5 - December 10, 1521

I see them, upstretched, walking on tip toes, circling around me as their white wings spill and tumble objects on my twin desks. Angels are knitting a web around me with strands of their long golden hair. They know demons will arrive soon to carry my soul to hell. The angels want the web they are knitting to trip the demons and make them plummet back to the underworld. They are like winged spiders surrounding me in a cocoon of light that can shelter me until I finish writing my story.

As instructed, I went to Julius II's apartments to drop the books and manuscripts I had brought for him from the Germanic States. He had his personal library in the new papal apartments, one floor above the Vatican library where we had recently spoken. The room was also called Stanza della Signatura, as it was where he signed official documents, adjacent to the chapel that his uncle Sixtus had built. I had not been there in two years—since I went on my journey.

When your life is without purpose, every step takes an effort. Every stride has to be calculated and measured. My arms ached with the weight of the manuscripts, but not as much as my mind did with conflicting concepts and ideas.

The first thing I noticed when I entered the new room was that the floors were laid with tiny mosaics in patterns reminding me of the highest workmanship I had witnessed in pagan Roman temples. It was a warm spring day, and the smell of flax seed oil and drying plaster merged with the sound of soft conversations and mortars grinding pigments. A radiant evening light filtered through an open window along with a current of cool air. My eyes instinctively followed the luminescent stream. The sight before me hit with a force as if the torrent of light from the window had exploded, filling the room with a summer meteor. My arms went limp, the manuscripts tumbling to the floor as my eyes dove into the magnificent murals covering the walls.

When entering, I had ignored the group of artists applying the finishing touches to one of the paintings. Raphael Sanzio was surrounded by his apprentices while he inspected progress and provided guidance. The manuscripts had created a commotion as they fell from my arms. He came to stand next to me. His eyes followed my gaze, and we united through the spectacle of his creation. He was seeing through my eyes, I was breathing light though the images in front of me. Christ presided over the celestial court with theologians debating at his feet. The composition made color a language of its own—one that I yearned to access—but then my eyes wandered to Apollo surrounded by poets.

Raphael had done it.

I could feel his pride through his gentle hand on my shoulder as he sensed the many emotions moving through me.

Raphael had effortlessly merged pagan antiquity with Christianity. There was only beauty, no conflict.

Amazed, I turned to the fresco next to me. I stumbled backward to get a better view but my legs failed, and I fell. In front of me, Greek and Roman philosophers and scientists gathered to speak amicably among themselves inside an area that reminded me of the half-raised walls inside Saint Peter's basilica. I fell to my knees and prayed. On his feet, Raphael prayed next to me as if we were in Sunday mass.

Before I could finish a Hail Mary, the magnificence of it all overpowered me, and I became like an epileptic body taken by a seizure. Inside this room, I felt protected. I could be the person my father wanted me to be. I could be myself. My spiritual struggle vanished. Plato and Aristotle could stand next to Saint Augustine and Saint Thomas Aquinas. My grandfather and his German friend would have found sense in their conversations.

I recognized Michelangelo as a lonely figure sitting by himself on the steps of the Basilica. Despite their rivalry, Raphael had paid tribute to his genius by incorporating him in the picture. I felt Raphael's hand clench my shoulder; he wanted me to look at him, not at Michelangelo's image. My gaze went to Dante and Petrarch, who were portrayed next to Apollo. Splendor co-existed in cultures old and new. The images reconciled pain and wonder, injustice and knowledge, filth and the sublime.

Raphael disregarded my sobs. He signaled to the poets painted as a group around a window: "Look, Federigo, Catullus is here. If it were not for the texts you gave me, I would not have understood his power. He became one of my favorites. Thanks to you, I even read him in Latin. While my understanding is incomplete, I relish the rhythm and musicality of his text. Plus the ladies love when I murmur his poems into their ears—even if they don't know what I am saying." Raphael's voice made me feel like returning to a home where my brother would be waiting safely for me. I was wailing. So much pain was surfacing to be washed away by shape and color. "Thank you for giving me Catullus in Italian. You helped me also with Virgil and Eneas and Homer...Look, I used the marble busts from the Pope's collection to copy their faces so they could all be here!" He signaled to the authors' images. "But Ovid and Catullus...they understand me."

I raised my wet face. His delicate and noble features merged with the surroundings. He was one with the great philosophers, astrologers, and artists of all times. Light channeled through him, and I was the vessel capturing it. In that room, young Raphael had seized the vibrant elements of mankind's spirit, understanding our dualities, accepting our imperfections and contradictions. He understood that human spirit is one. The past and the present cannot be separated in civilization, they feed on each other.

I prostrated and kissed Raphael's slippers as I had only done to the Pope. His apprentices watched from a distance, uncertain whether to mock or show gratitude to me. Raphael's hand stroked my bald head, resting on my ear, holding it very lightly, cupping it with his fingers. "Get up, Federigo. This stance only celebrates His Holiness Pope Julius II and his moment in history. We have been blessed to live during this time period where old and new converge to create the pinnacle of art and thought."

My tears subsided. I smiled at him, feeling connected. He returned a shy smile illuminated with accomplishment and recognition. He understood I needed more time with his creations. With an almost imperceptible trace from his fingers, he touched my eyelids and signaled to his entourage to follow him and empty the room so I could be left alone.

I remained kneeling, absorbing every detail in the murals while the sunlight entering the room became red and dimmed. For the first time in many years, I felt I was part of something.

CHAPTER 23

HEAVY FOOD FOR DINNER

fter the Transparency Conference meeting, Anthony gets time to work with Francesca at the Secret Archives study room. He reads the latest fragment of text sent by Akemi, then spends his afternoon working on his paper about the newly discovered *Catullus* poems. It is a very satisfying set of hours. Opening old Roman texts and cross-referencing the new-found verses offers a scholar's ultimate gratification. He scrutinizes every bit of Tacitus's and Julius Caesar's biographers that can help him to identify the historical moment and make connections to the text. For Anthony, the work is almost like erotic stimulation.

Francesca's hyperactivity is at its best. Her outstanding memory allows her to read a line and identify similarities with other writings. She reads a phrase and immediately gets three more books to support her intuitive revelations. She types on her laptop like a pianist at the climax of a concert.

Anthony's experience is almost musical, too. He reads and re-reads the poems, allowing himself to go with the tempo and melodic inflections. The overt sexual descriptions and tones, and the crass humor become intoxicating. This beat is ancient, a language that understands the primeval convulsions of pleasure, be they around a fire during the Stone Age or in Caesar's sophisticated court. The text acquires a voice of its own. Anthony understands how Carl Orff, a musician from the twentieth century could take *Catullus*'s poems and make them into a cantata celebrating sensuality. *"Da mi basia, Da mi basia mille, Deinde centum. Kiss me, Kiss me a thousand times, And then a hundred."*

By dinnertime, only the image of Akemi's thighs allows him to detach himself from the laptop and the ancient manuscripts.

He and Francesca go to *Osteria dell'Orso*, the oldest restaurant in Rome, situated in a palace dating back to the year 1400 and reopened in 2001 by Gualterio Marchesi, considered the creator of the new Italian cuisine. The venue was selected by Ahmed, Francesca's boyfriend, who is already seated at a table on the second floor close to windows overlooking the street. He is drinking a very expensive bottle of red wine.

"*Ciao, bellisima*!" Ahmed has dark skin framed by a very short and tight black beard. He wears a discreet Muslim headdress, a kaffiya, with a touch of jewelry, a delicate circle of small blue diamonds that match the ones covering his Rolex, on the black cord holding it. "Anthony! I have heard so many good things about you! Francesca could not have been luckier to get you as research partner."

"*Piacere*, Ahmed! Francesca is so much happier since she has been with you!" Their warmth makes Anthony feel a twinge of remorse. Francesca, one of the main suspects?

"Here, take a seat. I went ahead and ordered some wine. Walterio here has a great cava so I got us a Leroy Laticieres-Chambertin Grand Cru. It is amazing!"

"Sorry," and Anthony truly feels sorry, "red wine upsets my stomach. I'll have a sip of it and a beer."

"It is ok, ok. I will still order the tasting menu to please you. Their pigeon is exquisite."

"I'm truly sorry again...I am a vegetarian."

Ahmed laughs out loudly while Francesca holds his arm and admonishes with soft tenderness. "*Benne*, Ahmed, let Tony order what he wishes. We can ask the chef if he can prepare a vegetarian tasting menu for him. This is always the case with Ahmed, he is too generous. He wants everyone around him to experience the very best money can buy."

Ahmed passes an arm around Francesca's shoulders. "You will forgive me, my friend, but Ramadan is quickly approaching, and I want to enjoy eating before the time of fast." Ahmed's English accent is good; however, Anthony would have expected it to have a stronger British inflection.

"Where is your girlfriend?" Francesca slaps Anthony's face playfully while she winks at him.

"She is not my girlfriend, and she is submerged in work so I wonder if she will be able to make it." Francesca and Ahmed exchange looks.

"Is she the one leading the investigation of Giocatelli's murder?" Ahmed inquires with perfectly timed informality.

"She is part of the security team inside the Vatican. The Italian police is responsible for the case."

"Not the Central Security Corps or the Swiss Guard?" inquires Francesca with conspicuous interest.

"Everyone is involved! You can ask Akemi all you want to know when she arrives."

Francesca winks at Anthony and moves closer to him. "Are you very involved in the investigation? Is there any juicy gossip you can share with us? We'll keep it to ourselves. We promise!"

Anthony takes a moment to answer, he weighs his words. "It is a little confusing. First, the focus was to find Avinash's murderer, and now we are trying to find the killer of a killer. It all gets very complicated."

"Do you have good leads?" Ahmed sips from his glass of wine in a casual way—but deep in the darkest part of his eyes, curiosity is ablaze.

"You guys probably know more about the Italian police's *modus operandi*. To them, everyone is suspect. All of us in the Transparency Congress are suspects." Francesca and Ahmed exchange glances.

"I am sure your Embassy is helping…" Francesca rubs the big color stones in her rings with her index finger as if they were a magic lamp.

"Ellia Jones is not part of the inner investigation circle." Francesca releases an imperceptible sigh at Anthony's answer. "But we keep Ambassador Bradbury informed."

"Is Ellia in those meetings with the Ambassador?" Francesca plays with a piece of bread.

"She is. Since my arrest she has taken special interest in my 'well-being.' I think the Ambassador relies on her to get an objective perspective of events." The space between the three gets crowded. Anthony can feel the heat from Francesca's and Ahmed's bodies as they lean in too close, eagerly absorbing his every word and gesture—as if Anthony were the expensive red wine. "But you are friends with Ellia, aren't you, Francesca? Why not ask her directly?"

Francesca flutters her hands and leans backward. "She is just an acquaintance I met in Milan." From Ahmed's murky stare at his girlfriend, Anthony realizes there is more than what is being shared.

"How did you meet her?" Anthony asks.

Ahmed looks at his diamond-encrusted Rolex and exclaims, "Akemi seems to be running very late. Should we order some appetizers?"

Usually Francesca would be volunteering information in an exuberant way. Noticing she remains silent after his question, Anthony decides to change the conversation topic. "Are we waiting also for your friend the Los Angeles Bishop? Weren't you going to invite him too?" Anthony wants to know more about Gabriel Herrera.

"He won't make it. He has been very busy with the Transparency Conference. He is also working on a big, controversial study about the celibacy vows of priests and nuns. You know that has been a hot topic."

Anthony narrows his eyes, "Yes, it has been challenged over the last two thousand years. I can see how this could be a topic of his particular interest."

Ahmed has been reading the menu to select appetizers but he comments in an off-handed way. "Why would you think so?"

Anthony realizes he might have said too much. "Well, he is from Los Angeles, you know. It is not that celibacy is a big tenet of the entertainment industry. Last time I saw Gabriel Herrara was at one of the Transparency Commission meetings. I think he was checking the women around him while talking to Giocatelli. By the way, does everyone on the Commission know everyone else? Am I the only clueless one?"

Francesca chuckles in a forced way. "You are definitely the newcomer. The intellectual community linked to the Church is tightly knit. You should not be surprised by this. We all are connected in some way or another..."

"However..." Ahmed interrupts his girlfriend, "From what Francesca tells me, Giocatelli and Herrera were very good friends. Herrera had gone to many soirées at Giocatelli's. He is the kind of guest who would be welcomed at Giocatelli's mansion without an invitation." Ahmed raises an eyebrow.

"I imagine you know that because you were also invited to those soirées?"

Francesca repeats her forced chuckle, "You have met Gabriel. He is such a charming and worldly man that it is no surprise that he and Giocatelli would become close."

"I don't know if can call his skillset 'charming.' But I can see how he would connect to a big businessman in worldly matters. How close were you two with Giocatelli?"

"*Caro*, your girlfriend is running very late!" exclaims Francesca as she looks at her own diamond-encrusted Rolex.

"I believe she just arrived." The smell of orange flower fills Anthony's nostrils, sending small electric shocks through his lungs, heralding Akemi's presence.

Sometimes exhaustion distorts the perception of time. Akemi feels she is walking through a marsh as she crosses the room. She has been connected all day, sometimes working three conference calls at the same time while browsing information. She is wearing her Google Glass advanced prototype so all the information about the restaurant is flowing to the screen.

"Akemi, you have met Francesca. This is her boyfriend, Ahmed." Instead of answering, Akemi zooms the camera on her glasses on Ahmed's face and gestures in the air so a cloud-based program for face identification can run a background check on him. Ahmed and Francesca linger with their empty hands outstretched for a minute and decide to return to their seats when Akemi takes her place at the table absorbed in the images projected on her glasses. "She does not have the best social skills," apologizes Anthony, shrugging his shoulders to minimize Akemi's rudeness. He smiles to the uncomfortable couple. "Should we order? I am hungry!"

Akemi reaches for a glass and pours red wine to the brim taking a deep gulp. "This is good stuff. It is not only expensive but also hard to get." For the first time, she addresses her companions while reaching out to the bottle and zooming her glasses' camera on the label. The price appears instantly.

"I am glad someone will drink what Tony here will leave!" exclaims Ahmed testing how to work his charm on Akemi.

But Akemi ignores the comment. She leans and whispers into Anthony's ear: "I sent you more of the monk's restored text before I left the office. I am sure you relished it."

Anthony smiles to her, tense—like a wolf in mating season—by her proximity, but uncomfortable by her lack of manners. He decides the easiest course of action is to engage in a group conversation. "Akemi, our friends were asking me about Giocatelli's investigation. They want to know who is heading it up."

"You can read about it in the newspapers"

"Can you give them more details?" Anthony gives a soft kick to Akemi under the table.

"Ahem, yes. It is a collaborative effort between the Swiss Guard, the Security Corps, and the Italian Police. My company, Ghostwire, is providing the Big Data." Akemi surveys the menu. "I have not eaten since the morning. Can they make a tasting menu with only entrees? Forget about the fineries and the foams—the chef loves making flavored-infused foams—give me lamb and pork and pigeons. Online reviews say that the pigeon here is outstanding. They leave them pink in the center so you can taste the blood." The waiter takes notes with perfect efficiency. "What is your story, Ahmed?" she asks—although looking at Francesca.

"What Akemi means is that being a member of the royal Saudi family makes you very interesting. They are very private." Anthony is truly curious.

"No, I meant what is your story? What are you doing socializing with non-Muslims and dating someone with no money?"

Anthony tries again to soften the conversation but Ahmed extends his open palm for him to stop. "I like direct people. I prefer them much more than ones who try to be nice but are thinking that we Muslims are all terrorists. My culture is ancient and very sophisticated. The Saudi royal family is known to be discerning about its friends. I fell from grace with my family. I went to college in the US, and let's say I became weakened by the temptations of the West: too many drugs and alcohol, too many women. My family disapproves of scandal, and I became fodder for the tabloids. They tried to take me back to Saudi Arabia and imprison me in a palace. My brother visited me and declared I was no longer competent to make decisions for myself. To him, I had become insane. Fortunately, I had enough wealth of my own to dismiss his babbling. I escaped from his grip and traveled the world. The suffering I saw changed me. Misery does not discriminate based on religion. Human exploitation exists in all cultures. During my time in Milan, I met Francesca, who completed my transformation from vices with her zest for life and broad love of culture."

"I also became more stable, thanks to you...before I had too many men...and a few women; until I met you, I required a different lover every week." Francesca holds Ahmed's hand with both of hers. Her multicolored nails stroke his hairy, strong fingers like rings of living precious stones.

"His money was a big help. I am certain," Akemi snarls as she begins eating with eagerness, holding food with both hands instead of using cutlery. "Oh, my Lord, this is too good. Who could guess that foam could bring so much flavor to the crust on a Rock Cornish hen!" A reddish liquid drips down her chin.

Francesca extends one of her hands to hold Anthony's left hand. "I do not know if Anthony has told you my story. I come from a family with noble origins. There is a countess title in our lineage, but it was not relevant to my parents. They were intellectuals and disdained the pursuit of wealth. They had enough money from my grandparents. In their brainy arrogance, they became staunch critics and thus enemies of Berlusconi and his cronies. When he became a media super power, and later president of Italy, he crushed us like cockroaches. He fomented enough scandals in the media for my parents to become exiled from Italian intellectual circles. Their wealth was expropriated by the government when it was linked to fake frauds the president concocted. After a comfortable and pampered childhood, I experienced hunger and despair in my teenage years." She places in her mouth a crostini with cheese and fennel foam topped with Beluga caviar, savoring memories of her childhood. "We were always moving, from a bad to a worse address. Old acquaintances did not answer our pleas for help. Our day to day became more desperate. My parents became depressed. They were very tortured people. They committed double suicide. I discovered them coming back from high school. They took an overdose of Valium before sitting to read their favorite books on their favorite couches, the only remaining furniture from their former life." She sips the wine, hoping the alcohol will expunge the image. "I had to work very hard to pay college. Literature and art were the beautiful links to a happy past."

"Yes, I had information about you. It is always good to hear a first-hand account corroborating the data. After college, you became one of the brightest scholars in Italy on topics related to Classical literature." Akemi gnarls on a lamb chop bone.

"So you have checked my background?" Francesca leans away from the table.

"She checked the backgrounds of everyone in the Catholic Transparency Commission," intercedes Anthony while carefully slicing a wild mushroom frittata covered in a truffle and gold leaf foam.

"So then you know about the gifts that Ahmed has given me and about the house he just bought for us in Rome…"

"Yes."

"What else do you know?" Francesca and Ahmed stare at her, their forks frozen before poking a slice of meat.

"What else should I know?" Akemi wipes the lamb juices from her plate with a slice of rustic bread.

"Are we suspects?" ventures Francesca. The response is a long silence while Akemi chews her food with relish and Anthony cuts his frittata in little squares. "What else will you tell us about the investigation? Because if we are suspects we deserve to know and to prove you wrong."

"Should you be suspects?" As soon as Akemi asks the question, the screen on her Google Glass illuminates with the results of the face match. Ahmed is not a Saudi prince. The software cannot find him in Saudi Arabia or any Muslim country. In response to the surprise, Akemi extends her hand under the table and grabs Anthony's inner thigh. The contact makes him jump but he reaches out to his bottle of beer to cover the movement. The program also brings some information about the real Prince Ahmed. Distractedly, she starts caressing Anthony's leg. The story matches what Ahmed described. The real Prince Ahmed had studied in an American college. He had led a profligate life of drugs and excesses. His brother had tried to bring him back home and failed. The real Prince Ahmed had died eighteen months ago from binge drinking in a transgender bar. The family had hidden the news to prevent further scandals. For the media, Ahmed was still alive inside a private palace where he was rebuilding his morals. Now Akemi tightens her grip around Anthony's flesh as she evaluates her next move. Anthony gulps his beer trying to control his stimulated body from shaking.

"The food is outstanding!" remarks Anthony, signaling the waiter to get another drink. He reaches for Akemi's hand under the table but before he can touch her Akemi gets up and grabs her handbag.

"I have more important things to do now. I have to go." She does not thank them or say goodbye, only walks away.

"Is she always this pleasant?" questions Francesca.

"Oooh. Sometimes even more!" Anthony hopes the next dish on the menu is a light dessert.

CHAPTER 24

MICHELANGELO'S CEILING

O nly when he reaches his hotel room does Anthony let his body relax. The girls are sleeping with their grandparents. He is by himself. His clothes smell of Akemi, and he decides to sleep in them while collapsing into the bed. He notices there are more materials on his laptop. He is eager to read what Akemi sent so he props himself up with pillows. Somehow the rude woman at dinner and the one sharing letters seem to be two different people.

Day 5 – December 10, 1521 (Continued)

I have mentioned how Julius II had brought the best artists in the world to Rome. Despite being the youngest, Raphael had become the most celebrated not only for his talent but also for his pleasant demeanor. He always had a pleasant gesture or word for those around him. The most talented young apprentices lined up to work with him. This was in great contrast with the rude manners from Michelangelo, who was admired and respected but whose fierce nature made him very unpopular. Despite his recognized genius, Michelangelo's intensity was intimidating to most. He had locked himself in Sixtus's chapel to complete the project the Pope had assigned him: to paint the uneven ceiling with frescoes. Most of the time, he worked by himself as he would either fire his apprentices quickly or they would walk away offended by his mistreatment. All of Rome was impatient to see his work. Only gossip about the painting motifs circulated in the secret corridors and back alleyways of the palace. No one knew the facts. Rumor was that the Pope had grown impatient, too. Raphael was losing sleep. He worried that once Michelangelo's paintings were revealed, he would forfeit his status as the best.

It was in the middle of spring. I had been studying in the main papal library. The day was so warm and bright that the Vatican palace was almost empty, so I was relishing that the clamor from courtiers gossiping around me was not present. Suddenly, I heard someone dragging his feet as if burdened by a tragedy. Someone was approaching from the library room that held the Roman Classics. The movements had such sad intensity that I put down my book and discovered Raphael staring at me.

"You have helped me in the past, you can help me now." His breathing was agitated.

I questioned him about the matter with signs and gestures.

"It is the same matter as before, only worse. Come with me." He pulled my arm, making me stand up. I left my book open on the table as I followed him through corridors. He moved quickly. A few of the courtiers on our way tried to stop and exchange pleasantries with him but he pushed his way past, determined to show me the source of his distress. "Michelangelo argued with the Pope. They have not been on good terms lately. But yesterday, His Holiness entered the chapel unannounced. He had to force his entry as the doors were bolted and his knocks got no response. Michelangelo was painting close to the ceiling. Resentful of the intrusion, he threw a bucket from his scaffolding at His Holiness. He could have crippled him! The Pope is furious. They got into such a heated argument that Michelangelo had to escape from Rome during the night, afraid for his life. For certain he is seeking refuge in Florence..."

The fight should be a reason for celebration to Raphael, not grief.

"I had been trying to see Michelangelo's ceiling, so I went to Bramante this morning as soon as I heard that Michelangelo had fled." We stopped in front of the double doors leading into the Sistine Chapel. Raphael pulled a key from his pocket. As the Papal Architect, Bramante had the keys to every room in the palace and had given Raphael a copy. "Bramante was delighted to help me." Raphael's face drained out of blood as he pushed the doors wide open, ushering me into the empty chapel. As soon as we crossed the threshold, he slammed the heavy doors shut to block access to anybody who could be on our trail.

His expression struggled between dismay and ecstasy. His eyes had become a dark vacuum. The fear of not becoming transcendent created a void in his spirit. "What Michelangelo has accomplished in this chapel is the pinnacle of human creation." Parts of the ceiling were covered by the scaffolding but what was displayed on top of us was a marvel beyond my wildest dreams.

Raphael and my gaze merged again as we looked up, this time to admire the makings of his main rival. Our eyes traveled together across the Bible stories depicted above us, from God's creation of the sun and stars to Adam and Eve's downfall to Noah's story. No doubt was left for me; Michelangelo was a master of perspective and color! He was able to take the distortion of the uneven ceiling to create perfect scenes. I felt I was admiring God during the actual moment of creation. Michelangelo's lines and figures jumped out of the uneven surfaces as if they were colored sculptures made from a sublime, incorporeal stone with more gravitas than marble. He took the scenes from the Bible but the human spirit reigned in them. He painted naked bodies to decorate a chapel like the Romans had done to represent their gods! He had dared to paint naked human bodies in a Catholic chapel but their images were not erotic—they conveyed the power that allows us to rise above the filth. Nakedness became irrelevant when my gaze and Raphael's entwined in the movement and vigor held in the muscles and poses. Even the prophets and the image of God were a celebration of humankind. We could interpret most of the images except twenty paired nude male bodies seated around the biblical scenes. The first in the series were almost symmetrical, but to Raphael's horror—and my admiration—the scattered figures gained movement and freedom until each pair's postures bore no relation to each other. Maybe because these figures had no relationship to the Bible, we spent the most time admiring them. They represented the pure beauty of the human body without the need for any narrative. I then understood why His Holiness Julius II in his virtuous perception of every artist's potential had commissioned Michelangelo to execute this work. Raphael's voice brought me out of my reverie. His brow was wrinkled with a deep melancholy but his cheeks were glowing with admiration.

"I'm uncertain that I would have been able to tackle this enterprise with success. The ceiling is so uneven and my paintings appear so shallow compared to his. It all comes back to what I have told you before: Michelangelo was raised and educated in the finest court in Florence under the Medici. He can read and speak Latin. He understands the Roman thinkers and architects. He has studied their treaties on perspective and aesthetics. This has given him a power I lack. I don't know if I will ever accomplish something like this chapel's ceiling."

Talking soothed him. Little by little, the sparks I knew inhabited his eyes were returning. We sat on a bench for hours with our necks aching from spending too much time looking up. Raphael could talk freely as the chapel's emptiness provided refuge from indiscreet ears. As we sat, his hand touched a book abandoned on top of the bench. Raphael picked it up and read the title. "Michelangelo is connected to deeper ideas. Look, 'The Nature of Things' by Lucretius. I have too much work to study and think as much as I should. If only you could talk, you could become the part of my spirit that spends time studying. It would be our secret. You would read and then share ideas and challenging concepts with me while I kept working at the pace I am working now. Did you know that I have declined projects from the King of France because I just can't get enough time to work on everything I already have?" His face brightened; his forehead was proud. "My workshop is great, and each one of the artists in it contributes in unique ways with his talents, but still I have more commissions than I can deliver..."

I hesitated, but taking the book from his hands, my lips formed words and phrases paraphrasing what Lucretius had written centuries ago: "Humans are not unique compared to other living creatures. Our soul dies when we do and there is no afterlife. We all are made of the same miniscule particles. There are no angels, demons, or ghosts. All religions are delusions."

Raphael stood up abruptly, stumbling with surprise. If seeing Raphael's paintings had been a turning point in his spiritual struggles, hearing the mute speak was the miracle, the signal of encouragement Raphael had been seeking since discovering Michelangelo's accomplishment.

"The sound of your voice..." he babbled, "our existences always have new wonders as long as our spirit is strong." I explained that I was a spy for the Pope and because of this I had to pretend I was mute. The hole in my tongue was the invented proof for my story. When I said this, he held my tongue between his delicate fingers and poked at the hole with curiosity. His thumbprints tasted of flaxseed oil and mineral pigments that were too embedded in his pores for water and soap to ever remove. I continued whispering to him, and through my words he regained his strength as if each whisper was sustenance. "Raphael, please keep my secret. I'll be honored to nurture your spirit. Lucretius said the highest goal in our lives is the enhancement of pleasure and the reduction of pain. I have gone through too much pain already..."

"And I have had as much pleasure as anyone can hope for," he interrupted me.

"Lucretius not only referred to physical pleasure. He turned to knowledge because delusion is pain and the biggest obstacle to pleasure. Understanding the nature of things is the antidote to pain."

The sun had moved, and twilight obscured the paintings above us. "I don't agree with Lucretius because I believe in Jesus Christ. I find God in the beauty of Lucretius's verses. I hear God in religious music, and I see Him in your paintings. I am ignorant of pleasure. I am not a worldly man but I have felt ecstasy through human creation and thoughts. Maybe Lucretius is right, and everything is made of invisible particles floating in the void. Still, where Lucretius saw pleasure, I see God, and you—a true friend—are the embodiment of God's will not only for your art but also for your hunger to learn."

We remained silent for awhile, and he touched my lips with his fingertips still amazed at the miracle of my voice. Then he responded: "I believe in pleasure. If God did not wish us to feel He would not have created our senses. I find glory through my senses...ideas, painting...and women."

"I make an oath to help you. I will read and research anything you require. I'll help you create as much as you can. I'll read so you can use your time with brushes and pigments. We just need to meet in places where people cannot hear us." Raphael embraced me as a twin soul. The smell of lime plaster and wool came from his black clothes—the welcoming smell of a brother receiving me when returning home.

CHAPTER 25

GIVE ME KISSES - SIXTEENTH CENTURY

Day 5 – December 10, 1521 (Continued)

*A*fter the day we spied on Michelangelo's work, the new measure of time was conversations with Raphael. How we talked! He kept rejecting commissions from the most powerful and influential people in Europe because he lacked the time to oblige; yet I was surprised at how much time he allocated for our conversations in his busy life. We met at least four times every week. Finding areas where no one could hear us was easy; I had spent years moving in stealth through the Vatican Palace looming in its secret places. To arrange the meeting point, I sent notes to his studio. The writing was in invisible ink that he read by applying lemon juice to the paper.

In the papal court everyone is like a spider, crawling through corridors and behind walls, weaving thin webs in search of advancement—hungry to catch a fly and devour it—arrogant in their power while alive but becoming empty hulks and insignificant shells of dust after death. The difference between courtiers and me is that I was well aware that I was a predator ready to poison a victim. This led to my meeting place of choice with Raphael, a secret room on top of the Borgia bell tower. There, as if I were king of the nest, I raised spiders to harvest their venom. The walls, ceiling, and floors were covered with layers of webs that created the illusion of being inside the bulb of an Egyptian cotton flower. The only light in the venue came from two portholes that reigned over the city's red-tiled roofs, the river, and its bridges, the Pantheon dome and the cylinder of Castel Saint Angelo's walls.

Raphael and I would sit and dialogue safely inside our cocoon. He talked about his love conquests while I captured critters in glass flasks. I told him that the spiders were for my medical practice. I described to him how three days a week I served as physician for the court servants. Our conversations soon became personally disturbing to me as he introduced a unique perspective on beauty—that of the creator—and on kindness—that of the blessed and fortunate ones. This was a stark contrast to what I had to share with him, yet he seemed to relish the stories, as he could never have imagined the horrors of my tortures at the monastery and the vile corruption I had suffered under. At that point, I did not tell him that I had killed the deacons just that Christ had protected us all by making them die in a short period of time. Another topic that quickly leaked into our dialogues was the irrefutable and uncontrollable presence of carnal pleasures. He questioned me about the meaning of knowledge. Did it include the physical experiences and stimulations a man had with a woman? Did it include understanding the play of light on shapes and color in human bodies to evoke their sexuality, or was the human body's beauty sexless, as Michelangelo portrayed it in Sixtus Chapel? Did Lucretius focus only on intellectual quests or should our exploration include all bodily pleasures? Where were joy and suffering in this? What about humor? I was filling his voice and mind as he opened worlds for me; he was free to talk carelessly not required to measure the political impact of his every word as he usually would do. He could go beyond himself and explore his small role in the bigger Creation.

On many occasions, we would meet fortuitously at court parties or events, especially when I had to poison someone during a banquet. We would keep our distance then and barely exchange the words of casual acquaintances. Raphael was always surrounded by a crowd of admirers. When he engaged in a philosophical argument, he would pull me into his circle with a look and I would later provide perspective on the way he was tackling the arguments of others. With time and my help, the quotations from Classical text he would use to support his points of view rivaled anyone educated in Florence. He even memorized lines from Catullus poems: "Da mi basia, Da mi basia mille, Deinde centum. Give me kisses, give me a thousand kisses and then a hundred" to seduce educated women.

During those days, I forced myself to attend events I had avoided in the past. While I still did not participate in carnivals, I went to see a popular play: La Calandria by a cardinal named Bibbiena. So I could discuss how the complementary smaller performances during the intermezzos trivialized Roman culture as they portrayed myths like Jason's quest in a trite and base manner. We spent a long time laughing at a Venus chariot where the goddess appeared seated and holding a lighted taper in her hand while two scantily clad Amorini frolicked around the doves pulling the chariot.

But there was one palace where chance would bring us together frequently and integrate both of us into a privileged social circle. This was the Palace of Love, built by the banker Agostino Chigi, not to live in but to celebrate the most extravagant parties and gatherings in the city. The hostess and organizer of the many events, a woman called Imperia, enjoyed having Raphael and me as members of the colorful entourage she hand-picked for her patron. Despite his many affairs, Agostino had assigned this role to her because she was the most renowned courtesan in Rome, and her beauty and graceful manners at the dinner table, coupled with an intellect rivaling any of the men in the room, enhanced the finest furniture and decorations. I had met Imperia before, but after my conversations with Raphael I noticed that her pure skin smelled like cinnamon and her velvet gowns emanated a soft warmth whenever she stood close by. Imperia thrilled at participating in arguments with Raphael. Through great effort, she had educated herself so she could interact with aristocrats and cardinals. She was the rare woman accepted in men's discussions. Imperia had unique survival skills that included an acute observation and understanding of everything around her. She came to notice how Raphael and I secretly communicated by exchanging glances, and how, through simple gestures, I would provide support or direction in many of the arguments he had with other people, even as I stood far from him in the room. She made it her personal quest to stalk us—until, one night when Raphael and I were sitting next to each other during a banquet, she intercepted a note I was passing to

Raphael under the table with a quote in Latin to aid him in an argument he had been having with Baldassare Castiglioni. Without attracting attention from anyone else, she took the note from my hand and sat between us reading the note. After that she extended her hands under the table and placed one on Raphael's crotch and the other one on mine. I wanted to rush away from her touch and leave the banquet. Nobody had touched me there since I had been tortured, and her caresses both excited and made me sick but I controlled myself as she had discovered our friendship. She languidly kneaded our crotches for a few minutes, her skilled fingers following the contour of my member, until she was certain she had us hard and on the brink of staining our pants.

She relished her power over us and murmured so only we could hear: "I agree with the monk's perspective. I've been saying for years that if the Catholic Church doesn't change, it will crumble like the Roman Empire. I've noticed for some time that the mute has improved your intellect, Raphael. I'm proud of him helping you, and I'm proud of you being humble enough to get help from such a mysterious character. One thing is certain: the prostitute and the mute are smarter than the men gathered in this room! Smarter than the wealthiest and most arrogant of Rome!"

With our eyes, Raphael and I beseeched her to keep our friendship in confidence. With elegant movement, she rose from the table and walked to Agostino Chigi, embracing him and playfully grabbing his buttocks while winking at us as if saying, "Keeping secrets is part of my job." Raphael and I looked at each other with relief. My legs were shaking.

I liked Imperia very much not only for her beauty and brains but also because she was the central character in a painting Raphael was doing for Chigi. After he had commissioned him to paint the Chigi chapel at Santa Maria del Popolo, Agostino had Raphael paint a wall in his Palace of Love. Imperia posed for him, and he strived to surpass Michelangelo by capturing mankind's intellect and beauty in the movement of her naked body. Imperia as Galatea emerged from the water, her torso twisting gracefully, surrounded by nymphs, putti, and naked tritons. Raphael confided in me that sometimes, after a day of work, they would have sex in front of his studies for the mural. His hands caressed her, comparing the shape and lines of her body to those of the sketches so it would be easier to trace the chalk silhouette on the wall the following day. She was very adept in the art of lovemaking and enjoyed using her skills to drive him frenetic with sensual arousal. Chigi did not mind their relation. He saw the young superstar as a member of his family. While Imperia was his main mistress, he had many other women to entertain him. She was confident that the others did not matter to him. Chigi's main concern with Raphael and Imperia's lovemaking was to ensure that the painting reflected the spirit of his palace: a celebration of love and pleasure, a rebirth of mankind's sensual exploration.

After the night she discovered my friendship with Raphael, whenever I met Imperia at banquets she would look longer than usual into my eyes even if I tried to cling to a tapestry like a spider. She would approach me even if Raphael was not around and smile while she took turns gazing at different parts of my body evaluating my muscles and shapes. I would return to my quarters trembling, trying to ignore the image of her tongue moistening her lips as she conversed with Raphael and stole quick glances at me.

During this period, my nightmares became less painful. There were times when the monster in my dreams retreated and from its mouth would emerge the tempting body of a naked woman. Since my torture at Saint Benedictus, I had rejected lust. Just the memory of the ecstasy that the deacons had relished through my pain made me recoil from any sexual advances. One memory was the most difficult. One deacon, Guidobaldo, would blindfold me while I hung from chains with my arms and legs extended. He would slowly play with my most sensitive areas: my neck, my nipples, my inner thighs, and my buttocks. He concentrated on arousing me with his tongue getting me hard until I was on the edge. He then inflicted agony in the same areas he had just aroused using whips, pincers, and fire. The revulsion of being stimulated by a man, the pleasure and the pain, all three were entangled in my mind, preventing me from enjoying the touch of another person's skin. However, in my dreams I was able to experience many sensations with an unknown woman if protected by the distant shadow of Raphael. Somehow, I then did not feel threatened to reach out for carnal pleasures. The monster in my nightmares would allow the city to be a metropolis and man a free spirit.

I then spent time wondering how it would feel to lie with a woman in real life, to caress her long hair, and have all my body in contact with her body, my chest against her breasts, my knees rubbing her knees, our groins connecting. Would my mind explode with so many sensations coming from so many areas? I looked for forbidden books that talked about the art of lovemaking. The Romans had thought about everything.

Raphael's sexual experimentation became intellectual. He discussed Classical aesthetics with me to grasp the meaning the perfect naked gods had for the Romans and Greeks. He drew sketches for the Vatican rooms he still needed to decorate—sketches that included nude bodies. For the Stanza dell' Incendio, he added naked figures in motion—a man climbing a wall, Aeneas carrying his decrepit father—in an attempt to challenge Michelangelo's ceiling. He was never satisfied with the results. He sent some sketches to Dürer to get his advice. Raphael complained that sketching from the models he hired from the docks and tanneries provided great visual material as they were muscular but lacked the emotional depth to inspire him for the flesh to become spirit, to embody the spark he needed to create images that surpassed Michelangelo's.

Unfortunately, this was not the only way he dealt with his rivalry with Michelangelo. I never liked Donato Bramante. Not only had he torn down Constantine's basilica without the required care to save relics and treasures, but also he thrived on gossip and scandal more than anyone I had ever known. He reigned among all courtiers, and for fun spread stories that destroyed others. He had tried to obliterate Michelangelo with words many times and failed. In one instance, I had to use my skills to save Michelangelo's life. When the Pope inaugurated the Sixtus chapel, Rome fell in love with it and forgave all Michelangelo's trespasses and defects. Raphael became moody and irritated when hearing praise of Michelangelo's genius. I tried to help him focus on the wonderful projects he was working on, like the Stanza de Heliodoro. He ignored this and, with Bramante, started plotting behind closed doors. I soon learned that they wanted to poison the Florentine artist.

While Michelangelo was not my friend, I could not allow his early death. Through my reading, I had learned that some Roman emperors and Attila the Hun had protected themselves against poison by adding minuscule amounts of venom to their foods so their body would become immune against them. From that day on, I worked with Callisto the cook to prepare all foods for Michelangelo, adding minute traces of toxic agents to protect him. I also guarded his food and drink on the very rare occasions that he attended court banquets.

While all of this went on, the Pope had regained his strength after his sickness and defeat in Ravenna but kept his white beard. He would not shave until victorious. He was using all his energy to counterattack France, which wished to create a Religious Council and take power away from him. I had to murder several insiders who sympathized with this power grab. The Pope counterattacked, creating the Council of Saint John Lateran, which was completely under his influence and whose task it was to bring change to the Catholic Church. More than ever, he relied on Agostino Chigi's riches to buy and coax political forces across Europe in his favor. Sometimes I had to travel to other lands to perform my chores as papal poisoner. Raphael could not understand my change of white robes to lavender ones—he did not know that I was an assassin— so he would mock my change in fashion.

All this time I had kept going to the bakery owned by Lutti. Not only his bread provided comfort during these turbulent times, but most of all, my dreams of a naked woman had opened my heart so I was in love. Lutti's daughter was more beautiful every day. Her eyebrows curved in a perfect arc over wide almond-shaped eyes full with wonder. While I spent my life in stealth, Margharetta saw me. As she grew older, her eyes kept penetrating everyone's spirit around her with an ancient knowledge as if she had lived thousands of years in her virginal body. People liked her very much because under her gaze they felt alive and for someone living in the shadows, as I did, her gaze was brighter than sunlight. She noticed the change in the color of my robes. Being a young girl, she had taken to chatting incessantly and making small touching movements on my arms or shoulders while I admired her white skin and her lips ripe for a bite. She enjoyed serving me because, as a mute, I would not interrupt her talking. I was also a mystery to her with my shaved head and face. My lavender robes sparked her imagination even more, and many times I wondered if her dreams matched mine of a life together raising a family. Since Lutti's bread was the best in the city, I would buy bags of it for Raphael and his apprentices but never revealed its origin in spite of their inquiries. I wanted Margharetta to myself.

Julius II's health did not hold out for long. One week, early in February 1513, he strove for the shelter of his bed, away from sickness. He called me to his side, and I knew just by his looks that he would die soon. We had known each other for many years. He stopped in the middle of a sentence when he read in my features the encounter of his mortality. The gestures on my face did not lie to him. He realized the assassin mission he was giving me was pointless as his time was running out. Even close to death, he was wearing many rings on his fingers, which glittered as he grasped my hands, imploring to God for more years. The prospect of death was more powerful than his pride as he clung to me like a beggar desperate for sustenance.

"You have been a physician many years. You have cured many in court that my doctors had declared defunct on the spot. Is there nothing you can do? I just feel weak. My legs are unusually feeble and my breath short...maybe shorter every night." I closed my eyes. My lips trembled while I groped his hands, caressing the bright surface of the colorful gems in his rings with my right thumb and the fragile bones of his wrist through his thin skin with my left thumb. "You have been the best friend I could hope for in this court overflowing with hypocrisy and self-interest." He struggled for air for a minute or two. "I praise Jesus Christ for letting me know the end is coming. I dreamed I would see Saint Peter's Basilica finished but now I realize that I would need to live fifty more years and have a fortune larger than Chigi's. At least Christ allowed me to see what Raphael can do... and see Michelangelo's ceiling completion."

He gasped for air and remained in silence for a few minutes with his eyes slanted behind a cloud of thoughts. Panting, he resumed talking. "I will leave a letter to my successor. He must know about you and how priceless you are as a friend and through your skills. The promise of complete obedience you made to me will transfer to him unless he decides otherwise. If he releases you of his service, I release you of your monastic vows. I know you were forced to take them. You will not be a man of the Church anymore. You will be able to establish a practice, marry a good woman, and raise a family away from the politics that sully the Vatican." He failed to wet his lips with his tongue though his mouth was parched. I wanted to thank him, to share how he had opened up a new existence for me, and provided access to the art and literature I cherished, but he was short of breath and turned his head away from me with a dismissive gesture.

I knelt next to him and prayed. My voice joined his hoarse respiration, and they rose to heaven as chants in a monastery.

When I left his private chamber my mind was in complete disarray. What would my life be like if the new Pope allowed me to leave the Vatican court? Could I become something else away from the comfort of my chambers and my mastery of dark corridors? Would I stop being a spider? A part of me yearned for a different existence. I would be able to make a living as a physician, no doubt. My skills were already renowned through the city. I could marry the baker's daughter. I had enough wealth to give her luxuries she never dreamt of. I would protect her from any evil. After all, I had kissed the fleshless lips of darkness in the past and could see into men's souls.

The following night, I met with Raphael, this time in Castel Saint Angelo's basements, where I would gather insects and he would scrape minerals from the walls for pigments. He had met with the Pope too and was very downcast. Under the light of torches, we talked about our fears. I shared with him what the Pope had said about releasing me from my vows if his successor did not take me into his service. I did not mention Margharetta, the baker's daughter, as that part was too personal to share even with him but I mentioned that I would like to get married. He cocked his head, noticing my discomfort when talking about being with a woman to have children.

"I know monks are not supposed to, but I have met so many who have...Federigo, have you ever been in the company of a woman?" Under the torchlight, blood flushed my face like an embarrassing mask. Raphael thought for a few minutes while scrapping a rare yellow oxide blooming between rocks to a jar. "You cannot search for a wife if you have never been with a woman. Come with me tonight. I have a clandestine rendezvous with someone who also likes you very much." I tried to reject the invitation but the truth of his words echoed in my head.

Later on, we ascended the spiral rock staircase to escape the darkness and humidity below the fortress. Once in the streets, we moved through dark alleys. I trailed behind my friend, confused but excited. I was shaking. I did not stop to consider whether it was from fear or anticipation. The city was deserted, waiting for news about the Pope's health.

Raphael took me to a tall, elegant mansion raised side by side with other constructions on a crowded but aristocratic street. He manipulated the heavy brass knocker to create a rhythmic code. A silent butler opened the door and ushered us inside. The house was richly decorated with heavy red velvet curtains and brocade tapestries. The furniture was of exquisite woods, and I could see some pieces like a marble slab table that came from excavations of Roman buildings. I liked that the place had manuscripts and books on tables and shelves.

Outside the house, thunder rumbled. A huge storm was hovering over the city. Raphael knew his way around; after grasping a green apple from a fruit bowl, he guided me to a bedroom on the third floor. Sitting on an ornate four-post bed, with her back to us, waited Imperia. Her perfume of cinnamon merged with the heavy scent of the roses that filled many vases around the room. She was wearing a long black silk robe, its hem embroidered with large scarlet, gold, and silver roses. From the curve of her back and her clenched fists by her sides—one hand holding a handkerchief—we could see that she had been crying. I felt like an intruder. Raphael shuffled his foot to announce us.

Her proud melodic voice filled the room: "You came". It was just in time as it prevented me from changing my mind and leaving. "You would not allow me to be lonely on a night like this." The wind howled, shaking the windowpanes. "Agostino has brought his Venetian bitch to live with him at his residence. You know, his real residence, not the palace of love where we entertain the bastards and the bitches of Rome. I don't think it is because he is aging and prefers the flesh of younger girls. He has many of those and has seen that they won't rejuvenate his sagging skin and softening muscles." She raised the handkerchief to her face while we stood motionless, listening to her talking with her face turned away from us. I had heard the gossip about Agostino Chigi's infatuation with a new mistress. I never expected this would affect Imperia. She had always seemed above it. "Agostino is in love with her." Imperia choked a sob with her handkerchief. He has even called off his wedding to the Gonzaga bitch despite the woman's high and aristocratic class." I knew Chigi was engaged to a noble woman who would bring even more status to him but had not heard that he had called off the engagement. "He knows his money exempts him from any criticism. But with me...he has ignored that I have given him a daughter. His senses and memory only work when he is around the Venetian whore. How I wish he had never gone on the trip where he met her! But the Pope sent him there..." She lowered her head and her hair fell around her face like a veil mimicking the dense rain on the streets of Rome. "I did not mind when he kept her in a flat in the city as long as I continued to preside over his parties. I did not mind his pompous engagement with Margherita Gonzaga, everybody with money buys a marriage to improve the lineage...but he is blind now...what he hears drives him, and he only cares about Francesca's proximity to him, the bitch's heart beat makes him an idiot. He hears her steps close to him and he hears her moans of pleasure when they copulate...that is powerful enough for him not to listen to reason or anyone else." Her voice was angry, her body proud again. She turned to us, twisting her torso like the Galatea in Raphael's painting. As she turned, her robe slipped open, revealing the heaviness of her firm round breast the size of a ripe grapefruit, with a pale rosy nipple the texture of a flower in bloom. She ran her pleasantly surprised eyes through our bodies. "This is what I need tonight, not ONE warm young sensitive male body to satiate me..." She was thinking as her eyes grazed past every part of my torso, then slid down to my toes. Her mouth expanded into a salacious smile as she spoke to herself: "And even better if the Lord has sent me TWO strong bodies to please me for no commercial exchange. Tonight I feel like making a mute man talk!" My legs gave up and I had to lean against an armoire not to crumble to the floor.

With the windows closed and a hard rain outside, the air in the room should have felt saturated and hard to inhale but it was thin and energizing as if the fragrances of cinnamon and rose were wine flow-ing from my lungs to my temples. An icy layer of sweat covered my back and chest while my legs felt weak. For many years I had resisted the idea of someone touching me. Next to Raphael, the revulsion was gone. I felt protected as I became inundated with desire for Imperia but realized I lacked the skills to bed her.

"He has never laid with a woman..." Raphael explained as he swiped hair from his forehead, "as my true friend I thought I would bring him to you."

"I've always realized he is an unusual monk." Imperia chuckled. "Plus he is mute so cannot use false promises of love to attract women." She rose from the bed, the robe opening to show the area between her legs, shaved smooth, glistening with rose oils. Raphael approached her and they embraced lingering on a long kiss, their lips voracious, and their tongues expert in the movements to enhance sensations. His hands were under her robe, caressing her soft back. Her hands slid un-der his shirt feeling his taut stomach and chest.

I was paralyzed. I was enthralled and panicked by how their limbs in-tertwined. They kept standing rubbing against each other until Imperia took a step back and let her robe slip to the floor, the scarlet, gold, and silver roses at her feet. In my mind, her outline was that of a painting of an apocalyptic Virgin standing on a crescent moon, surrounded by roses, but once light hit the surface of her skin, revealing her naked-ness, she became Venus, her robe serving as the pedestal on which she stood.

She talked to me while Raphael leisurely undressed folding his dark clothes with care and placing them on a red velvet couch under the window. Imperia took one of my hands and placed it on her soft warm breast, my fingers coming alive, eager to feel guided by the indul-gent pulse of the veins around her nipples. She extended her arm and kneaded the muscles supporting my head; then she leaned forward and licked the base of my neck, first with the tip of her tongue and then with refrained greed making humid a path to my earlobes with patience and tenderness. Raphael watched with interest next to a couch as Imperia slowly disrobed me, ignoring that I trembled and discarding my clothes like a gluttonous girl unwrapping a cake. She revealed my chest and back crisscrossed with scars from the tortures at the monastery. The scars created a woven pattern as if my figure was an agglomeration of skin and muscle baskets. Imperia found the scars fascinating and used her fingers, her lips, and her nipples to follow the pathways on my body. I remained immobile as she ignited all the patterns on my skin with exquisite painful patience until she slid her hands down my trousers to clutch my buttocks. The memories of torture and pleasure at the monastery made my head spin and flush but I decided to let her continue so I could move away from my past. My lips were shut tightly but she made me lean against her and pushed one of her breasts into my mouth until her nipple opened my lips and my tongue exploded with her taste, first with small licks and then with wide circles. She finally pulled my pants off, admiring my engorged member, and appreciating the unexpected surprise of my hairless, clean crotch.

She guided me to her bed, where a kneeling Raphael was already waiting. He embraced her from behind while I explored the front of her body as if I were unlocking doors. I felt no guilt, just fascination with her physique. He sometimes would take my hand and guide it to crevices and nooks he knew were more sensitive. Imperia moaned in appreciation. They were good teachers, and she allowed us to adore her.

She guided me into her but I came almost immediately. She cuddled me for a moment, tender but not satisfied, and then turned to Raphael. I reclined on the pillows as I watched how he copulated with her with grace and artistry controlling their movements while letting go. After they came, Raphael went to a desk and pulled out parchment and a charcoal pencil. Meanwhile, Imperia returned to my arms, this time instructing on me how to last longer and allowing her to climax a couple of times by mounting me while I laid on my back before my time to ejaculate. Imperia took her time to teach me how to love a woman. While she performed tricks on me or guided me to do things to her, she called each movement with the name of a cardinal or aristocrat. "This is what Cardinal so and so likes the most; this is what the Count of so and so prefers to do to me..." Raphael sketched frantically fascinated by us.

When the rain stopped close to sunrise, Raphael rejoined us in bed. Our hands were touching while we played with Imperia's breasts. The tips of our toes rubbed while we stimulated her clitoris and kissed her all over, ensuring she kept on coming while she masturbated both of us, her right hand on me, her left on my friend, as she had done under the table when she discovered our friendship.

The world was vibrant with light and beauty when I returned to my quarters. I spent the following days dreaming of Imperia, but most of all, dreaming of the baker's daughter, our life together, and our love making every night. However, on the morning of Sunday, February 20, 1513, a cold wind blew through the city, halting everyone's chores, taking the words from conversations and replacing them with a silent pause that suddenly filled with the toll of bells conveying the death of the Pope Julius II. Wails erupted in the streets while I locked myself in my room to pray fervently for his soul...and for mine. I was hoping I could start a new life away from sin.

CHAPTER 26

GIVE ME KISSES – TWENTY-FIRST CENTURY

Akemi changes the room where she tries to sleep frequently—as if all the empty bedrooms in her houses are the many wives in a sultan's harem waiting to be chosen for the night. The one today is white and minimalistic with very few electronics. The bed's headboard is a white slab of marble with round, unpolished edges. There are no closets just a lone white bedside table in an otherwise empty room. No pictures. No rugs on top of the floor planks of white birch wood with a dark grey grain. She doesn't like to take sleeping pills, they give her nightmares; then again, everything gives her nightmares. She knows terror and guilt wait for her the moment she closes her eyes. But her mind is running at the speed of light with the day's overstimulation, and her body demands the rest. She takes a double dose of sleeping pills, longing to suppress the lust that torched her flesh while reading the monk's confession. The emptiness of her surroundings is enhanced by the light and noises from the street that filter through the thin curtains and shine on a half empty glass of water. The flow of tourists to *Piazza d'Spagna* never ceases. That was one of the reasons she chose this mansion, to always have anonymous company under her balcony and to prove irrefutably that the world did not care about her pain and that billions go on with their lives and their stories oblivious to her existence.

When Akemi buries her face in a pillow she sees screens, as if her Goggle Glass advanced prototypes never turn off. Akemi dreams in SQL, a computer language to manage relational data bases, the dominant form of data storage throughout the world.

```
SELECT      VisualID
FROM        Memory. Childhood. Restricted
WHERE       PeriodID IN
CASE
    WHEN condition1'Intercourse' THEN result1'Lust'  =  'Supress'
    SELECT CARDINALITY (FirstColumn || SecondColumn)
        FROM NIGHTMARE
    WHEN condition2 FirstColumn [Killedparents] = 'Desert'
```

Akemi dreams of a vast minimalistic landscape. The view is from her boarding school dormitory but there are no far away mountains in this picture. There is just a flat plain from which sparse shrubs emerge with sand extending in all directions as if gasping for traces of humidity in the air. The sky is dreary. She feels the sizzling air on her body as if she were contained inside the open mouth of a giant chameleon. The saguaros popping here and there only enhance the solitude she allows herself to feel. She is crying. She misses her parents. Her tears are also of anger. She feels betrayed because they sent her to this distant boarding school in America, far away from her homeland, Mexico. The heat is claiming all of the oxygen from the atmosphere. The sky is dull. The chameleon is inhaling, and the color of its skin is eternal emptiness. Akemi wants to breathe so she stumbles away from the window. Extending her arms to guide her, she explores the corridors opening every door to see if the oxygen and the color blue are hiding behind a closed door. Her legs move faster and faster but her feet want to linger behind. They fight each other and trip her repeatedly like the gnarly roots of an agonizing *guamuchil* tree abducted from its source of water.

```
UPDATE SLEEP
    Set JobTitle  =  CULPABILITY
            WHEN BoardingSchool  =  'Forsaken'
```

```
            THEN 'Anger'
      WHEN BoardingSchool  =  'Hacking'
            THEN 'DrugCartels'
      WHEN BoardingSchool  =  'Transparency'
            THEN 'Death'
   END  ;
```

The chameleon's gigantic tongue enters through a window. The tongue senses its way around the corridors. The BEAST that owns the world wants to digest her. She staggers down a staircase. On the lower floor, she opens a door and finds her protector, his only friend: the CATHOLIC priest who runs the school. He pulls her by his side, and his SACRED presence allows her to breathe again. He pushes her behind him. He raises a large silver crucifix that stops the tongue's advance. The chameleon exhales; the sky in the desert IS blue again. It has an atmosphere. The priest PRAYS in his loud, celibate voice. The mountains scramble to reappear on the horizon.

The school director, this priest, is everything she needed as a lone girl to endure. In her dream, she grows older, and as her body changes, grows curves, and has moisture and smells. She realizes that she does not want the protection of a priest anymore. Her body calls for the angles, moisture, and smells of a man. So the priest recedes into the corridor. She crosses the school's main doors and the desert fills up with buildings and streets. She walks into the San Francisco Bay and the Golden Gate Bridge. Presidio Island is far away. The pier is full of tourists, and Castro is having a carnival while streetcars extend imaginary lines to Mountain View, Cupertino, and San Jose. She cannot walk anymore because she is now seeing all of this through the window of her prison cell.

```
   SELECT FirstName, LastName
   FROM Person. Person
   WHERE PersonType  =  'Loved'
   WHERE PersonType  =  'Desired'
   AND FirstName  =  'Avinash'
```

Avinash is walking to her. She is in jail, but Avinash has come to release her from captivity. She is encircled by Avinash's strong arms, and he kisses her lightly at first, brushing her lips while caressing her neck with his strong hands, teasing her with his smell of fennel seed and cardamom. Then his tongue and hers play together, his full lips brushing away any metallic traces of desert sand. His mouth descends down her neck as if his lips were walking down its curve, following her veins in the direction of her heart. He opens her blouse so he can suck and blow small wet bursts of air on her nipples. He circles them with the tip of his tongue, with the heat of his fingerprints, while his hips grind against her open legs. His hardness nests on her genitals separated only by their clothes. Then she feels him pinch her breasts with enough pain to make her gasp as he descends the fluid movement of his tongue to her abdomen while she reaches for his erection down his navel into his pants and underwear

AND FirstName = 'Avinash?"
AND FirstName error.

But she looks at his face, and the dark skin turns lighter. His eyes change shades like the ocean when the sunlight changes. They become blue as if flooded by Caribbean water. His body loses the thick hair covering his arms and chest that she loves to trace and tangle. His smell changes its seasoning from heavy spices to green and red vegetables and fruits. She feels a lean tight body, all muscle. Her hands run over the new body with greed. They want to explore every crevice, every angle, and every pleasure point. Her fingers play with the man's ribs as if imitating the patterns of falling rain. Small contacts everywhere converge from his chest to his nipples, from his abdomen to his belly button, from his inner thighs to his penis. She is greedy with territoriality. She wants this man for herself.

She has accepted Avinash is gone. She is ready to move forward, have sex, and after that fall into deep sleep in the comfort of Anthony's warm body, but something is pulling her away. *The chameleon is back.* Rome is an ecosystem inside the chameleon's mouth. The beast tricked her. The chameleon's skin has assumed the colors of marble.

She calls for Anthony as the chameleon wraps its tongue around her waist, the tip stretching to nest between her legs, touching her clitoris. Anthony is looking at her, expressionless. His face and nude body are trapped under the skin of a Roman sculpture. Perfect like a god or emperor, but cold. Anthony is packed with erotic shapes but not responsive, immersed instead in his Catullus poems and the lust of centuries gone by; he ignores her. Akemi screams as the chameleon's tongue wrenches her away while plunging into her with greedy desire. The tongue violently penetrates her dry vagina. Her body is hauled, pulled by the tongue hooked inside her, through staircases and corridors in the Vatican, her hands clawing at the empty air but failing to grasp something to stop the beast from completely swallowing her.

This is the punishment she deserves for killing her parents. She must stay away from Anthony. To reinforce that thought, the chameleon's tail lashes at the marble statue that Anthony has become and turns it into wailing shreds, proving how toxic Akemi can be for her lovers. This is the punishment she deserves for killing her parents.

```
        CURRENT_DATE                    error
        CURRENT_TIME(1)                 error
        CURRENT_TIMESTAMP(2)            error
    END  ;
```

Akemi wakes to her own screams. The bed sheets are tangled and knotted around her legs and waist. Her sweat-soaked black hair sticks to her back like obsidian crawlers. As she sits, she covers her eyes with her extended palms unable to contain the overflow of anxiety and anguish.

• • •

In bed, Anthony's limbs feel heavy. The pillow sucks his consciousness. He cannot stop thinking of Akemi, coupled with the monk's story with Imperia and Raphael. With the fraction of awareness he preserves, he tries to wipe Akemi from his brain as the lust is so painful it won't allow him to fall asleep. He forces himself to think of *Catullus*, of his research on the newly found erotic verses. AKEMI. Anthony murmurs parts of *Catullus* poems in an effort to fall asleep lullabied by the rhythmic metric of the Roman phrases. His lips form the words in Latin; his mind says them in English.

Odi et amo	I hate you and love you
Quare id faciam,	Why do I do it?
Fortasse requires.	I have to be strong to do it.
Nescio?	Nescio?
Sed fieri sentio et excrucior. Ah!	I feel it and it tortures me.
Da mi basia	Kiss me
Da mi basia mille,	Kiss me a thousand times
Deinde centum	And then a hundred

Anthony feels small kisses fluttering down his forehead and cheeks: warm, moist, and brimming with sweet nectar. Taking their time, Akemi's lips follow his jawline, lingering under his earlobe to trace the tendons on his neck.

Dein mille altera,	Then another thousand,
Dein second centum	And a second hundred

Like exploring the tissue and the juice of a ripe pear, Akemi tastes his skin with the tip of her tongue, cool and wet, while her soft lips continue their way to his collar bone blue-printing the architecture of his bones. He wants to embrace her but his arms are immobile. His body is paralyzed, spread eagle, and open for her to pleasure him anyway she chooses.

Deinde usque altera mille,	Then still another thousand,
Deinde centum	And a hundred more

Akemi's lips are on his chest, around his nipples. They are light but precise caresses stirring him with small delicious electric shocks while her fingertips slide down his ribcage to his abdomen tracing his muscles, his ligaments, digestive system, and his hormonal glands while assembling the desire for her as the connective tissue.

Dein, cum milia multa fece rimus,	Then with a thousand more,
Conturba bimus illa, ne sciamus,	Until we are confused as to the count,
Aut neqquis malus invidere possit,	So that no one can be jealous
Cum tantum sciat esse basiorum.	Of the number of our kisses.

Her lips grasp both his nipples. She has two mouths that bite at the same time while her raindrop fingers scroll up and down his hard penis as they would on a screen pulsating with images of men and women of all races, all ages, and all body types, copulating in hundreds different positions, creating an undulating ocean of flesh and skin narrating the "Unabridged and Uncensored Complete History of Mankind."

Da mi basia,	Give me kisses,
Basia, basia...	Kisses, kisses...

Akemi's hands milk his penis, changing the grasps and pulses. Sometimes she holds the lower base of his penis following a quick rhythm, other times she rubs the mushroom head with her open palm while pulling his balls down to then switch to long hard strokes while her teeth pull on his nipples gnawing or teasing.

Anthony opens his surprised eyes as he ejaculates, soaking his crotch and the bed sheets. He went to bed with his shirt and trousers on to linger in Akemi's scent. Now the wet liquid on his groin forms small rivulets sliding down his thighs to flood the crevice between his buttocks. He raises himself to a sitting position pulling the covers away as if to expose himself to the untidiness of pleasure. Shaken, he switches the lamp on and still panting, admires the widespread stain on his pants. He is alone in the room as the girls are sleeping with their grandparents. This gives him some time to linger on the sensations, relishing the electricity humming under his skin. He unbuttons his shirt and runs his fingers through his chest and abdomen to check if his dream left any fingerprint of Akemi on his skin. Anthony has not had a wet dream since high school.

CHAPTER 27

MECHANICAL EYES AND THE INQUISITION

A shower makes Anthony feel tidy. The water soothes him as he relaxes his back muscles, his legs, and his shoulders—but his chest does not seem to respond to the yoga relaxation techniques. His nipples cannot erase the memory of the dream.

He picks up his smartphone from the bed stand and looks at the time: 4:00 am. The wet dream must have woken him half an hour earlier than usual. With the lights off, he opens the curtains and stands naked at the window. The Roman sky is dark. He can see the top of the American Embassy on one side and Neptune's Fountain down the street on the other side encircled by walls of confused palaces. Ancient bricks don't sleep. They are always awake with the insomnia hangover that centuries of hypocrisy, injustice, and violence can produce.

Down the street, a flock of nuns hurries to mass, their dark habits serving as camouflage against the dark walls. He wonders if they can see his nakedness. Do nuns and priests have wet dreams, too? Is that considered a sin? He runs his palms through his thighs and ponders a life of celibacy.

Anthony stops at the Excelsior Hotel to see the girls before starting his day. He is more distracted than usual but as he heads to the elevator, his mother-in-law hurries to catch up with him.

"I am seeing Sor Alegría today. Do you have any news I can share with her? She is hopeful that you have been able to present their ordeal to the right authorities within the Holy See."

"Not yet. It's been very crazy. So many things can be happening at the same time but I have a meeting this morning with people who can do something about Gabriel Herrera. I've been hesitant about how much I want to share and surface as this can become a big investigation on its own." Melissa is a petite woman, 5' 2" and thin, yet her shape seems to loom over Anthony with impatience. "But you are right to bring this up. I should not wait. What that man did is wrong."

Melissa jumps into the elevator, escaping the heavy mechanical doors as they close. "She has been in communication with some of the other victims in monasteries across South America. In their letters, several have gathered the courage to share their experiences and are willing to testify in a religious tribunal. It is no small feat for them to fortify themselves to do this."

In his mind, Anthony replays the image of the nuns running along the dark cobbled street hurrying to mass. He feels a pang of guilt for not having managed Herrera's investigation earlier. "I will find the right people to look into this case. I don't care if the investigation has nothing to do with the Transparency Commission or the murders of Avinash and Giocatelli."

Melissa clings to the fabric of his shirt keeping Anthony inside the elevator as they reach the lobby; its door opens and closes. The pulleys whirr as they move the metallic cube to a higher floor. "I have met with more nuns that were abused through Gabriel Herrera's activities. Some have broken their vows of silence to give me the names of the priests who frequented their monasteries and had forced sex with them." She frowns as she gets closer to him. "They want to come clean but worry about the scandal. I worry, too. The Church has too many scandals already." She takes a deep sigh. "These nuns want to keep helping the poor and needy but the sins they committed weigh heavily on them and they seek absolution."

The elevator stops and Melissa and Anthony remain silent as a couple of tourists join them in the small space. When reaching the lobby, Anthony jumps out with Melissa who continues talking while following him. "Every night I pray a rosary for the best outcome for the

Transparency Commission and that no new scandals come up. During the day, the girls keep me very busy with their questions. They are thinking about this transparency thing, too." Her steps are twice as fast as Anthony's to keep pace with him. "They are no longer girls. They want their future their own way. In my time, we had to believe what our parents said. We did not dare challenge them. We believed what radio and TV said. No one questioned the news or authorities."

"You believed in advertising, government, financial institutions, and the Catholic Church..." Anthony adds with a hint of sarcasm scrambling to reach the street. "The girls are different. We did not have smartphones and social platforms in our time. That is why I like studying the past. Things were linear." He pushes the door to *Via Veneto*. "Sorry, Melissa, I have to go. Take care of my girls." He kisses his mother-in-law's cheek.

• • •

For twenty-five minutes Anthony, Alessandro, the Head of the Swiss Guard, and the Security Corp commander wait in silence in the meeting room. Akemi is running late. Alessandro has texted her but received no reply. To keep himself busy, he scribbles on a small notebook. Anthony reads over his shoulder surprised to find the blurbs are fiction: "Alessandro, whatever you are writing does not read like a crime investigation. Sorry for snooping but the wait is unnerving me. We have the Transparency Conference meeting in a few minutes now."

Alessandro raises his head from the notebook and weighs the question. "I am writing a novel for my son. I don't spend much time with him so I write these adventures for him to read at night..." His body relaxes, and there is a hint of friendliness in his face. He takes a deep breath before changing the topic. "Akemi does this. She will go ballistic if someone else is late, but if she is late..." He taps below his left eye with a finger, "You'll see. She won't even apologize."

"Could we start without her?"

Alessandro considers his response. "That will create two conflicts instead of one. Everybody is stressed enough; we don't want her to be furious."

"Why do you put up with her?"

"Why do *you* put up with her?" He taps Anthony's chest. "You have more reasons than we do." The other men in the room type on their phones, unaware of the conversation. "Do you like her? Someone like you is right for her."

"Tell me more," Anthony signals with his hands to get more information.

"You seem to be a wholesome person. Your feet are on the earth, you follow the basics without getting distracted by all this technology, greed, and politics. She lives surrounded by sharks. The amount of information she processes per minute is more than the information you and I go through in a day. She needs a place where she can go and discover herself. Find some comfort, feel. Has she told you her story?"

"No. We seem to have just odd conversations."

"We got drunk together after she broke with Avinash. We had just completed a case and she asked me to go for dinner with her. Watch out, that woman can drink her tequila and *limoncello*. I was so sick the next day, I could not smoke. She doesn't talk about her personal life with most people, but I guess she felt like talking that night with me. Once she opened the floodgates, she could not stop." He pauses, remembering: "That's why I put up with her bad manners and attitude. I value friendship, and I think I became her friend in her own peculiar way." He examines Anthony for a moment. "I think that is the reason I disliked you for a long time. I did not think you would be man enough to control her." Anthony forces himself to remain expressionless. "Somehow you have been able to give her the good fight. She can be a brat."

Ignoring the references to his manhood, Anthony probes deeper. "What *is* her story?"

"She will have to tell it to you when ready. I cannot betray her confidence." Alessandro inspects his jacket pockets, finds his pack of cigarettes, and pulls it out. "Warning! You will admire her more after it." He lights a cigarette, ignoring the building's no-smoking regulations. He inhales a deep puff of smoke with relaxed, expectant pleasure. Anthony looks at his watch, the meeting will have to be postponed. He has to join the other members of the Catholic Transparency Commission.

• • •

Anthony drags himself into the meeting room. The members of the Commission are deeply engaged in their incessant bickering, acting like jungle animals, each one trying to gain personal advantage. Anthony knows he will have to use his yoga training to refrain from confronting Gabriel. He should have pushed a deeper investigation into the Los Angeles Bishop earlier. He should have championed the cause of the abused nuns. He ignores Francesca's festive welcome, her hair flashing like a flock of cockatoos flying in the hot blue tropical sky of an Amazonian forest. She is asking some follow-up questions from the previous night. Anthony slumps in his chair at the u-shaped meeting table, the only reassurance he gets are Akemi's micro robots scattered like sleeping dogs around the room probably to record the sessions. Ellia is sitting opposite him with a box of Kleenex and a bottle of NyQuil in front of her. Despite her runny nose and flushed cheeks, she is deep in thought, like a predator pondering where to position itself to devour the next victim. The other members continue their jungle racket. Someone talks with excitement about the masquerade party Google and the City of Rome have organized for the conference members at MAXXI, the city's amazing contemporary art museum. He reinforces that family members are welcome. Men have to wear tuxedos, women cocktail dresses, and all should wear masks.

Someone at the podium announces that the Bishop of Los Angeles, Gabriel Herrera, will be the speaker for the day. The robots around the room gyrate to take their positions.

• • •

The surveillance control room is covered in screens of all sizes. Every member of the Commission is pictured from many angles.

"Why did you miss the meeting this morning?" Alessandro looks for a place to sit among the light from the many monitors.

"I have a bad feeling about today. I brought a team early this morning to create redundancies in monitoring the room." Akemi is wearing prototype enhanced reality contact lenses that have cameras, allowing for 3D imaging into her retina. The contact lens prototype contains software barred for use in the regular Google Glass.

"Aren't you exaggerating with the vigilance? We can get into privacy issues if any reporter walks into this room."

"I have micro drones the size of hummingbirds patrolling the corridors."

· · ·

Anthony closes his eyes while Gabriel Herrera enters the room and takes the podium. If paying attention, Anthony would have noticed a thin white veil covering the Bishop's corneas like a membrane stained with milk. The jungle becomes silent as if waiting for a storm to strike. Nobody notices how Gabriel grabs both sides of the podium with exaggerated strength. The commission members are preparing themselves for another boring session, and each one prefers to concentrate on his or her own planning and plotting, making mental notes on how to act for the rest of the day.

For Gabriel this is no ordinary day. His nights have been plagued by images of his sexual escapades in the monasteries of South America. He has been the biggest supporter of removing the vow of celibacy to priests and nuns. That the Pope assigned him to work with a group preparing a point of view on celibacy for the twenty-first century is a source of pride to him, but Gabriel wonders if the Pope knows how he used monasteries as places for troubled priests to appease their lust. Research for the document has made him hypersensitive to his surroundings. He feels weak, as if the memory of his sins is making him sick. Were the first Christians celibate? It was not until the fourth century that the Council of Elvira, and later the Council of Carthage, ordered the priests to be continent. Gabriel repeats the text in his mind: "It is fitting that the holy bishops and priests of God as well as the Levites, i.e. those in the service of the divine sacraments, observe perfect continence, so that they may obtain in all simplicity what they are asking from God; what the apostles taught and what antiquity itself observed, let us also endeavor to keep..." The Catholic Church structures mimic the Roman army; it was in the best interest of the Church to ensure that priests did not have any other allegiance beyond the Holy See while in battle.

"We are here because we want to set guidelines so the Catholic Church can move into the digital age." His words sound so distant from the topic that is obsessing him. Transparency and celibacy? Yet he knows that in a world of many eyes—where the behavior of religious people can be watched by cameras—transparency is the primary motivation for bringing normalcy to the sexual life of the army of Christ. "But let me tell you, the Church has been there for a long time, as long as we have banned sexual intercourse for priests." His defiant and aggressive tone makes some start to pay attention. The plump priest looks like a hippopotamus lifting his bulky head as if emerging from a muddy pond, his tiny ears erect with interest. "We have bloggers in many countries read by large audiences. We have sites for the different orders. But there are also organizations that refuse to collaborate with the Vatican to find a peaceful resolution."

His disjointed speech is attractive to bored listeners looking for gossip materials. "We have sites like SNAP, "Survivors Network of those Abused by Priests." To our surprise and discomfort, some of our brothers in service have behaved in a way incompatible with their priestly commitments." Gabriel's eyes wander around the room. He can see what others can't. The commissioners seem to fade away and the hallucination of naked, brown skinned nuns standing in each corner of the room appears. He wonders how nobody is bothered by the noise their heavy breasts make when they walk—but then again he has been having such haunting visions in the recent days.

"These scandals are hard to understand. Even when we consider the aberration that making healthy men become celibate is. These scandals are part of the mystery of human behavior and involve moral and psychological factors, circumstances that..." Gabriel wants to talk about other things. About his difficult childhood in East L.A. How poor they were, and how his mother could not make ends meet, so he joined a street gang. He sold drugs and battled other street gangs to conquer new territories. Their headquarters was a trash-filled highway underpass where the lowest of the homeless retired to die.

One of the naked brown skinned nuns stops applying bright pink blush on her cheeks to order him to keep reading from his notes. "Celibacy is archaic. It was inherited from the Roman Army because the emperor wanted them not to have wives while in campaign. But they had wives when returning home. Not us."

On top of a table, he sees bodies writhing, limbs tangled, heads submerged in the flesh of others. The nun in the corner, eyes aflame and growing reptile wings, flies furiously around him. Gabriel reads his notes.

Akemi's mechanical eyes zoom onto his brow, covered in cold perspiration.

"We can always count on the help of the Holy See, so that with truth and transparency in a climate of fraternal and constructive conversations we can overcome our detractors. We need fortitude and a prayerful spirit..." He takes a sip of water from a glass on the podium. One of the micro machines at the end of one table moves closer to him. A priest who looks like a cheetah stares at the breast of the woman next to him. She is the one that looked like Medusa to Anthony, with her pomegranate hair and very revealing V-neck sweaters.

Guarded by two black-hooded inquisitors, a man enters the room covered in blood. Gabriel knows the man; Gabriel was under aged when he murdered him during a gang war. He shot him on the chest and saw him collapse. He hurried to the fallen body only to empty the rest of the bullets into it. He was the reason Gabriel became a missionary. Remorse is a powerful driver. "I was a missionary in South America and Africa. I grew up in the ranks overseeing several monasteries, both monks and nuns. It was the work there that gained me respect from the higher ecclesiastical authorities."

"Were they favoring you in exchange for the favors you got them?" thinks Anthony, who has sustained undivided attention.

"I also have challenged absurd norms..." His hands are shaking. Sitting on a bench in the last row, a line of women open and close their legs, their vaginas dripping moisture, inviting him to join them. "I helped many of my fellow priests find relief from the stress of their daily jobs. Men are men and have physical needs."

The commissioner from India, the wise panther, wonders where Gabriel is going with his speech. He tilts his head and narrows his eyes. "I had to return to Los Angeles when my mother died and my father's senile dementia required me back at home. I kept working hard there. I left the cunts and tits to follow my family obligations. Surely that should count in heaven."

Ellia is the only one in the room that does not gasp at his coarse language. Eyes are wide open. Jaws hanging open. The politicians murmur to each other, did they hear the same words? "Many see me as the successor for the Pope. The first North American Pope with an Hispanic background and an understanding of Africa. Also someone who knows how cunts want men to take them. All women are whores." Francesca covers her mouth to suppress an exclamation. The hippopotamus priest pushes his chair away from the podium and, with jerky movements, looks around. To Gabriel, the room, crowded with naked nuns, assents with laughter. The nun with reptile wings screeches with orgasmic delight.

In her control center, Akemi waves her arms and her gestures jolt machines and move cameras around. The robots' mechanic gears compute, gyrate, and swivel. Gabriel continues, "I don't care about transparency. The prying mechanical eyes and social media inquisition have ruined the privacy that allowed priests to fuck and bless at the same time."

The audience members remain sitting, their backs very straight. "Transparency is an American concept coming from the pampered minds of people who have not seen the misery the Catholic Church battles to alleviate. The Holy See requires total and unquestioning submission from its hierarchy and its followers." For Gabriel, the nuns are masturbating, the heavy smell of the fluids dripping from their vaginas creates a fog that filters down the clothes of the Transparency Commissioners. "All the bitches enjoy my long and thick cock." In response to his words, the walls expand to reveal modern dungeons where Spanish Inquisitors sharpen their torture instruments. The people in the room squirm in their seats uncomfortably. The medusa woman stands up in a burst of energy to snatch the microphone away from Gabriel. She marches toward the podium. Gabriel's white-veiled corneas zoom down the low cut of her sweater's neck. "The Inquisition will not stop this today. This is the twenty-first century." Gabriel's robes are soaked in sweat as he pulls a gun from his robes.

The woman stops in her tracks and screams, "He's got a gun!"

Gabriel shoots the approaching woman in the forehead, the eruption of blood matching the color of her pomegranate hair. The gunshot tears through the silence in the meeting room. Encouraged by the naked nuns, Gabriel shoots at the Italian politicians sitting close to the podium as if shooting birds on a fence. Three more bodies lie on the ground blood spouting from the wounds. Anthony rolls to the floor under the table covering his head with both hands. Others scream. Ellia hurries out the door, clutching her box of Kleenex and her bottle of NyQuil and runs in the opposite direction of the approaching Swiss Guard. The hunter is in the jungle, the animals are in chaos.

For God's sake, Gabriel, stop!" Francesca raises her arms and stands up for an instant before Anthony pulls her down by her thick Louis Vuitton belt so she ends kneeling under the table. Bullets graze the top of her colorful coiffure—bullets that would have pierced her heart.

The cheetah priest uses this distraction to dash to the exit but three shots in the back stop him in his tracks. Everything is happening in seconds, too fast to make sense of it. Akemi's micro machines have come to life. They speed and corral the bishop. From the ceiling, two square boxes that looked like speakers transform into drones. Akemi takes aim at Gabriel. The drones are equipped with weapons. Gabriel does not see them; he sees demonic hounds released by the Inquisition torturers, the beasts' fur ablaze with phosphorus. "They are coming for me."

Alessandro and the Swiss Guards cross the threshold. Anthony cannot cover his head as he gazes fascinated at Akemi's drones. The machines are whirling and ready to fire their weapons. Gabriel realizes the drones will kill him unless he pushes the gun into his open mouth and pulls the trigger. Blood, teeth, and brains burst and shower gore as his body crumbles with his hands still clutching the podium. The guards scream orders. Sobs. Six blood pools ooze on top of the delicate tile scenes on the floor.

Francesca sobs curled into a ball. "He shot at me. He wanted me dead."

CHAPTER 28

Do Not Trust the Women

Anthony waits at the police station for everyone to complete declarations. Francesca is next to him and has not stopped crying since the event at the meeting room. She has thanked him repeatedly for saving her life. Gabriel had tried to shoot her point blank.

"He was a good man, he was a good man." She keeps repeating to herself.

After a couple of hours, Alessandro Catzola calls Anthony and pulls him out to a side alley. Alessandro lights a cigarette. The detective's hair is messed up in ways that defy the laws of physics. His clothes have stains and wrinkles as if they had been in a hundred-year war.

"You want to interrogate me again?"

"I wanted to have a smoke with a friend away from the office for a moment." Alessandro puffs with greed. "The Swiss Guards and I were running to stop him. We should have been faster. We were almost there when he blew his brains out."

"I was not expecting the Bishop to be violent. When I met him, he tried to recruit me to save Avinash."

Alessandro lights a second cigarette. He offers one to Anthony, who declines. "How could he kill five more right under our noses? This is a catastrophe."

"Do you think he killed Giocatelli, too?"

"We just got the blood reports from the autopsy. Gabriel Herrera had substances in his system that made him violent and hallucinate. The laboratory identified different forms of opiates."

"Prescription drugs?"

"The lab noted that they were rare substances probably concocted in a small, rudimentary laboratory. It seems Gabriel must have been taking them for several days for them to have full effect."

"Someone gave him the substances..."

"That is our person. That is the person who gave the poisoned fruit to Giocatelli, too."

"Francesca almost lost her life in the incident, so that eliminates her as a suspect."

"But not her boyfriend. Still we don't have any evidence to arrest him."

"What about Jones? I have seen all the surviving members of the Conference here to give depositions, but no Ellia Jones."

"We are looking for her. She scurried away during the incident. We'll find her at the American Embassy."

Anthony leans against the wall and brushes his unwashed hair with a hand. "I have a terrible headache."

"I bet it's not as bad as mine..." Alessandro lights the third cigarette. Anthony inhales the smoke from it. The recent tension has made him forget how much he hates tobacco. "I just wish I could get a couple hours of sleep."

"Remember to take off your jacket and pants this time if you go to bed," Anthony jokes. Alessandro forces a smile in return to the remark. "How could Herrera pass a gun through the Swiss Guards' checkpoints? They check religious and secular visitors just the same. Same metal detectors and X-ray machine, same airport-like protocols."

"What, you don't enjoy when a guard runs his hands all over your body to check for concealed weapons?" jokes Alessandro.

"No, and they haven't done that to me."

"You are pretty enough for them to try at least once."

"Cut the crap with the how pretty I am references and jokes! It has become old and stale."

Alessandro inhales his smoke deeply. "We identified the weapon. The Bishop took the gun from the Prefect of the Secret Archives desk."

Anthony is very interested. "He took José Dosal's gun? I thought he kept it locked in his desk."

"He does."

"Doesn't this make José Dosal one of our main suspects?"

Alessandro scratches his head, creating further chaos in his hair. "The Prefect is out of Rome visiting his sister's orchard. We don't know how Herrera got the gun."

"The media is having a field day, isn't it?" The answer is a long silence. "Have you seen Akemi?"

"She has been in meetings and conference calls since the incident. Her micro robots provided great footage of the event. Let's go. I need to check if some of your fellow conference members are no longer hysterical and can give a coherent declaration."

"Do I have to wait until you finish with all of them?"

"Don't tell me the American police is more efficient..." Alessandro throws the cigarette butt onto a mountain of debris in the alley.

• • •

After 24 hours of investigation, they gather at the *Palazzo dell Governatorato*. Akemi and Alessandro have not slept. Anthony sits in a corner pondering the events from the previous day. His girls were so scared when they heard about the shooting, they clung to him at all times. Melissa attempted to get hysterical and coax everyone to return to America but the enormity of Gabriel's death kept her silent.

Angelo enters the room carrying a portfolio with drawings. "*Scusi.* Ms. Morishima asked me to bring these here. They found them in Gabriel Herrera's quarters." He enters and stands next to Anthony.

"Show them," nods Akemi.

Angelo opens the portfolio and starts laying out erotic drawings on the tables. "These are copies of the drawings you have seen at the workshop. These facsimiles came from the Giocatelli mansion." The men in the room are now gathering around the table, fascinated by the overt sexual content in the artwork. The police found these new facsimiles at Herrera's quarters. More erotic drawings by Raphael. They are facsimiles from a recent Sotheby's sale. They were acquired by different Hollywood movie stars and, it seems, given as a gift to the Los Angeles Bishop. As for the ones coming from Christie's, we have images of the documents' reverses. You can see they are covered in handwriting.

In the pictures, Anthony recognizes Federigo's body in the twisting torso crisscrossed with lines—the scars. Others appear to be studies for Bibbiena's steam bath: the faun with the enormous erect penis and the nymph combing her hair with one of her legs raised so you can see her vagina; or the image of a couple having sex in different positions: him kneeling between her legs while she holds his penis. There is one in which she is atop his arched body, standing up raising one leg that he holds under his arm while penetrating her. It is like a Renaissance Kama Sutra.

"In the bottom left side of the written pages, our monk numbered them. There are twenty drawings in the series," Angelo points at the drawings.

"What do these drawings have to do with the murders?" The head of the Swiss Guard cannot stop staring at one that shows the couple curled into each other in an overpowering embrace.

"We don't know, but it is a very odd coincidence that both of the recently killed men had these drawings in their possession." Akemi has been observing them. Taking off her Google Glass, she looks directly at the head of the Swiss Guard and the Security Corp. "Angelo, you cannot hear this, leave." She ushers the young man out. She now looks directly at Alessandro. She is making an effort to look directly at the people she is talking to. One of her robots becomes the projector in the room. It seems the truck-like automaton has been twirling after her through the corridors of the *Palazzo del Governatorato*. Another machine stops next to Anthony and fixates its camera gadget lens on him.

Alessandro explains, "The coroner found hallucinogenic substances in Gabriel's blood. Someone poisoned him into a psychotic frenzy that led to the death of six people, including his own."

"How did he get the gun into the Vatican? We have screening posts everywhere?" questions the head of the Swiss Guard.

"Gabriel was in the drug-induced stupor when he reached the Vatican. He was a friend of the Prefect in charge of the Secret Archives and knew José Dosal kept a gun in his desk. José is out of town. Gabriel managed to open the desk drawer and take the gun. We don't know where he got the key to the desk from. It was not with his belongings. His psychotic frenzy made him paranoid. Feeling threatened, he likely went for the gun to protect himself."

"Some kind of protection!" exclaims Anthony.

"Gabriel was one of the three suspects for Giocatelli's death based on the calls Giocatelli made on a disposable mobile phone before Avinash's death. We have two suspects left now: Francesca Malatesta and Ellia Jones."

A face appears on the screen. Akemi chimes in. "This is Dr. Francesca Malatesta's boyfriend, the one she calls Ahmed." Next to it appears a picture of another man with a white turban. "This is the real Ahmed. The Saudi royal family wants his death to remain secret. I have used all my sources and cannot identify the impostor, Francesca's boyfriend. He appeared out of nowhere and opened several bank accounts in London and Switzerland from one day to another. We cannot trace the origin of the money. We don't know why he or Francesca would want to block transparency in the Secret Archives." She gazes at each man to ensure that her words have sunk in. She skips Anthony.

Alessandro hands out paper folders he has taken out of his brief-case. "We have reached a dead end regarding the leak on Giocatelli's murder during the American Embassy press conference. We know Giocatelli wanted to get documents out of the Secret Archives in case the information in them became available to the public. What he wanted revealed the cooperation of his father with the Nazis during World War II. Someone, a tall man who seems to be American from his accent and maybe an ex-marine from his build, was able to acquire these documents, copied them and handed them to the press. This someone did not leave any electronic traces of where or how he got the documents. His handouts included information hacked from the Italian Police servers. We all know that the man who interrupted the press conference vanished into thin air. We have his picture posted at airports and train stations. Interpol and G5 are helping us, but so far, we have no leads."

"His face is also untraceable. Whenever we run software to identify him based on the footage from the American Embassy, we get nothing. This only happens when the systems have been tampered with." Akemi takes control of the meeting again. "This job could only be done by an insider in the American Embassy. It had to be Ellia Jones. She is my main suspect for these two murders. But is the US government part of this or is she an independent operator?"

"We are setting a private meeting with the American Ambassador for tomorrow. Anthony, can you join us?" Alessandro nods to him.

Anthony stares at Akemi. He wants her to look at him. She normally ignores the people around her, but today she is making an effort to connect with them. "Can you recap everything you know about Ellia Jones?"

Akemi turns to the screen. "Ellia Jones might look like an inconsequential middle-aged woman. She is really a ghost within the US Secret Service. Her background checks indicate a flawless record. Born in Michigan, college track athlete in Ann Arbor, joined the Foreign Service where she has held minor posts around the world. No family, no marriage, no kids, no close friends, no scandals. Her credit history is pristine. Her credit card transactions, predictable. An easily forgettable woman committed to her bureaucratic job. When we get into her Facebook account her conversations belong to that type of person always fading into the wallpaper during school reunions. People never bring her up in the conversations, never feel a need to reconnect with her but she is average enough to be recognized as an acquaintance. They all remember her vaguely."

Akemi turns and looks at her audience, skipping Anthony again. "I had to hack several systems, use my connections in Washington to get access to top secret data, and harness the best of my software to find the truth about her. All her data was planted in the archives. Her real life thumbprints have been erased globally from any and all archives by the CIA. I got the full report today at dawn." Her voice increases to an excited pitch. She is proud of the computing power inside her company—a hurricane of cloud servers orchestrated by the best program developers. "We have been able to find some traces of her existence combing gigantic data bases with face tracking and behavioral software. Ms. Jones moved through the ranks within a top-secret female marine unit and was selected for special ops. She is fluent in many languages and particularly talented with advanced mathematics. This made her suitable for espionage specializing in financial institutions and fraud.

Corporate, brokerage, and banking infiltrations are her core competencies. Her first assignment was in Milan in 1981 just before the collapse of the Banco Ambrosiano, a bank scandal that rocked the Vatican. Then she moved to Mexico in 1982 during the country's currency devaluation and crisis after the oil boom. She quickly relocated to Poland for the rest of the 80s during the Glasnost with part-time residence in Rome. During those years, she was the main liaison between the US, the Vatican, and the Polish Solidarity movement. She was stationed in South Korea during the 1997 Asian financial crisis. She was in New York in 2008, Greece 2010, and London 2012. During all of these years, she developed strong connections to powerful politicians and financial tycoons. Her file is one of the most secure I've ever encountered in my career, and you know I do internal investigations within the Pentagon. She is one of the untouchables in the system."

Without blinking, without moving his face for an instant to attract her gaze, Anthony asks: "Do you know why she is now in Rome?"

Akemi keeps looking at the screen, "No. We have been unable to determine why she is currently stationed at the American Embassy. Most of my advisors believe Ambassador Bradbury ignores her background and that she is here either protecting her own interests or representing those of someone incredibly high in Washington or on Wall Street. Ellia either retired, deciding Rome was a good place to live, or the Secret Archives hold something too important for her to allow transparency." She smiles to the floor pondering her last words. "She is no retiree." Finally she looks at Anthony and her black eyes reveal discomfort and fear, longing and constraint. "She has been investigating you and your family, Anthony, with obsessive compulsion. We have traced signals from secure CIA servers poking into your files and those of anyone who could be associated with you: your father and mother-in-law, your work associates, your daughters, and anyone related to them. They have placed tracking codes to every digital device your family owns. They have scrutinized the files and lives of any child that has been in class with your girls and tagged their Facebook pages. Ellia Jones wants something from you or your family. The searches are very deliberate and surgically precise. We ran a predictive behavior algorithm this morning with recent information. Your family is in danger. These modern spies, with their technology, can be worse than the inquisition."

Her eyes linger on his, concerned, confused with the variety of feelings Anthony provokes in her, but he is now frozen. He is retreating from her, panicked about his family's safety. Suddenly he remembers Jones telling him they were in danger. Was that an excuse to get close to his family? All those searches in his hotel room while he was in jail, the "burglar" in his in-laws suite, the burly man following them...they connect.

"We will talk with the Ambassador tomorrow. Using my Washington allies, we are preparing the paperwork for an arrest warrant for Ellia Jones related to Giocatelli's murder."

"This is another reason why we'll need you with us tomorrow. We will arrest her and need someone to soften any negative reactions from the American Embassy." Alessandro places a hand in Anthony's shoulder.

"I will be there." Now Anthony is looking to the floor. His attraction for Akemi is no longer relevant as he is informed that his girls are in danger. He wants to go back home and plan with his father-in-law how to protect them.

Anthony's subway ride back to the hotel is a haze. He follows rehearsed movements, his mind analyzing the data as best as he can. He arrives at the subway station at *Via Barberini* and emerges onto the square where the merman on Triton's fountain sits atop four dolphin tails with a conch to his lips where water sprouts unaware of the traffic and tourists around it. Next to the fountain, dressed in a simple black business suit and wearing a strand of pearls around her thick neck, Ellia Jones waits for him. She still carries a box of Kleenex. Her nose is red and runny, the skin on her face puffy. She grabs Anthony's arm as he walks, immersed in his thoughts next to her. Anthony's first impulse is to punch her, then he feels like running away but finally decides to control himself and walk arm in arm as if they were close friends despite the stench of sickness that emanates from her.

"We need to talk, Anthony." Her voice is hoarser than usual. Her bearing is infirm. She drags a mouthful of air to form her words. "I have to warn you of the dangers surrounding you."

"I am tired of your warnings," he proclaims, but she ignores his aggressive tone and tense muscles. His arms feel like an iron beam as she holds onto him. Up *Via Veneto*, Ellia nudges him into the Café du

Monde to sit in a sidewalk booth covered in long glass panels. He sits clenching his jaw and looking straight at nothing.

Ellia orders an extra hot double espresso and some pastries for both. "If you follow the traditional process to solve a murder, you will discover who poisoned both Giocatelli and Herrera."

"I don't know what you are talking about." Anthony looks directly at Ellia, clasping his fists under the tablecloth. Her breath stinks.

"Think about it. Who has the motivation to kill these people? Who would want to avenge Avinash's murder?" The possibility has never entered Anthony's brain. He knows where his alliances reside. "Akemi Morishima has a motive. She loved Avinash and revenge is a powerful motive. It seems Giocatelli held the gun but Herrera and others were his accomplices. She has access to enough information to understand who the accomplices are. She knew Giocatelli from her work in the Vatican, and her company provides services to Giocatelli's industries. She could have easily gone to Giocatelli's mansion with a basket of fruit to poison him."

"That does not make sense. Akemi was with me the day Giocatelli died."

"I know, José Dosal told me about your encounter in the underground files. I would advise you to check the time of Giocatelli's death in the coroner's report. Akemi had more than enough time to deliver the poison and then rescue you from Dosal in the underground vault. After that, what a better alibi than be a member of the party that discovers the body?"

Anthony's body is suddenly enveloped in cold sweat. He feels a deep bitter vacuum in his stomach.

Her hands quivering, Ellia lifts the small cup of coffee to her fever-blushed and cracked lips. "I understand Ms. Morishima missed the morning meeting with you and the Swiss Guard yesterday. Did you or anybody ask her where she was? She could have met with Herrera and guided him to José Dosal's gun. She had seen Dosal shooting at you in the underground vault. If she had been poisoning Herrera with hallucinogenic substances, what better idea than to guide him to a gun so he could see some more of Giocatelli's accomplices die? I know Dosal; he is suspicious of everyone so he leaves his office and his desk with triple locks when out of the city. Because of her work, Ms. Morishima is a unique person who has keys to all the locks in Vatican City." Anthony stares at his cappuccino, speechless. "She knew Herrera would not tell anyone she had given him Dosal's gun. If Herrera had not shot himself, Akemi's drones would have killed him, they were poised to do it." Anthony assents. "In her twisted mind she probably believes that everyone in the Catholic Transparency Commission should die. So far, seven are dead. Sweet revenge." A hoarse cough erupts from Ellia. She struggles for air and spits blood-stained mucus into a Kleenex.

"It doesn't make sense." Anthony wants to deny the possibility. "What makes you think Akemi is an expert poisoner?"

While Ellia ventures a hypothesis: "She has worked with the Secret Service, she could have picked up some of their techniques," Anthony realizes he knows the answer. He and Akemi have been reading the letters from the sixteenth-century assassin. Federigo Dottore was an expert poisoner. He had used poisoned fruit, and he had driven people to insanity and suicide just as Herrera had gone mad: "*I saved the final executions for Corpus Christi. That morning the monks woke up to the terrorized howls of Deacons Leonello and Guidobaldo. The deacons had gone insane and believed they were being chased by demons. In their terror, they had shredded their faces with their fingernails. Deacon Guidobaldo had gouged his eyes out.*" In his letters, the monk mentioned he had a notebook in which he annotated the recipes for all his venoms. The hymns book with the first letters and many drawings had recently surfaced. Had Akemi found that notebook in the Secret Archives, and was she using it for revenge? Was that the reason Akemi was so interested in confessions of the assassin working for the Pope?

"Anthony, I told you before, your family is in danger. Now I know *she* is the predator. Is there something one of your girls found the night of Avinash's murder? If you have it you should give it to me, not to Ms. Morishima. I can protect you."

"I have to go." Anthony pushes his untouched coffee away and pulls his chair back, his back is curved. "I don't know what you are talking about. I don't care if your theories are true or false. Stay away from me and my family."

While he hurriedly crosses the street toward the Excelsior Hotel, Ellia observes him with a smug smile. Her body shivers with a high fever.

CHAPTER 29

WHEN A POPE DIES

By the time Anthony gets to the Excelsior Hotel, the girls are asleep. While he wants them next to him, he refuses to wake them up. They can spend the night with their grandparents. He spies them from the room threshold, his forehead wrinkled with worry and guilt. The girls sleep peacefully hugging their stuffed friends.

Anthony closes the door and joins his father-in-law in the living room while Melissa prepares a cup of herbal tea, peeping out with trepidation from behind the kitchenette counter.

"Should we go back to America?" Anthony tiredly asks the question he has been afraid to articulate.

"Your mother-in-law and I have been talking about it all day," remarks Elmer. Melissa joins them with large worried eyes. "The girls have experienced revival in Rome. They are happy and interested in everything around them. They have had a respite from thinking about their mother. We think that despite the danger, Rome merits for all to stay."

Anthony releases a deep sigh, his eyes fill with controlled tears while his body slouches into the plush couch. "I am worried about everyone's safety. If something happened to the girls…" He allows the terrors he has kept at bay at the Vatican and the police station to surface.

Melissa kneels next to him and holds his hand. "This is your life. You know I have been against you participating in this Catholic Transparency Commission since the beginning. I've been thinking a lot. I've been praying for clarity and direction. There is a bigger reason for us to be here. Yesterday's events made me reconsider. Death brings unexpected perspectives. This bishop had to be punished and stopped. I don't know if the tension of the Vatican opening its files and revealing his sins or the remorse of his actions drove him insane, but justice was delivered…unfortunately he took other lives with him….Yesterday I told Elmer about my work at Mother Theresa's soup kitchen. The nuns there were distressed beyond anything I've seen." She keeps stirring her tea after the sugar has dissolved as if the small whirlpool in the cup could swallow up the recent events. "They felt redeemed but infuriated that he was able to go unpunished for so long. They felt guilty for the victims during the shoot-out as if they could have stopped him earlier…but I helped them. I was able to talk to them and comfort them. I described who you are and your values. I reassured them that while everything can't change in an instant, there are good people in the Vatican." She stood up and fetched more tea, uncomfortable with the intimacy. From the stove she murmured, "I am also experiencing a personal resurgence of life and faith in Rome. I was also desolate when Laura passed away. She was my daughter. God has put us here, in this place, this moment for a reason, a reason that might be too large for us to grasp, a reason that might give us some sense of our grief." Silence.

Elmer is the calmest of all. His businesses and Hollywood glitter have given him an escape valve even during the darkest moments of Laura's sickness. In Rome, partnering with an Italian production company keeps him young and partially isolated.

"How are the girls?"

"They saw you in the news again today during your press conference. They like that their father is a celebrity. They also like that you are a voice in this digital transparency conversation. They admire you. You might not be aware of it but the outcome is very relevant to them. They have been connected to the web since before they could talk through educational apps and toys. Claudia talks about how strange it is that she and her sisters' rights for information are being discussed by men who in many cases don't understand the changes technology has produced."

"How can we protect the girls?"

"I've been talking with my partners. They have offered their house in Ancona in case we want to vacation for a while. They are promising a bounty of truffles if we go." Elmer chuckles to himself. "That could be a great hide away, if needed. I have already bought train tickets in case we want to vanish quickly."

Anthony smiles, approving Elmer's plans, adds: "Meanwhile keep going to the Italian language classes AND stay away from the American Embassy. It is scary how ugly things get uncovered. I have reasons to suspect someone over there."

Day 6 – December 11, 1521

When a Pope dies, even the Tiber stops flowing to catch its breath and considers the new course. The surface waters remain calm because even the ocean takes a pause, its waves halting their roll, because it knows that in the blink of an eye the papal court and Christianity will be under new authority.

Courtiers prepare themselves for change. They clean their teeth with feathers, buy new clothes, and apply fresh pomades and powders to their complexions and hair during the day. At night, they stare at a dark ceiling with terror. Some spread like a flock of ducks landing on a lake so they can scatter favorable rumors to enhance their interests and weaken their rivals' positions. Others pack their luggage in a hurry to escape the city before the new ruling party takes power, before they become accountable for their actions.

This is also a sweet time for revenge. What better time to settle scores than when fortunes reverse so radically? Who will be audited and held to the standards others were held to, now that the Pope who protected and ignored their sins is gone? Everyone in Rome knows nothing will remain, yet everything will stay the same.

The doers proceed with their doing almost convinced their actions will speak for them. They gather working tools and documentation in fear that everything they have accomplished is questioned and, in many cases, demolished. The new administrators might think that what the doers have done was a bad idea—disregarding facts, destroying them in shifts of influence and the pinnacle of new egos.

Many crouch and wait, paralyzed, ignoring whether their lives will continue their flow or derail on a whim from the newly empowered. Nobody at the Vatican palace is safe. Nobody in Europe. Even the lowest servant and kitchen boy knows they can be replaced or thrown into jobs in which they have no skills. Just as well, the retarded boy who cleans the pigsties might be elevated to a position of eminence.

Innumerable voices fill the chambers. The acoustics pretend to know what will happen. A shred or a snippet of truth can go a long way toward weaving complete deceitful tapestries for the new reign.

Even mothers in labor delay to allow time for change to happen. Kings and princes far away wonder what threats and opportunities the new papal court will bring. Diplomats prepare their luggage, and ministers scan the markets and the guilds for the perfect and gracious inaugural gift.

When a Pope dies, the small rooms get tidied and furnished with a bare desk and two chairs for the unpleasant conversations where lives will be destroyed or disrupted while the elegantly furnished halls prepare the wines for the newly graced to toast to their good fortune.

Women get ready to sell their children. Men get ready to forsake their souls. The churches get packed with people praying for guidance and understanding. They wonder if their lives are part of a greater plan or depend on the whim of yet another man.

Without knowing it, many of the just and fair wait in the slaughterhouse for having worked instead of playing the game of politics. What does it matter how many souls they saved or industries they built to feed the poor and orphaned? They should have spent more time betraying for pleasure and creating fleeting alliances for personal advancement.

Close to the white smoke and the proclamation: "Habemus Papa." Followed by a name, servants and nobles frantically scavenge through closets, cabinets, armoires, desks, and drawers in the Pope's apartments in search of valuables: a gem, a bracelet, a coin, a note to blackmail a rich one. They yearn for anything to allow them to abscond with some profit from the adventure of having lived in the papal court, because when a Pope dies what is yours becomes someone else's.

The last carrion feeders take the doorknobs and window frames while all the echoes of old steps fade completely to be replaced by the bells of the city tolling the new Pope's name.

When a Pope dies, the Tiber takes new directions, flooding some palaces and houses and leaving others to die of thirst.

Callisto has interrupted me. He brought food but I prefer not to eat. He even sent one of the Jewish doctors Pope Leo X brought to court. While I was able to learn new techniques to treat my patients, I refuse to see anybody. I have no cure. The poison is corroding my entrails as I write. Yesterday, I spent all my waking hours writing my confession letters. Memories and activity ease the pain. I have run out of paper and vellum so I am writing behind the drawings that Raphael made of me and Margharetta. They are at the core of my soul so it is only suitable that they harbor the core of my story.

After His Holiness died, I remained in my quarters, waiting. I caught up reading manuscripts I had pulled from libraries around Rome in search of lost Classical knowledge and art. I used the time to perform extra cleaning rituals of my body and apparel. I spent hours with miniscule brushes scrubbing under my fingernails and in the crevices of my scars. I plucked any rebellious hair that had escaped the barber who shaved my body weekly. Inactivity allowed me to be cleaner, and my room became a cocoon against filth. My nightmares had been replaced by dreams in which Margharetta traced and sanitized the scars on my naked body and made them disappear.

One morning I heard uproar coming from the city. The peal of the bells was calling to celebrate. The new Pope had been elected and was entering Rome in a magnificent parade, the likes of which had not been seen since the triumphs during the reign of Trajan the Emperor. I have an aversion to carnivals and massive celebrations so I remained behind closed doors. I wished to find out if I would become an assassin for the new Pope or be able to rebuild my life with Margharetta. I realized there were more options. The Pope could condemn me to death for the crimes I had committed for his predecessor, or he could torture me to discover the executions I had carried out.

The new Pope, Leo X, came from illustrious Florentine aristocrats, the Medici. He was the son of Lorenzo il Magnifico, so everybody had high hopes for his pontificate. The city was exhausted after years of Julius II's never-ending energy. With Leo X, the center of the world completed its transition from Florence to Rome. This meant better business to all Romans. Ideas, art, and fashion will travel from here to the rest of the world.

Finally, the racket grew so loud that I opened my window. I saw that Leo X's official entrance to court after the parade was magnificent. There were fountains gushing red wine where men and women got completely drunk. Far away, a bullfight raised cheers from a crowd. The main avenues had been taken over by food vendors. Acrobats, magicians, and jesters gathered in every square. All the houses were empty; all of Rome's inhabitants were out partying. Even the invalids and the elders stood against walls watching the spectacle.

The festivity for the new Pope lasted three days and nights. Nobody was able to sleep with the racket. Some families who had found the affair entertaining at the beginning escaped to the countryside or camped around the Via Appia, away from street fights generated by alcohol consumption and other sins.

After the third day, the city became quiet and still like a drunkard under a pine tree. Even the birds paused their singing to regain their breath. The city bells became lazy, and the cattle and goats emerged from their hiding places to reclaim the Forum and the Palatino shrubs and grasses to graze.

I was reading, enjoying the silence that streamed through my open window when I heard an alarmed knock on my door. Through the years, my fame as physician had spread. Many palace servants who now lived in the city sometimes sent me friends or relatives. I think they also liked that I was mute and would not talk about their maladies with others. I charged very little or nothing at all while other doctors tried to squeeze every cent from them. Still people refrained from coming for me when I was not on my service hours. They were afraid of my power and stature inside the court. I wondered who had the audacity to venture into the palace, but the true surprise came when I discovered who was looking for me. Margharetta Lutti, my platonic love, the baker's daughter was there. She was not laughing. Her radiant white skin was covered by a black veil. Her dark eyes from under it pulled me away from my isolation as she asked for help. Through the many years of going to the bakery, our relationship had never gone beyond my gestures to order food and her incessant joyful chatting about everything and nothing. She always smiled and giggled, charmed by the mystery surrounding me. She made me feel that I existed. Her innocence and cheerful spirit was a light amid the filth that inundated the city, and her gaze made time real—as if she knew, without judging, all the secrets I kept. But she also smiled and chatted with others. My plan to marry her stemmed from the status I could give her. As a physician and with the wealth I had accumulated through the years I would be able to beat any other suitor.

She held my hand, her fingers soft despite the hard work at the bakery. "Please, I implore. You have to come with me. My father, you know him, Francesco Lutti is very sick. A rock hit him in the head during the festivities. He has been in bed for the last two days with a fever. He even sees things that are not there." I nodded and went inside for the carry box I had for emergencies. "He is in our house at Santa Dorotea. You have been there many times."

We rushed through the empty and dirty alleys. "We have heard of your talent from many people. They talk when they see you at the bakery. You can help us. I know in my heart I can trust you!" Her face revealed immense concern and her lips tightened at the drunkards we encountered lying on heaps of trash surrounded by wild dogs. "I have seen you all my life. I can remember you even when I was a child. You came to my grandfather's bakery first, and then you came to ours. I knew I could turn to you!"

Francesco was unconscious on his cot. His skull crusted with dried blood despite the efforts of his wife and daughters to clean it with rags and towels. He was in very delicate condition. The stone's impact had produced inflammation inside his skull—liquids and blood that would certainly kill him if untreated. But even if treated, it was extremely risky. I had learned the procedure from ancient manuscripts that described it as performed in Ancient Egypt. I had treated cases like this in the past and knew I had to drill a hole in the bone to release the fluids pressuring his brain tissue. Many patients died even when receiving the procedure correctly. I had seen terrible post effects, too, like the patient becoming paralyzed for the rest of his life or losing his mind. Despite being in my white robes, I asked Margharetta and her family to boil lots of water in the bread furnace. I needed to clean my instruments. I also requested clean rags, towels, and anything that could help me contain the blood. I expected the procedure to be very messy. They asked questions that

I answered as if playing charades, signaling at things and gesturing to explain what I would do.

I shaved Francesco's head and asked for only Margharetta to remain in the room while I penetrated his skull with a very thin silver drill. I was glad the city was silent and all my senses could be attuned to my tools. I had to stop drilling at the precise instant, or I would create irreparable damage. A murky viscous liquid flowed from the opening. As this happened, Francesco's face muscles relaxed. Not belonging to any doctor's guild allowed me to use whatever I deemed useful from ancient texts without having to follow approved procedures. I had also read about ancient practices to prevent infection. I looked for old bread, wondering if there was any left as the Lutti's would sell all their merchandise every day. Luckily, due to the celebrations, I found a loaf of honey bread covered in a white and green moldy surface. I made a paste adding some curing minerals and oils and applied it to the baker's head.

Before I departed, I gave the Lutti family opiates to reduce the pain and showed them how to keep the incision clean. I also left them money to pay their bills since they were not making and selling bread and thus had no income. Some gold coins would help them overcome any financial crisis. With tears in their eyes, the three women thanked me. Margharetta held both my hands and kissed them with devotion. Her moist face made me dizzy with yearning to cradle her in my arms. I gestured that I would return every other day to check the patient. If I had a choice, I would have stayed with them but I had to be available if the new Pope called for me.

It was late at night when I returned to the palace. I did not expect to find Callisto the cook with a suitcase in my quarters. He had been waiting for me to say his farewells. The new Pope had brought his household entourage from Florence. There was a completely new kitchen staff in charge, trained to satisfy His Holiness's taste. The Florentines were overtaking the palace from the humblest position to the Pope's treasurer. I could only imagine how Raphael and his workshop were adapting after Bramante had tirelessly built a faction of Northern artists and intellectuals to counteract the ones from Florence during the pontificate of Julius II. I extended my palms to the walls and ceiling in my room. Callisto could live with me while he figured out what to do. He would send his wife and children to Bracciano, where his wife's family lived. I gave him my bed as I did not mind sleeping on the floor.

The Pope did not call me in the following weeks, allowing my hopes for freedom to increase every day if he would not need me. I kept supervising the health of Francesco Lutti and was glad to see that he was one of the lucky ones to survive the procedure. I always left money for the family. As Francesco recovered with no side effects, they were able to make bread again. Francesco promised to pay me back, and I communicated that his family had become like my family – I did not say so, but I hoped to make that real and blessed in a marriage ceremony.

CHAPTER 30

THE NEW POPE

Day 6 – December 11, 1521 (Continued)

*H*e finally called me one day before dawn, at the hour of secrets, when the air is heavy, moist, and warm, when lovers say good-bye and burglars steal and murder for pleasure. Swiss Guards came and knocked at my door to escort me in complete silence through the empty palace to the Pope's private library. I thought the meeting place was a good omen as I would be surrounded by Raphael's frescoes. But when I entered the room, I realized that darkness encased them. Everything was obscured, and the opaque smoke of incense overpowered my senses. I could hear a murmur reciting a psalm:

"The cords of death entangled me, the anguish of the grave came upon me; I was overcome by trouble and sorrow. Then I called on the name of the LORD: 'O LORD, save me!' Be at rest once more, O my soul, for the LORD has been good to you. For you, O LORD, have delivered my soul from death, my eyes from tears, my feet from stumbling, that I may walk before the LORD in the land of the living. I believed; therefore I said, 'I am greatly afflicted.' And in my dismay I said, 'All men are liars.'"

As my eyes adapted to the gloom, I noticed a dim ray of light coming in through one of the windows where the curtain was slightly parted. This revealed the contour of a person sitting on a throne in the center of the room. The shaft of light illuminated only a pair of beautiful, graceful hands with long, proportioned fingers. Those hands should have belonged to another person. His face suddenly moved into the light, and I could see that he had a disproportionately large head and no neck. A triple chin connected his chest to his puffy, vein-covered cheeks. Surrounded by skin shining with sweat and oils, two brilliant eyes gazed at his surroundings with a spark that made you feel the center of a joke—a selfish gaze that judged you with standards that varied according to his needs.

He beamed at me with a welcoming but icy smile, and in the darkness I felt him hold my hands together with studied affection as I prostrated in front of him, the scarlet color of his slippers a surprising flash of red through the blackness. I dared raise my eyes and study his murky outline. His body was swollen with indulgence. His legs were curved and stodgy. To the court and other nations, Pope Leo X was charming and elegant despite his physique. He engaged with the best minds effortlessly. He smiled with ease. But to me, he was just this voice inside my head:

"I had my spies investigate you. You are a mystery, a well-kept secret. They discovered that your mother was a very pious lady who died tragically in a fire. The records show that your father, your brother, and you refused to listen to the word of God and only through her sacrifice were you redeemed by becoming a monk. It is still an enigma why Julius II had you in his service. My sources could not understand why, if you are merely a book hunter, you did not answer to Tommaso Inghirami, our head librarian and why you removed all of your facial hair and kept bathing yourself as if expunging some stain."

"Forgive me, Father, for I have sinned," I murmured, realizing he knew I could speak.

"Everything made sense when I read a very private letter that my predecessor left for me. I understood how you are expiating the sins you committed against your family." The voice entered my bloodstream like a flood of slush and mud suffocating me. I opened my mouth gasping for air and felt the smoke from the incense burn my throat and lungs. "Your soul is damned. You ignored the redeeming message of the Gospel and your recklessness caused the death of all your family members in tragic ways. May your service to the Vicars of Christ cleanse your spirit." He took a deep breath and seemed to inhale the last vestiges of light in the room. "His Holiness Julius II praised your skill, talents, and services. I can use a book hunter, spy, and poisoner myself. He explained that you only spoke to him. Here, my son, recite in Latin for me."

I coughed the words of Lucretius while a slant of his mouth curved precariously with delight. He believed he was the only one who could hear my educated voice. "You made a promise of service to Julius II. He also mentions that if I don't require your services, I should release you from all your vows and bonds." The new Pope signaled me to sit on a lower stool next to him. I could smell his body despite all the fragrant oils he used. "The Catholic Church is at a crossroads. I need to rebuild the Holy See spirit and mission after years of war and political turmoil with other countries, especially France, the Italian states, and the Holy Roman Empire. We need to continue the works of Jesus Christ." His voice was sweet and melodious like a cantor soothing his parish. Listening to him transformed his body into a gallant and heroic figure. "I have a lot to do with the Lateran Council happening. The Catholic Church has to be independent from the power of kings to achieve its evangelization mission. I need your services. I cannot release you right now. You should rejoice, as this will give you more time on holy service to cleanse your soul. I understand my predecessor's recommendation but I require your services at minimum for the next twelve months. Work for me, serve me, grant me the same loyalty you gave him in the past, and I promise I will do my best to release you of your obligations and vows. Think about it as a temporary job. A silent listener in the corridors of this palace is too valuable to waste. I find it fascinating that servants reveal to you indiscreet information when you cure them. It is delightful!"

He held my hands as if we were two matrons sharing confidences. "I am new here. I require eyes behind my back to survive. Your destiny is not only to be my eyes but also my ears." My heart sank. All of these weeks of dreaming while visiting the Lutti bakery appeared now to be a waste. Leo caressed my cleanly shaven head with interest and then traced the curve of my hairless brows. I disliked his touch, but this was my new master so I remained immobile.

"I can also use you as a book hunter. Knowledge is one of the main roads to the Almighty...and to have a better library than the King of

France...I am uncertain if I will use your skills as an assassin, but I will sleep better knowing you are a weapon in my personal arsenal instead of having you roaming around waiting to be hired by someone interested in killing me. Let me bless you." He wiped the sweat from his face with a delicately embroidered handkerchief.

I forced myself to kneel again in front of him and swore obedience. While he was used to being the only one with needs, I advanced two requests: to be released of my duties when ready and to reinstate Callisto as the head of one of the palace kitchens. I justified this by explaining I needed access to the ingredients and food in the kitchens through someone I could trust implicitly and who would not ask any questions. Despite being displeased that I had asked for things directly instead of using the court methods of procuring them, the Pope agreed to my conditions and dismissed me with a ceremonious embrace that confirmed I had just entered his inner circle of power.

I left the Papal apartments with the stink of mud and fragrant oils of his body infusing my flesh. The tears streaming down my eyes could not wash it. Running into the streets, I ignored the white robes I was wearing, allowing them to stain with the filth of the roads. I roamed the alleys while the sun came out, the hungry and miserable faces I found emerging from their huts offered companionship. After I while, I realized I needed my friend. While Raphael was particularly restrictive on who had entrance to his workshop, I was always welcomed there and I found him surrounded by his apprentices as they had just risen from their sleep. They were happy. It was the beginning of the day, and the sun streamed directly into the workshop bringing out bright colors and shapes. They were drinking wine and eating cured meats with cheese and bread for breakfast. Giulio Romano was making everybody laugh with his story about how he had seduced the wife of a street vendor during the recent festivities. Marcantonio Raimondi was coloring the narration with vulgar comments that made it even funnier. They welcomed me with warmth and slaps on the back offering me food. The Pope had recently confirmed Raphael's assignment to decorate the rooms of the papal palace, ensuring that they still had the best post in the city and an assured flow of income. The new pontiff was enthralled with Raphael's youth and intelligent energy.

Raphael sensed something was wrong with me so he told the others we would go get more wine. Once bathed in more warm light in the street, I told him of the Pope's decision to keep me at his side. Raphael did not know about my role as a poisoner but knew about my activities as a spy. He reassured me that if the Pope had promised to do so, he would release me of my vows as soon as he could. He confirmed his admiration of the pontiff as he himself had been overtaken by the Pope's cultured intellect and his love for music and poetry.

"He is a Medici! There cannot be any more highly educated patrons!" We entered the winery but he bought a small carafe. "We are not going back to my workshop. Agostino Chigi invited me to a breakfast in the garden of his palace of love to honor the new Pope's treasurer: Bernardo Bibbiena. Come along!" I felt so lonely and dejected that I followed him like a stray mongrel.

In the exuberant garden surrounded by salvaged statues of Roman gods and goddesses, I noticed that Raphael had become very close to this new cardinal who lived in the Vatican. He was called a family cardinal because he was living in the Vatican palace just a floor above the Pope and was considered one of Leo X's closest friends. Bernardo Dovizzi— nicknamed Bibbiena because his birthplace— had been instrumental during the conclave to influence other cardinals' votes in favor of Leo X. Chigi was hosting the feast, as he knew he had to become a close ally to the Pope's new treasurer.

Imperia came to us a few minutes after our arrival. She was wearing a long, blue velvet dress that accentuated her cleavage and a blue stone necklace around her neck.

"I am delighted to see you both. It has been a long time, and I still have pending work to do to make this mute speak one day!" she nudged me softly. "This is such a small celebration, only one hundred guests, but Agostino wanted the food to be the most exquisite. After the week of carnival to celebrate the new Pope, it became almost impossible to find the ingredients for today." Acrobats and musicians moved around the crowd while servants carried overflowing platters serving tables. Some men, Tommaso Inghirami, the papal librarian among them, sat through the morning, sampling every single dish. Bibbiena came to us, radiant with excitement from being honored at such a lavish party. He

was also well known for having written a comedy, La Calandria, that was to be performed at noon to guaranteed success. He was very adept in amorous matters.

After a short while, Raphael, Chigi, and Bibbiena sat roaring with laughter while they drank from gold cups that never emptied. Being lost in a crowd that ignored me helped me calm down, so with regained serenity I retreated to observe the guests. The day crept on until I felt Imperia's soft hand caressing my cheek. "Can you believe it, mute? Agostino brought his bitch to the party. I had to be a host for her. Of course I smiled gracefully and deferred to her as the lady of the house. She was not mean. Agostino must have told her that I am an important part of his entourage, especially with the recent arrivals from Florence. How many can brag of having a whore who reads Latin and quotes from Plato and Catullus? Yet...look at him!" A very young girl was leaning on Chigi's shoulder while he stroked her hands. Raphael and Bibbiena were more formal in their conversation not to offend her. She was very beautiful. Her face and body were made of thin fragile lines as if drawn with a very sharp pencil. "He is in love...He doesn't care she is ignorant! I bet you she cannot read or write." She held my arm. "It is humiliating but still I prefer to work for the richest man in the world than for a fat rich lover." Her fingers traced the lines on my face, and realizing I was very sad she stopped. "I have only talked about me. Why are you so dejected? Come with your friend after the party is over. I'll cheer you up."

The night had fallen when we got to Imperia's bedroom. Raphael was so drunk that he slumped into the red velvet couch and fell asleep immediately. Feeling protected by having him close by, I allowed Imperia to make love to me with painful tenderness. I ignored the heavy smells from her body; if my soul was already lost, why not dive into sin? Naked, she and I lay very closely together. I placed my leg between her thighs as she wrapped herself around me so that our bodies intertwined finding a refuge in each other. While I kissed and sucked her upper lip, she kissed my lower lip, and I felt as if we were prisoners of the city sharing our misfortunes. Then she slid down and took my penis in her hand as if it were the key to escape, she placed her lips around it and moved it inside her mouth, savoring it. She used her lips to press and release before pulling away softly so her tongue would lick and stroke my hardness, my senses converging on that point oblivious to other realities. She moved her body around so I could spread her genital lips with my fingers and brush them with my lips and tongue so she could escape too. Then I sucked and fluttered the tip of my tongue in her most intimate parts, making her scream with satisfaction and desire. We both required a measured passion, our hands and mouths taking infinite hours in every crevice, meticulously charting the most intimate corners where we would linger until moaning directed us elsewhere.

By dawn, with her breasts as my pillow, without noticing, I began sharing with her the reasons for my grief. In contrast she gave a thrilled shout, "I have finally made the mute talk!" She was used to miracles and manipulating their energy. With joy, she outlined the scars of my body while listening to the story of my love for Margharetta and how she and I would never be together, until her touch stimulated me such that copulating with her one more time was more urgent than speech.

When I returned my exhausted and unclean body to my quarters, I found Callisto waiting for me with a flask of wine. He wanted to celebrate that he had been reinstated as head cook of one of the kitchens. I drank a couple of sips but what I needed was a scalding hot bath to scrub away dirt and dreams.

The papal court under Leo X became an endless social event, frivolous and full of excess. I soon understood why the Pope had kept me in his service. He was fascinated by freaks of nature. He hired midgets as buffoons. It was rumored that a couple of the courtesans that frequented the parties were hermaphrodites.

One day he instructed me to be in the streets listening to what people were saying as they gathered to watch the entrance of a gift from the King of Portugal to the Pope. I moved with difficulty behind a group of clerics the Pope wanted to eavesdrop on. So engaged were they in their conversations that the first contingent of the procession caught them by surprise. It was a group of family members of the Pope and cardinals riding mules dressed in purple mantles. These were followed by the papal light horsemen, the footmen, and the cardinals' chamberlains. Within minutes, I could not hear any more of the conversations as the air was full with the sound of trumpets, pipes, drums, and brass instruments played by Portuguese musicians. On and on the procession went with courtiers and Portuguese Ambassadors followed by dignitaries and aristocrats from all of the Italian States. I was ready to go back home when the roar from the crowd forced my head to turn, and behold, the unusual sight of a rare beast: a white elephant from India, a gift from newly explored lands, and the centerpiece of the celebration. I was not taken aback by the gold, silver, and bejeweled decorations on the exotic animal. It was even wearing two red slippers imitating the ones the Pope wore. It was his eyes that hypnotized me, his sad, resigned eyes revealing a longing for a land he would never see again. Elephants are intelligent beasts, and he had realized that he had come to a foreign place, where he was nothing more than a curiosity. I felt the impulse to embrace the creature but the crowd contained me.

Soon the Vatican had the white elephant living in the Belvedere gardens as the Pope's favorite pet. Hanno became such an obsession to the pontiff that he asked Raphael to incorporate it as a recurring motif in the palace decoration. I felt I should stand next to the illustrations. I was the perfect match for Hanno the white elephant: a hairless, mute monk who was also a spy and an assassin—another precious oddity in the Pope's personal menagerie.

Leo X released Michelangelo from his services to the Holy See. Raphael became the uncontested premiere artist in Rome. The day he heard of Michelangelo's dismissal, he pulled me to the Borgia tower with a bottle of wine, and we talked surrounded by cobwebs and spiders. He was exultant. His workshop would have a big celebration, and Raphael promised to pay for all the whores that night. He asked me to join them at the brothel, but I declined, reminding him of my recent night with Imperia.

"Was that the day of Bibbiena's party?"

"You were asleep in the sofa."

He approved, entertained by the memory of the excess. "I did spy a little bit but was too drunk to join so I went back to sleep." The sun was setting and its crimson light made the cobwebs look like velvet fabric. He smiled like a child narrating an act of mischief. "My remembrance of the night when I did not fall asleep still makes me feverish," he confessed staring at me. "It was not the sex. Yes, that was really good. But it was the artistic possibilities that your body revealed. You are very lean and muscular, plus," he beamed, "you have no body hair so the light flows cleanly on your skin. Federigo, all of these things are enough to make you an excellent model for a painting but what makes you exceptional are the many scars and marks that crisscross your skin. The lines of your muscles rip and curve in one direction while the topography of your flesh presents a life of its own and flows in a different current with a unique texture. What the images in that room revealed to me was not a naked man but a human spirit enrobed in a surface of suffering and a struggle to hoist himself closer to God."

I drank my wine, unable to reply. For me, my scars were reminders of failures. A permanent emblem of how I had failed my brother, father, and even grandfather. Emblems also of the evil in men. If the great Raphael Sanzio could see more in them, I could only listen in awe.

"Federigo, can I draw you? I have some nudes in the murals I am working on. I'd rather use you as a model than hire someone from the docks. I want to experiment with the images. I see many worlds unknown to me in your suffering."

I assented. He could draw me. Just maybe in doing so I would be able to see in his drawings the man I did not see in myself.

CHAPTER 31

CLOAK AND DAGGER AT THE AMERICAN EMBASSY

The possibility that Akemi could be the one behind the recent deaths makes Anthony sick. The American Embassy is just a few blocks away from Hotel Modigliani, so Anthony drags himself there in the morning. It is housed in The Margherita, a nineteenth-century *palazzo* on *Via Veneto* that takes its name from Queen Margherita de Savoy who lived there after her husband's assassination. Akemi and Alessandro are waiting for him. She looks tired, her makeup failing to cover the black circles under her eyes. Alessandro's nicotine-stained hands offer a welcoming handshake. He also seems to have gone through another sleepless night. He is wearing the same clothes as the previous day and a heavy smell of sweat and cigarette smoke surround him. The greetings are feeble. Anthony refuses to smell the perfume of orange blossoms coming from Akemi, so he turns his head away from her. As they start walking into the building, Anthony reconsiders his attitude: "I need to give her a chance," he tells himself, so he reaches out to Akemi's shoulder but she shies away, briefly threatening him with a dark glance. "Does she know that I know?" murmurs Anthony in such a low voice that he cannot be heard.

"Leave her alone," advises Alessandro, "she is irritated because she cannot bring her robotic pets with her to the Embassy."

In response, Akemi raises her wrists to show what looks like two thick black ceramic bracelets. "Reveal yourselves," she commands, and they unfold on her forearms: two non-metallic robotic millipedes, one to record events, the other to shoot paralyzing darts. Just before the police checkpoint, they retreat to bracelet form.

"See? She is dangerous. She has always been dangerous. You have been staring at her boobs too long to see the danger in other parts of her body," Alessandro asserts.

Jonathan Bradbury, the American Ambassador, receives them in a private meeting room. His concern with the recent events is expressed in his apparel. He is not wearing a jacket, he has rolled up the sleeves of his impeccable white shirt, and the knot of his light blue tie is loose. He skips the pleasantries and jumps directly to the point.

"Lieutenant Catzola, you specifically asked for Ms. Ellia Jones not to be present or even remotely aware of our meeting. This is rather concerning. We are preparing for another press conference later today. Anthony, the PR agency will brief you about the key message points; but that is the least of my concerns right now. The office of the Secretary of State is alarmed by the chain of deaths related to the Transparency movement. They dislike that American citizens have been involved in these matters. They are outraged that an American clergy would go on a shooting rampage and then commit suicide. Now you are bringing concerns regarding Ellia Jones. My team here and our CIA liaisons trust her expertise as a Foreign Service diplomat. What is this all about?"

With businesslike precision, Alessandro and Akemi present a profile for Ellia Jones and why she is now the main suspect.

"Ms. Jones has refused to provide testimony about the events surrounding Herrera's death and shooting spree to the Italian Police. She left the crime scene during the shootings and is using the American Embassy as a safe house." Alessandro's hands shake, as he is respecting the no-smoking regulation at the Embassy.

"She knew this was going to release a PR nightmare. Her loyalty is to the American government. I endorse how she has been using her time."

"Yet she made time to talk to me," Anthony covers his mouth while forming the words he can only hear in silence.

"She has very high security clearance, and thus a powerful digital fence for all her information within Washington," Akemi adds. "She has been present in many of the world's biggest financial crises: Mexico, Argentina, Korea, Greece—the Vatican bank scandal. These facts have been erased from her Italian Embassy dossier."

The Ambassador's face becomes serious. "Well, there might be reasons why this is not there…"

"Are you aware that she is a highly ranked CIA agent not just a lawyer with a diplomatic career? Everything in her official dossier is a decoy. It is fake information. Do you know her line of command inside the Agency? The Pentagon shared all of that with me."

Jonathan Bradbury shifts uncomfortably in his seat. He realizes that his visitors know more than he does. "No, she never shared those credentials with me."

"That explains her 'good relations with your CIA liaisons.' She has been manipulating the situation to be close to the Catholic Transparency Conference. She volunteered for Anthony's case not because she was worried about a fellow American but because she wants something that she believes Anthony or his family has."

"What do you mean?"

"The information that was handed by the man Anthony calls the "linebacker" here at the Embassy's press conference about Mr. Giocatelli's death could only be obtained by a very skilled hacker. My company did not hack it; neither did the followers of Avinash Sullivan. Our only two remaining possibilities are the Chinese or the US government. The Chinese don't care about what is going on here—they have a very clear position regarding digital transparency."

"Are you accusing the US Government? This is a serious charge."

"Is Akemi doing all this to cover her tracks?" wonders Anthony as he stares at Akemi's high-heeled shoes.

"The PR conference was here in the Embassy. While this is one of the most secure places in Rome, the man who handed the information that day vanished into thin air after creating chaos. Coincidence? Fact number two: this same individual tried to snatch the backpack of one of Anthony's daughters. Is he an employee of yours? Are you part of this?"

Anthony and Alessandro become tense at hearing Akemi's direct and disrespectful questioning of the Ambassador. "I'm sorry, what Akemi means..." Alessandro jumps in to soften the accusation.

"I am not sorry. Ambassador Bradbury, either you are part of this plot or Ms. Jones has been operating under your nose. I know the answer but I want to hear it from you."

The Ambassador gets up from his chair, offended, ready to terminate the meeting, but then he pauses. He realizes he needs to acknowledge his ignorance. "I am not part of this." He sits down again. His forehead is pearled in sweat.

"You have to contact your superiors to communicate what we know."

"The Italian Police will act on an arrest warrant for Ellia Jones by the end of the day," Alessandro uses a smooth tone of voice.

"You cannot arrest her here inside the Embassy!" The Ambassador raises his hands.

"We know. We cannot arrest her in her home either, as she surely has several secret escape routes. She is a highly trained operative," Akemi adds.

"We will lure her to the Vatican building. Once in the *Governatorato,* we will be able to contain the situation. You also need to get us clearance so we can share her file with more people inside the Foreign Service, even if they don't have the security clearance from the CIA," recommends Alessandro.

The Ambassador nods almost imperceptibly. "Send her complete file to me first."

"My CIA liaisons are on top of this, too, so it won't be easy to get the approvals. You know I am a contractor for the American Government. So far my contacts have not found the answers I am looking for so I escalated the request to the head of the agency directly."

The Ambassador gasps listening to Akemi. "It is my job to be on top of this, Ms. Morishima, not yours."

"I had to confirm that you were not working with her. My contacts have given me consistently trustworthy references about you."

The Ambassador blushes with fury and answers in a controlled but offended tone, pausing between the words, "Ms. Morishima, mind your manners. May I remind you that you are talking with the highest representative of the American Government in this country? Your so-called contacts are mostly with the DEA and cyber defense units. You should have come to me directly instead of going to your 'contacts' in Washington."

"Why waste time?" Alessandro and Anthony close their eyes and cling to the arm rests of their chairs straining their torsos while listening to Akemi's retort. She is discounting every social clue that the Ambassador is throwing at her. Her lack of empathy irritates the man more by the minute.

"Why go to people who knew you in jail, Ms. Morishima?"

"The Head of the Agency did not know me in jail..." Anthony disregards any suspicions for a moment and steps on her foot to shut her up. She kicks his shin back, continuing: "I could not take the risk of you being involved. That fact would have hit the web and another scandal would have followed. We have too many of those right now. I want to solve this case and we are running out of suspects. We have limited time before they are all in graves, and the murderer disappears from the map. Also, Avinash picked the Catholic Church as a first step on a global crusade to change the world. His friends and followers share this philosophy. They want all institutions, governments, and corporations to open their files. That is why I required being 100% certain that neither you nor anybody else in Washington is part of this. The way technologies are emerging, sooner or later there would be a hacker that would get the information, and the transparency siege would move from the walls of the Vatican to the firewalls of the servers in Washington. I can hold back a sizable army with my cyber defense technologies but if the army is of billions, the walls will fall."

The Ambassador's chin trembles with indignation at being lectured to. "And on what side of this wall do you reside, Ms. Morishima? Wasn't Avinash Sullivan the person who pulled you out of jail? Were you not lovers until a year ago?"

Anthony's body trembles. Should he share Ellia Jones's theories with the Ambassador? Did Bradbury know the theories already? Wasn't Ellia a member of his close staff?

"I don't care what side of the wall you think I might be on. You are not paying for my contract with the American Government. I don't report to you on business or my personal life."

Anthony steps on Akemi's foot again. He addresses the Ambassador directly: "Sir, I will keep you apprised of any new development. Maybe you and I can chat before the press conference."

The Ambassador ignores Akemi, responding to Anthony. "Is it true that your family is in danger? Do they require an escort? Do you want them to move to my residence? My wife and I would be happy to have you as guests."

"I appreciate your offer, sir. However, at this moment we do not know who else in this building might be cooperating with Ellia Jones or who might be our true foe." He gives a side glance to Akemi.

The Ambassador assents. He then checks his watch and gets up, signaling the end of the discussion. The farewell pleasantries are staged and uncomfortable.

With stiff bodies, Akemi, Anthony, and Alessandro enter a large reception hall, moving in silence. The area must have been used as a ballroom in the past. There is an elegant crystal chandelier hanging above the center of the room. The floor and lower parts of the wall are covered in green marble and a plethora of cupids and generals look down from the ceiling frescoes that almost match the number of people moving in the area: embassy clerks, Italians on business, Americans living in Italy that need help for some matter or another. Alessandro asks them to wait while he goes to the bathroom.

Akemi is annoyed: "Anthony, you can wait for him. I have things to do."

"Wait, you and I must talk," he reaches out to stop her by the arm.

"I am too busy right now." Her bracelets unwind and threaten Anthony with glowing mechanical eyes.

"I don't care."

"This thing between you and me, it's never going to happen. We blew our chance on the first date and now we are too busy," Akemi declares in her typically blunt way.

"That's not what I want to talk about."

"We don't have any other topic in common. Don't bother me. You have a press conference to prepare for." She turns and quickly marches away.

Anthony controls the impulse to go after her. His body shaking with rage, he turns to the police lieutenant who has been watching the scene just as surprised. "Go, Alessandro. I'll wait for you here. We can get an espresso at the *Café du Monde* before returning to the craziness." He leans on the balustrade of a curving marble staircase and watches the people move around. "Is Akemi getting ready to murder me?" he sighs.

Anthony is lapsing into regret having come to Rome from Redondo Beach when something in his peripheral vision catches his attention. He turns swiftly to catch a glimpse of a person crossing the hall to enter one of the corridors leading to the administrative offices on the first floor. The person is the tall bald burly man who looks like a linebacker, the one who handed out Giocatelli's information on the thumb drives and accosted him on *Via Condoti*. Leaving behind all traces of self-pity, Anthony dashes behind him maneuvering so as not to crash into the other people moving through the hall. A couple of security guards notice his movements and communicate on a radio. The tall man is about to ascend an internal staircase, the one used by servants when the Embassy was a palace.

"YOU!" calls Anthony. The man turns, eliminating any doubt Anthony may have had about his identity. Their eyes meet for an instant before the man rushes up the staircase, two steps at a time. Anthony follows and they rush down a corridor. The man crashes into a clerk carrying several files. Papers fly into the air. Anthony hears the two policemen behind him.

"Stop, this area is restricted. Embassy employees only."

The tall man enters a service elevator. The door closes before Anthony can reach him. He turns to the policemen behind him. "Where does this go? You need to stop the elevator."

"I'm sorry, sir, but you have to come with us," each policemen grabs one of Anthony's arms.

"You have this wrong! I must talk to Ambassador Bradbury! Please. I was just in a meeting with him…" Each guard holds one of his arms.

It is two hours later when the desperate public relations executive finds Anthony locked inside an office.

"Nobody could tell us where you were. The reporters are waiting impatiently for you. I don't think we will have time for make-up…"

Anthony gnashes his teeth with frustration as he is guided to the press conference.

"Also, the Pope has requested that the upcoming masquerade ball stay on the agenda. He and the Google sponsors believe it is the best way to convey to the public that despite the recent events, the Catholic Transparency Commission will proceed with its mission. Be sure to mention this to the reporters."

Anthony nods while another PR executive hands him a fresh jacket. "The ball is with family so take your daughters with you. We could piece a very attractive story out of it. Make you even more human and likable for the American public." Anthony wants to snarl back but then realizes the safest places are where other people are present. He will talk with his father-in-law in the afternoon to set a date for the trip to Ancona. Meanwhile, having them at the ball might not be a bad idea.

· · ·

Outside, in Saint Peter's Square, the crowd calling for the Vatican to open its files swells in numbers. Similar crowds gather in front of Saint Patrick's in New York, the cathedrals of Mexico City, and Lima, Peru, while the stream of pilgrims to Santiago de Compostela in Spain expands like a river menacing to burst a dam. Some media outlets declare this "The death throes of the Catholic Church"; others say it is the beginning of the Apocalypse. Talk shows in every country debate the meaning of "Digital Transparency" and "Digital Privacy."

The social web sphere hums with the number of posts. Old and young are at their digital devices engaged in the conversation while the followers of Avinash's Transparency Movement stoke the flames. In Boston and Sao Paolo, Catholic Churches are actually set on fire.

CHAPTER 32

ENCOUNTERS

Anthony sits in silence at a deserted study room in the Secret Archives. He stares at a blank laptop screen while thousands of muted books stare at him from their bookshelves. Emails from his editor remain unopened, administrative tasks for his university sit unattended to, and essays idle as first drafts. On the table, books remain open and untouched around him.

• • •

Akemi is at Ghostwire's headquarters on the outskirts of Rome. Her office is a glass cube on the highest level of a smart high-rise. She is speaking with Alessandro, and he can notice with some surprise an undertone of anguish in her voice.

"The members of the new leadership of Avinash Transparency Crusade are here in Rome. They arrived two days ago. They are the ones spurring the street protests. They have demanded an audience with the Pope but they want it to be streamed live on YouTube. This request is unprecedented. It was immediately denied by the Communications Office. They are trying to acquire information, and have very skilled hackers trying to break into our systems. They have gone as far as to threaten the Holy See through the Communications Office. They are stating that Avinash was planning to accomplish his goals through diplomacy and pressure from the social web-sphere. They will not be so patient. They are angrier than Avinash. They are leveraging massive funding from Silicon Valley to bring hundreds of SNAP members, the Survivors Network of those Abused by Priests, to stand in front of Saint Peter and the major churches in Rome. Transparency is the foundation for their movement. If they can get the Vatican to open all their files then they can start legal proceedings and weed out lurking priest pedophiles." She is speaking quickly, balancing from one leg to the other roaming around her large office.

"Do you need me with you?"

She is not listening. She jumps in front of glass displays, signals an image to appear in front of her, and raises the volume for Alessandro to hear on his wireless phone. "Listen to the message they flooded into all Catholic newspapers and blogs."

The face of a man with a salt-and-pepper short beard takes over one of the glass panels. His piercing blue eyes reveal a deep-anchored anger. "The world needs God more than ever in its history. In every continent, people have lost their jobs and their homes. They are surrounded by greed and hypocrisy robbing them of their future. War and terror loom with fanatical and obscure agendas hijacking progress. In the Catholic Church, core territories, Latin America and Africa, sickness and violence from drug trafficking and war reign. Instead of providing spiritual guidance and comfort to its flock, instead of using its influence for change, the Catholic Church has chosen to use its assets to cover the actions of sexual predators and keep them away from justice systems. The cardinals have joined forces with the greedy who see people as a number to be erased on a spreadsheet. The Catholic Church believes they are still in the Middle Ages. They have to wake up to the twenty-first century." Alessandro listens, his palm resting on his messy, crammed office desk. "We need God's guidance. Catholics need the hope of Christ. There are already too many spin-offs of the Christian faith. We are demanding that the largest and most powerful one renews itself and embraces change. We don't need another Reformation. We need complete transparency in the institution so we can all believe again." Alessandro signals to a co-worker to lay a pile of papers on top of more papers in front of him—reports from analysts assigned to the case. "Avinash was a dreamer. The new leadership is made of warriors. Avinash did not have a family. Many of us are parents whose children were abused by priests. We will use the same ruthlessness our families were subjected to so we can bring justice and change. Many of us don't have anything left to lose. We won't hesitate to do what is right."

Akemi wishes she could see Alessandro's face in one of her screens. For an instant she wishes she could see Anthony too, but quickly discards the thought as unproductive. She is scared and overwhelmed. Her body would like to be embraced but her mind shuts the feelings into a drawer only to be opened during the deepest sleep. A blinking screen is showing the latest sentiment readings and attitudes across social sites in total and by country toward the Catholic Church and the Transparency Crusade. The faces in the screens change, summoning Akemi to a meeting with the PR and social agencies.

She ignores Alessandro's call and turns to the screens. "Damn it! How could you not do good regression analyses to foresee the trends on this?!" She is talking to the people behind the screens. "We have enough statistical models and big data from many sites to predict this peak. I want you to connect in real time so we can amplify any messaging we release to soften the situation. Amplify the right messages from key thought leaders. Crawl the web for them. I don't care if Google just updated its algorithms one more time. They do it all the time. Stay connected with our men in Mumbai. I am certain the Transparency Crusade will also try to trick the search crawlers. Talk with our contacts at Yahoo and Bing. Facebook has been messy for the last 48 hours after their new version release and is creating random posts; don't let the techy jumble confuse you on what we need to do. I need information releases that support the Vatican every time we see a change on trend. Talk to Amazon. I am certain the crusade is going to hack and trick their system so Amazon's internal search results and their Zeitgeist widgets bring titles defending their point of view regardless of the topic the shopper is searching for. It is all propaganda. They will be very pissed and willing to help if we can prove the Crusade is messing with their customer experience." Alessandro hangs up, realizing Akemi won't notice his silence.

Day 7 – December 12, 1521

Imperia roared with laughter when I told her about Raphael's request for me to pose naked and then encouraged me to pose for him. Raphael illuminated his studio with many oil lamps. I stood inside a circle surrounded by candles on the floor. There were lamps in crevices on the walls despite having natural light coming down on me from top windows as we were on the upper floor of his studio. I felt uncomfortable but forced myself to let go and trust my friend. The illumination made the scars on my naked body come to life and pulsate as well-defined threads on a cocoon.

"Those lines Federigo, they tell a story of death and resurrection. They are ancient runes discovered on a building before Roman times." His eyes were wide with wonder. He directed me to flex my muscles and rotate my torso in different directions until he found an angle that met what he had in mind for the drawing. He worked with carbon chalk and ink as if he were possessed by a devil, his eyes with the fire of many suns. "How could anyone get pleasure scarifying your body in such a way? But now your past seems to be just decoration on the façade of a cathedral."

I wished to become an object in harmony with the floor and walls. Let light and talent bring life to the surface of my skin where I had seen only death and evil for so many years. After he drew me the first time, he asked me to cover my body in oil to smooth the surface and better reflect the light. I stood there drenched and submerged in the smell from raw olive oil while he drew me in three more positions, my limbs slippery as if having emerged from a womb or as if I were a Roman athlete ready for the Olympics or a gladiator before entering the arena. Then he had me stand facing him, my arms at my sides. By that time I was tired and my mind rambled on its own. I closed my eyes and ran my hands over my chest running up and down my abdomen to keep myself warm. In my mind, I saw Margharetta's face on Imperia's naked body but the skin was fresher and suppler, the breasts fuller with the nipples pointing upward. Margharetta was seeing all of my scars as if she were discovering the geography of an ancient land. My penis started to engorge; I moved my hands to cover myself but heard Raphael's voice: "Don't move, imagine you are alone. I've seen you naked and excited before." I heard the chalk on the paper surface, and its rhythm allowed me to escape into reverie again. I imagined my hands circling Margharettas's breasts until I would make her moan with pleasure. I stroked myself slowly, at first imagining I was penetrating Margharetta with care and tenderness not to damage her tight and young sex as she murmured her love to me. Then I imagined we were rolling on the mattress, our limbs tangled as we fell to the floor while she demanded more from me with an unquenchable desire, so I increased my tempo. I exploded, the turbid liquid from my seed forming a small puddle at my feet while my body was shaking with pleasure as a butterfly emerging from her cocoon shaking away the old and dry walls that kept her trapped and protected.

The images had transported me from the studio where Raphael drew my body. But Raphael kept on working while my body relaxed preventing me from feeling any shame. He was absorbed by the task. I was drenched in sweat and soon became cold. Raphael asked me to open my eyes, and I discovered he had three sheets with sketches in front of him. He smiled like a brother and handed me water to clean myself before inviting me to get dressed again. I studied the pictures of my body and for the first time discovered beauty where I had only seen the memory of horror. Raphael had given a voice to my body, too, so it could express rebirth.

Smiling, and with the charcoal images vibrating in my memory, I threw myself back into the alleyways of Rome.

Back in the Vatican palace, my meetings before dawn with the Pope became more frequent. We always met very early, and in darkness, our voices a physical, tangible presence in the stale air, heavy with incense and aromatic oils untouched by sunlight. Leo X relished my retelling of gossip and conversations about the papal court. He had me sneaking behind cardinals and ambassadors at all times of day and night. He was particularly suspicious of popular cardinals and courtiers such as a certain Cardinal Petrucci admired by many.

Thinking back, I should have been pulled into his charm immediately. We should have connected. He loved music, and thanks to him I was able to listen to the most advanced musicians performing in the churches of Rome and the papal court. They came to the city from all corners of the world as the Pope paid handsomely for them to entertain him in events ranging from solitary suppers to magnificent feasts for hundreds. But the admiration for God in the music's lyrics was something he did not practice. He was Godless when ordering death. He had quickly forgotten he was not to use me as an assassin. He acted like a comedian performing during a tragedy, calculating his next move and selecting his next victim while becoming known for his many pious actions.

"Federigo, there is a new opportunity to expiate your sins by eliminating one of the emissaries from the Catholic Queen of Spain visiting Rome. Choose someone with enough importance to be noted but not important enough to create a political conflict. Make the death painful and vague so poison is obvious but untraceable so no conclusions can be made. Spend time listening to the emissaries talk. They seem to be a bunch of zealots that disapprove of the ways of the Vatican. They act as if they were holier than us. Choose the holiest one."

I wanted to like him. I desired to be charmed by him. But I always failed. Maybe it was an undertone in his sweet and elegant voice, maybe it was his effort to please those he manipulated.

I was hoping to go on a book hunt, but Leo X preferred hunting other prey. There were the beasts he loved to chase in the woods with hounds while leading a party of horsemen. Wild boars were good, but testing my skills as a poisoner was better. At the beginning, he had me kill as a way for him to understand the scope of my skills. The first victims were minor and frivolous choices—a clerk, a cook—that fascinated the Pope as he learned the variety of poisons and forms of death I could deliver. I had accumulated ingredients and death recipes through many years. If he experienced pleasure on having musicians performing during all his meals and during the masses he attended, he got more pleasure from knowing he could secretly kill. He would select the victim and then have his sources describe in every detail how the unfortunate person died.

"Federigo, I heard the deacon of Saint James died after a week of agony while his intestines became putrid. Is there a way to make the agony last two weeks?"

He was remorseless when selecting a victim and sending me on a mission. He could as well be selecting a new crucifix to wear at an event.

"For this week we have emissaries from Saxony and Portugal. I still feel obliged to the King of Portugal after the gift of Hanno, the elephant. Then again I already gave him a rose made of gold. We should test that wonderful poison that causes instant and permanent body paralysis on one of the minor servants from Portuguese entourage. May he rejoice on reaching the gates of Heaven sooner than he expected."

With ambassadors and nobles, he was affable and light. He soon had many followers and admirers that would swear on his piety and religious fervor. He was not rude to me. He conducted our business in a heartfelt manner as if he cared for the souls of others. While the court celebrated his sense of humor, I saw cold blood in all his actions. He experienced life in a calculated way. I learned through his actions that with a world divided by the immense powers of Spain, France, and the Holy Roman Empire, the Pope had to be the smartest of all the rulers of the world to protect the Medici family interests from the greed of other nations. When giving audiences, he never revealed his true feelings or plans. Graceful and smart, he would speak in ambiguous ways to make others believe they were advancing their interests.

"I can understand why this petition is so important for you and your town. I don't disagree with your point of view. Let's discuss this separately in a more private audience. Talk with one of my secretaries to set it up."

But then, in sessions with his inner circle, he would strike decisively with concise instructions to those around him never bothering to give context or explanation because only he would know the master plan.

"Burn the town. Make it seem as if the arsonists were spies who crossed the Alps. Kill all the children."

His delight with freaks, the unusual, and the grotesque stemmed from dark corners in his soul and hidden moral rationalizations. Dwarves and white elephants, acrobats, hermaphrodites, musicians and actors... and a mute hairless poisoner connected to moments of his life where he himself had been the dwarf. He had been the ugly toad in Lorenzo il Magnifico's court yet he had learned to shine and charm. He had strived despite the lack of grace in his body; his lack of beauty had become only a driver to becoming more educated and cunning. He had succeeded and now had become the head of the Catholic Church. While before he had been surrounded by preying courtiers plotting to eliminate or neutralize him; now he was surrounded by preying nations plotting to neutralize and manipulate the power of the Catholic Church.

As Akemi approaches her house, she sees them, waiting by the entrance of the building. Two of the individuals were once her friends, now she has to fight them. She left her Lamborghini in a parking spot close by; she misses the sense of security coming from the metal, glass, and leather drawn together by superior automotive design. There are three waiting by the door. The ones she recognizes are the man with a beard and the man in a wheel chair. With them is a woman in her late fifties, unkempt, overweight, dressed in loose jeans and a faded t-shirt.

Akemi is aware her social skills are deplorable even when pleased to see someone, which is not the case here. She has been able to prosper in business because of her dry lack of emotion and detached objectiveness when dealing with CEOs and other power holders in the world. They prefer data and unemotional recommendations. Her brilliance in what she does is the only thing that matters, cyber defense and social media being topics the powerful don't understand.

"Akemi, it is good to see you even if only to remember the time when you and Avinash were together," says the man with the salt-and-pepper short beard. He makes an awkward attempt to embrace her but she sidesteps him.

"Mike, Steve, we have been communicating a lot lately. Why do you require seeing me?"

"This is Mae, her son was abused by a priest and a result went into drugs that led him to a mental institution for life. She is part of the new leadership." The two women assess each other like two felines of different species before a fight. Mae dislikes that Akemi is working for the Vatican.

"We can walk to a restaurant close by. There is this place nearby called *Ottelo alla Concordia* which I love," Mike suggests breaking the uncomfortable moment.

In silence, they descend to *Piazza de Spagna* through a slanted side street that allows passage for Steve's wheel chair. They arrive at the restaurant and sit in an outside table of a small courtyard. It is still early so the place is almost empty.

They are sipping wine when Akemi breaks the silence. "I don't believe I can help you. I have a contract with the Holy See."

"What about Avinash? Don't you want to help his crusade to honor him? He died because of his cause." The man in the wheel chair approaches Akemi.

"He and I had major differences regarding transparency in the digital age. He shared with you the reasons why we broke up. You were his closest associates. I am sure he whined about my lack of flexibility with you. He is dead and so is our past."

"Is it?" Mike reaches for her hand. "You inspired him with your life story. It was you who planted the seed for a transparent digital society in his mind with what you once did. It is better to swallow the bitter data in one gulp than have a world that sooner or later will get bored with the scandals that can be uncovered by technology."

Akemi moves her hand away from Mike's. "Did he tell you so? Did he tell you the consequences of my actions? I made the information of several Mexican drug cartels transparent. I truly believed that exposing them would dismantle their operations. Instead I started a war among them, which killed hundreds of people...my Mother and Father among the casualties. You truly believe that was smart? I don't."

"You created enough strife for some of the drug organizations to collapse."

"They were replaced by others. It's human nature when it relates to greed and corruption, the moment one goes away, another takes its place. I was just a good fuck for Avinash! Don't try to hang your little saints on me for his beliefs."

The waiter avoids the table noticing the hostile tones on the voices. "His own life inspired this fucked up Transparency Crusade! Men and women are entitled to their private sins, so are institutions, corporations, and governments. How would you like your credit card information posted for anyone to see?"

"How would YOU like your son to be in a mental institution for the rest of his life, his brain destroyed by drugs, because the Vatican failed to control a sexual predator?" thunders Mae. "How would you like to find the Vatican knew of Monsignor Maciel's victims but decided to turn a blind eye because he was creating such a lucrative empire with schools? He swindled people out of their properties in the name of Christ. He was exceptional in recruiting new members for the Catholic Church, so why pay closer attention that as part of the recruitment he handpicked a few beautiful and vulnerable boys to abuse? Maybe transparency would have stopped him. Open files would have generated a timely outcry for the Vatican to reconsider their priorities."

"You are confusing the topics. You don't know what you are talking about when you refer to transparency. You are mixing the inefficient policies of an ancient institution with privacy. You are making generalizations on topics that are too complex for the masses to grasp." Akemi's body seems to rise as she looks down on Mae.

"Transparency within the Catholic Church could be a first step in finding the right balance of private and open information in the new world. Avinash had a plan to reveal to the Pope how allowing the information to remain locked was protecting criminal acts and false reputations. He worked on this for some time and had assembled the proof," Mike explains.

"Tell me something I don't know. Tell me how Avinash identified the individuals and who was his source in the Vatican. Those are the details I don't know and could help capture whoever is behind the trail of deaths following Avinash's murder. It should have stopped with him dying but many have been murdered after that."

"Look who is doing generalizations now," Mae derides. "What is your interest in this case? Why are you handling it directly when you are the leader of a technology company with thousands of capable employees? You won't fix the death of your parents if you stop the murders in this scandal. You probably feel what is happening is too close to home. This is a repeat of your worst nightmare. Welcome to my world. Every day when I read about a new Church scandal, I relive my son's downfall, but in my case there is nothing I can do about it when the information is hidden and the Catholic authorities protect the perpetrators," Mae snarls showing her yellow teeth.

"Avinash was very private, you know that," explains Steve, the man in the wheel chair. "He ran this by himself, keeping the information dispersed on cloud servers so nobody could trace it even if we were able to break his encrypted files."

"But we know he had a contact inside the Vatican to help him. Maybe even a whore. He might have gotten over you very quickly." Mae revels in breaking through Akemi's emotionless features. "She was her conduit to the ones who wanted information removed and to the ones that had access to the information. For a while we swore he had returned to you and you were helping him."

Blood fills Akemi's temples. Can she still be jealous? Fury? Indignation? Akemi turns to Steve as her dark hair falls like a veil of thunderclouds around her face.

"Mae is not very accurate. What she is saying are conjectures we made from Avinash's behavior and random comments. This is the reason we wanted to talk with you. We want your help in finding if this woman is real and, if so, her identity. If it was not a woman, we want to find who the contact inside the Vatican was." Mike continues to be conciliatory.

"We want to finish what Avinash started," adds Steve.

"They believe it will cleanse the waters," Mae glares at the men at the table, "but I believe this will tilt the scale so that the masses enforce justice and the Vatican walls will collapse under a digital mob. This is the day of reckoning the Bible talks about, why delay it?"

"I find all of you very confused and trivializing many important matters you don't understand." Akemi throws the unopened menu on the floor.

"Why would you think differently? You are one of the wealthy from Silicon Valley who has made their fortunes not caring about the other 99%." Mae picks the menu from the floor and throws it back at her.

The bottle of wine is empty. Akemi weighs her words carefully. "You are just a bunch of imbeciles. You lack data for most of your statements. I expected more from you and Steve, Mike." She stands up. "Hypocrisy is part of humanity's DNA. The Right for Privacy is one of the most basic rights stemming from the right to have property. This crusade is a waste of time and money. We can all stand naked and there will still be hidden secrets."

"You were once one of us…"

"I was never an idiot jumping to conclusions without diving into the data before I opened my mouth."

Akemi turns and walks away.

CHAPTER 33

THE UNDERGROUND PALACE

(Continued) Day 7, December 12, 1521

O ur Father, Who art in Heaven...I have strayed from my religion. I am a broken chalice that spilled the Light of God...maybe this confession will save me. I have been proud and lustful. I envied my friend, and I have let the fire of revenge inspire me to kill.

What if Lucretius was right? What if we are just particles floating in nothingness? My consciousness will perish with my body. Will Philosophy and Art justify my struggles? I have lived at the center of the world. I have witnessed how the world is changing from the events inside the Vatican palace. My name will be completely forgotten, fall down the crack of posterity like a peasant or an orchard tree that dries and becomes firewood.

Enough rambling. My time runs out. My muscles and joints ache and I dread that fevers might halt my writing. I have to go on...

On 1514, Bramante died, and by April, Raphael had been appointed the new architect in charge of building Saint Peter's Basilica. His new position confirmed his status as a prince of the church. He became even richer and more famous. An entourage of fifty people circled him wherever he went. Everybody who was anybody wished to hire him as an architect or painter. His studio grew in size and popularity, and they had so many jobs that they worked from sun to sun. His closest apprentices, Giulio Romano and Marcantonio Raimondi, became celebrities in their own right. Emissaries came from all lands to request their services, but Raphael was committed only to Rome.

Cardinal Bernardo Bibbiena prided himself in having made Raphael his protégé, although I don't think Raphael needed more patrons, as he already had Leo X and the banker Agostino Chigi. During one of the bacchanals, Bibbiena convinced Raphael that he needed to marry a high society lady and hence offered his niece, Maria, as an ideal option. A beautiful, elegant woman, she was flattered by the engagement, however, developed a frigid and distant relationship to the artist, who was in no hurry to marry her. He did not mention this to me but the rumor was that Raphael expected the Pope to grant him a red hat, a cardinal position, in the future to reward him for his services. To many, that explained the stalling of the marriage. I think Raphael was just having a great time with all the women in the city. I also heard through the patients of my medical practice that Maria Bibbiena did not favor men but preferred the favors from women thus welcoming the postponement of the wedding day. Nothing mattered as long as Raphael continued painting and marveling Rome. He revealed masterpiece after masterpiece on the papal apartments, amazing and delighting courtiers and ambassadors from all countries.

While our time to meet and talk became very scarce, sometimes I still brought warm bread for him and his apprentices to his studio on the mornings after I visited Lutti's bakery. On one of these occasions, when I arrived with a basket of warm loaves before dawn, Giulio Romano said Raphael had requested that if I stopped by to take breakfast for him to Hanno's, the white elephant, dwellings. After entering the city under a triumphal march, the gift from the Portuguese King had lived in the Belvedere gardens, but being the Pope's favorite creature, the elephant would now enjoy a mansion in a vacant lot between the Vatican and Castel Saint Angelo, to be built by Raphael. Raphael had left the studio very early in the morning because he had to supervise the construction of the animal's residence. Giulio told me that when Raphael left before sunrise, all he mentioned was that he desperately needed the warm rolls crusted with sugar and honey that I usually brought to him.

Raphael was exhilarated to see my basket of bread and dove into it with both hands as if the warm crusts and vapors were a fireplace from which to draw comfort amid the pre-dawn cold. He devoured my gifts, and we agreed—as we had many times—that these were the best bread and pastries in the city. "Federigo, we share many secrets, you can share this one with me. You MUST take me to this bakery." I lied and explained I had offered to take him there in the past. In reality, I had been content to keep Lutti's just for myself.

"I'm just too busy," he replied, "but today is an excellent day. My entourage is still in bed, and my work here went a lot faster than expected. The streets are deserted. This is a great time. I will enjoy moving unnoticed around Rome without a crowd around me for once."

Walking side by side, we hurried through winding alleys while Raphael described the scandals at a recent party he had attended. As we approached the bakery in Pigna, the foul air transformed from the stink of mud and dung to the sweet yeasty perfume of freshly baked bread. At the same moment, the sun rose over the horizon, illuminating church domes and Roman columns. We stopped and gulped the air with gluttony. The sun seemed to stop for an instant, while our senses were stimulated by everything surrounding us. The bell towers were pealing for the matins. Maybe the benevolent sun took a moment to look down at us before the world changed again.

When we entered the bakery full of customers, Francesco and his wife stopped attending to others to receive me with cheerful exclamations and arm waving. "But you were just here this morning! Did you already eat that huge basket of bread? This is so unusual, you are here twice in a day!" Raphael had worn a cloak to cover his face while we crossed the city. I signaled to him so they would know I was bringing a friend to the bakery for the first time. "Any friend of yours is a friend of ours! You are family." The Luttis knew not to embrace me as I disliked euphoric physical contact, so they raised their voices when they wanted to convey emotions.

"This is the best bakery in all Rome!" exclaimed Raphael uncovering his face.

"God Almighty! If it is not the great Raphael Sanzio di Urbino!" Everybody in the shop turned to look at him as excitement filled the room. They rarely got this close to a celebrity of Raphael's caliber.

Francesco and his wife embraced and then paraded, showing him shelves featuring trays with a variety of delights. "You can take anything you want! Federigo's friends are also part of our family. Just don't take my two daughters! We'll give you other treats!"

The customers murmured among themselves, and a few bold ones extended their hands to touch the artist. Smiling, Raphael grabbed his favorite sugar and honey loaf from a tray. It was just like the one he had eaten earlier, but all the same he wolfed it down, as a boy would devour a sweet. People stood still and watched in awe as if he were doing a spectacular feat. The silence was suddenly interrupted by Francesco's voice calling his daughters: "Come girls! There is someone you must meet!"

The young women appeared at the top of a staircase. After the morning chores, Margharetta had just finished combing her long, rich, dark hair and was holding a shell comb in her hand. She beamed at me but then her eyes widened and her pretty mouth dropped open as she discovered the greatest artist in the world standing in her father's bakery. Her biggest surprise was to discover how handsome and sensual he was, how each angle in his body promised to become archways to pleasures she had only dreamt of. Seeing his painting at the Chigi chapel, she had always imagined him as an old man.

Raphael's mouth also dropped open. His gaze explored every crevice of Margharetta's body, ready to dive into her brown eyes, holding his breath before the plunge. As a painter, he found no greater satisfaction than to be seen by others with enhanced visual perception. What greater invitation than to realize that someone in front of him could speak the secret language of images with her eyes? Noticing their mutual admiration, blood left my body and a fever burst into my temples. This was not what I had wanted—or expected.

Raphael ignored everyone else in the room and climbed the staircase two steps at a time to clasp Margharetta's hand in his. "It is a joy to discover you. Your father harbors not only the best bread in Rome but the most beautiful woman in the city." Margharetta lowered her eyelids while blushing a deep crimson.

"Come on, come on," called the baker, "I told you not to take my daughters. Margharetta is not for sale." He roared with laughter but I could read discomfort in his movements. He was worried for his daughter—although for someone of his status having a family member develop bonds with someone who was practically a prince could be the best thing that could happen to them.

The customers were already back to their business, still murmuring but eager to return to their mundane lives. Sitting with me at a small table, Margharetta and Raphael chatted incessantly, like birds chirping from one tree to another. Both were enthralled by the other's voice. They used me as a common topic. Both shared stories of how I had helped them in the past, praising me as the best of friends. In his eagerness, Raphael almost revealed that I could speak, but halted mid-phrase when he noticed he was about to say too much. From my bench, I did not know if I should run away or remain feigning a serenity I lacked.

Soon the bells tolled again reminding Raphael that he was late for an important appointment. He promised Margharetta to return as we left the bakery together. We separated at the first crossroad.

During the following days I convinced myself that the encounter was the best thing that could have happened. If I could not have Margharetta, then let Raphael become her lover. I was bound to the Pope and the Catholic Church and could offer no future. If Margharetta became more than a fling to Raphael it would be the best destiny for both. Still, I avoided visiting the bakery and Raphael's workshop for some time. The Pope kept me experimenting with new methods of eliminating his enemies. I had read about ways to make people sick, a slow poisoning approach that undermined their life vitality, allowing them to live but destroying their will. Another debilitating substance made the victim very weak and prone to sickness—a great way to cover death by poisoning. The Pope selected a monastery in Northern Italy and, with the excuse of dispatching me to procure old manuscripts, sent me to try my poisons on the monks and report back. After all, who would be surprised if a small plague swept through the population in a monastery? I disliked the mission but it allowed me to leave Rome for a while and stop thinking about Raphael and Margharetta. Also the manuscripts at the monastery had many rare classical texts for me to read during my spare time.

I returned early December, just in time to witness a major fire in the papal apartments. Flames engulfed part of the palace with infernal fury while the bells of the city tolled for its inhabitants to bring water from the river. I joined the crowd in the effort to contain the destruction. I was in panic that the flames could reach Raphael's or Michelangelo's frescos. Fortunately, only the quarters of two cardinals were severely damaged. As the papal architect, Raphael was assigned the repair job. My job became to spy and assess if the fire had been an accident or intentional. I cured the servants who had suffered minor injuries from the event. The tales they told suggested an accident. I needed to confirm the information so I moved in stealth to inspect the rubble and listened to people who visited the damaged area. Here is where I met with Raphael again. He had ten workers receiving directions from him when he noticed me bent next to the remains of a desk studying a half-burnt book. He dismissed his entourage and came to me with open arms, his hair a stroke of color like a blond wind in the ash-covered room.

"Federigo! I have been looking for you all over the city to share the joy that has filled my life. I cannot thank you enough for introducing me to the Luttis. Can you believe I am completely in love? The baker's daughter is the woman God intended for me. She is real, not the pretentious courtesans or the greedy low class women I have been dealing with all these years. When she looks at me, I know she sees me." I controlled my expression, displaying only happiness at the news. "My friends see me so obsessed with her beauty and charm that I need to escape the workshop for a respite from their teasing. They nicknamed her 'La Fornarina,' the baker's daughter. The funniest thing is that this is still a boyish love. I have not taken her to my bed yet. Her father is such a great man that I feel a touch of guilt about stealing her virginity. He is doing his best to protect her."

I smiled and nodded. Was he serious about her? Putting his face very close to mine he murmured, "I have a great plan for a New Year's celebration. We are eloping after midnight mass."

I did not want to hear the details of his escape with her, but I kept a grinning mask on my face while anger and rebellion against God and my destiny throbbed in my chest. I gestured, asking about his plans after she went away with him.

"Giulio Romano has come to my aid. He found a charming room for rent at an aristocratic mansion close to our workshop. She will live there from now on. I will cover all her expenses and give her luxuries she never experienced before. Since I am taking her from her father, I'll protect her now. I might not be as wealthy as Chigi—only God is—but I can keep my lady very well." He radiated anticipation and pride. He was truly a prince and behaving as one.

I took out a notebook and a stick of charcoal. I wrote: "Does B. know? Aren't you engaged to his niece Maria?"

His eyes twinkled mischievously as if honey were pouring into them. "He will be fine. He knows his niece is 'distant' and with other 'interests.' He will not be happy but he is a smart politician over all. He realizes that having his name closely and publicly associated with mine grants him stature among others in the Curia. Being a family cardinal, he does not have the mansions and material fortune of others and realizes that, more than others, his influence and connections are his wealth."

One of his assistants approached us holding a pile of papers with the layout of the burnt apartments. I was relieved that our conversation had been interrupted, and he went back to business. I took the opportunity to wave goodbye. Instead of going to my quarters, I threw myself into the streets with demons churning in my stomach. My head was high but I wanted to wander in the streets so the vision of the sick and crippled beggars would convince me of having good fortune despite my distress. I explored side roads and the back alleys behind churches where the miserable gather waiting for charity or death. My feet had a plan and without my conscious decision I walked to the construction that served as a stable for Hanno, the Pope's white elephant. The sun had already set but a dull light with specks of scintillating red dust lingered in the air. The stable was deserted. The elephant stood motionless while munching some hay appearing surrendered to boredom and melancholy for his native land. He stared at me with his taciturn eyes. We were two creatures forced to exist in Rome. I had heard that he was dangerous. Powerful enormous muscles and his mass made him unstoppable when irritated. He had killed one of his handlers by grabbing him with his trunk and thrashing him against a wall. Disregarding any fear, I reached to his flank feeling his coarse, thick, wrinkled skin. My white hand connecting with him seemed to be made of the same material covering his scarred body. As if responding to the extreme dryness of his body, tears flowed down my cheeks. I was gloomy for both of us.

We each had been snatched from good lives by interests and greed within the Church. The city would never offer life mates to us. We would remain as long as the Pope celebrated us as his favored freaks.

I leaned on the beast, seeking shelter. Was it because he felt the wetness on my face that he stopped munching and his breathing soothed? He moved his trunk and explored my back with caution, culminating his exploration on my hairless skull. I embraced the wall of animal with both my arms, and he seemed to understand I was weeping for both of us.

But I was not the only one crying because of Raphael and Margharetta. It was early in the year 1515 when I ventured back to the bakery at 21 Santa Dorotea. Francesco pulled me to a table as soon as he saw me picking a loaf of bread. He held tightly to my forearms and wept: "Your friend has taken my beautiful daughter. She is his concubine! You gave me my life back when I was injured in the head but you took it away when you brought Raphael Sanzio to this place." During this time, I grasped the loaf of bread I had picked up from a shelf. I could feel his grief in the loaf as the dough had not risen as usual, becoming flat and unsavory. I allowed him to talk while customers poured in and out the bakery. "My biggest sin is that I forgive her. I am only a baker, what kind of suitors would have approached her otherwise? Maybe she would have met an oaf that would fill her with children. At least she is the mistress of the greatest artist in the universe, the architect for the Pope and Saint Peter's Basilica, intimate friend of cardinals and bankers." He scrutinized me, his gaze intense and probing while allowing conflicting emotions to surface from his damaged heart. A customer complained next to us. She demanded her money back as the honey and sugar loaf was sour. "I don't want to lose Margharetta. I wish she would return and know she is welcomed. This is still her home if the affair ends. We don't care about what the people will gossip, we are her family. She and her confessor will have to figure how to save her eternal soul. I cherish her too much to shun her like all those families who reject their daughters after they choose to live unmarried with a man. She should know that we will always be here for her even if our parish excommunicates us."

I gestured for him to write a note to her. He was shaking when he acknowledged: "I can only scribble the basic letters; I can barely discern some words and use them to make my business better than others.

People of my stature cannot read or write, you should not mock me."
I gestured for him to dictate the message to me. I pulled a piece of
paper and a charcoal stick from my robes. Francesco was radiant. He
chose his words with great care to express his love to his daughter. He
promised not to judge her actions and invited her to visit the bakery as
frequently as she desired. As I folded the note, his rough hands covered mine, and his eyes shone with hope. "I am certain she will come,
Federigo. I am certain God Almighty's designs intended her to be more
than a baker's daughter. She is too beautiful and charming. Her gentle
heart has too much strength and will and zest for life. She can be the
right woman for a great man. I pray he is serious about her. Raphael
Sanzio is known as womanizer...but I saw how he looked at her, how
they talked and moved when together. She must be a lot more to him.
Their status is too distant for them to marry, even a stupid baker like me
knows that, but I pray that she remains next to him for the rest of her
life. She should become an inspiration for him to achieve even greater
glory." I assented with movements.

Raphael's workshop was frantic with activity as he was accepting
more assignments than they could manage, but still the work made everybody cheerful and energetic. Giulio Romano asked me for the basket
of bread I always brought to them. I had come empty handed; I refused
to reveal how unsavory the pastries had become in the last few weeks.
He complained that Raphael had not returned from Margharetta's room
where he had gone the previous night. "So much work, and he is in
mating season!" I requested directions to Margharetta's address. I hurried, fearful, but excited at the prospect of seeing her again.

The rented room was in an old magnificent mansion. It belonged to
a member of Rome's ancient aristocracy. However, their centuries-old
lineage had not prevented their decline into poverty, forcing them to
subdivide and rent portions of the house. The mansion was in disrepair
but still radiated an aura of class and patrician arrogance that missing and loose tiles and threadbare tapestries and worn out rugs could
not diminish. A servant let me in, and I quickly climbed the stairs to
Margharetta's room.

Margharetta responded to the knock at her door. She peeked first,
but opened the door widely when she recognized me. The room air

was saturated with the musky perfumes of a love-making night. She was only wearing a very thin white slip that whispered the colors of her skin, her nipples, and her pubis. She hugged me joyful and excited, and kissed me on both cheeks, holding me next to her body. I could feel her hard nipples and the moist warm heat between her legs through the thin fabric. Her dark hair smelled of the moon, chamomile, and lavender. I got hard instantly, so I had to gently push her away against my will.

"Let's make this clear, my love. Federigo is the only other man besides me who you are allowed to embrace and kiss in such a way," Raphael declared, half-dressed, from across the room. He realized he was late for some appointment and was violently stuffing his feet into his boots; his naked torso revealed dry streaks of saliva on his chest and armpits. "He and I are brothers. We are living the same life in two connected bodies. That was the universe's design so we could grasp more of this unique moment with one existence." His tone was half serious, half jest. Still, I felt flattered with his words—but looking at him, I could not help but wonder how he could not bathe every day.

Margharetta showed me around the large and once-elegant bedroom. Streaks of sunlight filtered through a worn-out velvet curtain illuminating Margharetta's back and revealing the shape of her body through the slip fabric. I moved my legs hoping they would not notice the erection protruding under my robes. Raphael winked as he slipped on his black jacket.

I extracted Lutti's letter from my sleeve and handed it to Raphael knowing that Margharetta could not read. He stared me in the eyes, his tousled hair creating an aureole around his head. "Federigo, you should read it to Margharetta. If we are truly connected you should not hold any secrets from her." This time he was serious.

She was about to reprimand Raphael for the comment when I took the letter and spoke: "It's a letter from your father. I saw him this morning." She gave a step backwards amazed and delighted by the discovery of my voice and the news. "You have to swear to keep the secret that I can talk. Your life and Raphael's would be in danger if it is known that I converse with you." Raphael stood next to me and passed his arm around my shoulders. The smell of his sweat mixed with Margharetta's lavender and chamomile suffused his jaws and shoulders. "But my voice is a topic for another time. I have to read the note from your father to you." She sat on the untidy bed showing fear and foreboding. Raphael took a step to her, his muscles taut like a spring. "He wants to tell you that he adores you and you are always welcomed at home." I read Francesco's phrases while her delicate hands covered her crying face. Raphael sat and hugged her, sharing the bliss and relief that Francesco's words delivered.

We remained some minutes frozen like that. Margharetta crying, Raphael holding her while I watched. Then she got on her knees and kissed my right hand. "Thank you, my lord, thank you, my friend, thank you, my lover's brother." Her dripping moist tears caressed my skin. Passion was surging again in me when Raphael uncoiled out of bed and pulled me away from Margharetta.

"I have to run! I am late to meet with Chigi and Bibbiena!" He pulled my arm. "I just realized you should come with me, too, Federigo. You will like this. We are going to an underground excavation at Titus Baths. You were the one who told me about them first. I always wanted an excursion into the digs, and Bibbiena was able to organize one for today. There is more than one reason you are here today. Come with me."

I accepted to join the excursion, as it was the perfect excuse for me to leave Margharetta's side quickly. I turned away as Raphael embraced and kissed Margharetta with a passionate farewell. She then stopped me before I walked out of the room and gave me a kiss on each cheek, her lips still wet with Raphael's saliva.

I knew we were approaching the dig site because the strong balm from the field of lavender flowers engulfed us, filling me with ambivalent memories. Agostino Chigi and Bernardo Bibbiena were waiting for Raphael under the shadow of a pine tree. The influential men were not used to waiting for anybody; however, instead of being irritated, they had their servants fetch wine and antipasto from a nearby tavern and had spread the meal on a makeshift table in front of them. The weather was delightful, sunny but cool. Purple rolling fields with ancient columns emerging randomly provided a perfect distraction from daily occupations. Both men greeted us with enthusiasm. They knew that Raphael and I had become good friends, so they allowed me to enter their inner circle.

Under the shade of a crowded canvas tent waited a cluster of ex-cavators and servants. They had a large basket with a thick rope tied to it to lower us down one by one into the dig. We had also a guide and torch bearers who would accompany us. Waiting for my turn to be descended into the pit, I rejoiced at the memories of my grandfather asleep while my brother and I played around. I could see the edge of the rock wall where we had found the entrance to the underground room where the tablets with the poison formulas had been. All this time, lazy bees obese with the abundance of lavender honey buzzed languidly in the hot air.

Lowered down inside the basket, I joined the party. With lit torch-es, we explored the tunnels. The chief excavator told us they had found close to a hundred rooms. We entered what felt like a cave but was a rectangular peristyle court backed against the hillside rock foundation. Triple and quintuple suites of dining rooms in many shapes and sizes faced the court. As we looked at the decoration of the rooms, the men were discussing how Bibbiena should decorate his apartments damaged by the December fire. Raphael was repairing them. Chigi was pointing at the wall and double ceilings with trap doors where flowers or treats were hidden to drop on the guests at the climax of the banquet. Exuberant frescos with landscapes depicting fountains and forests where frolicking cupids floated in the wind like minute clouds encircled us, and everybody was delighted with them. In one fresco, Zeus stood at the center while the youth Ganymede was his cupbearer. The marble and mosaic in most rooms had been stripped off and stolen a long time ago but frescoes re-mained. We were welcomed into the following room by roaring laughter from Chigi as he was the first to discover erotic scenes of nymphs and centaurs in love. They were painted inside decorative medallions under a high barrel vault decorated to evoke a cave with pumice stone. A small stream of water skimmed down the wall and crossed the room; it was the vestige of a waterfall once used to cool down the room now simply creat-ing a muggy atmosphere like a steam bath.

"Bernardo, why don't you ask the boy here to paint your walls with these types of motifs? I am certain Leo would have a good laugh and visit you frequently." Chigi pointed to the head of a centaur posed be-tween the open legs of a nymph.

"And if you could make one room as hot and humid as this one you could reduce many of my ailments!" completed Bibbiena, his face dripping sweat.

Raphael was enthralled by the images. He traced them with his index finger drenching the movement and overtly sensual and joyous depiction. I read in his forehead how he was linking the frescos in front of him to the drawings of Imperia and me when he had celebrated carnal pleasure. His eyes were ablaze with ideas and inspiration seeing how he could translate the sensuality of the ancient gods to one that celebrated the human spirit.

The erotic images reminded me of the ones my brother and I had discovered many years ago. In my childhood, I had seen just a small fraction of the underground palace, some of the outer, more private rooms. My heart was pounding in my chest. It was the ecstasy of discovery but also the perception of being in a different time, when a Roman Emperor—or even better, my young brother, Giacomo—would appear around the corner. I snatched a torch from one of the servants and decided to explore by myself while the members of my party continued to discuss ideas for Bibbiena's apartments.

The size of the place convinced me that the excavators were wrong in considering this site to be Titus's Baths. Based on my reading, this had to be Nero's Domus Aurea. I approached the rock walls since we had found the tablet room entrance in a crevice on the living rock. I was about to turn back to the group when something captured my attention: an intense crimson wall, partly submerged in rubble but revealing an orgy of gods, satyrs, women, and nymphs. Females were getting pleasure from females, males from males. In some portions, two men were having intercourse with one woman. Everything was very overt but maintained an elegance and grace in shape and line, as I had never seen. The lambent flame of the torch created the illusion of movement on the flat surface. I stared at it, aroused and admiring the work when I discovered the scene from a distant room. It was the satyr and nymph image that had welcomed Giacomo and me when we had found the clay tablets so long ago. I moved swiftly in that direction—maybe my spirit believed it could jump into my past. It was the scene we had discovered that had made Giacomo laugh at the shameless display of breasts and sexual organs, nymphs and satyrs contorted in suggestive poses. Mature now, I realized how beautiful the artwork was, and how it was connected to other frescos. I peeked into the orgy room and noticed that my party was there. Their conversations had ceased as they admired in awe the landscape of bodies. Whatever ideas they had discussed in the previous room now became grandiose and transcendent. Raphael's eyes could not have been wider with creative challenge. Bibbiena smirked mischievously to himself while Chigi touched the fresco with reverent and trembling fingers.

"How could they do this?"

"This is truly a celebration of human anatomy in a way Michelangelo would have never been able to grasp. Eros is triumphant. Mind, spirit, and flesh reveals they are merged as one substance," whispered Raphael. "Pleasure for pleasure's sake drives the human spirit since its inception."

"I have many ideas for the decoration of my apartment," chuckled Bibbiena.

"I have many ideas for my mistresses!" retorted Chigi.

I ignored them as I had discovered a half-blocked passageway in the direction of the clay tablets room. I wished to go there, so I scurried into it. Soon the passageway became very narrow, but that did not stop me. I dropped into a chamber. It was the place where the tablets had been. Part of the roof had collapsed on it, so rocks and debris obstructed part of it. I looked around in awe but then I discovered human bones in one corner. The bones were very clean. Wild dogs and rats had nibbled on them. The skeleton was far from complete. The skull and ribs were there but most of the other bones were gone. I pushed the skull with my foot and discovered the bones of a hand under it. One of the fingers had a gold ring with a large square ruby. I picked it up, wiping the dust from the surface to reveal two cart wheels connected by a cross engraved on it. It was my grandfather's ring! I sat down holding the skeleton's hand in my palms, flushed with relief, grief, and deep melancholy. This was the ring my grandfather had vowed to return to his friend the German archbishop.

The finding explained a lot. I envisioned how the night my father died my grandfather had ran away naked and bewildered from our burning home. He had searched for a safe house. His brain, unable to reason, had allowed his heart to guide his steps to the lavender fields he had frequented with my brother and me. He had found an entrance through the rock wall to the underground palace where had hid until a wild dog or hunger had killed him. I held the ring tightly in my fist. Guilt made me nauseated. I had failed to protect my grandfather. I felt my mother's presence next to me deriding the murals in the other rooms, reveling in my punishment for having failed to protect the ones I loved in favor of pagan culture. But I would not fail to return the ring to his rightful owner. I would fulfill my grandfather's promise to his friend. I opened the secret chamber in the ring to find honey still in it. Then I heard my companions calling for me. I took a rock and banged it on the debris so they could find my location. I wished for Raphael to see the room so we could talk about it later.

"He seems to have gone over there!" called the expedition guide.

"That devil, why would he go down that half-blocked alley?" exclaimed Bibbiena.

"Maybe he wants to enjoy the pictures in private! Pull your pants up, mute, we are coming for you!" scoffed Chigi.

I kept knocking on the debris so they would join me when suddenly the rocks and dirt groaned an unexpected response. The chamber shook as if struck by an earthquake and soon parts of the wall around me collapsed. Sprinting to the exit while holding tightly to the ring, I felt sand and pebbles hitting me. The dust choked me. The guide and my companions were shouting when an avalanche of rocks fell, projecting me into darkness.

I woke up three days later. I was in a strange bed. I smelled chamomile in my surroundings. I was in Margharetta's bedroom. The guide and my companions had pulled me out of the debris. Raphael had brought me to Margharetta's so she could take care of me. I noticed I was naked under the bed sheets. My body was clean, and my wounds had been treated. I trembled, wondering if she had been the one scrubbing my body with a sponge, water, and vinegar. The room was empty, but realizing where I was explained what I thought were recent dreams. During those three days, I had laid semi-conscious. Sometimes delirious, sometimes listening to the sounds around me with closed eyes. I made an effort and was able to reconstruct full conversations in my mind. I remembered the voices of Raphael and Margharetta. I understood that through Raphael, Margharetta was rediscovering the city where she had lived all her life. Rome had become suddenly an amazing place inundated with secrets and knowledge of the past. Art was everywhere. They talked of how the thoughts of the ancient thinkers eliminated guilt from carnal sins that so many priests held as a branding stick in their eulogies. He enjoyed teaching her things, guiding her as she experienced more...part of which were the sounds of their lovemaking. They had given me the bed, while they slept on the velvet couch next to the window. Half-conscious I had listened to their moans of satisfaction and their movements as they embraced and caressed each other.

The door opened. Margharetta came into the room and embraced me when noticing I was awake. She was carrying a bag of warm bread from her father's bakery she had brought to mix with milk and feed to me.

"Federigo! I prayed so much for your health." She covered my face with kisses and her hands caressed my cheeks. "Raphael and I were devastated! You cannot die before we do. Swear that you'll wait until he and I are in our graves! We could not stand the grief of losing you!" I extended my arms and held her next to me, her warmth filtering through my body, her breasts against my chest through the covers. "You know that if I had not met Raphael, sooner or later I would have fallen in love with you." She said standing up. "You are such a noble and wise man. Raphael has told me how you helped him and how much you have taught him. Now he is my teacher."

CHAPTER 34

MASKED BALL

The Vatican insisted on keeping the masked ball on schedule—odd, given that the Los Angeles bishop had been buried just the previous day. The Holy See doesn't want to make a bigger deal of Herrera's death. He was part of an insider movement against celibacy for priests, and the Curia is not ready to discuss any reforms with the press yet. The Vatican does not fulfill the image the popular media presents: a well coordinated, centralized organization. There are many departments and groups working inside their silos, not communicating and frequently with conflicting agendas.

The girls have taken all day to get ready for the ball. Their grandma took them for facials and manicures. Their grandfather took them shopping for fabulous new dresses. They are now taking showers, getting their hair done, and ensuring their shoes look their best. To have space to get dressed, they are doing all of this at their grandparents' suite at the Hotel Excelsior. Anthony hears the girls inside the suite fighting among themselves about who should wear a certain necklace. He wonders if he should intervene, but decides against it and stays working on his laptop. He reads the newspaper. Larry Page and Google's international president are in Rome for the masked ball. The balance between transparency and privacy in the web is a core topic for them. Anthony hears the girls' arguing escalating in volume.

• • •

"Is this going to end very late?" Thalia cuddles against her father in the back seat of a taxi cab as they wind up streets moving away from Rome's downtown. "Panda had a surgical procedure today, and we need to get back to him."

"Thalia has been feeding Panda small erasers with food shapes through a tear on his neck," explains Claudia to make sense of her sister's comments. "Thalia has been buying them from street vendors throughout the city, and Panda became so heavy that the small tear under its neck was at risk of decapitating him."

"He is still hungry," remarks Thalia matter-of-factly.

"What did you do with the 'food'?" Anthony passes his hand through his daughter's long, elegantly braided hair.

"I left it on top of the desk in our room."

"We just need to pick some and 'feed' them back to Panda. Grandma already fixed the tear and left it small again, but Thalia, you will have to choose which ones to give him. If not, he will tear again," explains Claudia.

"Does he have a favorite food?" asks Anthony as he pays the taxi driver.

"Hot dogs, I separated them from other 'food groups.' Panda will have a feast tomorrow morning."

· · ·

The MAXXI is an exceptional building with flowing angles and dare-devil design. It serves as the perfect background for a crowd of men dressed in black ties and women in cocktail dresses and feathers, all of them wearing carnival masks covering their eyes and nose. Religious men wear their black soutanes. Google has gigantic screens where 3D images stream without the need of special glasses. They are showing their latest technologies while serving a buffet prepared by top chefs flown expressly for the event from different venues around the globe. At the rotunda facing the museum entrance, they have a replica of the dinosaur skeleton at their Mountain View office complex.

Anthony arrives with his in-laws and his daughters. The girls walk to the building, leaning back in awe. At the reception, they enter a photography booth with a Google background. Their pictures are immediately photo-streamed to a stripe of displays circling inside the building like a ribbon. A guide welcomes them and gives them a number for a tour of the exhibits. A whirlwind of people in black ties and in colorful gowns envelops them. Francesca is wearing a dress from the Spanish designer Agatha Ruiz de la Prada multilayered and multicolored as if inspired by her hair. Ahmed walks three steps behind her in an Armani tuxedo.

"This is what I needed." She hangs herself from Anthony's arm. "I've been desolated since Gabriel's death." She has been drinking several of the vodka cocktails mixed for the event. She kisses all members of Anthony's family covering them in a cloud of alcoholic fumes. Ahmed has moved away to a corner at the bar lounge.

Anthony pats Francesca on her bare arm. "You and I need to catch up very soon. I called you many times but got the answering machine."

"I was too depressed. Ahmed had to take me to Milan to cheer me up, but even that failed to make me feel better."

"It's alright. We'll talk in the upcoming days. Are you planning to work next week? We have to submit a new draft of our *Catullus* paper."

"I will be there. Now let me go back to Ahmed…he does not like large crowds…he becomes shy as if worried someone might recognize him. You know these royalty types!" She winks at him.

A guide calls Anthony's family number for a tour. Anthony examines the sleek lines of the building, feeling as it were alive. The girls run up and down the ramps delighted by the large art installations and massive canvases. Their favorite part is discovering shiny solid aluminum toilets in the restrooms.

Claudia is analyzing information spread across the different floors, explaining the Transparency Controversy surrounding the Catholic Church. "You know, Papa? I think you are getting this Transparency thing wrong. You and your friends are *ooold*. Ancient by Internet standards." Her sisters agree with a playful smile. "You should have people our age discussing the topic. I see the pictures of some of the members of the Conference and wonder if they have ever used a computer." Anthony laughs at her comment. "It's true! We are the ones who had iPads in our cribs! *WE* should know better."

"Look, dessert!" Anthony does not want to invest any more time in the topic. He would rather stop at a *cannoli* station on the third floor. He is serving the girls when he detects a figure floating toward him. Anxiety shakes him, and his face is on fire. His muscles tighten, alert. Akemi is wearing a lustrous, black, long gown that matches the daring metallic lines of the museum. Micro robots that imitate-diamond encrusted jewelry encircle her neck and bare arms. The girls become silent noticing their father's distraction and follow his gaze.

Thalia releases Anthony's hand. "It's the same lady that looked for you at our hotel." She is angry that someone has intruded on their time together. Akemi stares at Anthony and his family with a longing look. Her body is paralyzed, sensing his distrust and lust.

"Is she your girlfriend? Is that why you and grandpa have been talking about sending us to Ancona?" Anthony is shocked by the accusing tone. Thalia steps away from him, her arms at her sides, curved and ready for battle. "Have you picked *her* over us?"

"No, sweetheart. You are more important than any woman out there. She and I have worked together—not that I want to work with her anymore." But even he can sense the layers of contradictory emotions in his words.

Thalia examines Akemi, pouting her lips. Claudia's eyes reveal she is evaluating the situation. Virginia is mesmerized by her clothes. Somehow Anthony and Akemi stay in their places, incapable of moving closer or away. There is vulnerability in Akemi's eyes, surprising and inviting. They just stare at each other, defenses low.

"She IS your GIRLfriend!" shrieks Thalia offended as she sprints away through groups of people, reaching the aerodynamic staircases that connect the different gallery floors.

Anthony snaps out of the trance and immediately races behind her. "Girls, stay here with your grandparents!"

The metallic stairs at the MAXXI have small perforations that make them semi-translucent. Thalia is escaping, propelled by her fury, but Anthony quickly closes the distance between them when he sees a burly arm in the distance. The linebacker! The tall, bald giant who had tried to snatch Thalia's backpack at Piazza d'Spagna, who revealed Giocatelli's secrets to the press, and who had just eluded him at the American

Embassy is there. Thalia is running toward him. The bald man's lips contort in a gruesome smile noticing the girl dashing in his direction. Anthony speeds up but the giant snatches the girl by the waist and pulls her into a gallery, carrying her without effort. Anthony hears Thalia's frenetic fighting and a high-pitched squeal: "PAPA, help!" His legs are his limit, he cannot move them faster, but as he turns the bend, he realizes that installation his daughter has been abducted into is a labyrinth made of marble blocks, mirrors, and flat TV screens.

"Thalia! Thalia! Let her go, bastard." His voice gets lost in the high ceiling. He navigates the twists and turns of the labyrinth realizing that the area is larger and more complex than he could have imagined. The sound coming from the TV screens is loud and unnerving, like a pack of hyenas howling at him.

After a turn, he comes face to face with a panting Akemi. She has taken off her high heels to run faster. She is wearing her enhanced reality prototype Google Glass so she can track her micro robots and drones launched in pursuit of the muscular giant. She is giving orders to the guards through her Glass. She looks directly at Anthony. "Follow me! I can see where they are going." Akemi moves through a tunnel made of rock while stating the obvious. "It's the same man from the American Embassy press release." Anthony sees the man in the distance holding Thalia. Guilt brings tears to his eyes.

The drones fly like a cloud of eagles with talons extended while Akemi's other robots scurry on the walls and handrails. The giant reaches the staircase and climbs it with surprising agility, ignoring the struggling girl in his arms. As he grabs the handrail, he feels a thousand needles puncturing his skin. Akemi's diamond necklace had become a centipede and has been waiting for him: a trap for the muscular man. The surprise and the pain make him stop. He grabs the micro robot in his formidable paw and throws it against a wall where it explodes into pieces. This gives time for Anthony to reach him, and he charges against the man's chest with his shoulder. His momentum is powerful enough to knock his opponent down. The linebacker releases Thalia as he an Anthony roll halfway down a short staircase. Thalia sits shaking when she feels Akemi's arms embrace her from behind. Akemi kneels to soothe the girl, distracting her from the brawl in front of them.

Security guards are pouring in from all corners. The giant gets up, raising Anthony by the neck, and then punches him in the gut with a powerful blow that propels him against a rail with all of the air knocked out of his lungs. The giant stands up and swats at the drones around him, making them spin out of control and explode as they collide against the walls. While the giant assesses his next move, the security guards have pulled out guns and surround him. When the man realizes the guards will capture him in a few minutes, he makes a desperate attempt to escape by jumping off the staircase into the void. Two drones shoot at him, and the impact of the projectiles makes him lose the balance to soften his landing. The people under him scream in panic while his plummeting ends with a crunching sound on the floor of the reception lobby where he lies inert—a pool of blood forming under him.

Thalia extricates herself from Akemi's hug and rushes to her father. Tears of terror wet Anthony's starched white shirt, torn and open since the buttons flew into the air during the fight. He is regaining consciousness and buries his face in Thalia's hair. He agonizingly stands up with Akemi's help and, holding Thalia's hand, limps down the stairs as fast as he can. Alessandro emerges from the crowd on the lower floor and touches the fallen man's neck. "He is still alive," he whispers into a radio. Akemi and Anthony reach the giant's body at the same time. Anthony urges Thalia to rejoin her sisters and grandparents. The scared girl obeys with no questions. Anthony's eyes push Alessandro and Akemi away from the body, defying them to investigate him before he does. He staggers to the motionless body and kneels next to it. He pats the man's jacket and, feeling something in the breast pocket, fishes out the giant's smartphone. Akemi is about to take a step toward him but Anthony makes her stop, extending his palm to her. He punches the phone to check recent calls.

E. Jones
E. Jones
E. Jones
E. Jones
E. Jones
E. Jones

Ellia Jones's name fills the recent calls screen—both received and made. Anthony drops the phone and rubs his temples with shaking hands. Akemi approaches now and instead of searching the giant she hugs the kneeling Anthony, just as she had done with Thalia, and her warmth and orange flower scent make Anthony cuddle against her.

. . .

Anthony reunites with his family. Virginia and Claudia surround their sister and join their tears to hers. Outside, sirens, police cars, and ambulances can be heard in the distance. The failed party is over, and the guests are being ushered to the parking lot.

Akemi approaches the three girls. She stoops in front of them. "Are you okay?" Thalia's eyes glisten when she discovers another robotic centipede as it transforms into a diamond bracelet around Akemi's wrist. She touches it with a shaking finger. The bracelet untangles and winds around the girl's forearm. Akemi caresses it and the girl's small hand and wrist with unexpected tenderness. Thalia ventures half a smile.

Anthony crouches next to Akemi, resting his hand on his daughter's shoulder. "Baby, did the man say anything to you?" Thalia closes her eyes and cries in silence, moving her head from one side to another.

"I think it is time to put the Ancona plan to work," Elmer declares behind them.

Alessandro has also joined the group. "I'll get a police car to take you to the train station."

"Melissa and I can go to the hotel to pick up a few things. The girls left their backpacks with us. We have travel luggage ready for this, too."

"I'll accompany the girls to Termini. I will join you as soon as I can in Ancona." Anthony turns to his daughters. "I need to stay to capture the bad guys. Is that ok with you girls?" The three nod in agreement despite the fear their faces reveal.

. . .

The express train to Ancona pulls away on the track. Akemi stands next to Anthony while the wind flutters through her disheveled black hair.

"How could I get my family into this mess?" he asks. Akemi passes her arm around his shoulder. "I want to get lost. Maybe escape every-thing for a night. Take the train and get off wherever it takes me."

She holds his hand and pulls him into the subway. "Let's go. Let's get lost in Rome's underground tunnels and maybe capture the illusion of moving away from this mess."

They sit on thick plastic upholstery in an empty wagon echoing with the sounds and smells from the day. They sit side-by-side, shoulder-to-shoulder. The darkness and the sway of the train lulls Akemi into sleep. She tilts her head and rests it on Anthony's shoulder, closing her eyes as he looks into emptiness with guilt and fear pulling at his stomach mus-cles and heart tendons. The train slides away from the city into midnight.

CHAPTER 35

AKEMI'S STORY

There is something about trains scurrying under the city while everyone is asleep. Maybe it is their white artificial light enhancing the emptiness of a space usually crowded; the fatigue of the wagons aware that soon they will stop at a station where a cleaning crew will strip them of the layers of human detritus (skin cells, spilled liquids, trash, routine, broken dreams, discovery, and day adventures); or the lingering smells merged into an encyclopedia of everyday stories from the inhabitants of Rome that if recorded would fill hundreds of volumes with narratives from the obscene to the sublime. Akemi cuddles against the warmth of Anthony's body while he protects her with his arm around her shoulder. Intermittent light caresses her obsidian hair. "Who is this woman? Who is she *really*? What lies beneath the efficiency?" he murmurs to himself, feeling protective, wishing they were at home—wherever that might be, sitting on a couch reading together while sipping a hot drink in front of a fireplace.

The train slows down and a distorted voice through the train's speakers declares that they have reached the last stop and the service has ended for the night. Anthony shakes Akemi lightly to wake her up from a sleep deeper than her usual. She opens her dark eyes stunned to be in a train wagon. She pulls away from Anthony, straightening her clothes and hair. She then walks to the exit with muscles tight, her face holding a troubled expression. She feels violated because Anthony has intruded with the unexpected intimacy of the mundane. He follows her, and when she stops trying to figure out their location in the darkness, he pulls off his coat and puts it around her bare shoulders, as the air is cold and humid. She overcomes her instinct to reject the coat, instead burrowing into it; the smell of his body permeates the fabric. Anthony takes her hand and guides her to a pedestrian bridge that crosses a multi-lane highway. They are in *Ostia Antica*, and he remembers having seen a small bed and breakfast on the way to the excavations he had visited with his daughters. They stroll under dormant umbrella pine trees. Akemi stops and tugs Anthony to a bench in front of the Castle of Julius II, a fortress built along the left bank of the Tiber commissioned to *Baccio Pontelli*, an architect that built some of the most beautiful castles in central Italy, by Julius II before he became Pope. He later used the construction as a sanctuary and personal retreat whenever he needed to escape from Rome. Anthony and Akemi avert each other's gaze by examining the crenelated walls and powerful round tower in front of them. After a while, Anthony takes a deep breath: "I need to know more about you."

"Yes you do." She responds matter-of-factly, no hint of doubt. She lets go of his hand and opens her bag, pulling a tablet and what seems to be a case for contact lenses. She hands it to Anthony and signals for him to put the contacts on. Anthony uses the tablet as a mirror to place the transparent semi-spheres on his eyes. Then she asks him to place the palm of his right hand on the surface of a tablet. Akemi also pulls her tablet out of her bag and starts scrolling on it. The technology irritates Anthony but before he can complain, two nano-cameras on the contact lenses turn on and zoom on his retinas, projecting images directly into his field of vision, creating the effect of an image on top of another image as the backdrop of the castle fades.

The first image that encircles him is of tomato fields extending far out to a flat horizon where green leaves stretch under irrigation systems and the sun. The horizon is verdant with globes of plump red poking their heads under rainbows created by miniscule drops of water, painting an otherwise desert land.

"I am a mix of bloods: Mexican, Japanese and American. This is where I was born, in a tomato ranch close to La Angostura, Sinaloa. My father was a Japanese-American engineer. He worked for Toyota in Los Angeles, and was a rising star. During the weekends, he loved to escape to Mexico. He had been obsessed by the culture of that country since he had been in middle school. He loved the food, he loved the spirit of its people, and he loved the history. What began as day trips to Tijuana soon became trips to its cities and pre-Hispanic archeological sites. He relished its beaches, and one autumn decided to venture on a road trip across Sonora and Sinaloa, two northwestern states. Some tried to dissuade him. The area he was going to visit had high criminality driven by drug trafficking. He ignored them. It was his destiny to meet my mother on that vacation. She was a beauty from Sinaloa, the daughter of a wealthy landowner who cultivated cotton, tomatoes, and white corn. My Mom and he fell in love instantly. He returned to Los Angeles, resigned from his job at Toyota, and loaded his car with all his belongings to return to Mexico, where he became an agronomy engineer."

The fields lead to an unpaved road at the end of which is a large house made of brick and painted white with chairs and tables on the porch where the family sits when the sun is setting to drink cold lemonade and eat sweet, freshly picked tomatoes fresher than cold-salted watermelon. Anthony sees a Japanese man and a tall black-haired Hispanic woman with a little girl.

"This is my first home. I created these animations to test new software developed by my company. I sometimes venture into them."

The image vanishes and, as if guided by the ghosts of Christmas, Anthony is in Akemi's second home. They are walking up the stairs of a concrete four story–high building in the middle of the Arizona desert. The sterile concrete grey walls look down on them. Far away in the distance is the spectacle of sliced mountains where rock strata create stripes of different colors from forgotten geological eras. Akemi hesitates to go in. Anthony wishes to comfort her, but she shies away and, rushing, pushes the very heavy metallic double doors open into the building. He runs behind her, but she is lost in a thick current of girls between eight and eighteen swarming around the foyer, corridors, and staircase. They are all wearing uniforms: plaid skirts, white button-up shirts, a red cravat, and blue vests. They ebb and flow as Sargasso algae on a field down an ocean trench. He pushes his way around as if fighting a mob. The air conditioning is blasting, but he sweats. He climbs the stairs and looks for the computer room in the different floors. He finds her there, sitting by herself surrounded by empty green desks. Her screen is on as she peeks at the world ignoring the desert sprawl out the windows. She seems to be waiting for emails from her parents, but a spreadsheet floating in the upper corner of the screen reveals that she has been waiting to hear from them for months.

"Without any warning or explanation, they sent me to a Catholic all-girls boarding school in Arizona. The head priest at the school was a very good person. I did not get along with anybody but him. He became my only family since I spent all my vacations at the boarding school. Nobody ever came to see me or pick me up. My parents paid punctually but I was isolated from them." Akemi clenches her fists until the lack of blood circulation turns them the color of white-hot resentment. "I disliked everyone. I made a point not to socialize. Father George, the head priest, noticed that I had a natural ability with computers so he allowed me to have a laptop and be connected to Wi-Fi as much as I desired as long as my grades were good. We struck a deal. I refrained from being too mean to others, studied hard—and, in exchange, had a digital window to look out of from the boarding school for the next four years. I read all kinds of books on my laptop. I saw places and talked to people in other countries. I forced myself to learn and practiced other languages, but most importantly I found others like me. They were also isolated misfits. Freaks too brilliant with math and programming skills that they became hackers. I joined their ranks. I learned their honor code while I cracked security systems better than they could. I paraded my anger inside heavily guarded servers. It was thrilling to be one step ahead of authorities and meddle in others secrets: big corporations, governments, institutions, and individuals. One morning during a summer vacation, I woke up and decided to use my skills to locate my parents and give them pay back."

Her black hair covers the front of her teenage face as if creating a vortex behind which to hide her sad eyes. A screen saver appears with two images of planet Earth. Japanese pop music blares from the small speakers out of the computer, and the two Earths rotate and counter-rotate on top of a muddy background. Anthony extends his arm and places his hand on top of the young girl's shoulder. As if she were a robot and human touch were the power-on button, she pushes her hair backward with both hands and places frantic fingers on the keyboard. Her frenzy hacks into forbidden places. Today she is determined to hack into her parents' world and disrupt it so they will return for her. Emails, documents, and pictures appear on the screen in a delirious flow.

"I traced my family's payments to the school. I hacked both my parents' emails and explored all the information in their computer terminals and electronics. I downloaded any and all data related to them, including credit card transactions, taxes, and medical records. I unveiled their illegal activities. Our farms grew drugs for one of the powerful drug cartels. Next to our tomato plants, poppies extended their seductive petals. Drug processing labs stood next to the corn silos."

They are back to her childhood home. The tomato fields wither and infinite rows of flowers—poppies in bloom—embrace them like a psychedelic LSD dream where the color of the petals heats the air so much that oxygen escapes around them, and the white house that was Akemi's home becomes decrepit. The porch collapses on top of the chairs and tables on the porch where the family once drank lemonade, and the white paint has peeled off, revealing heavy brown bricks. A glossy black pickup truck, with chrome rims and high tires crunches along the earth road and stops next to two sun-bleached wooden remains of a family area. The "banda" music is blaring a "narco-corrido" describing the fortunes of a drug dealer in an epic tale. The smiles under the mens' black Ray Bans and their thick mustaches reveal gold teeth. This is going to be a good harvest and the labs will get more than enough raw materials to produce premium heroin.

"I debated about how to send the information to the DEA, but then discovered that my parents had been forced to join this cartel. My father had been given the option to cooperate or to see his wife and daughter raped and tortured to death. My father had not found an escape route. It was during this time that they had sent me to the boarding school and made me disappear from the face of the Earth. They'd rather not see me again than risk my life." Akemi runs her hands through her hair and covers her face for an instant as if shielding herself from the memories. "My fury shifted gears. I now wanted revenge on the drug cartel. I wanted to make them pay and suffer what I had suffered. At sixteen, I believed that only my pain mattered. I hacked the servers from the Sinaloa cartel and from their rival cartels. I studied them to understand their operations: who helped them, which officials had they bought, and how they infiltrated the US and Europe with narcotics. My parents were trapped in an uglier and thicker mesh than I could have ever imagined. I also saw how many governments were failing to stop the cartels. I sat in my room during that summer vacation like a digital oracle seeing everything from a distant vantage point and understanding the horror of it.

One night, while I was immersed in the desert view from the balcony in my empty dormitory, it hit me. Could I create a war between the cartels? Could I break the walls of secrecy in their operations so the DEA and Interpol could use the chaos of their internal wars to destroy their operations? I had enough data and access to a network of individuals that I could create this mega-war and destroy them. I believed that by tearing through the mesh, I could liberate my parents, and we would be able to reunite. My strategy was Transparency. Open the cartel archives to the world so their enemies could poach them."

Anthony is frozen standing behind the teenage Akemi and cannot help but watch as she hacks into the servers of the men with dark Ray Bans and thick mustaches to make their data available to others. Pages of information flash on the screen, organizational charts with pictures of traffickers and assassins appear, supported by better IT systems than many Fortune 500 companies. The drug kingpins have money to pay for the best technology and run their business in the most productive and efficient way. Employees are very cheap to acquire—and to lose. Akemi's bright, open eyes reveal conviction that if she makes all information from the main drug cartels in Mexico available to each other and to the police, the DEA, FBI, CIA, and Interpol, Transparency will destroy evil. Her face is intent on her crusade.

"I did that. I blew their firewalls and connected the FBI and DEA and their rivals to the data bases. Millions of dollars of merchandise were captured in days. Their operations failed, and their covers crumbled. A war erupted among the different drug-trafficking organizations. Everybody's secrets were revealed, and there was nowhere to run. The following months were the most violent and deadly the state of Sinaloa and most of Mexico had ever witnessed. That is a remarkable accomplishment in a land known for its ruthless violence."

The screen fills with headline news of the violent blood bath. The picture are disturbing: tortured naked bodies hanging on bridges over a freeway, a bag of heads thrown onto the floor of a disco, a childcare center burnt to ashes with everyone trapped inside, the body of a woman raped and covered in burns from cigarettes ... the images are too many and too horrible for Anthony to keep his gaze on the screens, but the young Akemi cannot stop looking, accepting her responsibility for the events. The stroboscopic effect that all the content creates in the room suddenly ceases, and the pale static white illumination coming from the computer makes Anthony look again. In one of the front pages, he can see a photograph of Akemi's decapitated parents. Their heads are on a kitchen counter, the headless bodies, flat on a blood-soaked wood floor, are still holding hands. The teenage Akemi turns to run away and clashes into his arms. She is silently holding back her tears, but in her embrace he feels desolation until she pushes him away with unexpected strength, and runs.

"The cartels I targeted collapsed but inevitably new ones took their place. I was appalled by the death count. I could not sleep from the guilt. I had played a game, and the bloodshed proved it was not a child's game. I was skilled enough that they could not trace my tracks. I was an invisible force, but they reached me still. My parents became casualties in the drug war. I had killed them. Father George pulled me out of class one December morning to give me the news. I hid in a pantry for a week with tears and insomnia for nourishment. Father George found me and comforted me. I told him what I had done. My parents had pushed me out of their lives to protect me, and I repaid them by getting them and many others killed."

"The US intelligence services were able to track me. Not for the events in Mexico but for hacking into the CIA servers. I believe I wanted them to find me, so I had subconsciously left tracks the last time I visited them to gather information on how many of the corrupt American senators who were part of the drug network had died under suspicious conditions. I don't remember which government agency came for me. Father George tried to stop them, but I ended up in jail on major charges of cyber crime."

The Akemi sitting on a bench in front of Julius II Castle turns to look at Anthony, opening her eyes for the first time since the beginning of her story. "But you know what? I felt good in jail. I was there for charges unrelated to the drug war but I felt I was getting the punishment I deserved."

Anthony sees they are in her third home. Concrete walls and a space large enough for a basketball court, but not empty. In the center, she sits in an isolated jail cell in front of very advanced computer and servers, grey metallic boxes with small blipping lights, hardware for her to harness super-classified power. She is cooperating with the DEA and the CIA. She has recruited a community of world hackers to aid in her mission. Her work is a route to oblivion. In one corner of her room, paper books stack high. She reads the Greek and Roman Classics when her eyes want something more than pixels on LED or plasma surfaces.

"My eighteenth birthday was a very lonely event, marked by my transfer to an adult facility close to San Francisco. I did not know it, but the move had been motivated not by my turning of age but because the FBI wanted to recruit me for highly classified affairs of national cyber defense. They were impressed with my skill as a hacker and wanted me to break in into firewall prototypes for the State Department. Soon, I was coding programs to reinforce their cyber walls and creating protocols in case of cyber-espionage threats or terrorists attacks. My biggest breakthrough was a reftag that attached to any hacker, allowing the government to track and identify him or her. My digital activity served to atone for my previous sins. It also provided books of different places and lives. During that time, I kept reading the Classical texts: Homer, *Catullus*, Ovid, *Lucretius*…you name it. I read them all because, through them, I could escape to a very different time."

Anthony notices there is now a third person in the room. He is a slightly overweight man with incandescent green eyes that look at Akemi with longing. Anthony recognizes him as Avinash Sullivan, the wealthy Silicon Valley entrepreneur. Reading his movements—the careful cupping of Akemi's hand, the glee in his arms carrying gifts to the young prisoner, the never completely relaxed stance as he sits close to her for hours in front of the computer screen— Anthony sees Avinash is in love. He recognizes himself in Avinash's confusion.

"I was 19, a favorite of the FBI, Homeland Security, and the DEA when I met Avinash Sullivan. Since his company provided security programming to the government, he had heard about me from several sources. I had become an exotic technology celebrity. He was in his early thirties, a handsome man of Hindu and Irish ancestry. He hired me as a contractor while I was still in jail. When we were together, his extraordinary emotional intelligence attracted me as something new and unusual. He had a unique combination of charm, business acumen, and geekiness that empowered him to navigate from power one-on-ones in board rooms to innovative technological creativity with even the most dysfunctional savant nerds."

"Without consulting me, he hired the best law firm in San Francisco to work on my case. Their argument was that I had been under age and extreme emotional duress when hacking American government servers. My recent cooperation with authorities evidenced how I had matured and had abided by the ways of the law. After one hearing, I was released as long as Avinash would become my sponsor jointly with a sustained commitment to cooperate and work with government institutions."

The Glass prototypes project a very blue and clear day in San Francisco. The air is warm and welcoming. Anthony sees Akemi's new home, a small crammed place in the city overlooking rooftops and a tiny slice of the bay.

"My parents left me a fortune. Still, Avinash helped me settle in an apartment and start my own technology company, supervising my reincorporation into everyday activities. My startup was an overnight success because I had recruited many of the freak hackers I had known for years. I helped them make fortunes of their own. Cyber defense had become a very well-paying endeavor for everyone. Since my social skills were not the best, Avinash became a partner and the face of my company. That I was so young did not help either, especially when many of the people at the top do not understand technology or respect the wisdom of the young. Think about it, most C-suite executives became successful with a very different skill set. They don't understand that for people my age technology has been an integral part of our lives—much less how terrorism, espionage, and warfare have evolved. They hear things in the news but don't understand the depth of it."

"One of my first clients was the Vatican. The new Pope's charter was around reform, and he understood that a way to control scandals was to protect information—he is so vexed by how all of this is going now. He wanted a completely new system architecture and training programs for the Curia. We are still rolling those out. He did not consider how a millenary bureaucracy could slow things. I got the job based on a recommendation from Avinash."

The Akemi present in Ostia Antica remembers in silence for an instant. "Avinash was great in so many ways. He introduced me to his social circles. I discovered myself happy surrounded by intense geeks with their own social inabilities. For the first time, I belonged." Akemi takes another pause. "It was only a matter of time until I fell in love with him. He knew we were meant for each other the moment he saw me in my jail cell, but it took time for me to understand how to feel again. He had been a sort of technology playboy before we met, dating celebrities and models who got a kick out of appearing in glossy magazines with a Silicon Valley millionaire. He claimed that all of that had stopped when he met me, and I believed him. He needed someone complex with a big brain." Akemi smiles, savoring the past. Anthony sees a photo collage of the man Akemi fell in love with, but he forces his eyes away from the projections. The image of the castle and pre-dawn sky bring him back to the present. "We were a couple for eight years. I thought it would remain like that until I died because I did not desire any change or variation. In the end, it was our beliefs that tore us apart. Avinash had always believed in a utopia through transparency. Hypocrisy would become extinct through technology. Millenials already trust the wisdom of crowds. They doubt any construed communication. They are unstructured, creative, resilient, skeptical, and innovative. They realize they have to be masters of their future as the workforce shifts to become 70% self-employed some years from now. Avinash was a child of crowd-sourcing, social media, and authenticity for whom collaboration and transparency are big values. I had tasted the other flavors in the candy store, the toxic collection stemming from secrecy, lies, and information as a lethal weapon. Transparency slaughtered my parents and hundreds more. My sole purpose was to create bigger and better fences around information and privacy. In contrast, Avinash believed in a society in which all of your information—financial and personal—should be visible. He called it a "new digital order," the foundation for a new economic and cultural society. I like my secrets hidden from others. I refuse to learn the dirty facts about others if I don't need to do it to accomplish my job. For years, our points of divergence were the source of many spirited arguments over drinks that lasted through the night and attracted a passionate group of participants. They became real when he found out his brother had committed suicide after being silent for years about being the victim of sexual abuse from a priest. Avinashs's fury spurred him to action when discovering the priest had abused others before and that the Church had just relocated him to another parish. He started the Transparency Crusade so the Catholic Church would open its archives and procedures. By doing this, he stepped forward into his dreamed-of new digital society and economic order. He would transform the Catholic Church first, and then tackle other institutions, corporations, and finally governments. He realized enough techies would follow him and would provide funds, free technology, and hacking services. In his isolated thinking, he believed I would naturally stand by him. He was too self-centered and did not realize that I was on the other side in this war. My everyday centered on protecting others' privacy: people, institutions, companies, and governments. The long-winded, bohemian, hypothetical arguments from our past became concrete. They formed a wall between us, ousting me from his house when we accepted we could no longer live together. We loved each other. I have no doubt about how we felt, but we both had a higher calling that drove us to sacrifice anything that came in the way. Our friends took sides. Some of my best employees quit and joined his company. I recruited some of his."

Pause, the sound of breathing in the dark.

"Deep inside I hoped reality would force him to mature. He would realize his disruption could create more damage than benefit. He was a lucky pampered child too naïve for the violence of the real world. That killed him."

Deep sigh. Anthony reaches to her hand and holds it. "We will never be together again. It was very abrupt. My routines were shoved into a glass box. I can look at it through memories but I will never touch that quotidian existence again…Are ideas better than people?"

Anthony clutches her hand. They allow the silence to float like dust in the air as he embraces her body and she rubs her forehead against the unshaven stubs in his chin.

"…and then I met you. You are another child who has not experienced evil first hand and spends his hours in a land of ancient abstract ideas. The clean-cut American embodying the good of our country: family, principles, brains, strength to face all odds."

To break the silence that follows her confession, Anthony leans close to her and kisses her lips. Her body resuscitates as she clamps her arms around his neck grounding herself into his firm body. Dogs bark among the ruins of *Ostia* in the distant forest.

CHAPTER 36

SKETCHES ON LOVE MAKING

Day 8 – December 13, 1521

*T*o celebrate my recovery after the accident at the underground palace, Agostino Chigi organized a banquet at his "Palace of Love." Imperia received us in a pale brown dress embroidered with slightly darker roses—clearly her favorite motif. She had pulled her hair up into a bun to showcase her jewelry, as her necklace, earrings, and bracelets matched the solid gold plates and cups engraved with Chigi's coat of arms we used for the meal. The Pope joined us later in the night and roared with laughter at the stories and occurrences that were discussed when describing the erotic frescoes in the underground palace. The event soon became a scene of sumptuous merriment: fingers dripping pork fat stuck with lamb meat from the main dishes, and empty gold plates flung out the window into the Tiber as a gesture of supreme decadence by our host. A group of string musicians complemented the mood. Some of the guests danced. At one moment, Cardinal Bibbiena complained about the pain in his joints. He described how the heat and humidity inside the underground palace had soothed his aches. Chigi mentioned that the latest fashion in Florence for treating those ailments was to have a small steam room in which to rest and allow the heat to loosen the joints—like a bath, with a small stove, a stuffetta, where coals boiled water in an adjacent chamber, filling the room with water vapor through a grid in the wall.*

"Well, Raphael, you are the Master Architect. Build me one of those!" exclaimed Bibbiena.

"I could build it as part of the remodeling of your apartments," declared Raphael while he gulped the wine excited by the possibility of a modern project inside the Vatican palace.

"It is a brilliant idea," echoed the Pope. "Since your apartments are on top of mine, I could use it whenever I wished by climbing up the staircase into your private quarters. Master Architect, I order you to build it for us!"

Agostino spurted wine from his mouth as a thought made him laugh while drinking. "You should decorate it with erotic frescoes!"

"I don't believe we will have enough area on the walls to recreate the crimson orgy..."

"Paint scenes inside medallions. Didn't we see flowing breasts and monstrous penises in the other rooms?" inquired Chigi.

"You can paint a catalogue of sexual positions," suggested Imperia, covering her mouth at the idea. "But you realize it would be above the Pope's chambers?" she inquired, trying not to be too obvious about her fake modesty.

"Why not!?" boomed Leo X. "It would be our secret chapel, a secret to celebrate what the pagans taught us about the joy of carnal pleasures." He stretched his arms above his chubby body and, pushing his chair back, paraded around the table in creative fervor. "Let's celebrate humanity! I am exhausted by the superstition and lies I have to champion to keep the peasants in their place and gold flowing into the coffers. Others had their turn to relish their papacy. This is my time, my turn, and I can order you to do whatever I please!" Leo's voice was thick with alcohol, his movements grotesque like a toad out of the water. "Papal Architect, I command you to build the stuffetta for Bibbiena and decorate it with sin!"

Raphael, who had also been drinking in excess, assented. "I will have the bodies at the stuffetta do what Michelangelo's bodies will never do! This is the best project I have taken, and I toast to it!" We all clanked our gold cups, the red wine splashing over bejeweled rings. We then threw the cups out the window into the Tiber river. The music was overpowered by laughter and vulgar comments coming from the group while the servants steadily delivered libations.

I had drunk very little and, enrobed in my muteness, observed the spectacle of the most powerful men in the world behaving like pimps in *a tavern. This vision confirmed that under the enlightened thinking of Classical texts, Rome had become a festival of carnal love.*

I eat only bread soaked in warm milk. My teeth are loose and many have fallen out. My skin is sallow. I can barely walk from my bed to a desk. Praise the Lord that my vision remains strong and my hands can still hold a writing implement.

I look out the window and can't help but remember that the Vatican Palace was built on top of a pagan cemetery. We Catholics built where Saint Peter had been buried, and he was in a place where many other tombs covered the horizon. My city has taken on a mantle of funerary monuments that I wear as I become the monster in my own nightmares. It is as if all the people I killed were depositing their burial places around my quarters. At moments I see corpses scratching their way out of the earth and coming to get me. My time is quickly approaching.

What is death? I dislike its abruptness. Everything we believed we owned slips away as we move into a different state. Do we die when we leave our childhood home, never to return? Everything that was ceases to be in an instant, never to be recreated. There is no way of fixing it or to make events happen again. Routines vanish. The people we saw and cherished daily fade and wither. Isn't life a continuous death? It is a flower bulb that continually reveals petals in different colors until we get to a moment where the flower is no more. We can gather the petals but that will not bring the flower back to life. This is what I do in these letters, these confessions. I am picking the fallen petals of my days and organizing them as if they were a flower bulb, knowing they will never be anything close to what I experienced.

So when I eat my bread soaked in warm milk, I cannot help but force myself to deceive my tongue by telling it we are soaking freshly baked warm honey bread from Lutti. I instruct my remaining teeth to act if they were biting into a thin crackling crust and soft aromatic crumbs instead of a tasteless mush. This is when I know there must be more beyond this time and this existence. The flower will be dust, I will be dust, but the essence of the taste in that honey bread will remain somewhere. Maybe it will be recreated by a new baker in the future, or it will just linger in the Light, hovering over other loaves of bread until I exist again...and maybe on this round I will tell a different story on my deathbed: one of hope.

Every time I went to the bakery at 21 Santa Dorotea, the bread was better. Francesco Lutti was exuberant. No trace of sadness remained. He told me that he saw Margharetta frequently. He had made peace with her as she was radiant with happiness. He thanked me and gave me a basket of honey bread he had baked specially for me by adding lavender. I was not planning to visit Raphael on that occasion, but the bread basket was too big for me alone.

They all welcomed me with shouts of comradery and slaps on my back as they reached to devour my gift. The workshop was as hectic as I had ever seen it. Raphael cut through the chaos to pull me to the balcony where he shut the door tightly so we could whisper to each other. His eyes were blazing with inspiration; the muses were stoking the fire. I had seen him at work many times, and it was a sight of a god in the act of creation. When painting, Raphael would be transported to another place, his cheeks flushed with energy as he directed his associates and apprentices in the project; when he was holding chalk or the brush, his hands would be holding the fire of a hundred suns with the clarity of a thousand serene summer moons. At that moment, fame was irrelevant as if he were surrounded by a glow that animated pigments, oils, and lines into essential pictures of eternity. At those moments, his spirit was revealed. Today he was not painting but his cheeks were flushed as if he were standing on a scaffold, higher than our century, applying color to the dome of our starlit firmament.

"I have been pondering on how to decorate Bibbiena's stuffetta and create something above Michelangelo. He used a large space. I'll do it in a small room where scale will not be as relevant to obtaining the highest expression. He was right that the human body represents us in a quintessential way. Creation is what differentiates us from the beasts. With Margharetta I have understood that our sexuality crystalizes our expression of love, our flesh and blood physicality and the ultimate act of creation: that of spawning another human life. I am convinced I can do something unique. Nobody has done erotic frescoes since the Roman Empire. I could bring antiquity to our times and open the path for a new daring approach to art—like Leonardo did in Florence many years ago. I will have nymphs and fauns but most of all I liked Imperia's idea of a man and a woman in many intercourse poses."

He paused, looking out of the balcony as if an image had revealed itself far beyond the horizon, beyond streets and houses for him to contemplate. "In the recent days I have paid men from the docks and whores to fuck in front of me while I draw them. I have asked them to do it in different poses. I have asked them to let their carnal feelings go free." He took another pause, recreating in his mind the images he had captured. "I don't like what I am getting. They are as inspiring as two copulating dogs. I might as well get a horse and a mare. I only get the flesh and blood, the bestiality in us. There is none of the spirit that elevates humankind on these moments, no love. I observe their faces and gestures, and they are vacant. I will never get what I need from them. I have been struggling about how to enhance emotions and movement in my paintings. I compare the sketches with the ones I made of you and Imperia. I destroy them because they are no match."

I don't know what to say. I am not as experienced as he is. A heavy silence befalls upon us.

From that day on, whenever we met, Raphael would share his frustration with the models he kept procuring for his erotic drawings. The men were too filthy, the women's spirit never present during intercourse. He required subjects that could convey caring and intelligence. Each session would end with a bunch of empty lines or a blank piece of paper. The only pleasure, Raphael got from them was tearing the folios to shreds. "If only I could watch myself and Margharetta when making love. I know are bodies express different things. I know it because I have fornicated like these hired men and women do, immersed in the carnal pleasure. What Margharetta and I have is different. I know it because my muscles move differently when my skin comes into contacts with Margharetta. It is another rhythm, it is like painting."

One day he came with an unusual story: "Yesterday in my study, I had a bosomy whore on her knees sucking the cock and balls of a muscular iron welder, my sketch paper blank, when Margharetta entered the room by accident. You know she has this way of looking at other people? She makes them real, as if her eyes beam a unique light that makes objects and persons aware of their existence at that precise moment. The whore and the iron welder noticed her in the room, although she was in only for an instant—she must have felt uncomfortable and ashamed of having witnessed the scene—but during that brief instant, under Margharetta's gaze their shapes filled with human spirit as if the clouds had parted to allow the sun to shine through. They were not vacant shells of human fucking, they were a man and a woman together."

One evening, while I joined him to supervise the works at Hanno's stable, he pulled me aside when the workers had left and only the magnificent white elephant and we two remained in the dusk. Hanno was used to my presence by then—I brought apples to him and used him as a confessor when my sins weighed too heavily on my soul. The elephant tilted his head toward us as I scratched his shoulder and listened to Raphael's continuing frustrations about his exploration for Bibbiena's stuffeta. I am not sure I was paying full attention when my friend pulled me by the shoulders away from the animal and murmured close to my face. "I realize it is not proper to make this request from you. You can decline and it won't affect our brotherhood. When I have drawn you... your scars, your slim but muscular body, and the lack of body hair make you a superb model. I need superb models for this enterprise. I can also feel your emotions when painting you. It is your spirit I trace into the lines. During my life, I have only felt I that connection with two persons: you and Margharetta. I can sense what you two are feeling even when not looking at you...you are my brother...we are two halves of the same man...one emerging from the darkness and one surrounded by light..."

The elephant puffed as if sighing, he was captive in a hopeless existence. He had comfort and food, but he would never be able to accomplish what God had created him for. Hanno nudged me with his trunk as if knowing what Raphael was going to propose. "It has to be you. I cannot have anybody else...let me correct myself...I would not—could not—tolerate anybody else copulating with Margharetta for me to sketch."

I felt my breath trapped in the old scars and the hole in my tongue sucking away any answer I could possibly come up with. My stomach burned with acid...I had dreamed of bedding Margharetta for so, so many nights, yet what he proposed had to be forbidden; but most of all it would only be an illusion, a transient moment mocking my old hope of marrying and growing old with Margharetta. Hadn't I given my dead mother enough reasons to condemn me?

"I have talked about this with her, he continued. "She understands and she agreed to pose but emphasized that she would only do this if you were the man with her. I have researched the Ovid translation you gave me. I have already outlined the poses. I can show them to you whenever you are ready. This will be a secret among the three of us. Let others believe I went to a whorehouse for my inspiration."

I squinted while leaning my bald head on the bald skin of the elephant behind me. I imagined my grandfather encouraging me to accept. This was for art...Who was I kidding? I desired to be with Margharetta more than anything else. I was shaking and getting hard. "I will do as you please." The realization made my legs weak. I repeated in my mind: Raphael had offered me a pleasure bed with Margharetta. I adored her, I desired her. The idea was insane but I slowly nodded while Raphael embraced me with elation. I was shaking but I was going to let myself go with the flow. Enjoy life, saving guilt and self-pity for a later time.

For us to enact the scenes, Raphael rented another room in the upper floor of the aristocratic mansion where Margharetta lived. It was a late addition to the building and had large windows that filled it with a vibrant light. It had very high ceiling. The only furnishings in it were a large bed with white sheets, some chairs, and a desk.

Before our first appointment, I took a scalding hot bath, scrubbed myself and removed any vestige of hair. However, no matter how hard I scrubbed myself, I could not get rid of my misgivings about the whole affair.

Margharetta looked beautiful in her thin white slip, barely hiding the colors of her skin, her dark nipples and pubic hair revealed through the fabric. She nervously lowered her eyes when welcoming me. Raphael had his pens and pencils along with many folios of paper ready. He was flushed with excitement while he set his tools in place...

The moon is full and resplendent as it illuminates the pine trees weaving their foliage together as if there were only one tree with many trunks. The houses around Anthony and Akemi have closed their eyes, lulled as their roof tiles are caressed by a soft breeze. The sun will soon come out. The air smells of salt and algae and they can taste the nearby ocean. They leave the bench facing Julius II's fortress and walk down a path through the woods. She walks leaning her body against his shoulder while he holds her as if carrying a fragile object. Everything seems asleep, but in the distance Anthony can envision the howling pack of terminally ill dogs racing through the forest and the Roman ruins while celebrating a new day. Maybe they are chasing the ancient souls of Roman sailors and merchants. Maybe they are following the ghosts of lovers for a summer feast.

Down the path, Anthony discovers a small bed and breakfast. The windows are dark but he does not hesitate to bang on the door driven by the sensations awakened by Akemi cuddling his arm, her head leaning toward him. The smell of her hair mixed with pine and clay, her breasts pointing to his torso. After a few minutes, a sleepy and annoyed manager dressed in a robe opens the door. He is irritated but realizes that admitting the couple will allow him to charge full price for an otherwise empty room. The summer is the season to maximize profits for him so he welcomes them. Akemi raises her head as the stale air inside the old construction—tomato, clay, basil, humidity, burnt oil, and garlic—makes her search for Anthony's smells of wood and the musk of his perspiration. Her heart pounces, and now completely awake with anticipation she takes his hand and hurries him to their room.

I have the sketches in front of me as death approaches. They are my most precious possession—although I have been forced to use the back of them to scribble my confession. I am too weak to get more paper. They are more beautiful than any piece of art I have ever been blessed to admire. Better than any musical piece, better than any sculpture or building, better than the frescoes on the Sistine Chapel. Others won't see what I can because they were not present with Margharetta, Raphael, and me when we admired each sketch after the love making sessions. It was at that moment that I would fully grasp the previous hours making love. With our eyes fixed on the paper I would recreate each instant I had contributed to the lines and shapes of startling beauty.

On this one, before the moment was captured on paper, her hands had slid across my chest, tracing my scars while I touched her lips with my index finger. She traced the scars from my neck to my nipples, from my back to my stomach. At moments the memories of how the scars had been created surfaced: the whip, the blades, the hot coals. Her fingertips functioned like drops of healing water on a chalk drawing: diffusing the images, blurring the contours, and creating a new blank surface on which to paint again.

Looking at the sketches he had created, Raphael might have been remembering how he had given us directions as if we were in a play— but I could only see how I slid my palms down her neck, posing on her shoulders to go down her arms until I grabbed her buttocks at the same time she counted my ribs, rubbed my hip bones, and placed her hands in my inner thighs, smiling as she traveled down my legs to my knees and back to cup my genitals. I just embraced her and our lips searched each other. I held her face in my hands and licked it like I was a puppy. I wanted to capture all the tastes that made her, all the shades her skin could hold, all the smells that radiated from her wetness. She returned my caresses with enthusiasm, playful, letting herself imagine she was my wife.

"Do it standing up. Margharetta, raise your right leg as if you were climbing a tree. Federigo, hold her at the bend of her leg."

We stood close to each other as if by doing so we would never have to be separated again. She stood on my foot and wrapping her other leg around my thigh while I penetrated her with gusto each of our organs synchronized: our breathing, our muscles, our genitals. I was thrusting, and she was clasping me, escalating my body to give more space to my thrusts and allow more of her skin to rub against mine.

"Slow down. Control your cadence. Federigo, let your buttocks curve like ocean waves, I want the light of the candles to play with the bulk of their shape." His voice directed our sweat-dripping bodies and overrode the frenzy that we felt, so our pace became slower, controlled, *and the pleasure I got became languid, elongated, and stretched as if each heartbeat lasted for a year.*

Akemi pulls Anthony into the small bedroom and without pausing she tears his shirt open, the last couple of buttons remaining from the fight tear off. She slides her hands down his torso to open his belt and pants. She pulls his underwear down with a swift movement, his hard cock bobbing as it is released from the fabric. Anthony holds her, watching the light playing on her skin. Admiring her body, he decides to allow her to use him as she pleases. But before that, he pushes her against the wall pulling her dress up to her thighs and ripping the panties as he clamps her neck with his mouth inhaling the fragrance of her hair. He wants to penetrate her but remembers the condoms are in his wallet. He releases her with frustration, his flesh angry at the interruption. He crawls on his knees to grab his scattered trousers while smelling the mold in the old floor in the room, the synthetic fibers in the carpet abrasive on his knees. Meanwhile Akemi lies on the bed pulling down the cheap nylon bed covers. She pulls off her dress with a swift movement, and when he joins her, she pushes him onto his back with determination and mounts his erection guiding him inside her with demanding impatience. She sits astride him, riding him with her legs hanging to the sides of the thin and lumpy mattress. He lets her, concentrating all his will on the sensations her body brings. Her black hair cascades on his chest like feathers caressing his skin, producing laser heat signatures. She clenches him tightly between her legs and sways up and down starved for feelings. She gyrates with him as an axis. She can take her pleasure on him her way. She can be completely in control while he is drunk with the image of her body on top of his.

We had several sessions together. Always Raphael instructed us what to do, what poses to take, and every time we got into more interesting and fulfilling positions.

He asked her to please me with her mouth while I lay in opposite direction with my head between her legs licking her. Another position was with me on top of her while I lifted and stretched her legs against my shoulders forming a V shape while I penetrated her.

Imperia had educated her, and we never allowed my seed to explode inside her. When I was ready, I would pull away and she would grab my member with her delicate hand and make my seed shower her torso while we remained in the love making position. Because we took our time to create the images for Raphael, she was also getting satisfied, coming multiple times in succession when I penetrated her at last.

On one occasion, I took her from behind while she bent until her palms touched the floor, and she cried with joy and pain bringing back memories of my past suffering at the hands of the deacons, so I held her tightly while I sobbed burying my face deep in her hair. My hips kept rocking unstoppable with a life of their own. Somehow Raphael captured the suffering and the ecstasy in his sketch. I have looked and relooked at this folio through the years unable to decipher if he did it through the outline of our muscles, the light on our bodies, or Margharetta's half-hidden profile.

Other times, we would lie side by side, our arms stretched over our heads with our hands joining above us, our noses almost touching, taking the breath from each other's lungs as soon as it was exhaled from our swollen lips; and then we would do it again, enacting a new pose, as if we possessed an infinite night that was measured in the light of the candles and Raphael's materials.

Akemi comes with seizure force collapsing on top of Anthony who catches her in his arms clutching onto her with desperation. The saliva merges and drools as they lick each other's faces. Now it is his turn. He wants to give her new pleasure. Yoga has provided an excellent foundation for tantric love making. He places her back against the bed and draws up her knees until they rest against the curves of her breasts. Seeing her allowing him to curl her in such an exposed position makes him kiss each of the round of her knees. He takes her feet and puts them under his armpits feeling the softness of her heels. Then Anthony guides her hands to cup her buttocks so he can penetrate her varying the tempo and depth of his strokes – **1**, 2, 3, 4 - 1, **2**, 3, 4 - 1, 2, **3**, 4 - 1, 2, 3, **4** - until she screams and his mind blacks out for a second as he comes inside her.

They rest side by side, staring into each other's eyes with awe under the moonlight streaming through the thinning old curtains unaware of the mattress's uneven coils punishing their backs.

On this sketch, Raphael instructed us on what steps to follow from notes he had taken from Imperia's advice. He stood next to us and moved our bodies on top of the mattress, one hand lifting Margharetta's hips by the small of her back, another hand grabbing my buttock to pull me closer. Imperia had told him that there were ways to enhance the pleasure women got from sex, and Raphael was intent in capturing such experience. He lifted Margharetta's left leg, stretching it and resting it on my shoulder while he asked her to rotate her torso to the right. I could feel her clitoris against my groin as Raphael guided me into her, his hand sweaty, warm, and tense on my skin with the obsession of a perfect image. She gasped with pleasure and squirmed against me but Raphael leaned forward and kissing her lightly on the lips asked her to remain motionless for a few minutes feeling me inside her. He then rushed to his desk and vigorously traced the paper with a pen. My legs trembled with the effort while my penis seemed to expand even more against Margharetta's minuscule squirming as if the labia of her organ could move on their own caressing me in secrecy so the artist would not detect that we were submerged in a rhythm and pleasure of our own. I pushed her foot closer to my lips and to control myself sucked on her toes until Raphael's voice commanded me to rotate while still inside her so both our torsos, her face and mine, would be in his direction—bathed in light, our eyes fixed on his face. But his eyes did not meet ours, they climbed up and down our skin and the landscape of our muscles while Margharetta and I kept our secret conversation through the slight swaying of my buttocks as I softly increased their tempo and arch—at the beginning in an imperceptible way, as her timid gasps of air became moans, and my movements a hammer wielding hot metal until our voices in heat could be heard in the street mingled with Raphael's voice consenting to our squirming against each other. The scratch of chalk and pen, and the shuffling of new paper could not cover his own panting and short breath.

Lying side to side, Akemi pulls her tablet from her bag. Anthony realizes he is still wearing the holographic contact lenses. Two small molecular cameras project images to his retinas. Akemi and Anthony have learned the rules. This time they start sideways. No one is on top. Both are using enhanced reality technology as they immerse in an overlapping digital world where Anthony flies with white angel wings when Akemi approaches him and wraps him in cold metallic tentacles made of cables. He knows they don't exist but can feel them against his back, winding around his arms like ropes, curling around his right thigh and crotch in a bondage ritual coming from a wire central. Anthony forces his focus on the physical world because it is his skin that records every inch of Akemi's body, and his lips that never tire of her large round nipples while she learns the new tantric positions of love making: the jewel case, in which they lie side by side with legs parallel and toes touching while their thighs embrace and they squeeze each other in a pulsating rhythm. Then she lies on her back, her thighs pressed tightly together to completely embrace Anthony's penis as he penetrates her, his wings and tentacles intertwined, creating a shelter. Later they lose the virtual appendages, and the digital blue sky is replaced by holograms of Rome. Akemi sits down with her thighs up high wrapped around Anthony's waist as he forcefully pushes in and out of her, surrounded by the imagery of Piazza Navonna where passers-by and crowds of tourist move around their love making in a Bernini fountain. Akemi and Anthony are equals, moaning until they run out of condoms. The inn keeper is knocking on their door because they are disturbing the guests. Their genitals ache. They are puffy and red from usage, so Akemi calls her driverless car and instructs it to pick them up. For the next hour, while waiting for the car to arrive, they lick and kiss each other's bodies, paying special attention to crevices never explored, like canines cleaning and curing their mates protected in a cove behind a waterfall.

It has been many years since those nights, and I can recall precisely every position Raphael directed us to perform. I close my eyes and can replay the smells and even the smallest minutiae. When I don't have nightmares, I dream I am lying in bed while she is standing in front of

me, one foot close to my head, one foot between my legs as she low-
ers toward my erection while gazing at Raphael's eyes until she impales
herself in me—her body lowering to a folio of drawing paper where the
contours of her body become ink traces that merge into the surface of
the paper. Sometimes I lift the sketches to my nose, wondering if I can
discover in them the scents flowing from her during those long-gone
nights.

They arrive at Akemi's house. The car enters the garage so they can
hop on the stairs. While Anthony takes off the enhanced reality contact
lenses, she brings some juice from blood oranges. "You can keep those
and the tablet. They will help with your research more than your old laptop," and then asks him to wait while she takes a shower. With the glass
in his hand, sipping the juice, Anthony wonders if he should join her but
remembers he has no more condoms. There will be time in the future
for both of them to shower together, but his heart still beats fast, so to
distract himself he roams—with small steps so his pants won't chafe his
groin— through the rooms, exploring the books and objects that are
part of Akemi's life while the Roman sun bounces on the rooftops on
Piazza d'Spagna and enters through the curtains enhancing colors and
shapes.

It is hard to recount how many weeks the affair lasted. It all became
one, long beautiful night to me. Raphael drew many folios but chose
twenty and destroyed the rest. I had to escape from it on a night when
he directed her to stand behind me, her back resting on a column.
Then I leaned with my back against her and raised my arms clasping
my hands behind her neck as if captive while Raphael instructed her
to play with the most sensitive areas. My body was wide open to her
caressing fingers: my nipples, my inner thighs, the fold of my thigh
on my groin. Her touch breezed on my penis while her hand lightly
weighed my testicles. I was wild with desire and tried to disentangle
my hands from the back of her neck but he approached us and lean-
ing very closely held my wrists in place with a strong grasp while she
continued touching my chest. There was something uncomfortable
with all of this. His smell mixed with hers, her breath on my neck, and

his on my face. I did not realize it at the moment but I was in a pose similar to the one my tortures used when taking their pleasure on me at Saint Benedictus, however Margharetta's caresses absorbed me. Raphael was hard under his trousers. He stared at my eyes and I could tell he and Margharetta had replayed in their intimacy many of the scenes we had enacted for him, but something had awakened as he saw me bound against her and the column. When Margharetta started masturbating me, he cupped her hand with his and kissed me on the lips. "Thank you my brother," he whispered before he plunged his tongue in my mouth. But as his beard scratched my chin the memories flooded back to me. The memories of how the scars had been cre-ated were pushed to the surface: the whip lacerating my inner thighs while the deacons had sex between them; the blades that marked the surface of my skin while they masturbated to then spread their semen on my wounds, mixing my blood and shreds of skin with their seed; the hot coals glowing a mere inch in front of my abdomen forc-ing me to remain perfectly still as they took turns violently fucking my ass, pushing me closer to the glowing coals with every vicious thrust! Disentangling my arms, I used them to push Raphael away from me with force. Surprised, he allowed me to step away from Margharetta. They watched and said things I did not hear as I was violently shak-ing and hurried into my robes trying to warm the ice on my flesh. Margharetta was also surprised. She embraced me as if to stop me, her body still trembling with desire but I pushed her aside to the bed with one decisive shove.

"I cannot do this anymore," I called from the threshold. Both were the mutes now. I want to believe their eyes burst with sadness after I banged the ornate door and rushed down the decaying elegant marble staircase of the aristocratic mansion to dive into the city passageways. My heart sought to return to their arms but my feet followed the course of the filth floating in the Tiber River. Suddenly I was inundated with guilt and I felt sinful and dirty.

I required the company of another freak, so I went to Hanno's stable close to the Castel Saint Angelo only to find it empty. Early in the year, the Pope had acquired a rhinoceros to make him com-pany. But Hanno needed a female mate, not another scarred freak like him, so shortly after he had died of loneliness. The building was empty. I sat on the floor on top of the decomposing hay and dung. The walls oppressed me with their silence. Had I lost my voice again after leaving Raphael and Margharetta? When my brother and I went to the first monastery I had healed by singing in the monks' choir. In the stable's darkness I groaned and then, as if a hand propelled down my throat to pull me back into the world, I started humming, the notes bouncing on the arched dome of the stone building as I vocalized the words of a Miserere. "Misereremei, Deus." Have mercy on me, God. I praise you for your gifts but forgive my sinner's nature. I stood up and sang, feeling as empty as the stable and as dead as the Pope's elephant.

Back in my quarters, I sat at one of my desks and pulled the notebook with the poison formulas from its secret drawer. God had created me to be an assassin. I read the recipes to myself as if praying. The ingredients that had come from ancient Egypt to Livia in Rome and finally to me replaced the words of Psalms and the Gospel. God wanted me to be in service of the Pope. God had created me to murder.

Anthony listens to the shower as he scans the scarce contents in Akemi's bedroom. This is minimalism taken to another level. The only piece of furniture besides the cocoon bed is an aerodynamic small white desk with a stool in front of it. On top of the desk is a very old notebook. Anthony recognizes the handwriting. Holding it with shaking hands, he is afraid to open it.

"Akemi, what is this notebook on your desk?" he calls, feigning calm as she turns off the water.

"Something Angelo sent me related to the monk's letters. It is the notebook with the poison formulas."

"How long have you had it?"

"It just arrived. I haven't had time to scrutinize it." She calls, still in the bathroom.

With utmost care, Anthony flips through the pages. Here is the recipe to create poisoned fruit—Giocatelli; here the one to make someone insane so he would kill others before committing suicide—Herrera. Why had Akemi not mentioned she had the notebook in her possession? Why had Angelo not mention anything about it either? Akemi enters the room in a white robe while drying her black hair. "You should take a shower, too." Anthony wonders if the water would erase the recollection of Ellia Jones's warnings. Was the book in his hands the proof of Akemi's guilt in the murders?

PART 3
THE ART-LOVING ASSASSIN

CHAPTER 37

THE IDEA TO SELL INDULGENCES

Day 9 – December 14, 1521

I needed to escape from Rome. Everything reminded me of Margharetta. I dreaded encountering Raphael within the Vatican palace, so I paid special attention to travel only along the most secret corridor and back alleys. He sent for me several times. I chose not to answer. I even stayed away from Lutti's bakery. A somber deep melancholy enveloped me. I chose to wear grey robes because I felt that no matter how much I scrubbed my body during my daily baths, I could not remove the sensations lingering on my skin as a constant reminder of what my life would never be. I isolated myself in the Papal Library studying old texts during the day. Having found the ring in the underground palace, I forced myself to find the German parish where my grandfather's ring had come from. I held it in my fist for hours while I browsed book after book with a catalogue of heraldic images from the Holy Roman Empire—until I found what I had sought for years: the two cartwheels joined by the sign of the cross on a heraldic coat of arms that were identical to the engraving on the ring's ruby. The coat of arms belonged to the city, and thus to the Archbishop, of Mainz. It was time for me to fulfill my duty.

The next time the Pope summoned me, I pleaded to be sent to the Northern Countries. This was a request he was happy to grant as he was in peaceful conflict with the kingdoms of France and Spain and wished to assess the strength of his alliances in the Germanic states. There were also two old bishops he wanted me to poison so he could sell the positions and make a profit.

It was the fall of 1516. Seven years since my last visit, yet nothing had changed. Equal despair and abandon filled the churches and the souls of the poor in the countryside and cities. I wondered what else I could have done to save these unfortunate souls. Why was Christ allowing me to participate in missions of poison and death, and not of life? When I reached my destination, I realized that the Archbishopric of Mainz was one of the wealthiest of the Empire. Since I was a visitor from Rome, I received a lavish welcome and offered a very comfortable room. Nevertheless, I was disappointed with my reunion with the archbishop. Instead of the wise old man I was expecting, a man in his thirties with effeminate movements embraced me while his servants prepared a rich table baring wine, cold meats, and elaborate dishes. His name was Albert of Branderburg. Being mute, I had a written missive with my grandfather's story for him to understand my quest. I handed him the ring along with the letter. He explained that he had purchased the archbishopric when his predecessor had passed away of old age. He could not help me. He returned the ring to me, offering it as a gift in exchange for my carrying personal correspondence back to the Pope and making me swear that I would ensure that his Holiness read it. I accepted the exchange. He explained he was in financial trouble since he had bought the archbishop position with a loan from a bank, and the revenue stream was not as good as he had forecasted. He wanted the Vatican to advise him on how to increase his fortunes.

To accelerate my return, he emptied part of his library to fill my wagon and, suspecting that I was also on a reconnaissance mission, briefed me on the political allegiances of the German prince-electors. Due to his financial urgency, he instructed me to gallop back to Rome by myself but supplied two soldiers to travel with me, while the rest of my party and the wagon with the manuscripts trailed behind.

I requested an audience while still on my way to Rome; the Pope was intrigued by my entreaty to see him. I had reported completion of all the assassinations he had ordered so he wondered about the rush. He received me in his private library looking like a gigantic poisonous toad in a scarlet robe. Agostino Chigi was sitting by his side reviewing the latest profit reports from the alum mines around Rome. The Pope asked me if we needed complete privacy, and I negated with my head handing him the letter from the Archbishop of Mainz.

He broke the seal with his elegant hands and read out loud in a clear aristocratic voice. Chigi noticed the letter was about financial matters, which stirred his covetous interests. Unlike France and Spain, where the kings appointed key ecclesiastical posts, the Pope appointed these in the Holy Roman Empire. One reason for the deep resentment by German aristocrat was that the Holy See received substantial revenue for these placements. It was against the Church's interests if Albert of Brandenburg went bankrupt.

"What do you think of this request, Chigi? Some people believe that because I am God's representative I must shit solid gold. I damn Julius II for leaving me the expenses for the new Basilica of Saint Peter. Constantine's basilica was fine, he should have repaired it instead. The treasure is depleted, and you know we are trying to ideate ways to raise incremental money to finish this glorious construction. I am in no position to give money when we must hold onto every coin!"

The burly banker rested his head in his hands in thought. "There is something we could do your Holiness. Let's send a pile of printed indulgences to Mainz for the Archbishop to sell. He can keep half of the money he raises to pay his debt as long as he sends the other half for us to use in the construction of Saint Peter's Basilica. Mainz is a very wealthy area."

Leo X's expression animated his bloated body. "Brilliant idea! I will send that Dominican monk, Tetzel, to be in charge of the indulgence sales. He has proven to be the most apt for this type of chores. By helping others, we will help ourselves."

I swallowed a protest upon hearing their plan; after all, I was a mute in front of Chigi. I had shared with Leo X my concerns and pain at seeing the abandonment of peasants in the Holy Roman Empire Northern States. He had shown pity and apprehension listening to me, but here he was making decisions that would not provide hope and peace of mind to so many desperate souls. It was unsettling to see his charming and cheerful demeanor as he and Chigi calculated the profits they could accumulate from the enterprise. My legs had the impulse to run and seek shelter at Raphael's studio but I had decided to stay away from temptation. Christ had created me to serve the Pope.

"And think about how we will allow many souls to spend less time in purgatory by buying the indulgences from us!" Leo X chortled at a remark from Chigi. He then addressed me. "Thank you for your services, Federigo my son. Without a doubt you are one of the few treasures that Julius left for me. I wish he had left more gold and gems, too." He waved his hand, dismissing me. "Every day you complete a mission for me you allow your father and brother to get closer to salvation. You can leave us alone now." But, reminded of his favorite pet by my peculiarity, he added: "Go see the brilliant life-sized fresco of my late Hanno that Raphael is painting at the entrance of Saint Peter. The white elephant is the perfect gatekeeper to the holy site. I know you and Hanno had a lot in common. At least that is what my spies believe after reporting your frequent visits to his stable. Some even are stupid enough to think you sang a miserere on one occasion. That would have been a miracle for a mute!" His brow wrinkled and his eyes glowed with a threat accentuated by the skin on his neck bulging further.

I realized how stupid my actions had been and promised myself to be extra watchful for spies. I wished to see Hanno's fresco, but I had heard rumors in the ballrooms and back alleys of Rome about Bibbiena's stuffeta and its decoration. It was the hottest gossip in the street— delighting noblemen and peasants alike. I had to see this room. Would the wondrous images of Margharetta and me be on its walls? I climbed an internal staircase to Cardinal Bibbiena's apartment. Bibbiena was away. The loggetta decoration was finished, but I spent very little time admiring the spectacular motifs that covered walls and ceiling. Raphael had succeeded in transplanting Classical Roman art to our time, portraying scenes of the Bible in a fresh and new manner. I rushed to the small steam bath next to Bibbiena's bedroom. Raphael and his workshop had painted the erotic scenes inside medallions as we had seen in some of the rooms of the Domus Aurea. He had chosen this delicate approach versus murals covering the walls because of the small surface. He had kept the red backgrounds. My surprise came from seeing very few of the drawings from Margharetta and me replicated on the frescos. He had kept the best and boldest for him. The scenes chosen were beautiful, resembling the mythological images we had seen in the Roman palace. There was a naked faun with a large engorged penis staring lasciviously at a nymph combing her hair while sitting with open legs. While I recognized poses from Margharetta and me, the quality of the workmanship allowed me to notice that Raphael had marked the contours and had his apprentices finish the job as if he desired to stay distant from them. They lacked detail and tension in the lines, the faces were not ours. Somehow, all the passion he had discovered while working on them was gone, with the execution becoming just another enterprise. They were still good—even if they were not the magnificent sketches the three of us had admired after each session. I traced the contour of the nymph with my tongue, tasting lime plaster and earth pigments.

In the following weeks I listened with extra care to all conversations and gossip. I was correct. Giulio Romano and Marcantonio Raimondi had applied the color and completed the stuffetta after Raphael marked the outlines. I heard Raphael had been absorbed by his work on sketches for a series of large tapestries that the Pope had commissioned him to cover the walls of the Sistine Chapel. I could see how that had become his main focus. He had a chance to place an epic work, twelve tapestries, side by side to Michelangelo's ceiling for posterity to decide who was the greater of the two. His only distraction, I heard, was his work on the painting of a lady with her hair covered with a veil. Rumor had it he was painting his mistress. Since he could not marry her because of his engagement to Maria Bibbiena, making a portrait of Margharetta was a way of evidencing her importance and standing in his life. He painted her under a light that softened her facial lines so only those who knew her would recognize her immediately but still making her different enough to protect her identity. He placed a pearl in her hair, a symbol of eternal love with her right hand on her heart. I can describe the painting now because I have seen it—but at that time I stayed away from them, continuing to ignore the notes they sent to my room. I declined attendance to parties to which he was invited, and if I had to be there to complete a mission for the Pope, I would wear a disguise that included fake hair and a fake beard. Sometimes I saw them from a distance, and my skull felt as if it contained molten metal. I wanted to reclaim my voice, my conversations with my friend, and the pleasures with Margharetta, but I kept my distance and returned to the nightmares that plagued my sleep.

CHAPTER 38
MESSAGE ON A SMARTPHONE

Why would Angelo send the original notebook instead of a facsimile or a digital copy as he had done with every other material? Why had Akemi not mentioned anything about it during the hours they had spent together? The monk's story was a link between both of them. In a way, it had gotten them together. Anthony needs answers. He crosses the Swiss Guard checkpoint and heads directly to the restoration laboratory for the Secret Archives. His steps are quick, all the glow from the previous night has dissipated, its place taken by the pit in his stomach, the apprehension for his family, and the malady of certain betrayal.

Loud voices reach him before he can open the door. The restoration shop is in chaos. Everyone is cringing in a corner watching two figures arguing next to a lighted table. The Prefect for the Secret Archives, José Dosal, holds a handful of papers—the Raphael sketches—while Angelo stands defiantly, with his hands on his hips, in front of him.

"You cannot take those away! I have been working on my dissertation for months!"

"I can take anything I want from here. I am the Prefect of the Secret Archives and only the Pope tells me what not to do. These are unique treasures by Raphael." José waves the drawings and raises his chin.

"Ms. Morishima and Dr. Hibbert have been studying them, too. The sketches are part of a larger investigation." His voice is barely controlling the fury boiling inside him. He would like to punch the man in the face.

"As if I cared what Akemi has to say, *imbécil*...That woman thinks she can come into my archives and take control. She doesn't belong to the Church. Her arrogance will destroy her! You report to me and should have told me about these sooner. Next time I'll fire you and ensure you will never work in the Roman art world."

Anthony approaches the center of the room. Conciliatory, he raises his hands, palms exposed. "José, Angelo was getting the information together before sharing it with you. He wanted to have the best product before getting your input. He respects you too much."

"Respects, my ass! This scoundrel was trying to publish behind my back." José's face is beet red.

"Every time he talked with me and Akemi about Raphael's drawings, he mentioned that he wanted to publish this in conjunction with you, thus it needed to be up to your high standards. You drive these people hard."

"*La mierda con eso*! You stay in your research and Transparency Commission. Nobody asked your opinion on this matter. And you, Angelo, go tomorrow to my office so we can talk about what I should do with you. Right now, I am too angry to deal with it." He turns to other terrorized white coats in the shop. "That goes for everyone else here. Don't try to do research behind my back. Remember I am the boss. *El jefe*." Thrusting his body forward, he glares at the other investigators like a predator choosing which small field mouse to devour. José turns his compact body with surprising agility and storms out of the room, shoving Anthony with his shoulder on the way out.

Angelo holds on to the lighted table with both hands. He is shaking with fury, and his eyes are red with restrained tears. Anthony pats him on the back. "It will be alright. We will make it right."

"You don't get it. I will never have access to the Raphael sketches again, and he will force me to give him my research paper so he can publish it under his name." He punches the table with a fist. "Damn it! I knew this would happen! I'm so stupid."

Everybody else in the shop is still watching them, not daring to move. Anthony passes an arm around Angelo's back and softly pulls him away. "Let's go to the cafeteria. Some fresh air will be good." Angelo allows himself to be guided to the open courtyard.

Tears are streaming down his cheeks as he sips on a small espresso cup. "I should quit. This place under José sucks!"

"Calm down. Stay put. Francesca and I can help you get another job if that is what you want but don't make things worse with Dosal. You are very talented, and you will shine in any research you do."

"This one was too perfect. The Raphael sketches will be huge news in the art world. They will tell the story of what he could have done if he had lived. Plus we have the story of the models who posed for them: an assassin for the Pope and his mistress. This is a once-in-a-lifetime story. You do research; you know it is too perfect. I will never find a story as good for the rest of my life. Raphael could have done creations Picasso brought to life three hundred years later with his erotic drawings. This will put Raphael back on par with Michelangelo and Da Vinci, as he used to be for before the Pre-Raphaelites…"

Anthony lets him ramble on about his dissertation about Renaissance geniuses, noticing that this has a calming effect. He does not need to hear the complete thesis; he needs other information, but hesitates to probe. "The story of the Pope's assassin is unique. Just that will make headlines. How many times can you get a firsthand narrative as powerful as this one? Plus, Angelo, finding the poisoner's notebook makes it an even more sensational piece."

Angelo raises his head to the sun. His cheeks are dry but his eyes are still clouded with dark disappointment. "What do you mean?"

"The notebook you sent to Akemi, the one with all the assassins' recipes. The one he mentions in his letters."

Angelo stares blankly back at him. "I have not sent such manuscript to Ms. Morishima. I never send originals. You know that."

"I saw it this morning in her bedroom. If not from you…"

"Akemi must have found the notebook in the underground archives. This notebook must not be something new to her. Remember—she was interested in the drawings and Federigo's story before you and I even met. Despite her incredibly busy schedule, she was making time to help us decipher the story behind the drawings. Can you ask her to return the poisons notebook, however she might have acquired it? I cannot get into more trouble."

Anthony feels a knot on his throat. "Are you sure you did not send it to her?"

"You have seen me give thumb-drives to her. Only thumb-drives—digital facsimiles. I might not like José, but I take extreme care to protect Vatican property."

"Could someone send it to her by mistake, using your name?"

"Who? Only the three of us know about the monk's letters. The others in the lab are afraid of José and have stayed as far as possible from the Raphael sketches. These are feeble men who have spent their lives in that lab and would not risk losing tenure by sending anything to anyone."

"You will be fine." Anthony knows he must talk with Alessandro Catzola. "Let me think how I can help."

"This sucks at so many levels. I was planning to visit Bibbiena's *stufetta* later today to take some pictures and add them to the file. The drawings and the monk's story center on it, and I have not been there in a long time. There is no sense in taking those pictures anymore." Angelo takes a deep breath half closing his eyes as he feels the hot summer sun on his face. "You might have to get me a job in California. I hear there is sun year round over there."

"I have to go now. I'll call you later." Anthony shakes Angelo's hand.

"Bibbiena's *stufetta*—I should go there. Maybe there is a clue in the paintings that helps me solve everything and exonerate Akemi," Anthony mutters to himself as he hurries to retrieve his belonging from the storeroom at the entrance of the Secret Files. "It is ridiculous but I don't know where else to look."

Reaching the storeroom, he hurries to pick up his phone and briefcase from his metallic locker. He is organizing his briefcase when he feels a hesitant touch on his shoulder. Francesca is standing behind him. Her big hair is limp and small, her face has no make-up and looks grey under the white neon lights of the storage room. She is wearing no jewelry, and her eyes are colorless.

"I think he is going to leave me. I discovered that Ahmed is not who I thought he said he was. He is no Saudi royalty."

Anthony's heart pumps sending echoes from his chest to his throat and ears. He quickly decides the *stufetta* will have to wait but his phone vibrates with a text message: "I have information from the American Embassy that explains why the man was trying to get to your family. – Catzola." Now Francesca will have to wait, too.

"Francesca, you don't look well. Take a coffee in the cafeteria and then wait for me in a study room. I must see Lieutenant Catzola." She nods in response and slowly drags her feet away while Anthony dashes to the *Palazzo dell Governatorato*.

• • •

Alessandro beams through a cloud of cigarette smoke.

"The burly man's name is John Petersen. He was identified by the American Embassy this morning as minor diplomat, a financial attaché. In his office, we found the tapes the American Embassy requested from the Excelsior after Avinash's murder. It is true that the Ambassador did not know about them. Petersen had kept them for himself …and for Ellia Jones. While they kept their tracks clean—he did not officially report to her—others in the Embassy saw them frequently together. We traced substantial unidentified deposits in Petersen's bank account. The type you get if you are a hired gun. They came from a Swiss bank that Jones has used in the past."

It is just Anthony and Alessandro in the cramped office standing in front of a computer monitor. Anthony's hands are clammy. He feels exhausted.

"Look, these are images from the surveillance camera the night Avinash died on the Excelsior. It captured the corridor of the suite where his room and your in-laws' room were. I'll fast forward. Here we can see a man knocking on Avinash's door. Clearly, he is aware of cameras as he is wearing a long coat—in the summer! A hat is covering his face. He cannot be more suspicious. Yet we can see Giocatelli's profile for an instant—here." Alessandro stops the image. Anthony nods. "Next, we see the door open. We cannot see Avinash but we can see Giocatelli pulling the gun from his coat and firing. Immediately, he gets into the room, clearly in search of something. After a few minutes, he leaves holding the 'something' in his hand. He is wearing gloves and his hands are shaking so he does not notice the small object slip from his grasp when he thinks he is putting it in his coat pocket. Giocatelli knew that Avinash was planning to give the Pope a thumb drive with information and scanned documents from the Secret Archives that told his grandfather's story. That is the 'something' he dropped."

Anthony nods as Alessandro fast-forwards through the images. "Here you are, covered in red wine, back from your dinner to pick your daughters. Just a few minutes, and here you are again. This time you are with your girls." Claudia is telling something to Anthony, who is carrying Virginia and her backpacks since she is asleep, and he had been unsuccessful waking her up. Thalia lingers behind them. She hugs Panda wishing she could hibernate with him when she notices something on the carpet, the "something" Giocatelli took from Avinash. "Your youngest daughter picks a small object from the carpet, examines it in her hand and pushes it inside her backpack in a hurry when she notices you are asking her to speed up. This is what Ellia Jones and John Petersen saw, and that is why they have been after your family. Whatever is in that thumb drive must have information and documents that incriminate them, too. This reinforces Ellia as the main suspect."

Anthony gasps, he wants to tell his suspicions to Alessandro but is taken aback by the policeman's certainty. "How can I force this into the conversation?"

"What?"

"Sorry, I was murmuring to myself. Alessandro, do you have access everywhere in the Vatican?"

"Right now I do. What do you need?"

"Akemi and I have been...reading something and...it might be related to the case. Remember the erotic sketches we found in Giocatelli's staircase and then in Herrera's room?"

"An odd coincidence, yes." Alessandro wonders if the stress is shattering the American's mind.

"I'll tell you the story but you need me to take me to the third floor of the Vatican palace. There is a place called Bibbiena's *stufetta* next to a restricted area that the Holy See uses to receive international dignitaries."

"Let me make a call to security, and I can take you there." Alessandro is surprised to find that he is concerned for Anthony's well-being. He never imagined he could feel empathy for him but realizes that if his son had been in danger, he too would be shaken and a little incoherent.

. . .

"Just wanted to be certain I heard well: the place you mentioned, is Bibbiena's *stufetta*. Why do you want to go there? It is now used as a supplies closet."

Anthony flushes and nods. Stuttering a little bit, he narrates his finding in the Secret Archives, meeting Angelo, and discovering that he and Akemi shared an interest in the writing behind Raphael's erotic drawings.

They walk through the empty corridors of the Vatican palace. Alessandro wants to get back home to his kid, it has already been a very long day for him, too. The beautiful furniture and artwork seem to look down at them wondering what the strangers are up to.

"What is that smell?" Anthony asks, interrupting his narrative as they cross a room furnished with an elegant table where representatives from many countries customarily sit when visiting the Pope.

"It is summer in Rome. I wouldn't be surprised if someone left some antipasto to rot in a corridor or meeting room and the cleaning crew has not gotten to it. Activity here has been at its minimal level since the Pope has spent several days in Castel Gandolfo."

Anthony is thankful to be distracted as he admires the frescos covering walls and ceilings around him. "This is all Raphael's. We are overlooking the *Cortille del Maresciallo*. You can see the many religious motifs on the ceiling. Look, there is Hanno, the Pope's white elephant incorporated into a Biblical scene." Anthony exclaims more to himself while he gawks with pleasure. "This is such an unexpected treat. I guess most visitors are not allowed in this area."

"You are correct." Alessandro wonders if he should get a doctor to examine Anthony. He cannot understand the man's mood swing but the images are bringing back the wonder Anthony has experienced in the last weeks as he read the monk's story while starting a relationship with Akemi. The images on the ceiling and walls smell of dry chalk, and in them Anthony remembers the fragrance of Akemi's hair. He longs for her. He longs for the laziness after love making, safe and tranquil in her arms.

Alessandro points at a door. "You can keep on telling me your story on the way back. Let's get into the glorified *stufetta* closet and go back as quickly as possible. I am glad I can help. Anything for my American friend." He moves the doorknob in a couple directions to unlock it and then throws the door open with a grandiloquent gesture. In response, a thick, putrid stench hits them in the face.

"God, what is this?" exclaims Anthony, covering his nose and mouth with both hands. The sexual arousal the memories had conjured is wiped out in a second as Alessandro turns on the light inside the *stufetta*. The scene before them makes them turn in disgust. Raphael's frescos cover the walls but time has taken much of their color and grace. They are faded and forgotten as they are an inconvenience for a Vatican administration condemning carnal sins. The faun's gigantic phallus is hidden by white plaster, the nymph's open legs are washed out, as is the look on the nymph's eyes; her hair has grayed, and the scarlet color used in some areas is now a pasty salmon. Cardboard boxes holding stationary occupy several areas. Towers of plastic cups and plates sit on what once was a bench to rest while inhaling the restorative water vapors. To complete the image of time's ability to extinguish all human activity, in a clearing at the center of the room lies a half-putrefied human body. The decay has bloated the corpse, and a thick obscure liquid—emanations of the rigor mortis—forms small puddles around it. The image is so gruesome that it silences any words.

Alessandro is the first one to react. He sprints down the corridor to get the Swiss Guard.

Anthony remains immobile and dares himself to look. The body has ballooned. The black tongue and the bulbous eyes are protruding out of the skull. The gelatinous liquid around the body is solid with stench. The room is very hot, accelerating the decay. The body must have been there for at least a couple of days. Studying the clothing and the size of the corpse, Anthony makes a nasty realization: he is looking at Ellia Jones's death body.

He leans and examines the copse, pushing it with his foot. Alessandro has returned and, covering his mouth and nose with a handkerchief, checks the cadaver's pockets and pulls out a wallet. Opening it, he confirms their suspicion. Ellia Jones. Their main suspect is dead. Something else has attracted Anthony's attention. In one hand Ellia holds a crumbled Kleenex, in the other she clutches her smartphone. He signals to Alessandro, who takes the handerchief from his mouth to cover his hand as he retrieves the smartphone. The screen comes alive instantly. Surprised that no password is needed, Alessandro opens it. Letters on a yellow background: the app to write notes. Anthony peeks at the message Ellia had written as she was dying. The reek in the room freezes on his forehead as terror claws up his esophagus with jagged nails.

"Akemi Morishima has poisoned me. She made me sick, and now she dragged and locked me in here to die. I am one of many. Justice be made in the name of God."

CHAPTER 39

THE CONSPIRACY AGAINST THE POPE

"The preliminary autopsy shows bee poison mixed with honey on Ellia's mouth and trachea. She had been sick, and the bee's poison closed her bronchial tubes making her die of *asphyxiation*."

It all made sense to Anthony. Federigo had killed making people sick and using bee poison mixed with lavender honey. "Did they find traces of lavender?"

Alessandro assents. "How do you know? Oh, yes! The assassin's story you have been telling me about." He stares at the Vatican gardens with an empty look. "I cannot procrastinate arresting Akemi anymore. Even your far-fetched explanation ties nicely with the case. We have a motive for her to kill: revenge Avinash's death. We have a weapon: the old poison recipes. We have timing: she could have seen Giocatelli before she met you in the underground vault; she could have seen Herrera before the Transparency Commission session when she missed our meeting; Ellia died the afternoon of the day of the masquerade. Akemi has access to every room in the Vatican. She could have lured Ellia to meet with her before the event. She has no alibi. She lives alone, and you and I know she barely sleeps at night."

"I don't want this to be true." Anthony joins Alessandro in blankly staring out the window.

"We have assembled the needed force. We will wait at her home. We want a discreet arrest, as this will make headlines around the world."

"What about her wearable robots and drones?"

"If she fights that would just prove her guilt. We have snipers positioned around the area with dart rifles to knock her out if she pulls any tricks."

Anthony exhales, the beautiful gardens seem empty of color. "Will I be able to communicate with her?"

"We won't allow any electronics. She will be isolated for the next 12 to 24 hours. You can visit her after that. I'll arrange that."

Anthony hands Alessandro several papers. "I imagined she would be isolated. Can you give her this? I printed the latest we have on the monk's story. It will give her something to do."

Alessandro breezes through the paragraphs and assents. "On days like these I hate my job. I wish I could do something else." His phone rings. "I have to go. Two of the representatives of the Transparency Crusade have just been interned in a hospital with 'food poisoning.' I have to stop Akemi."

"Ellia said it in her note: I am one of many. Justice be made in the name of God."

Day 9 (Continued) – December 14, 1521

Pope Leo X was very different from His Holiness Julius II. Leo X never communicated his complete plan or intentions. With him I felt used, an unquestioning instrument at his service but I knew I had to pay for my past sins. On most occasions, I would comprehend the role I had played at court months after carrying out the assassination and only after carefully piecing together the information I gathered in the palace corridors. Most times, understanding the role I had played made me feel stained. Pious and charming to the world, I knew that concealed under his mask was a man with the instincts of a cornered beast: scared and ready to murder. Maybe that was why he loved to go hunting. To him, everyone was his enemy: Spain, Venice, the Northern Italian States, all the bishops, all the cardinals, all the kings and queens—even the Emperor of the Holy Roman Empire. Their interests yanked him around like chains on the neck of a caged lion. He was the Vicar of Christ and, as such, he had to be above all of them. Through the years, I understood his hatred for anyone but the Medici family.

As months went by, I questioned my decision to separate from Raphael and Margharetta. Right and wrong were confusing. I had sinned with them against God and Nature, yet the memories of those nights were the sweetest. My penance brought death and destruction and enhanced my guilt instead of cleansing it. The Pope made a point of reminding me that I had failed those who depended on me. I could not fail the Catholic Church, or I would condemn those I had loved to damnation.

In 1517, the Papal States went to war with the Republic of Venice disputing the Duchy of Urbino. For Leo X, this meant his cage got smaller as he did not have enough money to finance the war. His primal instincts heightened, his claws extended, and his throat parched with blood thirst. He summoned me one night to his hunting villa outside of Rome and gave me a detailed mission, according to which I had to commit several murders. In the recent weeks, I had heard many swirling rumors of a conspiracy among the cardinals against the Pope's rule. I knew from my sources that the rumors had been initiated by the Pope's minions. The conspiracy was an excuse to replenish the Vatican coffers by profiting from the punishment several cardinals would receive.

Riding back to Rome, I considered vanishing from the city forever, searching for a different life in a faraway kingdom. The Pope would find me, I knew too many of his secrets. My thoughts drifted back to Raphael and how he would be disgusted if he ever discovered who I really was. Deep in thought, I returned to the Vatican palace and glided through the secret passages to the corridor leading to my quarters. I was revolted by what I had been instructed to do but my unconditional obedience to the Pope took precedence. Surprised, I found Raphael waiting for me at the door of my room. My first impulse was to open my arms to him, but I refrained.

"Federigo, brother, we have to talk." His face was somber.

I unlocked the door, looked around, and ushered him into my room, shutting the door in haste.

Raphael confronted me: "Why have you ignored our letters? Why are you evading us?" I remained silent. He sat on my mattress, moving both his hands through his blonde hair. "I should not have asked you to pose for the stufetta. It was sinful and only misfortune can come from sin. I apologize. I was possessed by the demonic illusion that I could reinvent pagan art."

But he had...I remained silent and looked out my window. A street vendor inviting people to buy his wares echoed in the deserted streets.

"Federigo, have you seen it? Have you been to Bibbiena's steam bath?"

I turned to him. "How could I not when all of Rome is talking about it? It seems you, Chigi, and Bibbiena have a bet on who can show the erotic frescos to more people."

"It is not what I envisioned, but still it is something new and daring. We have brought the past to life again in this century, and people cannot have enough of it."

I sighed, letting my shoulders fall. In the recent weeks I had missed the intensity in Raphael. "You used almost none of the drawings of Margharetta and me..." He lowered his face. "You did not execute the final frescos. Your apprentices applied the paint. You only created the traces." A dog howled in the distance. A spider hung on a thread on my windowsill, illuminated by the rising moon.

Facing the floor, he answered, "I could not use the best drawings. They are too personal. Bibbiena and the Pope don't deserve them. While it is fun to have all of Rome talking about the stufetta, I don't want the populous to look at our drawings. I believe they are just for me and Margharetta....and you. They are a sliver of an opened door through which I can peek into what art can be in the future, or in heaven—when we can celebrate our humanity and our bodies. During the process, they became too personal, too intimate. My great inspiration took a life of its own, went out of control....appreciating the beauty of the lines while two bodies fornicate, expressing the true feelings can bring, becoming light—conception....I could not bear the prospect of anyone looking at them and making a vulgar comment. The images represent humanity at its most basic, our desire to perpetuate our existence, the ecstasy of creation, and the pleasure of the now when we break the bonds with the hours of our moment in history to become part of the unstoppable current of further generations....I could not bear somebody comparing these images with decorations for a brothel." He took a deep breath. "I am not equipped to paint like that right now. Rome and the world are not ready to grasp the meaning I want to convey."

He slowly raised his head, his chin trembling. "I have brought multitudes to the stufetta to receive their praise for my work. I laugh with them and their indecent remarks. I gloat when they tell me I am the most advanced artist of this era." He paused, looking at the moon that glossed directly on his face while the spider knitted continually on my windowsill. "But I am not the greatest artist of this era. I am vain and enjoy praise, and then when I get home I look at the drawings and realize I am nothing because I cannot use what I sense is the ultimate expression I should recreate on a wall or a piece of cloth." If the spider made any sound spinning its web it would have been the only sound in the room. "Federigo, I need your conversations."

I paced the room, feeling trapped. It was my turn to confess to him. "I should not go back to you and Margharetta. I am not what I seem. You know I am a manuscript hunter and a spy for the Pope...I also work for him as an assassin. I excel in the art of poison. In the past, I promised on my father and my brother's souls to follow the Pope's commands without question. I am damned but maybe I can prevent them from being condemned for their sins. I never wished to be your friend, or for that matter, anybody's friend. Every moment, awake or asleep, I fear that one day the Pope might order me to poison you or Margharetta...

"You should not worry. I am one of the Pope's favorites . . ."

"Mark my words. The Pope has no favorites. He uses everyone around him. He will not hesitate to have me poison you if it is advantageous for him. He has no loyalties except for the Medici clan...and even there he falters. He will keep you if convenient but discard you on a whim if you become too inconvenient or expensive. With your profession, your popularity, and your influence you can become both at any moment."

"What you do...it cannot be so terrible...you are a good man, one of the best I've ever met."

"I am just a predator servicing the Pope." I trembled, remembering my new mission. "I'll prove it. Come with me tonight, Raphael. I have been ordered to poison five people. Join me in my journey. I was instructed to cover my face with a hood. You can wear one, too. You will witness the suffering I inflict, and the Pope's lack of scruples. If by sunrise you still want to be my friend, so be it! I have looked at your love and spirit of creation, let's see if you can bear to see the executioner in me."

"But you are not only my friend...."

"Cease your foolish words. Witness tonight, and we can converse when the sun comes out. Young Cardinals Petruzzi and Sauli were apprehended while you and I have been in this room. They are being charged with plotting to murder the Pope."

"You must be mistaken. Cardinal Bendinello Sauli is a noble man! And so is Petruzzi..."

"I am uncertain if they are guilty or innocent. Meanwhile, the Pope has sent his Swiss Guard to apprehend five bishops close to them. His orders are clear. With the horrible manner he wants me to carry the executions, he wishes to send a message to the College of Cardinals. He wants them terrorized to prevent them from siding with Petruzzi and Sauli's cause when they go on trial in a few days...You still want to join me?" Raphael thought for a moment and then assented.

We raced two horses to the old Via Appia, where we found a chariot where guards transported the prisoners and had been instructed to meet me. The bishops' hands were bound, and their mouths gagged as they kneeled on hay on their prison carriage, blindfolds covering their eyes. One of the Pope's dwarves was the chief of the operation. Nobody suspected he was in charge of doing His Holiness's dirty jobs as he was a court jester. We connected, and he ordered us to follow them.

We trotted on the millenary stones gliding between vegetation and old constructions until we reached the church of San Sebastiano fuori le mura, erected at the entrance of an ancient Christian catacomb. From there, we followed the procession that moved down through the bone-covered tunnels to the deepest chambers. The bishops walked in a row, still blindfolded, with guards on their sides guiding them while the dwarf chuckled in the lead thinking of their fortune. Raphael and I trailed behind them carrying our own torches. The area we selected was a circular enclave with niches around it crowded with skeletons from the early Christians. We pulled the gags and, ignoring their protests, I forced a potion down the throat of each of the bishops; it was a strong hallucinogenic concoction that delivered a slow death. Once we were sure they had swallowed the venom, the Swiss Guards completely stripped off the mens' clothes to humiliate them and, ripping off their blindfolds, shoved each one of them into a sepulcher carved on the stonewall until the bones of others immobilized them completely. We left them in the humid underground cold with the sputtering light of just one torch. As we retreated, we heard their supplications and shrieks of terror. The dwarf laughed in the darkness while the rest of us hurried, thirsty for open air, and eager to forget the insane eyes of our victims as we abandoned them.

The guards would return for the bodies two days later and drop the horror-contorted carcasses in different parts of Rome. By that time, the Pope had captured other cardinals accused of being involved in the conspiracy, including Cardinal Riaro, one of the richest and most respected men in the city. The dead bishops delivered the message suppressing opposition to the Pope's actions as he triumphantly claimed to have suppressed the conspiracy to murder him. With this, he also opened posts to appoint new lucrative allies inside the College of Cardinals and obtained vast wealth after beheading Petruzzi and charging exorbitant fines to Riaro and others in exchange of forgiveness. His war chest for the Urbino campaign was replenished.

But let me go back to the night at the catacombs...Raphael stood next to me and held the bishops' heads as I forced the toxic liquid into their mouths. He also watched as they contorted and screamed when the hallucinations commenced. His pace was steady as we abandoned the site. He never looked back but I could sense how shaken he was.

He and I separated from the group and reached the Tiber in time to remove our hoods so our faces could be blessed by a sunrise. We dismounted and sat on the muddy riverbank looking at the water currents. When we finally dared to look at each other, we waited for the other to speak first. The horses huffed with their flanks covered in sweaty foam impatient to return to their stables but we could not find any words to say. Finally, I gathered my courage, and asked: "Raphael, do you still want to be my friend?"

His hair flowed in the morning breeze, light and resplendent. He creased his brow in deep thought. He cautiously responded: "I am your brother, now and always, Federigo. I have only one condition for our friendship and you have to swear you will act on it."

"I'll do anything you command me."

"If and when the Pope orders you to poison me, you will not keep it secret from me. Furthermore, you will allow me to hold the cup of poison and drink it on my own will. I would rather receive death from you than from a hired coward. Despite anything the Pope might direct you to do, you will give me a poison that delivers death slowly to allow me to settle my affairs and say my goodbyes."

I held his hands in mine. "We are friends again. Our pact is sealed." I mounted my horse and, as I galloped away from him, screamed: "So be it!"

That winter, I returned to Mainz. The indulgence sales had become such a good enterprise that the archbishop had been able to pay his debt to the bankers and make a handsome profit. The Vatican was also enthusiastic about the profit they were making. They had been able to re-start Saint Peter's Basilica construction plus add to the war coffers. Business was so good that the archbishop sought to increase the allotted number of indulgences for sale and, as a good will gesture, had gathered crumbling manuscripts from churches and monasteries in the area as a gift for the Pope, so I was asked to travel and bring them back to Rome. The Pope also wanted me to spy for him around the town on a certain monk who had recently irritated him. The man's name was Martin Luther. He had directly sent him a letter outlining 99 arguments against the conditions of the Catholic Church in the German states and protesting the sale of indulgences. He criticized that the indulgences had been sold under the false promise that whoever bought them could get pardon now and sin later. They could also be used so their deceased loved ones could spend less time in Purgatory. Leo X felt threatened by the impertinence of having a "nobody" questioning his authority. If he allowed this to happen, next kings and emperors would challenge his power. In response to the letter, he publicly declared that as Pope and representative of God on Earth, he was above everyone and everything, even the Bible. Nobody had a right to question or challenge his judgment.

Unfortunately, the news I brought back in early 1518 was not what he was expecting. His bloated face turned red with barely contained anger when I described how Luther's ideas were spreading throughout the Holy Roman Catholic Empire. I showed him a reprint of Luther's 99 arguments that someone had produced in a clandestine press. The Pope kept me in silence a long while by his side as he plotted his next moves.

Exhausted after my meeting with him, I went to look for Raphael only to be surprised in finding that he had moved from his studio to Agostino Chigi's palace of love. The banker had commissioned him with the decoration of a large hall called "the Psyche Loggia," because the frescos covering the ceiling celebrated Roman pagan gods and goddesses. Chigi had convinced Raphael to bring Margharetta to live with him there as he had noticed how distracted and unproductive the painter was when away from her.

She was the one to welcome me to their new dwelling. I had not talked with her since our last session, and I felt she was somewhat distant and angry with me for having evaded them. She was stunning, having bloomed into a mature and worldly woman. My legs buckled at the sight of her, and proximity to her made me ache. I longed to embrace and kiss her but instead we made awkward small talk. She was not chatting anymore with me, yet her eyes kept that luminosity that made everything come to life. Still, she told me of the latest events. The Pope had a new treasurer, so Bibbiena had temporarily left his apartments in the Vatican and was living now at the French court. Nobody knew if he was there as an ambassador, a spy, or a resentful traitor.

Margharetta's mood improved when Raphael joined us for a lunch of bread, cheese, olives, and wine. She seemed to make a special effort, embracing him and repeatedly touching his body. He just grinned receiving the signs of affection and later took me to see the work in progress. Noticing my childish delight and fascination with Raphael's work,

Margharetta appeared to forgive me and soon the three of us were laughing together as we examined the walls and ceiling of the hall.

Anthony wanders through the streets of Rome immersed in reflection and sadness. Reaching the Pantheon, he decides to stop for a moment. He enters the circular Roman temple transformed into a church and looks for Raphael's tomb. The marble plaque inscription welcomes him: "Here lies that famous Raphael by whom Nature feared to be conquered while he lived, and when he was dying, feared herself to die," and next to it a plaque for Maria Bibbiena, claiming she had been Raphael's wife.

"But they never got married...." clarifies Anthony to no one. "I wonder why she is here." It doesn't matter. He is tired and wants to take a taxi to his hotel, call his daughters, take a hot shower and, if possible, sleep.

CHAPTER 40

PANDA'S DIET

In the morning, Anthony skips his yoga routine. He jogs through the Borghese Gardens, more than doubling the distance he covers every day. He wants to run away from the discoveries of the recent days and the pictures that fill the newspapers in all the kiosks in the city: Akemi's face under large black letters with sensationalist phrases about her arrest. His legs dash through *Via delle Magnolie* as if he were in a 100-meter race and the finish line at the *Villa Borghese*, where he sprints—his heart pounding in his ears, his legs cramping with effort—to the temple of Antonino and Faustina. Akemi is so different from Laura. Akemi is a criminal. Early morning tourists trying to escape the heat of the day during their adventures stare at him with surprise at his energy. His speed and intensity contrast with the summer laziness of the city. Anthony covers the paths around the Zoological Gardens, around the *Viale dei Due Sarcofaghi* all the way to the *Viale dei Muro Torto* into *Piazza del Popolo*. The pictures in the newspapers torment him. He envisions Akemi in the same prison cell he was detained earlier in the year. Same oppressing walls under a white neon light sucking color and life from everything: every object, every wall, and every unfortunate soul trapped behind bars. He never slows down. He hated arriving the previous night at the hotel: his empty room without the girls, his empty bed without a woman. He is short of breath as he maintains his pace through the crowd on *Via del Corso* as if Ellia Jones's minion were still chasing him. People move out of his way escaping contact with his almost-naked body; his t-shirt is tucked around his waist. A group of teenage girls blushes, giggles, and gossips as he passes them. The stores around him make him long for his family, make him wish he was back in Redondo Beach where life was simpler and the ocean could lull him to tranquility. His skin has stopped sweating. It is already so hot that he got completely soaked for most of the race but now his body is becoming dehydrated. Anthony stumbles into *Piazza de Spagna* and kneels in front of the *Fontana della Barcaccia*, where he plunges his face into the water pulling his dripping hair back with both hands as he straightens up. He is breathing violently, gasping air like a fish out of water. His body is shaking slightly with the effort as he remains kneeling. Anthony raises his face and looks up the stairs connecting to the Piazza, to the obelisk, and then to the steeples of the church of *Trinita dei Monti*, up to a clear and intense blue sky when he realizes he has to take a position regarding Akemi. He has to decide if he believes she is guilty and sever her from his life or trust in her innocence, even if it is a lie, and remain close to her: support her while in jail, bring her food, and magazines, make love during conjugal visits and— most importantly—stay permanently in Rome to be close to her prison cell, to her "for life" captivity after committing several murders.

He walks up the stairs wishing he had carried some money to buy water on his way back to the hotel. His tongue is parched and thick. His matted hair sticks to his forehead. He has slowed the race into a nice jogging pace looking for signs in the stone buildings around him to make a decision.

He puts his t-shirt on before entering the lobby of Hotel Modigliani. The man at reception stops him.

"Mr. Hibbert, you got a basket of goods a couple of nights ago but the employee who received it got sick. We found about it just this morning. We apologize for our error but we have sent it to your room." Anthony assents cordially and gets into the elevator.

The basket is on a table but he ignores it to grab a bottle of water from the mini-fridge. He drinks with voracity and desperation. Opening a second water bottle, he catches a glimpse of the fruit on the gift bas-ket from the corner of his eye as he opens the door to the terrace to get some fresh air into the room. He approaches the basket and grabs an apple when he notices the basket contains also cheese and salami. Someone seems to have sliced small portions of them. Feeling suspi-cious, he reaches for the card in the basket, refraining from biting the fruit in his hand.

"Thanks for your support in the investigation. Akemi," read the typewritten words.

"Akemi?" Anthony plays with the cardboard card in his fingers. "Why and when would Akemi send this to me? Why didn't she mention it while we were in *Ostia*?" his voice fills the empty room as he returns the apple to the basket. The salami is artisanal; it comes from a convent in Tuscany. The red meat and white fat morsels glisten on the exposed area where a chunk was sliced off. "Akemi knows I don't eat meat..." Making a sudden realization, he jumps to grab his smartphone charging on the bed's side table. He punches in Alessandro's number quickly, impatiently.

Alessandro is on his way to the station. He picks up the call in his car and assents as Anthony requests that the police department analyze the gift in front of him. He is certain they will find poison in it.

Anthony's heart beats as if he were still sprinting. He has made a decision about Akemi. He holds the phone tightly when it vibrates and rings, signaling he has a call and startling him.

"Papa, we miss you," Thalia's voice is sweet but a little resentful. "We did not talk yesterday."

"How are you, sweetheart? I miss all of you immensely." He walks out to the open terrace. The air's temperature is rising.

"This place is beautiful but I am calling you with a follow-up. Have you put Panda's food in a safe place?" Anthony remembers Claudia explained that Thalia had been "feeding" her stuffed animal food-shaped erasers through a small rip below his neck but had to take them out the night of the masquerade because of the risk of the slit becoming larger. "I haven't sweetheart, but I will do it right away so they won't get lost, and Panda can have a banquet when you return. How are your sisters and grandparents? I would also like to chat with them."

He goes to the dresser, on top of which is a pile of small rubber shapes. Amused while he speaks on the phone, he analyzes them one by one as he puts them into a Ziplock bag: a mini-cake with pink frosting, a pizza slice, a variety of sushi rolls, a hamburger, a hot dog, and another hot dog...he pauses looking at this rubbery shape. There is something different in it. It is larger than the other erasers and while it is rubbery it feels like it is covering a hard object. He squeezes it repeatedly. He is no longer listening to the conversation. "Sweetie, something just came up. I'll call you a little later."

"But Papa...." Anthony ends the call and uses both hands to explore the gum hot dog. There is a line around it close to one of its ends. He pulls the end and discovers it reveals the metallic connector of a thumb drive. He wheezes, this is what Ellia Jones's minion had been looking for all this time, this is the thumb drive Avinash was going to give to the Pope with information showcasing secrets he believed society should be aware of. He jumps to his laptop.

• • •

Via Venetto was once the gathering center of Italian movie stars and paparazzi. The *Café du Monde* was at the core where Gina Lollobrigida and Marcello Mastroianni would be dazed from the camera flashes. Today, it is an area for high-end hotels frequented by businessmen and tourists. Anthony meets Alessandro there after sending the gift basket away in a police car to a forensic laboratory. Sitting on a table on the sidewalk, they wait for the laptop to turn on while the waiters—aged gentlemen from another era—serve them overpriced goods.

"Let me show you! Avinash's data confirms what we had found and expands the information in some areas."

Alessandro lights a cigarette.

"The three cases from the Vatican Secret Archives that Avinash was going to share with the Pope were Giocatelli, Herrera, and Jones. The three of them were trying to retrieve the documents from the Archives before they were accessible to the public—Avinash does not reveal their inside source but he investigated further and complemented the findings." The light at the end of the hot-dog USB drive lights up as information flows from it into the laptop.

"Three dossiers. A brief summary for the Pope and then scanned papers, pictures, and meeting summaries. The examples of what Avinash believed society deserved to know and that a holy institution should not cover up. The files on Giocatelli evidence how he was trying to protect his family name. Meeting summaries from Vatican investigators into Second World War infiltrators reveal how Giocatelli's father had been a spy for the Nazis preying to stop the activities the Catholic Church had undertaken to help Jews escape the Holocaust. There are intercepted documents—they never reached the Nazis—in which Giocatelli Sr. reveals a list of convents in Rome where Jewish people were hiding. Now, there is a letter that Giocatelli sent to the Pope Pius XII. In it he asked for an audience. The documents narrate how Giocatelli Sr. had visited Castel Gandolfo in the summer of 1942. While there, he had infiltrated the Pope's private bedroom in hopes of finding more evidence against his Holiness. He found it. In the Pope's bedroom, five pregnant Jewish women had found refuge to have their babies and care for them until they were strong enough to travel to another hiding place. They slept in the Pope's bed while his Holiness slept on the floor in his office. Here are the pictures that Giocatelli took that day. He gave them to the Pope during his repentance audience when he asked for absolution. Seeing the women changed Giocatelli Sr. He became a double agent. After the war he stayed in Rome where he began his toy business and buried his past."

The screen images from many documents evidence Giocatelli's Sr. activities as a double agent working against the Nazis. Alessandro sips his espresso and exhales a cloud of smoke. Their eyes are fixed on the computer screen. "That would have been the end of Giocatelli's story but as a response to the Vatican's support of Glasnost in the 90s, the Soviets orchestrated a campaign to discredit Pius XII by placing documents in the Secret Archives alleging a conspiracy between the Catholic Church and the Nazis to exterminate Jewish people. They claimed the Pope had been supportive and complicit with the Nazis. These documents were placed in a convenient area so they were found by scholars and revealed to the media. During the crisis, Giocatelli Sr. was called to inspect the documents and assess their authenticity—or lack of authenticity, in this case—because he had known the identity of the true Nazi agents during the war. Giocatelli Sr. went further; he worked closely with Vatican investigators to uncover documentation that proved Hitler had a plan to kidnap and murder Pius XII. The Soviet's ploy was revealed but shadows have been cast over Pius XII ever since stopping his canonization."

"With his father redeemed, Giocatelli did not need to kill to protect his family's secrets." Alessandro has seen the futility of crime too many times in his career.

"Giocatelli's father was ashamed of his past. He had become a proud Italian citizen and did not wish anybody to learn he had been a Nazi. As a young man, Giocatelli had heard a confession from his father. On his father's deathbed, the old man made his son promise that he would do anything to ensure that the family's past remained hidden. We know this because there is a letter from our Giocatelli petitioning Pope Francis I to destroy all evidence in the Secret Archives of Giocatelli Sr.'s acts. That letter is also among the documents Giocatelli paid someone to remove from the Secret Archives when he became aware of the possibility of them becoming transparent. Avinash got a copy of all the files—as I said, I cannot tell from whom based on what I have read. Giocatelli had to murder Avinash to protect his family's honor."

The keyboard clicks as Alessandro browses through the file directory. "The amount of documents is staggering. The media would have a field day and a great run publishing and analyzing the documents if they had access to them. Avinash must have believed that Giocatelli's family had nothing to be ashamed of. In his view, here was an example how transparency allowed people to understand history better."

"Here are the documents regarding the investigation on Gabriel Herrera's effort to convert several convents into whore houses for his fellow clergymen. There is unequivocal data that reveals Herrera as the head of the operation: the Big Pimp. The file contains confessions from a priest who repented and accusations from nuns who were forced to provide sexual favors to traveling clergy. It has some chilling stories about the abuse they received and about nuns who killed themselves as a consequence. All of it matches what I heard from Sor Alegria, the nun I met through my mother-in-law here in Rome. The surprising data is the resolution from the Vatican investigation. Since Herrera provided 'entertainment' for his fellow Church members, he had many friends at high levels—plus a long list of powerful names he would compromise if he accepted they had been his "clients." He was reprimanded, but the evidence was locked in the archives. The results were never shared with the Pope. As "punishment," Herrera was transferred to Los Angeles after spending a month in a monastery in Italy for penance."

Anthony's blood chills as he browses some of the nuns' declarations. "Avinash intended to make this case very public as an example of how transparency could stop corruption and abuse in the Catholic Church. This was one of his prime examples of how the Church should not be above any country's laws. Avinash was infuriated to see that Herrera could be a candidate for the papacy. He describes him as a poster child for hypocrisy and his actions as those of groups without morals within the Church. Avinash believed the Catholic Church should not spend more time dealing with scandals by eliminating them but by exposing them and focusing the public's attention on the Catholic Church's charitable actions to make these larger and more extensive. Transparency for the sake of the most. Transparency for a positive balance of happiness in favor of a majority." Anthony quotes from Avinash's essays.

"We get now to the last victim: Ellia Jones. Jones was able to erase her traces from the CIA and FBI data banks but she could not remove non-digital accounts of her actions in the Secret Archives. In the 90s, Ellia Jones was a key liaison between the U.S. government, the Vatican, and the Solidarity movement in Poland. She had been the money man— or money woman, I should say. She handled the flow of funds from the US to Poland via the Vatican to support the demise of the Soviet system. The files in the Secret Archives are meeting minutes documenting when Jones provides instructions on where and how to transfer the fortune to support the rebellion. However, there are also documents revealing an investigation because the Vatican realized that Jones was taking a generous percentage from every transaction for herself. The amounts Jones took made her a multimillionaire. Jones silenced bureaucrats of the Vatican Bank by giving them cover from the US Government in the mafia money-laundering schemes. She also got a cut from these. The file ends with a note explaining that the investigators in charge of the Jones case had mysteriously died before sharing the findings with the US government or the Pope. Whoever wrote the note had the evidence and the complete file in his hands. He knew his life was also in danger so used the Secret Archives as a place to hide everything. Jones had been looking for this information for several years. She knew that proof of her deeds and a file accusing a list of powerful names in the US government was hidden within the piles of paper in the underground archives. The threat of Avinash's campaign to open the files to the public just increased her sense of urgency. Avinash enjoyed getting a copy of the Jones dossier. He says as much in his essay about this case. He took the information and expanded the investigation. He was able to obtain a list of Jones's many identities, and with it trace her actions in many other CIA financial missions: the Asia crisis, the Argentinean collapse, the 2008 banking crisis. Managing the transfer of 'secret' funds was Jones's specialty, and based on data in this thumb drive she always took a cut. I can understand why Jones was very pleased when Avinash was murdered. I understood why she would encourage Giocatelli to commit the crime. The information in this thumb drive would throw her in jail for the rest of her life along with several high-ranking corrupt officials in Washington. I now understand why she would pay her wingman, Petersen, to harm a child if needed to recuperate the thumb drive. In a way, this piece of evidence was what created the largest danger for my family, but until she could obtain it, also ensured that we were kept alive. That reminds me, we need to share this with the American Ambassador for him to reach Washington and take the proper actions."

Both sip their coffees and watch the cars driving down the street.

"Did Akemi know about the content in the thumb drive?"

"I don't know. I wonder if she is also after it? Has she been using me to get it?"

Alessandro smiles sardonically and punches Anthony in the shoulder. "Look at the American, he has become a man! She used you? You had sex? I can think of many worse things happening to you!"

Anthony doesn't answer. "I think she is innocent. Whoever killed Giocatelli, Herrera, and Jones wants to make us believe she is the criminal. The assassin also tried to poison the new leaders of the Transparency Crusade and tried to poison me, as we will find out when you analyze the food in my room."

"You can become a police investigator now," Alessandro seems almost proud, "but my advice is that you should not let a pair of breasts cloud your judgment. She has also been my friend and having her in jail doesn't make me happy. I really wish she would be innocent."

"My instinct tells me that whoever retrieved the information from the Secret Archives is also our assassin. I don't know if this is the same person who gave the information to Avinash."

"So you think we have been looking in the wrong places?"

"Giocatelli made three calls: Herrera, Jones, and Francesca. I think we will find the answer with my research partner, but before that I want to see Akemi. Can you arrange that?"

"This sounds serious between the two of you." Alessandro nudges Anthony with his elbow like two tweens talking about girl matters. "You are playing with fire, my *amico Americano*. That woman can devour both of us and spit out our bones as an appetizer. Everything points to her as the assassin. You have to tread lightly on this terrain. This is not America. Intrigue has been Rome's specialty for thousands of years."

CHAPTER 41

THE WEDDING

The City of Rome frowns, exhausted by the heat wave gathering grey clouds, lightning, and thunder in the distant horizon. It closes its eyes and exhales gusts of wind heavy with water vapor as premonition of the approaching storm. Abandoned newspapers take flight in the gale, and dust particles become darts hitting the exposed skins of tourist until they protest only to discover that doing so allows the dust to invade the crevices between their teeth.

Anthony rushes into the police station, ignoring the weather. He clutches a folder with printed paper in both hands to prevent it from becoming trash in the wind. He finds Akemi in an isolated cell, a cage in the middle of an empty larger room. She is sitting on a bench with her tangled dark hair covering her face—looking down—stretching the curve of her slouched back. Alessandro has intervened to allow him to speak to her; however, the police commander has chosen to keep Akemi in her cell. He is concerned that she might use some kind of "cybernetic magic" to concoct an escape as if she were a digital witch able to fly away using a cloud server as a broom.

"Akemi, I found the thumb drive Avinash had for the Pope." She is unresponsive. "The information in it supports what we found on Giocatelli and Herrera and adds more information on Ellia Jones. You were always right."

Silence.

Anthony notices cameras swirling from mechanical arms in the ceiling observing them. "Thalia had picked the thumb drive because it has the shape of a hot dog. Why would Avinash use a thumb drive like that for the Pope?"

"A hot dog?" Her voice is barely a murmur. She tilts her face up as if her neck was in a lot of pain. "A hot dog?" Her dark eyes collide with Anthony's only to startle him with an amused smile. "That imbecile was a character until the end. He once gave me a huge piece of jewelry in the shape of a hot dog… "

"Akemi, help me find the assassin."

She looks at him with contempt. "Technology is a sham. Everything failed: all my data, all the hacking and monitoring. Someone is moving outside the web—a rat moving on top of the cables, above the Internet connections. He is no part of any social network, does not communicate through emails or IM's… and knows technology is my strength and weakness." Anthony waits for her to keep on speaking, but she stares at him, studies him from an unemotional distance. The guard shuffles his feet, impatient. He looks at his wristwatch. The visit will soon be over. "It would have been nice. The two of us, getting to know your family."

Anthony takes a deep breath and forces himself to control his stance. He relaxes his back muscles stretching his spinal cord with subtle grace. "I brought you the latest printout from the monk's letters. We are about to finish deciphering the records. Between facsimiles and authentic ones we have 18 out of the 20 sketches. We are missing the last two. Angelo dreads we will never read the final chapters…although his biggest concern right now is how to deal with José Dosal, who has taken all the originals."

The guard removes the folder from Anthony's hands, scans the contents one last time, and hands it to Akemi through the bars. She stands up to receive the typed pages. She holds the paper folder with its contents tightly against her chest, protecting them. Anthony approaches the bars wanting to hold her through the bars but the guard stops him with a hand on his shoulder. She seems so small and fragile with her arms crossed on her chest holding her only belongings in the stark cell. "You have to help me, Akemi. You were investigating Francesca's boyfriend. How can I get that information?"

She looks at him as if he were speaking in another language, takes a step back, and collapses back in her bench. She shakes her head, and

the black hair becomes a veil around her shoulders and face from behind which she can hide.

"The time is up." The guard holds Anthony's arm.

"Akemi… " He walks away from her but stops before exiting the
large empty space with the cage in its center. Defying the guard, he
turns to see her. She is watching him from her bench. "For God's sake…"
he whispers to himself.

"Find Lucca, he might know," she whispers.

"Where?"

The guard pulls Anthony out of the room.

Day 10 – December 15, 1521

*My strength has withered. I have to skip part of my story and go di-
rectly to the most relevant events for my confession. I cannot linger on
the happenings at the Papal court or delve into Imperia's story or the
many intrigues that touched me or the people I killed, the music I discovered, and the magnificent art that was created in the city. Or can I?
I am dying. I will only say that the time between my re-encounter with
Margharetta and Raphael felt stable and benign, but then the year 1519
hit us with all its force. I had become immune to the expert manipulators around me. I kept enjoying access to study forbidden manuscripts
and the warmth of my friends. God is a trickster. At times we have a
sense of stability that seems it will stretch unchanged until we become
elders and pass away. We don't realize everything is temporary: our occupations, our influences, our friends and lovers, even our cities. We are
temporary beings, and He knows it.*

*I quickly wither . . . In the year 1519, a new and more powerful
emperor came to the throne of the Holy Roman Empire. He was the
young Charles I of Spain, Charles V of Germany. The sun never set on
his dominions. After this emperor reached his ascent, the Pope's deepest insecurities were inflamed. He knew he would have to be on top
of his conniving game when dealing with the King of France and the
Emperor. Both wanted his allegiance against the other, while being eager to betray Rome. Both sought to control the world. Leo X initiated
secret negotiations with both sides while he figured who was the least*

treacherous ally. I was a mute messenger between courts and, on many occasions, I killed to smooth the communication exchanges. However, the Pope soon discovered that Charles V was a religious fanatic. Spain's Tribunal of the Holy Order of the Inquisition was very active. Charles V followed doctrine with fervor and campaigned for morality and virtue in his territory. The Emperor followed the scriptures to the letter and was forcefully condemnatory of sin. He was offended, and opposed the loose morals in the Vatican court. He did not approve of pagan knowledge and art, believing they resulted in decadent behavior. To him, the stories of a steam bath decorated with obscene sexual images within the Vatican palace was the ultimate manifestation of the sins that infused all clergy in Rome. How could Raphael bring groups of people to admire this stufetta that was better suited for a brothel than the apartments in the upper floor of the Pope's quarters? How could they keep such indecencies in proximity to the sacred relics at Saint Peter's Basilica?

The Emperor also sent several missives to the Pope complaining about Agostino Chigi. Stories about his lustful and legendary Palace of Love were repeated in courts everywhere. How could the Pope's closest banker and aide be a man living in sin with his mistress? Agostino had kept as his favorite Francesca, the young woman who had usurped Imperia's place so many years ago. Francesca had given Chigi five children in the seven years they had been living together, and Chigi was happy with her.

The Pope yielded to the Emperor's pressure and convinced Chigi to marry Francesca. Leo X himself officiated during the wedding surrounded by a crowd of courtiers and cardinals. Magnificent ceremony. I can still hear the choir—or are those Angels of Death around me humming to themselves before taking their prey? I was there, holding Imperia's hand as she cried behind a curtain so nobody would see her. She later performed her chores as a radiant hostess during the wild celebration that followed the union ceremony. The best cooks in the city provided the feast. There was dancing and jousters. Leo X's favorite dwarf clowned while listening to the conversations around in search of treasonous talk against the Church among the guests.

Leo X was scared. The Emperor and the French monarch had too much power. Black circles appeared under his protruding eyes. The spiders in the clandestine corridors became restless from the fear in the air.

His Holiness—the Toad Pope—also forbade Raphael from bringing any visitors to Bibbiena's apartments and locked the stufetta—he barred the door—prohibiting entrance to it. Cardinal Bernardo Bibbiena was still living in the French court so his chambers could remain vacated. However, Bibbiena's extended time with the King of Frances was another reason for the Pope to worry. Spies were sending him messages that his once close friend was now the close friend of the French King. Bibbiena had known him since childhood. Did the Pope feel the foreign intrigue choking him as I now feel sickness filling my throat? Did Raphael feel this while dying? Tell me, Angels of Death. The Kingdom of Hungary had a pact with the Ottoman Sultan. Francis the I, King of France, had a greater library than ours. Charles the I, V of Germany, was the child of the Catholic king and queen. Was coitus sinful to him? My lips are parched and covered in dry blood— (interrupted text and spots of ink on the paper).

I fainted. The spills in the paper are my vomit. Luckily, my stomach has been empty for a couple of days. The stains are just bile and sorrow. Forgive me, reader, if I am repeating parts of my story. I cannot think straight anymore. I have not moved from this desk even to sleep. I just slump on top of my filth, which drips from the chair as I defecate and urinate in my place. I have stopped writing only to pray for God to give me strength. Good God allow me to finish my confession. Forgive me Father, for I have sinned...WE all have sinned...only art was above us... but that was also SIN. I passed out...the first segments of my confession letters I was able to hide in a book I placed in the Secret Archives library, and I chose a book that had been with me during my time of need at Saint Benedictus Minor. But I cannot walk any more. I have been writing on the back of the sacred drawings—the true holy sketches—that Raphael made of Margharetta and me making love. Love can be made. It is spun out of thin air, like colors and shapes in painting, like tangible music you can taste on your tongue. Everything that Raphael touched is sacred, his hands were blessed, and these drawings cannot be destroyed. Nothing he created should disappear from the face of God's Kingdom but I could not find any more vellum or paper folios. These were the only white surfaces I had. I think it is a proper place to reveal their origin. If you found them, you will have broken into the secret compartments of my twin desks. My most precious possessions will be there with this: my grandfather's ring tied to the book in which I have been recording the recipes for poison, MY GRANDFATHER'S RING NEXT TO THE BOOK OF POISON because I concealed poison behind the gem on top of it—also I hid my father's copy of "The Nature of Things" by Lucretius...nothing from my Mother, nothing from my brother...MY GRANDFATHER'S RING AND THE PAGES OF POISON—these drawings from my friend and from the only woman I loved—these sketches so they cannot be torn into shreds—everything that Raphael created should be protected. Giulio Romano gave me the erotic drawings after Raphael died. He came to me...wait, I hear the wonderful music that Leo X brought to Rome. The musicians must have left their churches and cathedrals to serenade me. During the last papacy, we had the best music in the city...the best musicians...I don't know what I am writing about anymore. I'm covered in sweat but my mouth is dry, my tongue swollen. My body is shaking. I am very cold. I need Margharetta's arms around me to cure me again, like the time I was rescued from the underground palace. I cry at times but only foam comes out of my eyes...I want the heat from Margharetta's body—my scars are like a net tightening around my chest, making it harder to breathe. I need to finish this. Nobody will find it ...the pieces are scattered. If you are reading this, look for them. The drawings are in both desks, there is a psalms book, and my father's book with hidden pockets where I put the letters... LEAVE THE RING TIED WITH A STRIP OF LEATHER KNOTTED TO THE POISON BOOK. I need to finish this...I can hear Raphael's voice commanding me to proceed but I also feel Margharetta's soft hands pulling me away to the fires of Hell, enticing me to receive my punishment. It will be impossible for me to join them in heaven, even if I wish for nothing else once I die. God will not have mercy on me. I killed a Pope. No man has given me an absolution...I have too many sins...I have brazenly ignored my mother's religion during my life. But didn't I obey the Vicars of Christ? Everything else was done for love. Leo X said he was above the Bible. His Word more powerful than any sacred scripture, his wisdom more profound than that of Jesus.

I keep vomiting. Angels...white, tip-toeing around me in concentric circles carrying candles. I see their translucent bodies and hear the air parting for them. They are also coming for me—maybe I still have a chance for Purgatory—but I must finish my confession. God have mercy. Condemn me but let my story remain! Let the part that revolts me the most be known in the future so the fires of hell are stoked forever to torture me! Where was I? I need to remember ...I know the part but don't want to relive it...it's painful. I can take twenty deaths like the one I am going through if I could have prevented the events that followed.

It was early 1520. The Pope desired Raphael to finally get married to Maria Bibbiena and quiet the gossips from other courts. I listened when emissaries came from Spain for private sessions. The Emperor threatened Leo X to make him change his ways. The emissaries were clear when repeating their spoken threats. They were only spoken because Charles I wished not to leave any document trail of his anger. I poisoned more than one of the emissaries. Sometimes the Pope would join me to watch them die; other times, we made them sick so they would perish on their way back to Spain. It was the only satisfaction the Pope could secure from the communication exchanges. He would watch with amusement, his thick neck bloating in rhythm like a toad's. Sometimes he even allowed me to dissect the victims while alive so I could understand how to improve the venoms. It was entertaining for him to see the internal functions of the human body.

The Emperor kept condemning the stories he heard from the Papal court. The German states were ready for revolt. Leo X had sent a representative—a Johannes Eck—to challenge Martin Luther, the monk who had dared question him on the sale of indulgences. The monk who had written so many books and papers challenging the Catholic Church not understanding that the Pope is infallible in all matters of faith. The encounter between the Pope's representative and Luther was held in a public forum. It became a debate. That is NOT what his Holiness desired! Luther was protected by the Elector of Saxony. The Pope demanded that Luther retract his criticism of the Catholic Church. He wanted to admonish him through Eck but Luther answered with reason. There was a large gathering at the public debate. Everybody wished to hear the arguments from both parties first hand. The peasants needed guidance, the aristocrats wanted control and benefit of controlling clerical appointments in their territories. After the event, the crowd favored Luther—even when he declared the Pope was not infallible in all matters of Faith. He had dissertated with his head high, educated and rational. As someone who was raised with the illuminated thinking of Greek and Roman philosophers, I have to confess I agreed with Martin Luther's logic when he attacked the promises people had been made when buying the indulgences. I read Luther's forbidden papers. How could Tetzel, the salesman the Vatican had sent, claim that "as soon as the coin in the coffer rings, the soul from the purgatory springs"? Luther asked the crowd, "Why does the Pope, whose wealth today is greater than the richest Crassus, build the basilica of Saint Peter with money of poor believers rather than with his own money?" But the Pope's emissary was not there to engage in an educated conversation. He declared in a loud and proud voice that nobody could challenge the Pope's commands as he was the representative of Christ on Earth. He reiterated that the Pope was above all kings and emperors, even above anything written in the Bible. Based on this, Martin Luther should abide by the Pope's instructions to recant his 95 theses without questioning the Pope's authority, or he would be excommunicated.

What happened next was contrary to the reaction the Pope expected. Martin Luther escaped and hid, protected by the people and the nobles. The messages the Pope got from the Emperor regarding this matter were uncertain. The Emperor was not taking sides. The wording of the missives was open to many interpretations. At first, they seemed to express support of Rome but letters from many parts revealed that the Emperor sympathized with his German aristocracy in their requests to be independent from the Vatican. Spain was able to appoint its bishops and parish men. It did not make sense for the Emperor to have power to do this in Spain but not in his German territories.

Leo X's exterior exuded his usual charm, but behind closed doors he doubted everyone as he manipulated double negotiations with

France and the Empire. This ruse all came crashing down when he got a missive from Charles I that he would cease all negotiations until he was convinced that the Papal Court was the decent place it should be, as it corresponded to the spiritual center of the world. Furthermore, in his written message, the Emperor expressed his disgust at the Pope for having officiated at Agostino Chigi's wedding. He had requested that the Pope's loyal banker stop living in sin but he never requested the Curia to patronize a union stemming from years of concubinage with cardinals toasting as Imperia, a harlot, hosted the banquet so the bride could be free to enjoy the evening!

During the following days, the Pope called me for different missions, continually changing his instructions. HE WAS GOING INSANE. One day he asked me to go to Spain and poison the Emperor's closest advisors. The following day he cancelled this mission realizing that it could backfire in an ugly way and asked me instead to find a way to eliminate Martin Luther. Next morning, he asked me to stop my plans. Killing Luther would just increase the fervor people had for him by making him a martyr. "FIND A WAY TO BURN EVERY PAPER HE HAS WRITTEN." Every time it would be just the Pope and me in a secluded room. I had never seen him losing control like this. Usually he would be three steps ahead of me, but not this time. I got a glimpse of the constant terror he lived in speculating on the actions the other expert manipulators could execute. Francis I, King of France, glory to him. At one moment he had intentions of sending me to French court—oh, the glory of entering that library! He had confirmation that Cardinal Bernardo Bibbiena had indeed changed alliances and was now faithful to the king of that country after residing in that damned court for two years. He did not acknowledge that he had exiled Bibbiena from his circle of power when he found more apt and reliable courtiers than his lifelong friend. I did not say it but I could not blame Bibbiena for looking for a new patron. The Pope only saw liabilities as he regained his cold blood. Bibbiena was a liability. After all, his famous stufetta was one of the major reasons the Emperor was irked. "BAR THE STUFETTA. DON'T ALLOW THE EYES OF ANY MORE MEN FALL ON THE OBSCENITIES IN IT." Bibbiena had also written a very popular vulgar comedy: La Calandria. The Pope censored it now while he had roared with laughter watching it in the past.

He ordered me to go to France to poison Bibbiena. "MAKE HIM HAVE A PAINFUL DEATH, MAKE HIM WRITHE IN HIS EXCREMENT." He feared Bibbiena was sharing too much information about the Vatican with his enemies. Bibbiena knew him too well. I had to retract my mission when he realized that Bibbiena's death in French territory would jeopardize his secret negotiations with the King of France.

Soon the Pope was dissatisfied with Raphael, too. VERY DISSATISFIED. In public, he rejoiced and celebrated the magnificent tapestries Raphael had created for the Sistine Chapel in a extravagant event to reveal them to the public. They were so heavenly. I stared at them for hours. I would have been content to have died in their presence. They were the ultimate counterpart to Michelangelo's creation covering the ceiling of the Sistine Chapel. The Pope had praised Raphael during the recent inauguration for them but turned his back when the artist had approached him later that night. He did not spend any time with the artist. He also assigned other architects to work with Raphael on Saint Peter's Basilica, taking authority away from his Papal architect and delaying the work as his choices were sometimes very elderly men whose glory in architecture had withered with age.

Truth is, Raphael was also upset with Leo X. The construction bonanza was destroying the remains of Imperial Rome. The builders were exploiting ancient monuments and buildings as stone and marble quarries. The Colosseum was shedding its marble skin. Raphael and I had talked about it as we noticed the islands of ancient edifices that had once emerged on the lavender fields on top of the underground palace disappear. He and I watched from the Borgia Tower as the city changed and the past was being annihilated.

Raphael looked for occasions to talk with his Holiness. He was scandalized that everything Roman was being poached and destroyed. Raphael's audiences were denied. Since the Pope evaded his principal artist, Raphael wrote a letter to the Pope pleading for him to protect the remains of our glorious past. It was a fantastic letter, enumerating the monuments that had been destroyed, and consolidating the voices of many who were upset with the events. That got him an audience— but, to Raphael's surprise, the topic was very different. Leo X had no appetite to protect paganism at the moment; instead he coerced Raphael to throw Margharetta Lutti from his mansion since she was now living in his workshop. The Emperor did not approve of the Pope's favored artist and architect living with a woman he was not married to. He encouraged Raphael to marry his fiancée of many years, Maria Bibbiena, even if that alliance was not advantageous considering Bernardo Bibbiena's role in the French court.

I had to calm Raphael on his way back to his studio from the Pope's audience. His face burned with fury but destiny was to spare him having to make a harsh decision. As soon as he entered his workshop, we got word that Maria Bibbiena had passed away. I hurried to the convent where Maria's secret mistress lived. The nun was devastated by the news and collapsed howling from sorrow in my arms. Raphael and Margharetta perceived the news very differently. To them, Maria's death was a signal from God for them to get married regardless of their differences in social status. I received the news the following morning. Margharetta rushed to knock on my door at daybreak. She was laughing—if only I could hear her perfect laughter again. Her pale skin was flushed with the excitement, her large brown eyes brimming with the future, illuminating everything around her with the purest light. Since the last session, we had not had sex. I had already accepted she and I would never make love again. I was truly happy for them. During all these years, Margharetta had been very careful not to get pregnant by following Imperia's advice. Imperia had taught her well but for some time now she and Raphael had wanted children. While they recognized their social status differences, Chigi's marriage to Francesca had showed them the way. The people of Rome had accepted this alliance with gusto. If the wealthiest man in the world could marry a peasant, could the greatest artist in the universe not marry a baker's daughter?

I cautioned them. I advised them to be very discreet. I told them the Emperor had not been pleased with the way the Chigi ceremony had been officiated, thus the Pope was not pleased. Raphael and Margharetta married in secret. They would reveal their union little by little to the court and the city. The ceremony was a pastoral affair in the chapel of a farm in the Via Appia, close to Caecilia Metela's mausoleum. Giulio Romano and the rest of his workshop apprentices were present. Agostino Chigi was there, too. He came with Francesca and their five children. Imperia came with her daughter. All the Luttis participated in the celebration. THE PERFUME OF FRESHLY BAKED BREAD. While it was only the closest friends and family, Raphael was so popular that a hundred guests assisted. Knowing it was clandestine made it the "must go" event of the year.

Before the priest arrived, Raphael pulled me away from the crowd to thank me for having introduced him to his soon-to-be wife. He was carrying a large rolled up drawing under his arm. We stopped near an aqueduct, and he unfolded the drawing under the soft sunlight. Since Raphael had met Margharetta, all the women he painted had the same common facial features regardless of the sitter: a perfectly proportioned oval face with a small chin and immaculate curved eyebrows on top of almond-shaped eyes. He was repeating Margharetta's face in every painting. This one was a picture of Margharetta but it went beyond. Her upper torso was naked, her pristine breast exposed. She was surrounded by myrtle and quince plants, symbols of fertility and fidelity. She had a pearl in her hair and a large ruby ring, the marriage ring Raphael was going to give her that day, in her left hand. She was stunning, and I could not help but long for her flesh. Why was Raphael torturing me?

"This is for you. I know about your love for Margharetta. The night of Chigi's wedding Imperia got so drunk that Margharetta and I brought her home to care for her. In her inebriation, she told us about your feelings for Margharetta at the time of his holiness Julius II's death. She told us how you had planned to marry if the Pope had liberated you of your vows."

The sun did not feel warm anymore. I felt betrayed and exposed. It was degrading that my friends knew the secret I had shared with Imperia the first night she had heard my voice. My movements were shattered by anger and sadness so I remained in front of Raphael when I wished to sprint away.

"Don't blame Imperia. You are a priceless friend for her, too. The following morning she did not remember having told us anything. You have to understand she was in pain. Regarding Margharetta and me...I should not have asked you to pose for those drawings...it was not only sinful...but then if you had not loved Margharetta the scenes would have been imperfect. The merging of sexual passion and spiritual feelings created images so powerful I could only keep them for myself."

My body was shaking. THE IMAGES ON THOSE SKETCHES ARE SO PERFECT, SO BEAUTIFUL.

"Our respect and love for you has grown even more. If this were a different world, if I had not sinned already so much, we would live together. The three of us." He caressed my cheek with a finger. I smiled at him with friendship and acceptance. "The last years have been a celebration of sensuality, a return to pagan gods. This is all changing. I can feel how we will return to the folds of doctrine and Catholic piety. The world is changing again. This is not our time anymore." He extended his arms and held my shoulders at arm's length staring at my face. "This drawing is a study for an oil painting I am doing for you. I have commenced the work on a canvas you will soon be able to take to your quarters. Your spirit will be with us. I have found no other like you who could overcome pain and torture, sin, hypocrisy, and cruelty, to immerse himself in art and ideas to help others transcend. I would not be the artist I am without your help and education. I would not have found Margharetta. This painting will be a token of my gratitude."

An eagle shrieked in the sky as Raphael embraced me. The rest of the evening was joyous. Food and wine flowed, enhancing the joyful day.

When I returned to the Vatican Palace from the wedding celebration, I shred Raphael's drawing of his new wife into tiny pieces and threw them out the Borgia tower to the wind.

The Pope was maddened to discover Raphael's wedding. He immediately rejected the plan to let the news be broadly known. He already believed it had been an appalling mistake that so many guests had attended the ceremony. He even threatened to annul the union if the news spread. I could feel the tension between the King of France, the Emperor, and the Pope was reaching its climax. The Pope would soon have to make a decision of whom to ally with. The treasure was again empty. For all I knew, Chigi owned the Vatican, Saint Peter's

Basilica, and the Sistine Chapel if he claimed payment of the Church's debts. Chigi owned the Catholic Church. Even the Vatican treasure, the jewels and crowns, was in his house as if they had been sent to a pawnshop.

Charming in public, the Pope walked in circles around the many courtiers showing a pious façade. While in private, the Toad was different, his voluminous body moved with unsuspected agility and his chubby face dripped with tainted sweat as he meditated on his next moves.

CHAPTER 42

THE TOWER OF THE WIND

The city remains dry for now but menaced by a ring of thunderstorms and pouring rain in its suburbs. The protest marches at Saint Peter's square become disorganized with their leaders in the hospital. The heat and storm looming in the distance makes the protesters anxious and uneasy. Perturbed by the dust caked on their foreheads, the protesters leave one by one as if the gathering had become a clod of dirt crumbling under a dry spell. In other cities, the flow of posts in social media dries up. The forums become distracted with the other fast-trending topics. They lose interest in knowing the suspected assassin is in jail—and their summer is almost over. They have to catch up with shallow news.

When Alessandro picks Anthony in his small Fiat, they can see the lightning in the distance and taste the electricity in the air. Anthony is wearing the enhanced-reality contact lenses. He knows where to find Lucca. After seeing Akemi, he returned to his hotel room and used the tablet she had given him to research the identity of this Lucca. He had found a Lucca working at Rome's Ghostwire headquarters who had been communicating with Akemi regarding the investigation of Ahmed, Francesca's boyfriend.

Anthony pushes some papers from the passenger's seat and realizes they are a story scribbled by Alessandro. "Any dream jobs?" he asks holding the papers in his hand.

"Write children's stories or TV shows." Alessandro smirks, mocking himself.

"After all this is over, I can introduce you to my in-laws' Italian partners. They produce children's shows."

Alessandro grasps Anthony's shoulder thanking him. "One never knows."

In the pile of papers Anthony also finds a laboratory report.

"Your gift basket was poisoned. We found some substances similar to the ones in Giocatelli's apple."

"What about the hotel employee who received it and got sick?"

"He ate a piece of the salami. He is in intensive care and will survive."

Anthony wedges himself into the passenger's seat. The stench of tobacco and ashes is revolting so he quickly opens the window despite gushes of wind carrying thick particles of dust and city debris. "Can you get me into Ghostwire?"

"I've got all the paperwork here. Normally I would not do any of this, but I feel guilty for putting Akemi behind bars."

The Ghostwire building is a tall black skyscraper made of curving glass and towering chrome. "This is Akemi's office?" Anthony asks. He wonders about the size of Ghostwire's headquarters in California. Somehow he never connected the woman with a gigantic multibillion corporation. "Is all the building Ghostwire?" he asks Alessandro in case he is making incorrect assumptions.

"This is the main building. Akemi's company has grown so much that they have a couple of secondary offices in Milan and Naples. The European Union are her clients, but she decided to have her regional headquarters in Italy. Don't ask me why."

The lobby of the building is a whirlwind of movement. People are registering at multiple desks and then going through security scanners while their bags, shoes, and belts are X-rayed. It resembles more a futuristic airport than a corporation. As they approach one of the desks, a page approaches them. "Mr. Hibbert, Mr. Catzola, Lucca is expecting you, please follow me." Anthony is a little amazed by the announcement. Alessandro never said who they were looking for in his communication with Ghostwire's security department. The man guides them around the checkpoints. Alessandro is satisfied he can keep his gun inside its holster not having to check it before entering the building.

As they approach the elevators, the enhanced reality contact lenses turn on automatically and the molecular cameras project messages into Anthony's eyes. He is getting instant debriefs of any employee that crosses their path, but Anthony doesn't need that information. He is more interested in the very informal dress code—employees wearing short pants, t-shirts, and sandals—and the dogs of all sizes and races stroll next to their owners. "San José in Rome," he comments under his breath "Only the shorts, the t-shirts, and the sandals are high-end Italian designer brands." Then it hits him. Could he spend the rest of his life with the woman who is leading this technology conglomerate? When he thinks of Akemi, he thinks of different things, and then how her lack of manners contrast with her tenderness and need to be loved. He remembers the long conversation about books written during the origins of Western Culture in the driverless car returning from Ostia. Binary language and code developers have never been topics for him—maybe that has changed without him realizing it. He wants to protect her, yet as he looks around at the army of men and women working in her company, he realizes she is able to protect herself very well, much better than he can take care of himself living on a college's professor income, even with tenure at UCLA.

They are escorted into an elliptical meeting room overlooking the old city— the storm looms in the distance. While the architecture is breathtaking, the furniture is minimalistic and Spartan. Translucent plastic planks, a chrome metallic table and chair legs, shelves almost floating attached to the walls.

"*Bon giorno*. I thought you would want to see me, Mr. Hibbert. I got a security alert early today of someone investigating my background on a company-connected tablet with high security clearance. I traced it and realized Akemi had given you the required credentials. I then linked this to a request by the Italian police to visit our offices." Lucca, a man in his early thirties obsessed with personal fitness and outdoor sports, speaks without looking at them.

"He behaves like Akemi," Anthony's lips form the words with no sound.

Lucca proceeds without introductions. "I know who you both are and that Akemi wouldn't have given you access to the restricted servers within the company network if she did not trust you."

"She trusts me," Anthony asserts, feeling warmth in his chest.

"I researched your interaction with her in recent weeks. Here is what I will give you. Nothing more." He moves his hands and a projector starts revealing images on a wall while the windows darken.

"How many employees work in Ghostwire?" Anthony asks.

"This is not a company tour," he signals the images. "I have found the information you are looking for. We had to send agents to Bosnia to complete the picture. Ahmed Vladek was a boy escaping from his burnt village during the Bosnia-Herzegovina War. His family was murdered as part of the ethnic cleansing the Catholics were doing against the Muslim population. Ahmed, a child with a very high IQ according to his school records, hid in a bombed mansion he found in the richest suburb at Sarajevo. From stories he told some of his comrades, he discovered the secret passage to a subterranean vault under the mansion where he found refuge while bombs decimated the city for months. The inhabitants of the house had long since been killed, and somehow the perpetrators had not discovered the vault so he was able to hide undisturbed. He was surrounded by bottles of fine wine and cans and preserves coming from the best delis around the world. He did not starve while he dreamed of revenge against the Catholics who had murdered everyone in his village. In the vault he also found a fortune in diamonds and gold. A modern Count of Montecristo."

On the wall are images of Ahmed's village before and after it was burned to the ground. Now an image of Ahmed as a young boy and of an elegant mansion in Sarajevo.

Anthony looks out of the darkened window. The wind is so fierce, he can see newspapers suspended high in the air as if levitating above the city. Trees bend while the streets become deserted.

"After the war he used the money to establish a new identity. He moved to Italy while forging a plan. He spent time in Milan and Rome where he observed the coming and goings of Vatican insiders for years. He identified Francesca Malatesta as a key connection he could use when the time was right. She had slept with many powerful men inside and outside the Curia. I surely don't need to go through that list in detail. I don't have all day." It would have been funny if Lucca had not said it with an unemotional voice while walking back and forth.

Anthony suddenly recalls to himself: "Francesca, I was supposed to meet her yesterday. Crap. Where is my brain lately?"

"Simultaneously, when the Transparency Crusade started, Ahmed sent large donations to Avinash Sullivan. We have been able to reconstruct the story from encrypted, very private communications between them. They both knew who each other was but they took all the precautions for nobody else to find out. Ahmed believed the biggest scandal of all would be to expose the dirt from the Catholic Church in more than one area. Avinash and he communicated frequently, both frustrated by the possibility of failing to unearth documents and protocols. They became allies in the campaign. That was the moment when Ahmed's plan fell into place. He had heard about several of Francesca's connections being alarmed and concerned at the possibility of having their secrets exposed if the Secret Files opened to the public. He seduced Francesca, making her believe he was a Saudi prince. He worked behind the scenes, convincing Francesca to help her friends and orchestrating the exchange of files from the Secret Archives for Raphael's erotic sketches. The exchange was to happen between Francesca's friends—Giocatelli, Herrera, and Jones—and a Vatican insider with free access to the underground vault who could extract the files—I'm still digging to figure out who this person is. I'm sure you have your own theories. Whoever this person might be, he is an outlier who doesn't use the Internet and moves in a physical world. The Vatican insider sent photocopies of all archives to Francesca to share with her friends and show in advance the originals they would get if they paid in rare artwork. Ahmed was living with Francesca when the envelope with photocopies from the Vatican was delivered. He made more copies of the information and sent it behind Francesca's back to Avinash who then use this as proof that secrecy only breeds more corruption as he prepared for his private audience with the Pope. That meeting never happened because Ahmed helped Francesca and her friends become aware of the information that Avinash had 'somehow' gathered. After that, we lose trace of his involvement in the murders. Is he the killer? We doubt it, as he was not dealing directly with the victims. He always operated behind the scenes, manipulating his girlfriend. Is she the killer? We also don't think so. We have analyzed her profile with the top criminalists around the world, and we don't think she has what it takes—"

"Could Akemi be the killer?" Alessandro interrupts. "If she had all the information you gave us right now, she knew more than what she shared with us."

"The complete profile of Ahmed came together in the last 24 hours. We knew about his relation with Avinash but not his motive. We got the information about his past in Sarajevo twelve hours ago."

"Still Akemi had enough information. Could she be the killer?"

"She could." The practical and unemotional answer from Lucca makes Anthony's stomach contract. "She had a motive and she definitely has the cold blood. Where I think the argument is flawed is that she would not have wasted resources investigating Ahmed's background and gathering information of all the members of the Transparency Commission if she was the killer in the first place."

The logic answer stuns Anthony. "Then who?"

"I only do electronic espionage. Find Francesca's Vatican connection and that will lead you to the assassin."

People are standing behind the glass door to the meeting room. They look inside with irritated glances. A dog whimpers. Lucca glances at a clock on the wall. "Gentlemen, our time is up. I only booked the room for an hour."

As they walk to the lobby Anthony discovers a wall display featuring magazine covers with Akemi in them: *Fortune, Fast Time, Entrepreneur, Time, The Economist, Vanity Fair* and business magazines from Italy, Germany, and France. Anthony realizes he has only been a regular to the UCLA's History and Classic Literature gazettes.

● ● ●

Cold heavy raindrops falling in a compressed pattern hit Saint Peter's dome like a furious waterfall aiming to erase all the sins from the Holy See. The square is empty, and only a few unfortunate tourists seek shelter under the balustrade curving around the plaza. When Anthony reaches the lockers at the entrance of the Secret Archives, he is already soaked, his shirt sticking to his torso. He hurries across the deserted open-air cafeteria half closing his eyes to protect them from the gales and the water. Thunders roar in the sky as if Zeus were laughing at contemporary human misery from atop Mount Olympus. Anthony must see Francesca. He has to speak with her and find out how much she knows about Ahmed and the identity of the Vatican insider. Is it Angelo? Is it José Dosal? Is it someone she slept with and has never mentioned to him? Is it someone higher in the ranks?

His hair is stuck to his skull, his shoes inundated, but still Anthony enters a deserted study room to find Francesca sitting alone at a work desk. She has faded more since he last saw her. She has lost more of her color. Her blank stare and blank face betray the lack of make-up. Her hair is flatter and the roots reveal her natural brown color. She is not wearing jewelry. Her suit is timeworn and grey.

"Francesca, what is going on?" Anthony lifts her limp hand and holds her. Maybe it is the water running down his sleeves that makes her turn her face to him. For an instant, she seems startled as if suddenly realizing her whereabouts. Maybe she is surprised to see her friend standing in a puddle of water ruining the ancient carpet beneath his feet.

She whispers. "Please, *Caro*. Let's go to a private place. I am losing my mind. I have many things to tell you although I am not sure I can. I am sorry I got you involved in this mess." She closes her eyes, and he can read the apprehension in the deep lines around her mouth. Thunder shakes the glass in the windows. A librarian looks at Anthony disapprovingly but then fluctuations in the electricity distract her and make her hurry to the front desk where she can be closer to the exit if the lights go off.

"Where do you suggest we go to?" Anthony tries to make Francesca stand up but she feels like dead weight.

"The Tower of the Winds. José showed me a way in. I don't think anybody is there right now." Francesca yearns to be surrounded by paintings on the walls depicting boats sinking during a tempest. Maybe the waves will drown her confusion.

Anthony pulls her up. Dragging her feet, she wobbles behind him around a cordoned area and then up the concrete tight spiral staircase leading to the upper floors of the first planetary observatory in the Vatican palace. They climb up slowly. Clearly her health is suffering, and it is hard for her to move. Anthony worries that she might trip. They enter the Meridian room, where markings on the floor reflect the passing of the seasons through the movements of a single ray of sunlight entering through the open mouth of the image of the God of Winds. For now, lightning creates the illusion of a god with sporadic heaving. Francesca slumps down onto the floor. Seeing her, Anthony kneels at her side shaking with cold from his wet clothes. They are a perfect fit with the images on the wall where people crouch on a boat hoping not to drown.

Francesca looks around like a captive animal. She leans and says in a low voice: "God forgive endless documents confessing bad actions. The deaths are entirely my fault! I am paying for meddling in other people's business." Her body is shaking as if she were the one soaked in cold water. "I should have told you many things before. Please forgive me."

Anthony pats her hand and then pulls back his wet hair from his forehead. "It is all right, my friend. I have never thanked you before for the things you've done for me but I have to do it now at the risk of sounding corny and melodramatic. You were there for me when I needed you. If it had not been for the invitation to join you in Rome—"

"I should have told you everything from the beginning. We had our research. If we had focused on that, we would be celebrating our discovery of Catullus poems instead of being embroiled in this dark situation. I feel as if rats are queuing outside these walls waiting for my carcass."

"I would not have met Akemi," Anthony tells himself, and then in a louder voice: "Your secrets are safe with me." She hesitates. He cannot let go of the opportunity to gather her information. "I have the Italian police on my side. I can get you protection."

"I know my career will end if I speak up." A flash of light, the roar of thunder, and the electricity goes off in the building.

"Things can be fine again."

In the half light, Francesca observes the human bodies covered in water around her. The hurricane in the frescoes intrudes on her reasoning. She is losing hope; she has to take the risk of confessing. "It's time for me to open up. I think I will die next . . . I met José Dosal at the University of Milan during an art conference. I found him so cute! This chubby but strong Spaniard priest so passionate about art, especially Renaissance art. He bought me coffee, and we talked for hours. He was entertaining, funny, and knowledgeable. We became inseparable for the next days, going to the same roundtables and seminars. I gave one talk about how we reconstruct literature and literary history based on information in paintings, sculpture, and architecture. That was the night we slept together for the first time. He was entertaining even in bed!" While her voice is still low, her phrases are inflected. "After the love making, we imagined ourselves living different lives. He would be a millionaire art collector, and I would be his kept woman living in luxury. We laughed. The following day, we went to a great presentation about the drawings that Raphael made for the tapestries in the Vatican. The presenters were from the British Museum and…That night, to impress me after love making, he confessed that, while cataloguing some materials, he had discovered in the Secret Archives two erotic drawings made by Raphael. They were so wonderful and unique that he had taken them home. Nobody knew they existed so nobody would ever look for them. We giggled as accomplices. Then he told me that he was intrigued as it seemed these were the last two drawings of a series of twenty but despite all the research he had done he had not found any mention of the other eighteen in any art book or publication. I promised to help him find if others existed."

Anthony's instincts become heightened. Goose bumps on his arms and back transform from reactions to the temperature to those of an animal alert during the hunt. He needs to remain serene so Francesca can keep talking, but her eyes are wandering in their orbits following the hallucination of sea urchins carrying syringes brimming with drugs.

"Like many others, José was not just a name I wrote in my notebook of lovers. We became friends, and I helped him locate private collectors that owned other Raphael erotic drawings from the series. I talked with some of the owners but everything was very scholarly. José did not have the means to acquire art, and I did not think about it again...until some months later. I was already dating Ahmed and getting calls from other members in my lovers' notebook. At that time, the Avinash Sullivan Transparency Crusade was gaining force. Rumors swirling inside the Vatican were that there was a strong possibility of the Secret Archives being completely open to the public. Many powerful people were panicking at the prospect. The Vatican prefers to do most things behind closed doors. Surprisingly, everyone is so willing to talk in the dark! My friends were very worried about the opening of the archives. They could not risk reaching out directly to clergy because clergy loves gossip—religious men love gossiping—exactly what my friends were avoiding. My friends required files that would certainly damage their public image. They had a lot to lose if the truth were exposed."

Anthony notices she is speaking quickly, repeating herself as if reliving everything in her mind in fast forward. "They needed an outsider to be their liaison with exactly the right insider. The operation had to be done with surgical precision, and they knew I had one of the best networks in Italy. I have slept with anybody that matters except the Pope. At least this one. I remember mentioning what was going on to Ahmed, and he suggested that I reach out to José Dosal. As the Prefect of the Secret Archives, he had unlimited access to everything and knew where the compromising files could be located. My Ahmed..." Francesca smiles for the first time. "God blessed me with him during these grueling times, and now I have lost him, too."

She clutches her heart, and closing her eyes listens to a centuries-old artifact used to measure the speed of winds on top of the tower. "Ahmed knew about José because he had been browsing through my lovers' notebook—I was so in love with him at that stage that I had not cared. He seemed to enjoy whenever I told him the stories of my crazy affairs with clergymen, college students, and celebrities. He particularly liked when I shared my experimentation with other women." She leans away from the Christ standing on a floundering boat in the fresco as if concerned He might hear her. "Ahmed pointed out that José Dosal could extract the information without any questioning from his superiors. I had doubts because while José can be crazy and take some artwork as a loan from the Holy See, he is not a corrupt man. He cannot be bought for money. So Ahmed questioned if there was something José would want as barter for the documents. At that moment, I remembered the series of Raphael's erotic sketches. José Dosal would do anything for those. Since I had already contacted the collectors who owned them, I reached out to José to assess his interest in the plan. He loved the idea of completing the Raphael series in exchange of dusty files nobody read in the miles and miles of underground archives. Did you know that lined up, the files in the archives are longer than the Panama Canal?" Her eyeballs slide to her right side as if peeking at something approaching her. She coughs, struggling to regain her breath, certain to lose Anthony's trust with her confession. He almost expects to see her coughing seawater out of her lungs.

"I knew the price to acquire the artwork was not going to be cheap so I only offered the deal to the two ex-lovers who could afford it: Mr. Giocatelli and Ellia Jones. Gabriel Herrera was not wealthy but he kept calling me for help. He had been my lover many years ago, but today I did it as a favor to my friend. When I mentioned what it would take to get his files eliminated discreetly he reached out to his Hollywood connections and obtained the money. He was the confessor of choice to all Catholic Hollywood stars." She chuckles while Anthony braces himself trying to regain body heat. "In the next weeks, we used Christie's and Sotheby's as brokers. They got the drawings from the owners as they could smell the profit in the matter. While I had located most sketches, we were still missing a few to complete the series."

"The ones Angelo found..." Anthony enunciates without making a sound. Talking to himself is getting worse.

"José worked on his side of the deal. He looked for, identified, and extracted the documents from the Secret Archives and an exchange was arranged. To prove the value of his findings, José sent me photocopies of the records. I shared those with my three friends and scheduled the meetings for the handover. Everybody was happy with the timing as Avinash's Transparency Crusade was gaining momentum. Damn Social Media." The storm pounds the tower making it creak with the arthritis of many centuries.

Anthony moves his arms up and down as if warming up before a boxing match. His hair is drying but his clothes feel heavy with water as if he were being dragged down to the bottom of a lake. He wishes Alessandro had joined him for the encounter with Francesca but Alessandro's son had an important soccer match, the final in his summer camp tournament. He wonders how the children are playing in the storm. Besides, Francesca would not have talked in the detective's presence.

"It would have gone smoothly. The exchange would have happened with no problems. As I said, we had already set dates for each of the interested parties to meet directly with José. However the gossip machine at the Vatican is powerful. Almost in real time we found out through internal sources that Avinash had made an appointment with the Pope, and that during the audience, he was going to share the files of three powerful persons who were extracting files from the Secret Archives to protect themselves. *Merda*! It was not hard to realize that my correspondence with José had been intercepted by Avinash's agents in Rome. José was in a panic, and so were my three other friends." Francesca sighs slowly. She gains courage to continue with her narrative. "The afternoon before Avinash landed in Rome, we all got together at Giocatelli's mansion. He decided that he would take the matter into his own hands, slightly cocking his head toward the cabinet with his gun collection when he said this: 'I did not want to get involved in a murder plot but this had already gone too far. I only wish to give a little help to my friends.' When Gabriel tried to coerce Giocatelli to reveal his plan details, Giocatelli smirked and declared it was better for us to remain ignorant. José Dosal was so worried about the Vatican finding out his actions that he encouraged Giocatelli to do whatever was necessary. Ellia Jones had smiled—it was convenient for her that Giocatelli would do the dirty work. She was used to doing it herself so she encouraged the businessman to protect his honor."

Francesca's eyes fill with tears. Without eyeliner and color mascara they look diminutive and sad. "Forgive me. I should not have involved you in this. It was shortly after the reunion at Giocatelli's mansion that Gabriel and I pulled you into the restaurant to recruit your help in warning Avinash of the danger. We were unsettled about how far this had gone. We did not wish for blood to be spilled. "

Sobs interrupt Francesca's words. Anthony hugs her, and her tears flow into his already wet shoulder. He struggles with his feelings. One side of him wants to comfort and reassure his friend; another is irate, making his heart pump with fury. He had known for a while he could not trust Francesca, but had always kept a sliver of hope that she would come out fine from the tangle of events. There is no doubt now about her complicity in the first murder. She had been the catalyst that brought all of them together. Giocatelli had been the hit man, but who was the poisoner?

"You know the story of what happened next, Tony. Avinash was killed and the files he was going to share with the Pope were never found. We all believed the ordeal was over. We were relieved for an instant. We could proceed with the document/drawing exchanges as planned and would have quickly forgotten everything happened. We did not stop to accept we were now accomplices in a murder. I evaded reality. Ahmed had promised me a luxury trip around the world as soon as things slowed down. You and I had found poems by the great Roman poet *Catullus*. The future could only be bright!" She gasps for breath. The veins in her hands and forehead protrude revealing a murky purple color. "Then Giocatelli was poisoned by that horrible woman and the drawings he was going to use for the exchange were stolen. Since then I have been terrified for my life. I am glad Signora Morishima is in jail but what if she had accomplices?" Her words are slurred and hard to understand as her Italian accent gets thicker. "Then Gabriel loses his mind—goes completely psychotic—and shoots at me before killing himself! Did the pressure drive him insane? Did Akemi give him hallucinogenic substances, or did he take them himself to have the courage to kill me and other members of the Transparency Commission? He pointed his gun at my face! I would be dead if you had not pulled me down!" Francesca breaks into sobs again.

Anthony looks at the delicate light coming from a window. He needs to keep on listening. He has to find out if there is any clue to direct him to Akemi's innocence. Francesca's body shakes with sorrow. Anthony does not hurry her. He waits until she is ready to proceed. "I'm desperate now and I am not feeling well anymore…" Her voice is louder. Her hands are shaking. "I wake up at night screaming! I have hallucinations! I think Ahmed left me because he saw I am going crazy. Maybe he realized I had gone through his things and discovered an old passport from the time Bosnia was part of Yugoslavia. He was just a kid in the picture and had another last name."

She clutches the front of Anthony's shirt, clinging to it until one of the shirt's buttons tears off. "Why would he lie to me? I would have accepted him as he is. I love him. I didn't confront him, I never mentioned what I had discovered, but I think he read it in my eyes. He just left without any reason…" Anthony worries that somebody in the study rooms below might hear them. Francesca stands up with unexpected energy. She begins to pace around and wave her arms as she speaks. "But he had been good. He installed alarms in our new home and he even hired armed guards for the entrance. YOU know Ellia Jones is dead too!" She stares directly at his eyes like an insane eagle before her prey. "My affair with HER was one of the MOST unpleasant events in my life. I SHOULD HAVE NEVER HELPED HER!"

"Calm down, Francesca. They will hear you downstairs. You don't want José Dosal knowing you are telling me all this."

She paces frantically with uncertain steps. "It was FUN at the beginning—some woman-to-woman action—but then IT turned dark." She moves like a drunken actress performing in a Greek tragedy. "THAT woman was twisted! Sex reveals the other's soul!" She bends her back while walking and lowers her voice again talking to the floor. "We remained friends but I kept a healthy distance …yet I also discovered how powerful she was during the nights I spent with her. She was a woman you can never escape. You could never say no."

Francesca is crying again. Terror is creeping into her voice while her body shudders. "Whoever was strong enough to murder her IS COMING FOR ME NEXT, and Ahmed is no longer at my side to protect me." She screams and raises her trembling hands, pleading to God. "Ahmed got me tranquilizers from his doctor, but they are not working. What if Akemi set the wheels in motion for my execution before she was captured? What if she has an accomplice? José Dosal and I are next!" She is an actress in a Greek tragedy as if performing for a Roman Emperor, yet the tragedy for her is real.

"Anxiety and terror wrap around my veins like barbed wire. The air I breathe makes me choke with thorns! Sometimes I wish to be bound in my bed so I CAN SCREAM AND THRASH!" Her body contorts with fear.

Anthony watches her, unsure of how to calm her. "Maybe that will free me from this hell I have driven me into! Maybe I should end this BEFORE SHE GETS TO ME!" Confused, she approaches the spiral staircase. She trips with her own feet. Anthony reaches out to catch her but she tumbles down before Anthony can stop her, leaving him with extended arms as he hears her body bouncing down the stone stairwell. The sound of bones breaking mingles with the sound of rain pounding on the walls.

CHAPTER 43

THE SPIDERS DURING LENT

A kemi leans on the bars while sitting on the hard bench. She is holding the folder with the transcript from the monk's confession. This is the last part Angelo has; she will imagine the ending. She closes her eyes and visualizes herself resting her forehead on Anthony's bare chest. That will never happen again. Her future is an Italian prison, and she knows they are worse than the American ones.

She forces herself to think of an alternate universe in which she is having breakfast with Anthony and his daughters. It is a simple house, with a simple round breakfast table next to an open kitchen. They are having cereal, and she is leaning toward Claudia teaching her how to hack into a blog that is not feminist enough. A cold draft of air brings her back to the prison cell. She opens the folder carefully, feeling the physicality of the paper between her fingers.

Day 11 – December 16, 1521

The emissary visits from the various European powers kept increasing in number. There were many days when French ones were in one room while the Spanish representatives were in another. For the first time, my secret passages and back corridors in the castle were blocked by guards. I could not move freely anymore or listen behind walls. The Pope stopped requesting my presence for a couple of weeks and I felt afraid, excluded from his inner circle. The courtiers forced their smiles and graceful manners but avoided looking at each other. Was the City in danger? Would the Emperor or the King of France escalate his aggression against Rome?

One morning in March, I got a message from the Pope to meet him at Bibbiena's empty apartments before dawn. I arrived, scuttling through the alleys with rats and other vermin. The door to the loggia was left half open and, when I entered, Raphael's marvelous biblical decorations on walls and ceilings danced in gloomy and contorted captivity under the flickering light of sparse oil lamps. I had seen these wonderful images many times. I had stood under them and admired their simple storytelling—but in semi-darkness, they seemed grotesque, like the stone crevices and nooks at the entrance of a cave leading to hell.

Leo X sat on a heavy wooden chair with exaggerated carved motifs and plush velvet on the seat and back like a throne pulled from a crypt. He was waiting in one of the living quarters, in a dark corner—like a vampire seeking refuge from the sun. I could only discern the bloated shape of his body under a simple robe and a black mitre encrusted with precious black stones. A simple ray of light was precisely directed on a wide and friendly smile. His hands were crossed on his lap as if he were contemplating a bucolic scene. He seemed completely serene. All the strife and tension from the recent months had evaporated. He was in control. I knelt in front of him to kiss his feet and ring. In his proximity, I noticed he was wearing a black velvet stole around his neck as if in mass, and a large pectoral cross encrusted with jewels that swallowed the glitter and sparkle instead of reflecting the light. The Pope's smell reminded me of the tunnels in the catacombs and the dungeons under Castel Saint Angelo.

He stood up and helped me to my feet. Placing his fat arm around my shoulders, we walked the cortile back and forth like old friends strolling on the paths of an obscure and sterile garden. He was nimble as if he had been cured from his gout. His conversation was graceful. He invited me to a private concert at the Sistine Chapel. He had brought the best musicians from Germany to play what he believed was innovative music. He patted me on the shoulder with appreciation, his hand heavy with rings. His voice resonated under the arched ceiling. One of the musicians in the group was also his hired informant and had brought news about Martin Luther. The rebellious monk in hiding was publishing books with inflammatory ideas that further criticized the Catholic Church and challenged the Pope's divine rights. We knew that, and I wondered why he was bringing up that topic now. Leo X was very upset that the Emperor did not have his house in order as the news was that aristocrats and peasants continued to avidly consume Luther's ideas, taking his side. I kept following the Pope's obscure path. As we approached a threshold, the lamps became scarcer, and the darkness entered my lungs as if it were water and I was a drowning man sinking alone on a subterranean lake. He opened a door to reveal the only brightly lit room in the apartment. I was blinded for a moment from the many oil lamps and candles that illuminated the small space inside Bibbiena's stufetta. I had seen the images many times but now the color was as sensually vivid, highlighting the enormous erect phallus of the faun close to the nymph combing her long dark hair with her legs revealing her pubis. The Pope was satisfied to observe me cringe, dazzled with color and light. I confirmed that his robe, scarf, and mitre were different shades of black. His eyes were bloodshot. The only white was on his teeth. He wore an icy smile, perfect and pleasant.

"This is a very charming room. Bibbiena, Raphael, and Chigi had a lot of laughs from it, and I am sure the hot steam baths alleviated Bernardo's ailments." He leaned his heavy body on the white marble bathtub. He had brought jewel-encrusted candle holders and silver incense burners, placing them around the room. He had taken the naked sculpture of Venus from the central niche replacing it with a gold monstrance, the sacred vessel for displaying the communion host. "I have no doubt Nero would have been very pleased with this place. Unfortunately, the Emperor is not. After all the talk in the City about this place, the Emperor's spies infiltrated this area and copied the images in chalk for him. I've been told that he burned the drawings before soaking them in holy water for a day." He scratched his greasy hair and pondered. "I did the same thing with the letters he sent me reproving the existence of this place inside a holy site. I soaked the letters in urine and burnt them in this very room using the water heater that produces the steam." His smile beamed piously. "Unfortunately I cannot make the Emperor disappear as easily as his words or the detailed account his spies provided of Raphael, Chigi, and Bibbiena's activities around this room. He vehemently condemns that Raphael, the papal architect and painter, was part of this creation and is using this fact to hinder our treaties. He accuses me of allowing Chigi to promote carnal sin in Rome in exchange of money. He believes Bernardo is behaving like a spoiled child rebelling against his father through treason in the French court. He also used these arguments not to sign a favorable treaty."

He talked about a musical performance instead of politics. His teeth flashed an elegant smile—a gesture he must have spent his entire life perfecting to appear agreeable while hiding his true feelings. He crossed his hands in a royal stance. His voice became shriller, as if sharing a happy story. "I am very sorry for the mission I have to give you today." He articulated the word "sorry" in a practiced manner, lacking any emotion. He adapted his smile and inflection as if to convey a hint of sadness, but that digressed into a courtier manner, delightful but focused on the business. He listed my victims, his voice echoing out of the brightly lit room into the night. "I will not remind you of the promise you made to my predecessor and renewed with me to follow my orders without questioning. You made this promise over the souls of your dead father and brother, both sinners who preferred the pagan word to the text in the gospels. You have proven faithful, and I am certain that their souls must be approaching the Light of our Lord Jesus Christ in heaven. No man would wish to change that."

My eyes wandered around. I looked at the scenes of sexual ecstasy framed in flower garlands. The crimson background that framed them seemed pale in contrast to my blood, which had turned into the scorching orange color of molten iron. "I want the triad that conceived the aberrations in this room to die. My love for them blinded me to how unholy these decorations are. While it pains me, it's time to make amends." HIS SMILE NEVER VANISHED. "Bernardo Dovizzi Bibbiena, Raphael Sanzio di Urbino, and Agostino Chigi must die." His diabolical smile never left his face. "The sooner, the better, although I understand that we will have to wait until Bibbiena visits Rome to complete that part. This should not delay you on the other two." His frog-twisted smile never left his bloated face as he issued me my orders.

For a moment, I considered pleading for Raphael's life. I grasped that Agostino's destiny was sealed. He was too wealthy, and his death would give the Pope an avenue to escape his debts to Chigi and recuperate the papal jewels that had been given as guarantee of the many loans to the Vatican. As for Bibbiena—the Pope had not needed him for some time. But Raphael? He was the noblest of men. He had obeyed the Pope in everything, even when the Pope had commanded him to paint Hanno's fresco at the entrance of Saint Peter's Basilica. The Pope had known all the time about the stufetta. He had endorsed the plans to build and decorate it. We walked out of the steam bathroom, and I was grateful to be shrouded in darkness so as not to see his smile any more.

The Pope confirmed his instructions with a levity he would have shown in selecting the desert for a banquet. "Chigi and Raphael go first. Bibbiena, later in the year. You don't have to go to the French court to complete the assignment."

He turned for a moment to the room behind us and stared though the open door several steps away. He gazed at the crimson walls with superiority and contempt. He stood in the darkness, half of his body illuminated by the brightness escaping the stufetta, the skin on his pudgy face wrinkled in thick folds. He pouted as if he were a huge ball of wax melting under the summer sun. The pain in his leg from the gout had returned making him limp as he marched to the stairs that communicated his personal quarters with Bibbiena's.

That afternoon, I prayed while listening to a choir in Saint John Lateran. If the saints and angels could not hear me, maybe the music would elevate my prayers. I knelt on the floor for hours asking that the Pope would change his mind. I tried to remember the prayers my Mother had taught me as a child, but instead I heard Lucretius's words inside my head. I offered God my body and soul in exchange for my friend's life but I knew my soul was already worthless. I volunteered a hundred different penitences and pilgrimages. I would go on my knees to Jerusalem or Saint James of Compostela in Spain. I would burn all my pagan books. I would never read again. I would never look at pagan art. Back in my room, I lacerated my back with a whip adding to the blood, pain, and scars that the deacons had inflicted on me during my torture. I offered to God to retreat inside a diminutive brick room until my death with only a sliver to contact the external world to get nourishment. I visited other temples in search of answers and realized the Church was looking back at me with blind eyes. The buildings I visited followed Roman pagan designs. The doors of Saint John Lateran had been the doors of the old Roman Senate, the columns of Jupiter's temple were next to the main altar. Even Saint Peter, a new building, was emulating the markets that the Roman Emperors built and was using marble and stone from pagan centers. The pagan world had melted and merged with everything around me. I could not escape or lie to myself. The past was everywhere, reminding me that imperial politics had not changed either. Just as easily as Nero had ordered the execution of thousands, the Pope had ordered me to poison my friend.

While I prepared the venoms, the city went wild celebrating carnival. From my quarters I could hear the depravity of a crowd cheering during a bullfight and could smell the fried dough from the many food and drink stands throughout the city. The voices and vulgar laughter from street plays hung in the air and merged with the music from the masked celebrations. Flies, drunk from the spilled wine, tumbled against walls in swarms covering the bodies of unconscious drunkards prostrate in puddles of mud. The whores became courageous and invaded every street, leaning against the columns on many churches' atriums eager to make a profit from those in a rush to sin before lent.

I had promised Raphael before that I would give him enough time to get his affairs in order if I were to poison him. I concocted a twelve-day death. For Chigi, I had something elegant and quick. He had been kind to me so I prepared for him my favorite potion. I poured the bee venom in lavender honey in the secret compartment of my grandfather's ring so I could put it in his drinks at the first opportunity. I had time to think about Bibbiena.

When I asked Raphael to meet me at our secret room at the Borgia tower, we were already deep into lent, Rome had become silent and grey. The streets were deserted and the wine had dried. The whores were all wearing black veils to cover their faces as they prayed for forgiveness to the altars heavy with black and purple cloths. The smell of incense and myrrh formed a fog that floated to the bell tower in the

Vatican. The Borgia spiders have kept knitting their insect traps during these years, transforming the whole area into a thick cloud. They ignored the colors of mourning around the city. Their temple was built with translucent filaments and dead insects. Raphael was waiting for me under a white cobweb dome when I arrived. We could hear monks chanting in the distance, calling for repentance, knocking on the heavy doors of Rome's palaces.

Raphael wanted to share with me the progress on his latest work, an oil painting called "The Resurrection" that he was particularly proud of because of the way he had been able to capture the expressions on the crowd around a crucified Jesus Christ. Raphael's face was patrician, as his inner fire contrasted with the soft light of the afternoon. He was only thirty-seven. God knows what he would have painted if he had lived longer. I listened to him with courtesy until a bout of nausea made my interrupt him abruptly. Heat and cold had taken over my muscles. Raphael grasped me by the arms, sensing something was terribly wrong. As if realizing what I was about to reveal to him, he blanched. His lips became white, the skin on his forehead almost transparent.

I did not want to see his face. Through the wall opening overlooking the city, I could see a procession of penitents advancing on their knees in the direction of Satin Peter's tomb, their torsos naked as they flogged themselves. Some were wearing crowns made of thorn They left a trail of blood on the cobblestones in their wake.

The peal of a bell brought me back to the moment. The murmurs of a rosary crept from a crypt. "I promised you I would tell you if and when the Pope ordered me to terminate your life..." My voice cracked as I sobbed involuntarily. Raphael lost his balance. He kneeled, reclining against a wall where the cobwebs engulfed his back like a funeral shroud made of spiders. I knelt in front of him and held both his hands in mine as if we were praying. "The Pope has given the order..." I lost my voice again, convulsing with tears. "Tomorrow at dawn I will seek you dressed in my purple robes. The poison will give you twelve days to put your affairs in order while your life withers." Raphael's body became limp in my arms as if he had already passed away. Sadness and fear overpowered him as he looked into the vortex of death. Fire filled my arms and legs. Instead of blood, acid pulsated in my temples. "If you wish to escape Rome in the shadows of the night, I will understand." I said holding his trembling body.

The bells of the city pealed again. This time the bell above us on the Borgia tower resonated, shaking us and sending the spiders scurrying to their nests. It was a magnificent bass like the voice of God not only deafening but also felt in every fiber and bone of our bodies—a grieving judgmental presence in itself calling for penitence. Raphael's eyes regained vitality in response. I felt a pulse return to his wrists, and he pulled me back to look at me. "No, my brother," he said in a feeble tone evidencing an immense effort to mutter words. He was gasping with vowels and consonants beyond language as his essence communicated with me almost without a sound. "No, brother. The Pope's spies would find me and in the process destroy my loved ones."

The bell tolled again, calling for the vespers, the sound covering the city with despair as wailing penitents approached the altar on top of Saint Peter's tomb-surrounded columns lacking a dome to support.

"I will not run. Lucky is the man who knows the time of his death." He struggled to get up, pulling the cobwebs off while spiders delighted by playing on his golden hair. He leaned against the wall while his legs pushed him up. "I could stay and talk with you but we will have eternity for that because I am certain we will be reunited in the afterlife. Tonight I will celebrate my physical body, relish its health and the pleasures I can find with Margharetta. I will wait for you at dawn." He coughed dust and turned to leave. I also stood up and he paused, retraced his steps to embrace me. "Federigo, it was good while it lasted."

"I'll look for you at dawn."

"I'll be ready and waiting for you." Then he left with the pride and elegance of a king.

New tolling of bells resounded across Rome. A lonely dog howled in the distance at the scent of carrion. I stood at the window looking at the rooftops. I felt a flurry of movement on my right hand as I clasped the windowsill. Spiders had mobbed my hand, attracted to the lavender honey I kept inside my grandfather's ring. My hand looked like it was covered with a black glove, and as I removed it from the wall I noticed spiders drop to the floor as soon as they drank the honey left on the *borders of the ruby with the inscription of two cartwheels joined by a cross. My poison was quick and deadly even for them.*

She feels a strain on her shoulders and her temples pound into her numb skull. Akemi's black eyes merge with the empty space around her prison cell. The walls have metallic bars. She is like an animal in a cage at the center of an empty warehouse—only if she really were in a warehouse Akemi could look forward to large, threatening grey rats for company instead of the immense solitude of the defective, humming air conditioning pipes. The air is like a vacuum made of inert neon light glimmering on the last line printed of the paper she has been reading. *"My poison was quick and deadly even for them."* The letters tremble under the flickering light. There is nothing more after this last phrase. She will never know how this story ends. Just as she will never explore what a relationship with Anthony and his family can be like. She will never be allowed to touch a computer or web-connected device. She has always been a loner but has never felt as lonely as she feels now.

CHAPTER 44

NIGHT LIFE

Like lonely wolves howling at the moon, the sirens of ambulances entering and leaving the hospital wail with voices of despair and pain to a city that never listens to them. Anthony sits in a deserted waiting room in which empty plastic chairs, the smell of sour coffee, and lingering body fluids reeking of distress, malady and death are the only alternative to once-glossy gossip magazines. His briefcase still holds the tablet Akemi gave him, but he cringes at touching or looking at the glass surface because everything that is sleek reminds him of her. He prefers to stare at the empty nurses' desk where a phone rings with none of the overworked and underpaid nurses picking up.

Finally Alessandro emerges from a flat, colorless side door with a stained opaque window. His whole body has the appearance of a crinkled paper doll. Even the parts with bare skin—his neck, his hands, and his forehead—look polluted and covered in tiny unnatural folds. The nicotine stains on his teeth and fingertips have spread to completely cover him. His shirt and pants have dark brown blotches; his eyes are brown on a sepia surface.

"Francesca is stable." That is it. No greeting. Both are exhausted and wish there would have never been a Transparency Crusade. "They found traces of poison and hallucinogenic compounds in her bloodstream. Whoever was doing this has taken her time to murder her."

Anthony asks the obvious, "You believe Akemi did it?"

Alessandro pulls a pack of cigarettes out of the pocket of his dilapidated jacket, hesitates for a moment when he realizes he is inside a hospital, then places the cigarette carefully between his lips and lights it up. He inhales with greed, seeking the comfort only a bed and being close to his family would bring. Anthony looks around. No response from a smoke detector, no infuriated doctor or nurse shouting at them. The emptiness of the hospital waiting room on a summer night is like stagnant water in the middle of a road. The two men stand next to each other at odd angles; both are considering where to go next. With a fingertip, Alessandro brushes the red ash on top of the cigarette expecting the burn to bring him back in motion. "*Buona notte*, Tony. I still have to stop at the police station."

Anthony returns to retrieve his briefcase sitting next to the empty orange plastic chair. Akemi's tablet pokes from the open zipper. He crouches and tenderly traces the corner of the flat surface with his index finger. Maybe he should go to Ancona and join his family for a few days off. The girls would be delighted.

He walks to the exit into an empty parking lot. He realizes there will be no more public transportation so late at night. He will walk until he finds a taxi. If not, he will walk all the way to the hotel. Rome is not that big. The hot air after the storm sticks to his body immediately. In all his life he has never perspired as much as he has during this summer in Rome, he ponders as new dampness runs along the crevices of his skin, reminding him of Akemi exploring his naked body as he lay immobile, his arms and legs extended for her. He has to stop thinking about Akemi. He will surely meet other women. He is still young and can rebuild his life. Akemi hit him so hard because she was the first woman after Laura. She caught him on the rebound. He walks toward the *Palatino*. The hill with Roman ruins is illuminated in the darkness; its shapes and contours appear through the fog. This is not the best way home but he crosses the avenue and moves to the center of the Roman Circus, an empty grassy esplanade, an oval field with a tower that only tourists look at. Once it had two obelisks but one is at the center in *Piazza del Popolo* and the other in *Piazza di San Giovanni Laterano*. Nothing more remains of the track where chariots raced in antiquity and where bets were made to choose which wild animal would survive in a fight. He stands at the center of it. The wild grasses are pricking his ankles. No cars are moving on the usually very busy avenues that frame the *Circus Maximus*. The fog opens for a moment, as a courtesan opening her robe to reveal rows of magnificent stone arches on top of each other looking down at him. For an instant, he breathes the centuries: from the time emperors were building their palaces to the Renaissance, when Federigo and Raphael had looked at the same wall from the *Palatine* and marveled. This realization jolts his senses, making him blush with excitement and aware of every detail on the enormous support structure in front of him. The City looks down at him with the eyes of a goddess demanding more from her chosen ones.

The letters from the Pope's assassin…He can do one last thing for Akemi. He will find the two missing erotic drawings. He will end the confession. He can give her the gift of a complete story. Francesca said the Prefect of the Secret Archives had found some of them. He shifts his weight from one foot to another as he ponders his next steps. He must go to José Dosal's house and get the missing sketches. How to do that? Angelo would know where Dosal lives. He remembers Angelo gave him a card with the name of the club where he DJs some nights. Anthony strides to a light post on the sidewalk and under the yellow light digs for Angelo's card amid an excess of crumbled papers and business cards in a side pocket of his briefcase.

• • •

Before midnight, the line at Borgia's goes around the corner. Since it is much later, Anthony has to wait only a few minutes behind the red rope to be allowed in. However, noticing men in tight pants and silk shirts with buttons open to expose half their chest and women wearing almost nothing, he realizes he has to adjust his appearance before trying to enter the club. He throws his conservative jacket and socks into a trash bin, rolls up his sleeves and the hems of his pants to show his ankles. Then he tucks his shirt inside his pants to make it look as tight as possible. The sweat soaking his body helps. He knows he looks like a tourist trying to be cool but it works. He just needs to ignore the look of sympathy from the muscled doormen.

Borgia's is inside the hulk of a thirteen-century church burnt and rebuilt mixing glass surfaces with brick ramparts. Deconstructed glass chandeliers hang from the curved ceiling where frescos of a modern day orgy have been plastered by a contemporary artist. The electronic beat shakes the building while lasers and lights encircle a crowd moving in synchronicity on the dance floor— once the church's nave. Arms are in the air and legs are jumping as if praying to the DJ who overlooks the crowd from the raised altar, where his gold leaf–covered desk with turn-tables and synthesizers reside. The performing DJ is wearing a papal ti-ara and an embroidered gold velvet stole over his naked torso. He is not Angelo so Anthony cruises through the hypnotized bodies trying not to stare at the topless torsos of many women. He gets a drink from the bar, outmaneuvering the many blonde, green-eyed prostitutes target-ing men just like him. He can't deny that he is tempted to make contact with them and just pay for a passage into oblivion. He moves around the area where chapels and confessionaries once stood. There are private booths, half open where naked bodies are tangled. There are couches with tables where millionaire tourists shower their guests in champagne after shaking the bottles and spraying them with the bubbly high-end drink that soaks their remaining clothes and water-resistant couches. In one area, a large white mastiff sleeps on top of a couch ignoring the bustle around him. A black cat licks his hind leg sitting under the dog. What is it with Italians and lazy live animals in hip places?

On the last table at the end of the right transept, Anthony discovers Angelo sitting with his head between his hands and a bottle of cham-pagne and limoncello in front of him. The beautiful women and men next to him are deep into their own business: kissing and fondling, talk-ing or laughing, or snorting coke. They are ignoring their friend, letting him get drunk without hassling him with preaching advice. Clearly all of them are locals and regulars who don't lift an eyebrow as Anthony crash-es on the couch next to Angelo. Anthony refills a glass with champagne and gulps it down before talking. Since there is no reaction from his friend, he realizes that he will have to scream to be heard over the mu-sic. Not getting any response, he shakes Angelo's shoulder. The young researcher turns to him in a stupor. He is completely wasted. His face lights up with an idiotic smile with a hint of recognition.

"Mr. Hibbert! Look at you. You have become an Italian. You even have a coffee stain on your teeth!" He embraces his friend, and Anthony is overpowered by the scent of alcohol, a citric designer fragrance and sweat with basil undertones. "You came to listen to me!" Angelo shouts and touches his friends so they turn to them. "This is my best American friend. He came to listen to me!" They all nod their heads politely, refill Anthony's glass, and return to their affairs. "I won't DJ anymore tonight but come, let's dance!" He tries to stand up and fails, but before he collapses to the floor Anthony catches him and helps him straighten his legs. Angelo's head and all his body weight are resting on Anthony's shoulder.

"Come, I think you need some fresh air." Anthony pulls Angelo away from the table, his feet dragging on the floor.

Angelo murmurs to Anthony's ear while he is carried across the church's nave toward the exit. None of the muscles in his body are helping on the journey; he is just dead weight. "I wanted to publish the paper with you. The story of the Pope's assassin would have been a blockbuster in research circles. Not only we would be able to talk about Raphael's erotic sketches discovery but would have a first-hand account of . . . " Angelo starts sobbing while Anthony picks his briefcase from the coat-check. The lady working the turn takes his ticket holding his hand longer than needed as she winks at him while moistening her glossy lips.

The night humid air is as hot as inside the club, and as soon as they exit the guarded club entrance Angelo disentangles from Anthony's support and quickly stumbles to a side alleyway where he leans with his extended arms against the wall for support as he vomits with a reptilian croak, the hot acid liquid splashing on his shoes and skinny pants.

Angelo is too sick to drive his Vespa. He is also so drunk that he would not be able to stay on the seat even if Anthony drove the moped.

"Here my friend. Lean on my shoulders and let's look for a place where you can get some coffee."

Angelo props against his drunken comrade. "There is a small bar that never closes around the corner." His breath saturated with hydrochloric acid and champagne makes Anthony recoil.

The bar is in a dingy crevice occupying an area where stables stood in the distant past between two baroque palaces. It is in character and looks like a makeshift stable with walls of rotten wood, hay on the floor, and tables covered in many layers of dirt. Angelo drinks a triple espresso while Anthony sips on a single. Coffee is clearly the main merchandise sold.

"There is no more. No more letters." Angelo takes his phone out and pulls the text from a book through an app. "This is Giorgio Vasari and his wonderful primary source: 'Lives of the Most Excellent Painters, Sculptors and Architects.' I enjoy how having been a painter in Rome during the sixteenth century, he got to write a book of all the artists from the thirteenth century up to his era. Let me read to you what he says about Raphael's death: "...*pursuing his amours in secret, Raffaello continued to divert himself beyond measure with the pleasures of love; whence it happened that, having on one occasion indulged in more than his usual excess, he returned to his house in a violent fever. The physicians, therefore, believing that he had overheated himself, and receiving from him no confession of the excess of which he had been guilty, imprudently bled him, insomuch that he was weakened and felt himself sinking; for he was in need rather of restoratives. Therefore he made his will: and first, like a good Christian, he sent his mistress out of the house, leaving her the means to live honorably. Next, he divided his possession among his disciples, Giulio Romano, whom he had always loved dearly, and the Florentine Giovanni Francesco . . .* ' He keeps on with the things he did before dying but let me read further on: '*Finally, he confessed and was penitent, and ended the course of his life at the age of thirty-seven, on the same day he was born, which was Good Friday. And even as he adorned the world with his talents, so, it may be believed, that his soul adorns Heaven by its presence. As he lay dead in the hall where he had been working, there was placed at his head this picture of the Transfiguration, which he had executed for Cardinal de Medici; and the sight of that living picture in contrast to the dead body, caused the hearts of all who beheld it to burst with sorrow.*' I guess we will have to use Vasari's text as the final chapter in Federigo's confession letters."

"Angelo, I MUST find the two missing drawings from the Raphael series. I know who has them."

The researcher rubs his forehead with ice, his dark curls stick to his skin. He wants to have a clear mind. "I've been obsessed with it, too. I think the Prefect has them."

"I KNOW he has them. Francesca told me about it."

"That is what drove José Dosal to scrutinize the restoration shop the morning he found my work. He knew too quickly what I was restoring the instant his eyes fell on the paper."

"When I arrived that morning both of you were arguing. What happened before?"

Angelo takes a deep breath and slurs slowly. "I was the first one at work that day. It was odd to find the door to the lab unlocked. When I got in I discovered him opening drawers. He noticed my presence but did not stop. Clearly he was on a mission. I asked him what he was looking for but he ignored me. Others were arriving then and he gave orders for everyone to hand him their keys to bookcases and cabinets."

"Did he take anything else from the shop?"

The speech becomes faster as he reconstructs the scene. "When he opened the drawer on my work station, he discovered the sketches. He knew they were Raphael's without taking a minute to inspect them. He threw the facsimiles to the floor and took the originals with triumph. He was smiling and gloating about his finding. He pronounced that nobody should do research behind his back." Angelo snaps his fingers to ask for another coffee to a taciturn, obese waiter. "I tried to stop him. That was when you arrived."

"I remember him saying they were sketches made by Raphael but I thought he had seen your notes or you had told him. Now I know."

"He was looking for the originals." Angelo shakes his head as if trying to shake the sorrow of having lost his research. "He found the last two drawings of the series in the Secret Archives underground vault, and he was looking for more sketches. I don't know when he found them but he on that day at the shop he knew what he was doing."

"It's before dawn; can you get into his office and find if he is keeping them there? We could recuperate your research—"

"*Our* research."

"We could recuperate our research and find the last two drawings of the series with the end of the monk's story"

"He has no space to keep them there. That place is a useless document hoarder's paradise. At the lab, we have wondered where he hides the artwork he finds and our only conclusion is that he either sends it to the Vatican Museum or keeps it at home." Angelo smiles, adding, "I've checked and he rarely sends pieces to the Vatican Museum. This is one more of the reasons I wanted him away from my findings."

"Aren't his actions considered theft?"

"I have no proof he has these pieces."

"Do you think José Dosal could also have found the monk's book of poisons? You know, that notebook Federigo kept with his recipes?"

"Federigo says in the text that he put it away with the ruby ring from his grandfather in one of his twin desks. The Prefect could have found both...but we can only speculate."

Anthony's heart is pounding as if he were still back in the club following the beat of the electronic music. In contrast, at the bar a very old song by Nicola di Bari wafts in the background. "Do you know where José Dosal lives?"

"He is very private about his address and has not given it to anyone I know. Sometimes he sleeps at the Vatican on the couch in his office—he is a very lonely man. A fellow researcher once saw him asleep at the library inside Saint Peter's Dome, the one that keeps historic architectural documents." Angelo rubs his eyes trying to remember. "Once on my Vespa I saw him entering an apartment building. He might live there but this is not a proper hour to make visits."

"I don't care about the hour. Go submerge your head in water and drink another coffee. You have to be sober enough to take us there."

Rome can be a labyrinth. While the ride is not smooth, Angelo is able to drive his moped through empty streets populated only by puddles of dirty water and traffic lights sending their signals to no one through the fog after the storm. Thunder and lightning still rumble as if they were emanations of a grey summer dream, but the inhabitants of Rome sleep with their windows open.

Anthony and Angelo stop in front of a century-old apartment building, a lone island surrounded by middle class multifamily high rises built in the 60s and 70s. There is an antiquities store selling old things that no collector would pick and a coffee shop/mini market on every street corner. The stands where street vendors offer their wares during the day are covered in canvas, and many of their owners sleep next to them under a tarpaulin tent. The air is finally colder so the sellers pull their blankets tightly around their bodies.

The apartment door is made of black iron and glass. It is triple locked and doesn't budge when they try to open it. The building's interphone has a directory with shiny buttons, the names of the inhabitants written in faded blue Dymo plastic labels. Anthony rubs the raised white letters next to an apartment number, amazed to find a relic of the 80s still in use. "J. Dosal" is there, indicating where the Prefect lives, so Anthony pushes the brass doorbell button three times. The windows on the building are completely dark, too close to the street to be open, and the protruding balconies loom in darkness above them. Anthony pushes the button again. They can hear a buzzer far away. He keeps pushing, unafraid of waking up the neighborhood.

Angelo is sitting on the stone doorsteps with his motorcycle helmet between the knees. He is debating between vomiting again and curling up to take a nap. Distant lighting shines dimly in the stale air. Anthony bangs on the heavy metal and glass door with his fists but the door barely makes a sound.

"There's no use, Tony, he is either not at home sleeping on his office couch or just refuses to answer the door at this unholy hour."

"Can we climb to his balcony?" Anthony inspects the wall, there are small crevices simulating blocks of rock on the facade.

"That is crazy, sir." Angelo stands up and holds his friend's arms. He has decided to vomit but has to get some sense into his friend's head before he can lean on the closest tree and throw up. "I think it is time to go home and get some sleep. We can look for him tomorrow." He feels the acid filling his esophagus but has to contain it as a feeble voice reaches them from the building's intercom.

"*Pronto, pronto.*"

"It must be the concierge lady. It is common here in Italy to have someone like her living in one apartment to clean and take care of the building."

"Tell her José Dosal phoned us and said he was feeling very ill and that we stopped to check on him as we are worried and that we might have to take him to a hospital." Angelo translates muttering in Italian to the intercom. "Tell her that since José is not answering his door, we fear he might have passed out and that his life might be in danger, and since he lives alone there is no one else to look out for him, and we don't want her to find him putrefied in a week next to his bathtub when the neighbors start complaining about the stench!" Angelo opens his eyes amazed at how quickly Anthony can come up with lies. He twitches his mouth before translating again. "Keep on talking Angelo, I would do it but a foreigner's accent is not convincing, it would be suspicious to this old Italian lady."

"She says she has keys to the apartment. We really scared her."

They ascend a spiraling staircase that has seen better times. The soot and grime of human use and contact have eroded the granite and iron that once made it grand. The old lady in charge of the building is wearing a light cotton nightgown, revealing sagging arms with hanging flesh. She must have been pretty in her youth but like the building, the decades have washed down her skin to make it flaccid, her mouth twisted so as to give her a permanent frown—unless she can gossip. José's apartment is in the last floor, and between Angelo's stupor and the lady's age, the ascent is slow. Anthony is jumping from one foot to another as the lady puts on her thick glasses to inspect her key chain. Finally, she pushes the door open as she calls out into the darkness: "*Signore* Dosal! *Signore* Dosal!"

Anthony searches for the light switch. The apartment has three spacious bedrooms, a living room designed to entertain guests with a long dining room for twelve. But what leaves them speechless is that every cubic foot is crammed with art objects. There is barely any space to move inside. Decades of objects cover every surface like poisonous fungi. Boxes are scattered everywhere. Painting canvases stack against the walls. Marble sculptures and bronzes of all sizes stand in clusters on top of tables and furniture. Anthony leans to inspect his surroundings and discovers many of the books include original etchings by famous artists. He pulls one out that seems to be missing the covers and realizes he is holding an authentic nineteenth-century edition of an illustrated Bible with Gustave Dore engravings. Instinct makes him push the book away, realizing that he is holding it without gloves—but seeing that it lands on top of the box with other treasures, Anthony realizes that José has been stealing artwork from the Holy See. The lady is checking the rooms in search of José while Anthony pulls himself together and explores other books. He realizes that many have been extracted from religious libraries in countries where José has lived. Treasures forgotten from places that lack the intellect to appreciate them (small monasteries and churches around the rural areas of poorer European countries) or that are too wealthy in art (the Vatican) to bother rescuing them.

Angelo's exclamations pull Anthony away. He is holding sculptures in his hand. Some are religious images of saints but others seem to be clay or small bronze models for larger pieces of art. Angelo holds the bronze miniature of a woman enrobed in folding cloth, her face turned to the heavens with an ecstatic expression.

"This is Bernini's Santa Teresa. This is a small sculpture Bernini made when working on the large marble sculpture at *Santa Maria della Vittoria*! Jose has priceless art objects cluttered together as if they were trinkets!" The concierge pulls Angelo's arm. She is requesting they leave the apartment since José is not in. They ignore her, and she pulls harder while raising her voice. She threatens to call the police—and, at that instant, Anthony's eyes wander into the bedroom, where leaning against the open door of a closet are the two Franz Marc paintings and the small Modigliani that were stolen the night Giocatelli was murdered. Anthony pulls his phone and dials Alessandro's number. "*Si, polizia!*" but he stops as Angelo calls from the bedside table. It is a wide piece of furniture but the lamp has been moved to the floor to make space for a stack of drawings. It is the complete set of Raphael's erotic drawings—including the originals from Sotheby's and Christie's that Giocatelli, Herrera, and Jones had offered as payment to José Dosal in exchange of him extracting information from the Secret Archives. Here are the ones taken from the restoration shop and the two missing ones that José had found with the first stack of objects sent to the Secret Archives for classification—the ones Anthony has become obsessed with finding, the ones that complete the assassin monk story. Anthony lifts them with infinite care, muttering in wonder: "He wanted art. He had been stealing what he deemed were unappreciated objects and when he found the first Raphael drawings he realized he had to have them all! Francesca knew he could not be bought with money but art would do it."

Angelo spreads out the drawings on top of the bed covers. "We got them back, all the originals. The series is complete! All twenty. They are so beautiful. You can see so much love in the tracing of the naked bodies." There is an extra drawing. It is an unexpected one. It is not numbered, like a bonus sketch in the series but very different. Here, the bodies are not making love. Three naked figures relax while walking forward. In the front is a woman, Margharetta, her hair barely contained by a scarf with a pearl brooch falling on her shoulders. She is pushing her body to the spectator, the right leg extended to the front as if she was taking a step. Her chest is also pushed forward as both her arms rise and bend likes the wings of a swam to touch the faces of the two men behind her in an almost unnatural pose as if she was blindly reaching for them. Her body covers half of each man's body. They are leaning toward each other while moving forward, half of their faces covered by Margharetta's. One man is Raphael. At his feet are models of buildings and painting instruments. The other man is Federigo, his scars converging toward his friends like lines on a map. At his feet are manuscripts, books, and lines that look like scars that have peeled away from his skin and fallen to the ground. Both men seem to be approaching each other as if to clash and become one, while Margharetta advances with them. The three are smiling.

Anthony massages his scalp to stimulate circulation to his brain and realizes he needs a haircut, having taken the last one in Redondo Beach. "Angelo, can you stay here and wait for the police? I am going to call Lieutenant Catzola and then go to the Vatican. This is too important. Can I take your Vespa?" The concierge lady is blabbering in a very loud voice and a couple of neighbors are opening their doors disturbed by the racket. "I must find José Dosal."

CHAPTER 45

A CARNIVAL OF MOURNERS

Day 12 – December 17, 1521

*I*t is so silent. The city monster is asleep. He doesn't have to fight to be fed. I'll go into his jaws soon. The angels lean inside the bell towers, making the bells mute...or maybe the poison has made me deaf already as it starts closing my senses off from the living. All my life I have been so clean and tidy but as I approach my final moments I'm covered in filth as if my sins have come to the surface of my body like feces floating on a corrupt river. I have to go on. Time has run out, and the many I murdered are clamoring for me.

I spent all night at the Borgia Tower awake and motionless hoping that the poisonous spiders would crawl on me and finish my existence before I could carry out my mission. But the spiders were afraid.

At sunrise I went to my quarters and cleansed myself with a sponge and water. Wearing my lavender color robes, I crossed the streets in my journey to Raphael's workshop. Pilgrims were sleeping in groups in many places. While there were still two weeks until Easter, many were coming into the city on a quest for redemption and forgiveness of their sins. Those who could not afford an inn gathered in groups keeping a watchman during the night to protect them from robbers. The rest bundled against each other waiting for the sun so they could visit the many relics and temples that could bring miracles to their lives. Their sentinels looked at me as I passed and cringed with fear sensing an incarnation of Death before their eyes.

I arrived at Raphael's workshop and for the first time I saw it as the palace built by Bramante rather than his studio. The large wood doors reminded me of the entrance to a church. Raphael received me with open arms. I could see that I had pulled him out of bed. His body was scarcely covered by a bed sheet around his waist as if he had been baptized in a river. His exposed skin was marked with the remnants of love making: red patches around his neck and nipples, thin scratches on his ribs and shoulders, dried fluids on his inner thighs. His eyes were blood shot. His hair completely tangled and matted with sweat. He smiled welcomingly, leading me into his empty studio. The arched ceiling created an altar for his paintings. None of the other artists or apprentices had arrived. He bragged about the canvas he had been working on: "The Resurrection," showing me how he had captured the many expressions of the crowd when Christ resurrects. Then he took me to where he had the half-finished portrait of Margharetta. This was the painting he had promised to me as a gift me during his wedding.

"I won't have time to finish it." He apologized. "Her face and upper body were already colored. The oil pigments were drying on the painted naked torso. In one of her hands, she had the huge ruby ring Raphael had given her for the wedding. The image made my chest ache as deep despair rushed to my forehead.

"Would you like to cover yourself before we get to business?" I signaled to his semi-naked body. The sun was peering through the windows but I felt stabs of ice on my back.

"Clothing won't warm me from the cold of death," he replied, brushing one of his erect nipples with a playful gesture. "Once we are done, this will make the return to the warmth of Margharetta in my bed better…even if it is the last time."

I paused and pulled a glass vial. "Would it please you if I mixed the poison with wine?" I looked around for two jars to use as my potion cruets.

He kneeled in front of me, his lips levered with my hand as if ready to kiss my ring. It was the same pose and gesture he had used when kissing the papal ring on innumerable occasions. "I'll take it straight. I want to feel it. I want my tongue and throat to recognize the moment when everything will change with the abruptness of a never-tasted flavor. I can have the wine after. I must rinse my lips and mouth before I kiss Margharetta again. She cannot get any traces of what is only mine." With that, he held my hand in both of his, pulled the top of the glass vial and emptied its contents in his mouth. I watched the thick fluid move with laziness. Impatient, he pushed the tip of his tongue into the glass container and avidly sucked the poison. Tears covered my face during this. He lowered his face and murmured as if he were in a confession booth: "Forgive me, Father, for I have sinned."

"Receive the Holy Spirit. If you forgive the sins of any, they are forgiven them; if you retain the sins of any, they are retained." I responded with the same words Jesus used when he sent his apostles to evangelize after his death.

A rooster crowed in the distance. Raphael stood up and cleaned the tears from my face with his open hands. "I have much to do now," he said, drinking water mixed with wine and eating some bread to cleanse his mouth, "I have to ensure all my matters are in order. Margharetta has to receive money for the rest of her life. I have to write a will." His beautiful face turned to the rising sun streaming through the windows. He smiled with peace as if he had just been blessed after confession. "But now I have to return to Margharetta's bed and get a peek at heaven." He emptied the bottle of wine and turned away from me dropping the bed sheet around his waist to stroll naked into his bed chamber. I caressed my grandfather's ring with my right hand feeling it had betrayed me and threw myself into the street.

During the next twelve days, Raphael had time to arrange his affairs and testament. To protect Margharetta from any censorship from the Church, he made her leave the studio the morning of my visit. He also did not want her present when the many doctors bled him and supplied futile remedies. He knew he could not be cured and did not want to give her any hope. She moved back in with her father at the bakery at 21 Santa Dorotea Street. The Luttis received her with no recrimination and plenty of love.

Giulio Romano gave me a package from Raphael. I got the twenty-one drawings he had made of me experiencing carnal pleasures. While in the studio I noticed that Margharetta's oil painting had been modified as Raphael agonized. The apprentices had retouched the hands covering with new paint the ruby ring and all traces of marriage symbols. Only the pearl brooch remained in her hair. The marriage had to remain secret for her sake. The painting was no longer for me. Some high-ranking person had seen it and offered a fortune for it. Raphael had accepted to sell it to add the money to Margharetta's inheritance. He knew I would agree with his decision. He left all his possessions to his apprentices, but Giulio Romano received an extra portion of his fortune to look after Margharetta in case she lost the considerable wealth left directly to her.

I visited every day but was never able to be alone with him. I watched him wither; I was a bystander to a public spectacle. I knew I had poisoned him to expiate my past sins but his slow agony reinvented the meaning of having committed a sin.

Raphael died on Good Friday, exactly twelve days after the morning he received the poison communion. Saturday during Holy Week signals the end of mourning. In the Catholic tradition, Christ dies on Friday and heaven opens to receive him on Saturday, making this day an occasion to celebrate across the city. The streets become a tapestry of street vendors, food stands spring up in every corner, bullfights and street plays are organized in open spaces. Musicians dress in bright colors to roam playing happy melodies so people can dance and party. The taverns open their doors and serve any passerby. After Lent and the repentance during Holy Week, all of the inhabitants of Rome rush out to sin again for a few hours before Easter.

As I mentioned, I never liked carnivals, never joined street celebrations even when Julius II returned triumphant from his military campaigns or when Leo X entered the city to take his post as Pope. I disdained the vanity in them. But when the bells of the city tolled incessantly all night on Friday until Saturday morning to announce the death of Raphael, I trod into the streets and piazzas getting lost while roaming aimlessly with the crowds to discover that this time the mood on Holy Saturday was dark and the laughter had ceased. The food stands remained closed. The bulls lived to die in a different bull fight. Actors abandoned their masks and costumes to join the sorrow, forgetting the lines from their comedies. The carnival to celebrate the opening of the gates of Heaven to receive Christ had transformed into a mourning *procession walking aimlessly, submerged in the grief of having lost the greatest and most loved artist the inhabitants of Rome had known. It was a painful march. The prostitutes and the tavern men joined the dock workers and the scribes marching in silence. A mass of silent people converged toward the funeral procession, merging with hordes of monks who had lost their voices and could no longer chant. I had always been aware of Raphael's celebrity status in Rome but did not expect the tears of sorrow from men, women, and children alike. After all, he had not only been an unstoppable creative force in building and decorating palaces and churches but he had done it with a joy that had touched anyone who had come into contact with him. He had not possessed the scary melancholic genius of Michelangelo or been the arrogant courtier Bramante and others had been. Raphael had thrown himself as a young man into Rome to experience everything around him—from the ancient ruins to its women and now even the ruins of palaces and temples that belonged to emperors turned grey and opaque letting brambles grow in their crevices with prickly leaves and dry undergrowth.*

I flowed with the river of people radiating deepest grief like a metal so cold it shone with a blue light. For once I was one of them, no longer a freak. For once, I belonged as my feet became covered in mud and my robes stained from the tears and running noses of those surrounding me.

Before sunrise, Rome seems to fall into a deep slumber. Very few cars and people roam the empty streets. Rome is there for Anthony to take as he rushes across *Via Labicana* next to the Colosseum into *Via dei Fiori Imperiali* and into the *Corso Vittorio Emanuelle*. He drives the Vespa as fast as it can go, its small engine whining as Anthony never slows down for the red lights next to monuments he doesn't admire for the first time. Red after red after red, he speeds until he crosses the Tiber on an ancient bridge into *Via della Concilizione* where he can see Saint Peter in the distance waiting for him as if he were a pilgrim or a meteor on collision course.

Saint Peter's Square is empty. Even the pigeons are asleep. The 140 saints on the 284 columns of the colonnade dream with their stone eyes open. Only the echo of the Vespa converses with the lonely Egyptian monolith on its center. Anthony doesn't stop to grasp the precious moment of solitude of a place always teeming with tourists. He drops the moped and runs to the Swiss Guards at one of the entrances, flashing all his scholarly credentials and permits. The guards are also half asleep and give him access mechanically, without assessing the unorthodox hour. Anthony runs to the Secret Archives.

Under a weak sun, I joined the procession following the coffin where Raphael was carried to the Pantheon where he was being put to rest. As night fell and advanced, torches illuminated the landscape of heads making a winding line waiting to enter the temple to pay homage. Everyone was there, even the robbers who did not care that the rest of the city was deserted and vulnerable with doors and windows wide open. Despite the late hour, cardinals, aristocrats, bankers, and intellectuals stood in line with beggars and peasants to bid farewell. Everyone was there except Margharetta, whose pain had immobilized her keeping her captive at the bakery. I looked for her face in the throngs. If I had known she was not present, I would have gone to her side.

Usually, the celebration on Holy Saturday reaches its climax at midnight with a paroxysm of drunkenness and lust, but not this time. Around me, people prayed and murmured repentance to the Almighty as if Lent had started all over again. The silence of the earlier march had transformed into a sea of voices pleading for meaning. The moon was high when I entered the Pantheon. Here we were, in a building where the Classical perfection of Roman architecture had merged with Christian icons. This had been a temple for all the pagan Gods and, as such, was a suitable place for Raphael to spend eternity. The moon shone through the oculus in its perfect concrete dome, bathing the altars in a white luminescence and spotlighting on the open coffin at the center of the circular construction. Raphael's last painting, The Resurrection, had been placed behind his coffin. Looking at it, we all expected to discover Raphael's soul leaving his body and ascending to heaven. The Pope had paid homage earlier. It was rumored that he had been crying so inconsolably, he could no stay through the wake. Agostino Chigi stayed all night dressed in black next to the close circle of people from Raphael's workshop. He kneeled and prayed incessantly.

The beaten floor, where the Roman designs had yielded to time, was wet from tears. I also glimpsed Imperia pushing her body behind a column as if she could become one with the marble and in the coldness of the surface diffuse the fire of her pain –

Forgive me reader. I am coughing blood so I must hurry. I cannot linger any more on my memories of that night. I have to finish my tale.

I poisoned Agostino Chigi three days after Raphael's funeral. I selected something quick and painless for him: the lavender honey with bee venom. He opened his palace to his friends after a rosary for Raphael. It was easy to pour the poison into his drink.

Bibbiena returned to Rome from the French court in the summer. I arranged for a fruit basket to be placed in his apartment. The substances I selected made him suffer in his death bed. When news of his death broke, the Pope beckoned me to his presence. This time the Toad chose the middle of the night to be in complete darkness. I did not want to see him so I welcomed the black void of his body sitting on a throne. He commended me on how efficient I had been in completing my mission. For the first time since I had served him, he paid me compensation for my services. He gave me a small chest with silver and gold from Spain. It was June.

I had seen Margharetta at the end of April and then in May after Raphael's death. She was dressed in black with a veil hiding her face. She barely ate so her clothes hung loose on a frame of bones and traces of flesh. Whenever I went to the bakery, she spent all the time crying. The day I got the coffer from the Pope, while I was walking back to my room from the audience, I decided to propose marriage to her. I would give her the coffer as a gift and ask her to run away from Rome with me. We would start our lives anew in a different place, with different names. After all she had already been my woman. But when I arrived at my quarters I found two guards waiting. After I left the coffer, they escorted me to the lodgings of one of the Jewish doctors that the Pope had brought to court. I knew the man well; he worked hard to do his job. He was very spiritual although I did not understand his religion. He realized that the surgery the Pope had ordered for him to perform on me was an abomination. Leo X was very concerned about the amount of information I had on him especially after the unrest in the city resulting from Raphael's death and the anger and mistrust that Chigi's passing had generated among businessmen who dealt with the Vatican. While everyone believed I was mute, his Holiness still desired to protect his interests. The doctor cut my tongue. Leo X wanted me to remain silent even if I was tortured by his enemies. It all seemed to fall in place. Raphael had returned my voice, and with his death I was losing my voice forever. The procedure left me sick and relegated to my bed for several weeks.

During that time, Margharetta's brother-in-law came looking for me because Francesco Lutti had fallen very ill; the hole in the baker's head that I had cured years ago was infected. I was delirious from the surgery. I barely remember him talking to me and imploring me to get dressed and follow him. Lutti needed me. Only I could cure him again. Margharetta needed me. But my body was too feeble and my mind so tormented with fever that I ignored him. When I regained strength I wondered if the visit had been real or an hallucination. Once I could get dressed, I stumbled to the bakery only to find it closed and deserted. Lutti had died. Since then, Margharetta had remained in her bed.

I found her in darkness, shying away from the sun curled in a worn out blanket obscured with the smoke of incense that burned at all times. In her grief, she had shorn her hair very short as a damned woman would. Her mother had been taking care of her, feeding her broths as if she were feeding a baby. But Margharetta's mother was not well herself. The grief from her husband's death had covered her face in wrinkles and turned her hair white. Concern for her daughter's health had kept her active every day. Since the bakery had closed, they had been living off the money Raphael had left to Margharetta but now Margharetta's sister wanted the mother to go live with her. I stood on the street in front of the bakery, my hands digging into the dirt in search of an explanation when I saw Giulio Romano coming my way. He had arranged for Margharetta to join a convent. It had been only four months after Raphael was gone, and my beloved's existence had turned to shreds. I did not return to the Vatican Palace for the next few days. I stayed next to Margharetta, nursing her until she could walk again. She never looked at my face, as if she did not want to recriminate that I had not *gone to her father's side when she needed me—or maybe she did not want to remember Raphael by looking at me.*

One morning, with her eyes downcast, holding my arm, she and I walked to the monastery of Santa Appolonia where she locked herself away. She was as mute as I had become, and her only farewell was brushing her lips to the back of my hand before the Mother Superior took her inside the stone cloister.

The entrance to the study rooms is locked and so is every door in the Secret Archives. Anthony moves from one doorknob to another impatiently testing them until he hears shuffling feet on the floor tiles down the corridor. He rushes to the sound to find an aged cleaning lady with a cart full of supplies. Her small body shivers with surprise to see Anthony. It is before dawn, and she likes to take her time to sweep the floors and swipe the tables before anybody arrives. Anthony asks in his accented Italian if she has the keys to the Prefect's office.

"*Shhhh. Il dorme.*" *He sleeps.* She winks while covering her lips with a twisted finger.

"*Per favore*, open the door!" and after she turns the key with care not to make noise, Anthony stares at José Dosal asleep on the couch in his office dressed in his black priest robe. He is embracing a large hardcover book about Raphael's tapestries for the Sistine Chapel. He has a smile on his face as if dreaming of beautiful paintings and magnificent buildings. His fingers caress the images on the cover of the book as if stroking a beautiful woman. His right index finger has a large ring with a ruby stone where two engraved cartwheels join through a cross. It is the assassin's ring. José Dosal had found the poisoner's notebook with the ring and two of the drawings. After Avinash was killed and it became big news, he realized that if Giocatelli, Herrera, Jones, or Francesca talked the police could find his connection with the erotic sketches from Raphael. He could not take the risk of Vatican authorities discovering that he had stolen art works from the Holy See for many years. He could not be discovered or he would lose all his treasures. That's when he decided to eliminate the liabilities. First Giocatelli—he was known by the businessman and had access to his mansion. Then Herrera—José had given Herrera the poison to drive him mad. Jose had also supplied the gun for Herrera to kill others and kill himself with. Why kill others? He hated the Transparency Commission. Finally, he had killed Ellia Jones who believed she was smarter than José and did not expect to be poisoned by a malady. Noticing that the police were getting close to discovering his involvement in the case and finding how easy it was to kill, José tried to eliminate Francesca and Anthony. He also hated the Transparency Crusade against the Vatican—they had started everything so he tried to poison the new leaders. Akemi was too smart to fall into a trap, so José had framed her. He had sent the poisoner's notebook to Akemi's address. He had also written the message on Ellia Jones phone accusing Akemi after Ellia died removing the screen lock so the message incriminating Akemi would be readily visible.

Leo X kept me busy. He had a big agenda and bigger opponents. Did all the murders help him succeed? He excommunicated Martin Luther in the same summer that Margharetta joined the convent. While the Emperor claimed to side with the Pope, he allowed Martin Luther to defend himself in facing the Diet of Worms, an assembly of all the nobles and heads of state in the Holy Roman Empire. When the Pope received the report, he threw a tea set and vases against the walls of his study hitting the images painted by Raphael: Plato in the face, and Apollo in the genitals. He remained serene in court dealings, smiling while he listened to music or organizing a hunt accompanied by three hundred courtiers. I stopped reading or curing others in the palace and resumed the Pope's directive to explore new poisons. Knowing of my love for music, the Pope ushered me to churches around Rome where he knew the best performers would appear. He also told me that while there, I had to choose a random victim in every parish so the deaths from my experiments would seem random and go unnoticed by anyone.

These irrational killings redoubled my solitude. I soon started conversing in my head with the images of Hanno the snow white elephant that were omnipresent in the Papal Palace, the tapestries in the Sistine Chapel, and the decorations on the apartments to the entrance at Saint Peter. I started seeking my drinking water only from the fountains in the city that had elephant sculptures—luckily, there were many. The beast and I talked to each other and understood each other. I was grateful that he had become part of the fabric of Rome and would remain long after I would be gone.

During this time, I became even more of a shadow at the palace. I scurried around so as to avoid seeing the Pope unless he summoned me. His presence revolted me. I was hiding in places even the spiders disliked.

It was the autumn of 1521, a year and a half after Raphael's death, when Giulio Romano came looking for me. Margharetta had died from grief at the convent. She never spoke with anyone while there. Margharetta had not become a nun so she had to be buried outside the convent. Giulio wanted me to be present at the ceremony. I had other desires and wrote them for Giulio to follow my lead. Margharetta had to rest next to her husband for eternity. We had to figure a way to place her in a niche next to Raphael at the Pantheon.

"That's impossible!" exclaimed an exasperated Giulio. "We could never justify that to the deacon at that church. We even run the risk of infuriating the Pope if he finds out we are trying to follow through with this crazy idea. The wedding was secret, and the Pope rejected it! Also, she was not of a social class to which the Pantheon can open its doors. You are not talking of a Maria Bibbiena! That would be different!" That gave me the solution. We buried Margharetta next to Raphael claiming to the church authorities that we were burying Maria Bibbiena. It was a tight logistic trick to perform. First we had to unearth and move the decayed body of Maria to the open grave we had acquired at a cemetery for Margharetta close to Santa Appolonia. Then we dressed Margharetta's corpse so she would look like a grand lady and placed her in the very expensive niche next to Raphael.

As only very few of us knew who really rested next to our friend. We wrote on the tomb "Maria Bibbiena. Here lies Raphael's wife." Those who knew Raphael realized Maria had never married him.

So the Pantheon, or as it is called now, the church of Santa Maria of the Martyrs, became the place for me to go. I would sit for hours tracing the letters on Margharetta's stone and reading the ones on Raphael's: "Here lies the famous Raphael by whom Nature feared to be conquered while he lived, and when he was dying, fear herself to *die." And engraving those words in my soul, I came to realize that I had promised on the souls of my brother and father to serve the Pope, but had never promised not to kill him.*

Anthony observes the sleeping man in front of him. He realizes Akemi will be free. No more jails for them. The new mystery to solve is how to live together with her? Will they even want to live together? Will she fit with his family? He knows he won't let her go. They can have the next year in Rome. After the sabbatical . . . who knows? He'll see what happens then. He'll worry about it later. Rome is a city that promises lots of adventures.

There will have to be a next step on the Transparency Commission. Maybe he will become an adviser to the Pope to figure out how to completely open the Secret Archives and make the Church operation transparent to the public. In Anthony's mind, there is no doubt about the need for transparency. The question is how to do it so it doesn't become a bigger destructive force. How to create checks and balances on the powerful while protecting people?

What does it mean to poison the Vicar of Christ? The Catholic Church had murdered all the pagan gods. By murdering the Pope, was I murdering the Catholic God? If so, this is what I had been preparing to do all my life. I had found beauty in Classical literature. I had found truth and acceptance of our virtues and defects. The true Christ could not be a hypocrite. His Word has been lost through the centuries and is not what we read in the Bible today. Maybe Martin Luther was right: We need to find meaning in the Bible by ourselves and not by what the Church tells us to think.

After the Pope had ordered me to explore new ways to murder, I knew I could apply my new potions to his Holiness. I started adding ingredients to his water and food to weaken his body, which intensified his gout and other ailments. He would howl at the smallest contact of anything with his swollen leg. The Pope's demeanor became very nasty. He could no longer feign kindness so he stopped attending events to showcase his piety. He was continually in pain and sick. To feel better, his courtiers organized one of his favorite past times, a magnificent hunt in a forest close to Rome. But the Pope got sicker. Some thought it was something in his lungs but his legs became putrid and maggots crawled out of them. He never called for me, or for anybody. He had his personal physicians and God's representation on Earth. He thought he was above all of us. He died in November 1521. Many suspected foul play, but nobody suspected me.

Anthony closes the door to José's office and bolts it from the outside. As he walks to the exit through the corridor where selected letters from the Secret Archives are displayed, he hears the police sirens in the distance and his mind reverts to all the things that can and will happen. He cannot wait to work with Angelo and publish the paper on Raphael's erotic drawings and the monk's story—that will give the art world something to talk about for more than a year. Meanwhile, he and Akemi can figure how to rewrite/reprogram their lives.

I decided to join Raphael and Margharetta while the Conclave is still adjourned. I took the same poison I gave Raphael. My breath is short. I am almost blind. I have lost all hearing. The hair has regrown all over my body and head only to fall out in patches from my malady.

Since art is the world around us, an artist's work is the description of himself. Raphael's soul belongs to heaven, and I, his brother, to hell. We were the two sides, the artist and the observer, the one living and the one thinking, the loved one and the one loving.

If you find this, give it to the Authorities. I pray that by the time this is discovered the Catholic Church is no longer governed by hypocritical and power-craving individuals but centering its efforts on evangelization and bringing education and hope to the unfortunates. I will put everything away in my desks. The angels are tip-toeing in concentric circles again. Chanting and carrying the candles. The undead are awake in the grounds surrounding the Vatican Palace since the times of Nero. The Roman nobles, the persecuted Christians, the forgotten soldiers. They are coming for me...so I put my pen down and open my arms.

About the Author

Andres Amezquita is a world traveler who fell in love with Rome many years ago, bewitched by the many layers of history and the secrets kept by the city. Once he learned of the existence of a steam bath with erotic frescos by Raphael inside the Vatican Palace, writing a story about it became an obsession that merged with his daily experience in the digital world, where he has resided for the last eight years.